SHADOW OF THE MAST

L. J. MARTIN

WISE WOLF
BOOKS

WISE WOLF BOOKS
An Imprint of Wolfpack Publishing
wisewolfbooks.com

Cover design by Wise Wolf Books

ISBN 978-1-953944-78-8(paperback) 978-1-953944-79-5(hardcover) 978-
1-953944-77-1(ebook)

Print Edition

For Ron Clausen,
The quintessential—and not in the order of importance—editor,
neighbor, attorney, superlative fly fisherman, constructive critic,
and damn fine friend.

FOREWORD

The legend of the 'tusuat' and of 'Chinigchinich' came from the oral history of California's Juanero Indians, who made their home near San Capistrano, California, where the swallows return every spring.

This novel was inspired by Richard Henry Dana's *Two Years Before the Mast*, which the author enjoyed while his ketch was moored in beautiful historic Dana Point Harbor, Dana Point, California.

SHADOW OF THE MAST

Boston, Massachusetts
September 3, 1827

LATE AFTERNOON SHADOWS darkened the cobblestoned streets.

Without breaking stride, the young man bent and retrieved a small loose stone and tossed it into the air, wondering what distant sea had polished it smooth, knowing it had arrived as ballast in the hull of some wandering vessel. He glanced back at the harbor, its ships toy-like now, and thought fleetingly of far-away lands he would never see. Then stately brick town houses again blocked the sun, enveloping him with a shudder, so he quickly strode on, continuing his own small journey.

A frigid nor'easter varnished the early fall landscape with ice. Trees adorned with a million diamonds glistened in the slanting late rays of the sun.

Even though the snow had not yet come in earnest, ice crackled underfoot and chamber pots froze beneath beds and had to thaw upside down in the sun to be emptied.

But Samuel McCreed Mueller didn't notice the cold. He

was on his way home from the school. On his way home to his mother's cooking.

It wasn't a particularly pleasant walk, when merely breathing the biting air was painful and the passing scenery no more than stark leafless trees and barren fields. Nor was he looking forward to facing his stepfather, Edward Mueller, a frugal man whose hard ways made Sam particularly enjoy his time away from the farm.

Since keeping a horse at school for a full week while he was attending classes would be a waste of good horseflesh, Sam was obliged to ride shank's mare the ten miles from Boston to Mueller Manor each Saturday afternoon. But with the long strides and boyish energy of a gangly youth who had nearly reached his height, he covered the cold ground quickly.

As the spires and shops and row houses of Boston gave way to open fields and pastures, Sam caught a lift with a neighboring farmer returning from a delivery. The wagon clattered and clanked down the bumpy path, and the sheep it carried left enough manure so Sam was obliged to ride crouched on his knees to avoid staining his breeches. His legs tired almost as much as if he had been walking. Nonetheless, he gave the farmer a hearty wave and "thank you" as he jumped out at the Mueller Manor gate.

It was still a quarter mile to the house along the poplar-lined road. Dairy cows turned their heads and lazily watched him pass, their breath billowing in the cold as they lowed a greeting. They went back to curling their tongues around the last of the dry, brittle pasture.

As Sam mounted the stairs to the back porch of the big farmhouse, the sweet smell of baking bread mixed with that of a pork roast cooking. Entering, he shucked his scarf and coat, then stood for a moment inhaling pleasant aromas. Hearing the door slam, his mother poked her dust cap covered head out the kitchen door.

"Sam... you're early! Good, you can sit with us for supper for a change." She motioned him in with the wooden spoon she carried and her eyes took on a special warm glow at the sight of him. "Wash up and fetch your brothers." She brought the spoon playfully across his backside as he passed and flashed her a smile.

Sam's natural father, Eric Schroder, had died shortly after Sam was born, leaving his mother to support her young son. Since Mueller Manor needed both a house-keeper and tutor, Kathleen McCreed Schroder, had hired on as an employee. Edward Mueller's first wife, the mother of Sam's four stepbrothers and two stepsisters, had died just one month earlier.

Edward took on Kathleen, waited the proper year after his wife's death, discarded his black arm band and promptly asked Kathleen to marry him. She was a beautiful slender woman with shining dark hair, fine features, and gleaming gray eyes. She had a quiet manner that belied a quick, fiery Irish temper. Only in the last few years had she begun to show the effects of hard farm work. Lines etched the corners of her eyes and mouth; still the men at the market-place gave her admiring glances.

Born a Catholic, after her marriage she had become a Lutheran at the insistence of her first husband, a hard-working German merchant. She had quietly instructed Sam in the old Catholic faith, though his father had decreed he be baptized Lutheran.

She stood at the wooden sink pumping water, watching Sam, her only natural child, cross the barnyard. He vaulted a four-rail fence in an easy motion and made his way across the corral. Her chest filled with pride at the way he had adjusted to the farm, and now to the rigors of school. He was a child no more, and without a father his childhood could have been a difficult time for both of them.

Again the back door slammed, and Kathleen smiled as her husband settled his big square frame into a ladder-backed chair and bent his thinning blond head over his generous belly to tug off his boots. She bent over to help him, wrapping her apron around a muddied one.

"It's a good thing the apples are all gone, Edward. A few more pies and you wouldn't be able to see your boots, much less pull them off."

"I always fatten up for the winter, Kathleen." He smiled then groaned as she removed the second boot. "Thank you. That feels better." He stood in his stocking feet, wiggled his toes, then retrieved his long-stemmed pipe from the rack on a shelf near the stove. He sat contentedly, tamping it as she worked.

Kathleen glanced up and saw her son disappear into the hundred-year-old Mueller Manor barn. He had just turned seventeen, his frame not yet filled out, but his eyes were a soft golden brown and his dark brown hair was thick and wavy. With his honesty and intelligence, she believed he would grow into the best kind of man.

In the double doorway, Sam paused to let his eyes adjust to the darkened interior of the large dairy barn where his stepbrothers tended a calving cow. He arrived just in time to see the calf drop. It was lucky to be born in the Mueller barn. Fresh straw covered the birthing stall floor and it was always spotlessly clean. Massive timbers supported the snows in the heaviest winters and tightly fitted caulked siding kept out the strongest winds. The lofts couldn't hold another fork full of hay and the split wooden hay forks hung neatly stowed with other tools. Hand swaths, broad-bladed hoes, hammers, saws, axes, adzes, braces and bits, planes, and huge collars and tack all hung neatly arranged along a far wall.

The newborn calf bleated a complaint of its ordeal, rolled, and tried to gain his feet as his mother proudly licked him clean. Klaus, a barrel-shaped man with blond pork chop sideburns and the ruddy red cheeks of the Muellers looked up as Sam approached and the cow, exhausted, collapsed to the straw.

"No sooner does this little fellow see daylight, and the sausage maker appears. It's a bull calf, Sam. You'll get this one." The little calf's luck had faded almost before it began.

One of Sam's ongoing responsibilities on the farm, school or no, was the making of sausage, scrapple, and souse. While the heifer calves went to the dairy, the bull calves were fattened for meat and by-products.

"I think I'll wait for you boys to get a little weight on him," Sam responded, as Klaus strained and tugged the cow to her feet. "We're called to supper," Sam added, jumping down from the stall fence where he'd climbed to observe.

Sam still had to look up to all the Mueller brothers. They were half-a-head taller and more powerfully built, a little like hog's head barrels.

As they entered the kitchen his mother bent over the stove. "Sam, fetch that plate of biscuits," his mother said.

He pulled the tin plate from the warming bin over the stove and added the heaping plate to a table laden with the fresh pork roast, baked apples, steaming green and yellow squash, gravy, and greens. The usual home-ground mustard and homemade mayonnaise flanked breath-catching horse radish ground to a fine paste, and sticks of expensive imported cinnamon for the cider. Fresh black bread and churned butter sat on the table, and a pitcher of buttermilk was as close as the potato cellar at all times.

Grace was offered—perfunctory but reverent. Little else was said other than "pass the…" or "a little more, please."

When the meal neared its end, Klaus, the eldest, leaned back in his ladder-back chair, dug his short-stemmed pipe out of a trouser pocket, and tamped in his tobacco. He turned to Sam, the only dark-haired Mueller besides Kathleen.

"Well, now that you're becoming an educated gentleman, Sam, maybe you can tell me how to get the corn to yield a bit more."

"Na," countered Sam, "you'll have to check the Almanac. My corn class doesn't start till next year." His brothers knew his school had no agricultural classes, much less a corn class. But his mother was proud of the education he was getting.

"With this farm divided among six families, someone will need to figure how to get it to yield more... too much more, I fear."

Sam held his tongue, but inwardly he cringed. As the youngest at the table, and a stepson, he felt the outsider. Even Edward Jr., who was closest to his age, had always remained distant, preferring the company of his older blood brothers.

Edward Sr. crinkled his liver-spotted brow. "This farm has provided well enough for us all, Klaus, and it will continue to do so." He turned his attention to Sam. "Have you seen your cousin Ernst about? Wilhelm tells me he does not do well in his studies."

"I haven't seen him since the first of last week." His cousin was two years older and attended the university. "I had hoped he would do better, but I do not think he will. He has no interest in school. It's too bad he couldn't live on the farm." That remark brought a groan from the others, but they kept their remarks to themselves.

"You'll not have to put up with me," Edward Jr. put in. "Not if Father will speak to our congressman about my appointment to West Point."

"Humph," his father grunted, clamping down firmly on the pipe stem, the red veins in his ruddy complexion standing out, particularly the ones on his balding head.

"Have you, Father? Have you written the congressman for me?" The look the boy garnered was enough of an answer. He wisely left the subject alone and turned to the cobbler Sam's mother set in front of him.

Edward looked sternly at Sam, shook his head, and continued, "Well, I know that Wilhelm is disappointed. He had so counted on Ernst joining him in his medical practice. I know you two boys are friends. Why don't you speak to him?"

"Yes, sir." Sam felt closer to his step cousin, Ernst, than to any of his stepbrothers. Ernst spent his summers at Mueller Manor and the two of them, along with Tug, the Mueller

6

Manor black Freedman, spent endless hours hunting and fishing. Sam never felt the competition with Ernst that his stepbrothers constantly thrust on him.

As the smallest, as well as the youngest of the boys, Sam had borne the brunt of many a joke and rough teasing. As they grew up, it had never been beyond the Mueller boys to thrash Sam severely at the slightest provocation. Only in the last two years had they learned that he could fight, and would do so, anytime he felt wronged or imposed upon. Blackened eyes and swollen lips taught them to remember they had been scraping, even if they bested him. Now at least their teasing was tempered with mutual respect.

Sam excused himself early. He'd done enough reading during the week so he didn't join in as Edward read aloud from the Farmer's Almanac. Instead, with a full stomach, he curled into his feather bed and was soon asleep.

The Sabbath was well respected on Mueller Manor, but the work on the farm waited only for the short respite of prayer and the paying of respect to the church—cows still had to be milked and meat not cared for would spoil. After a four-mile ride to and from the church, Sam spent the afternoon in the lean-to at the side of the smokehouse, making souse and scrapple for Edward's delivery to the markets in Boston.

The day went quickly, and by the light of slender tallow tapers Sam completed his schoolwork for the following day.

They had been on the road for an hour Monday morning before lemon yellow washed the eastern sky. With the birds singing their welcome to a sun not yet warm enough to melt the ice from the road, Edward dropped Sam off at the gate to his school.

"See you next Saturday, son." Edward extended a hemp sack to his stepson. "Do well, and try to encourage Ernst."

Sam grabbed the sack full of souse prepared especially for his teachers and jumped down from the wagon, waving to his stepfather but worried about his cousin. He knew the family would soon be in an uproar over his slovenly habits and lack of ambition.

———————

"EDWARD!" Edward's brother, Wilhelm, smiled from the top of the stairs. "You're just in time for tea. Come into the kitchen. The drawing room is full of patients." From the entry of the brownstone, they made their way down a little hallway past a roomful of people who glared at him. Edward knew they believed he was usurping their turn to see the doctor.

"It's good to see you, Wilhelm."

"How are things at the farm?" his bother asked. Although he was thinner and had a fuller head of hair, Edward thought his brother looked older than he. His thick mane had gone nearly white, and lines abounded around his eyes and mouth.

"Everything is fine, and here?" Edward sat down at the kitchen table.

"Not as good as they might be." Wilhelm sighed. "I had a visit from Ernst's schoolmaster this Sunday. He's suggested my son withdraw from the university and investigate other areas of endeavor." He averted his glance as he poured their tea.

"Ah, these boys." Edward shook his head. "Sometimes I wonder." He reached out to take one of the cookies that sat in the center of the table, thanks to Mrs. Foxe, Wilhelm's housekeeper, who doubled as his nurse.

"What do you think, Edward? I so wanted him to take up here as a physician. Now...well, he has no trade, no prospects. What do you think I should do?"

"Maybe a job as a clerk will help settle him down. Nothing like good steady work to turn a boy to seriousness. Or perhaps the military. Edward Jr. keeps pressing me to get out congressman to get him an appointment."

"But Edward Jr. had the marks for it. Ernst does not."

Wilhelm pulled a small kettle from the stove and freshened their steaming tea.

"He has enough education for the trades," Edward suggested, biting into a cookie. "You know every merchant in Boston. Maybe you can find him an apprenticeship of some kind?"

"I don't know." Wilhelm swept back a tendril of white hair that fell across his eyes. "I just can't see him as anything other than a physician."

"We would be happy to have him on the farm. You know that." Edward rested a large hand on his brother's shoulder.

"No...no, I made it off the farm and so shall he. I'm sorry Edward; I didn't mean that as it sounded. I don't mean to belittle the farm."

"No offense taken, brother. The farm is already stretched with so many, and another family would be difficult. Still, if you need us...."

They continued to talk until Mrs. Foxe leaned her buxom frame into the room and sternly reminded the doctor there were patients to attend.

———————————

STANDING AT THE CORNER, young Ernst Mueller ran a hand through his carrot-red hair and watched his Uncle Edward's wagon clatter away. He approached the brownstone, then hesitated, kicking at a multi-colored cobblestone. It rolled off down the slight incline of the street, cracking and clattering its way in front of the other townhouses. Finally, as it was growing dark and the last of his father's patients left, he walked as far as the doorway.

"Why, Master Ernst, what are you doing home on a weekday?" Mrs. Foxe looked at him sternly as she let a last patient out the door.

"Has father finished for the day?"

"He has. He'll be down to supper in a few minutes." She gave Ernst a pointed look and started to say something but

9

reconsidered and turned toward the kitchen. The strong smell of lamb, which normally would have whet Ernst's appetite, almost sickened him as he crept quietly up the stairs to his room.

His father was well into a mutton chop when Ernst made his way to the table. "Sir," Ernst mumbled, taking his seat.

"Don't 'sir' me, young man. You should be using that address to your professors right now. What are you doing home from school?"

"Father, I just don't think I was cut from the same cloth as you. I don't..."

"You mean you're lazy," Wilhelm sputtered, "and you don't study and you lollygag."

"Father, I don't like school or my instructors. I don't want to attend anymore." Ernst's face reddened until his freckles were almost imperceptible.

"Professor Keets was here yesterday, Ernst. You haven't been to class in a week. How do you expect to do well when you don't try?"

The food cooled on their plates while the argument heated. Soon Wilhelm stalked from the brownstone, leaving Ernst to try his first bite of cold lamb. The suet stuck to his teeth and gagged him. With a grimace he pushed away from the table and made his way quietly up to his room.

———

WILHELM THREADED through coils of line, nets, piles of ricking lumber, and sails being mended as he walked the street along the quay. He always looked to the sea to heal his spirits. His argument with Ernst had put him in such a temper they surely needed healing today.

With deep calming breaths, he inhaled the moist salt air and made his way along the rough board docks. After walking for over an hour, he turned into a waterfront pub, making his way across the straw-covered floor. A rough place, men crowded together, laughing and shoving. Smoke hung over dim whale oil lamps and the dank air reeked of sweat, ale, and the pungent odor of shellfish cooking. It was not a place he would normally frequent, but frustration demanded a drink.

"Doctor! Doctor Mueller, it's good to see you. Would you care to join us for a drink?" A tall broad-shouldered man in a braid-trimmed tailcoat and white cravat extended his hand. Wilhelm thought the man well-dressed for this rough place. "I'm Bryant. You treated my mother, Adele...Adele Bryant, just last week at the hospital."

"Yes, yes, I recall. I trust she is doing better? I haven't seen her for the past few days."

"Fine, thanks to you. May I buy you a mug and a pipe of tobacco in appreciation?" The man led him to a corner table where another equally well-dressed man sat sipping a mug of ale under an old-style tri-cornered hat and drawing on a long-stemmed pipe.

"This is my friend and partner, Mr. Sturgis," Bryant said, "Mr. Sturgis, meet Dr. Mueller."

Wilhelm sat and gratefully accepted a mug of rum and a pipe from the supply kept at hand by the blue-aproned publican. As the evening wore on, and more mugs disappeared, the conversation turned to his reason for being at the dock, his confrontation with his offspring.

"Sons are most always a problem," Sturgis said, his dark brow furrowed together. "You should let us try a hand at the boy, doctor. Our trade will test the mettle of any man."

"And what is that, sir?"

"Why the sea, doctor. Mr. Bryant and I own two of the finest ships and four of the finest brigs ever to round the horn. We sail to Alta California with trade goods, and—a gracious God willing—back with hide, horn, and tallow."

"Nothing like the sea to put iron in a man's backbone," offered Bryant.

"Hard work. Plain food. The salt spray in your face. Exotic ports. Nothing like it! Many a rebellious boy leaves for a year or two on the sea and most always a fine man returns."

Sturgis offered his comments while Wilhelm took a deep draw on his pipe. "If I were a young lad trying to find my niche in the world, it would surely be the sea for me." He reached across the table and laid a hand on Wilhelm's shoulder. "We're in need of bright young men with strong backs, and it sounds as if your boy is in need of some honest hard work. If for no other reason than to show him the wisdom of a good education."

Wilhelm drew on the pipe and released a cloud of smoke into the room. The words rang true. Smiling, he began to question both men at length.

The following morning at breakfast, listening to his father's words, Ernst left the table thinking school might not be have been as bad as he had earlier thought. His father, with a well-earned headache adding to his gruffness, had offered him an ultimatum, sign aboard the brig Virginia, or be written out of his father's will and tossed out of his house. He was to begin packing at once.

2

SAMUEL MCCREED MUELLER reined the hired little sorrel mare into the livery a block behind his Uncle Wilhelm's stately townhouse, the note his cousin had sent tucked into his pocket. He ducked as the mare sidestepped through the low entry.

"You must pick many a gentleman's hat from the mud with that low door," he said to the young boy who ran up to take his horse.

"How long will you be, sir?" the boy asked.

At seventeen, Sam didn't get many "sirs". Dismounting, he gathered his gangly, youthful frame to its full height. "Only tonight. See that she has a fair share of oats. She has earned them."

Ernst was sailing on the Saturday morning tide and the note said he wanted Sam to come and celebrate—or commiserate—with him before he left. As Sam strode up the cobblestone street, he felt a twinge of envy. His cousin was not a man to admire, certainly not by his stepfather's standards, but still, he couldn't help it. Although Sam knew he was quicker than his cousin mentally and physically, Ernst had always been larger and stronger. His cousin's two-year age advantage and added bulk set the stage for admiration, even though his slovenly habits detracted from it.

Sam bounded up the stairs between carved limestone lions and opened the door. "Ernst, you old sea dog, where are you?"

"Lord, Lord, Master Sam." Mrs. Foxe stepped back as Sam slammed the door. "It's a good thing the doctor's not home. He'd have your hide for raising such a stir."

Sam smiled at the buxom lady. She always smelled of fresh bread and sweet cakes—and treated Ernst like the mother he'd hardly known.

"Mrs. Foxe, you blaspheme and Gabriel will have you in Beulah Land before you have a chance to grow old and fat. Where's my rascal cousin? Hanging from the yardarm already?"

"Now don't you tempt fate. I don't sleep now for worrying 'bout the young master."

Sam left her in the hallway, wiping her hands on the apron she wore, and entered the drawing room. He was surprised to see his stepfather, Edward Mueller, deep in conversation with Ernst.

"Father," Sam said. "I'm sorry. I didn't realize you were coming to see Ernst off."

"I came with a delivery for the merchants," Edward replied with his usual gruffness. "Since you're here, it won't do any harm for you to listen to this, too." Edward filled his pipe from the small tobacco table near his chair. Behind him, Sam's cousin rolled his eyes in exasperation.

"Now, where was I? Yes, unacceptable behavior at the university is one thing, but at sea... at sea it could cost you your very life." He removed the pipe from his mouth and using it as a pointer, tapped Ernst in the chest with the stem. "There will be instances where a mistake or misjudgment could have a permanent effect, not only on you, but on your shipmates as well." Edward sat back and drew on the pipe. "The sea is unforgiving, no place for foolishness."

Between drawing on the pipe and pointing with its stem,

he warned Ernst of every potential problem from too much sun to syphilis, which he referred to as "the French sickness"—a subject which brought knowing glances and hidden smiles between the boys. Although they knew of men who'd gone crazy with the malady. It was no laughing matter.

Finally, Edward pulled his watch fob from his waistcoat, snaked the simple iron-cased watch out, gazed at it, then looked sternly at his nephew. "Do yourself proud, my boy, for you and your family... but above all, for yourself." He paused, looking suddenly uncomfortable. "Come home a man, Ernst, but come home to us in one piece. I'll say no more on the matter."

He turned to Sam. "Son, you and Ernst fetch a sack full of hams and souse from the wagon. It won't do to have the boy come home skin and bones."

The two escaped to the street. Sam filled a sack with hams and bacon, souse and cup cheese. "Eat the cheese first as it will spoil in a fortnight." He handed the sack to his cousin, then his mood changed. "Aren't you a bit afraid? It's far to the wilds of California."

"Na," Ernst replied smugly. "Many men would pay for the chance to see what I will see. It's a good thing father is a friend of Mr. Sturgis and Mr. Bryant. They took me to visit the fine brig I'll be sailing on. I do feel, considering my education, that I should be aft the mast, not fore—that means I should have been made an officer—but that will come soon enough."

"I'm sure it will, Ernst."

His red-haired cousin smiled. "Enough of that. I promised you a romp with a buxom lass if you came to spend this last eve with me sooo...." Ernst's pale blue eyes twinkled mischievously in his freckled face.

His note to Sam had indicated an unforgettable time, if only he would come. There were definite advantages to having an older cousin, Sam thought. Especially one who lived in the city. Sam was a country boy with limited knowledge.

His few walks in the woods with a neighbor girl had been little more than heated kisses until he'd finally summoned the courage to undo the ties on her blouse and touch her breasts. She enjoyed it for a moment then indignantly threatened to tell her father about his brazen actions—a threat that would have resulted in a severe thrashing from his stepfather at best, or a trip to apologize to her parents at worst.

Ernst placed an arm around his shoulders. "Well my young friend, you may be in luck. My father's good friend and neighbor in yonder town house has been kind enough to journey out of Bostontown. It so happens that his house-maid is a lovely Norwegian lass, who has, or so she claims, an equally lovely sister. You'll not have to take a buttered bun but will have your own tasty morsel."

In a worldly manner, he added, "She has been kind enough to invite me in for a bit of tea and a romp in her attic room several times over the summer past." He lifted a red eyebrow in an attempt at a look of sophistication. "And we've been invited this very eve, if her sister can slip out to join her."

"Do they not live together?"

"Na, the sister is indentured to the money changer who lives in the next block. They're fortunate to be so close. I haven't seen the sister, but Ingrid is a pleasure, quick of mind and equally quick with a corset string." He winked at Sam.

"Don't we take a great risk, trifling with another man's property?" Sam nervously shifted his feet.

"You will find, my country cousin, that a swelling of your breeches results in a shrinking of your restraint." Ernst laughed. "Once that happens, you will hardly worry about such trifles."

"Boys," Edward called from the house, "are you finished gathering the sausage? I must be on the road. It will be dark now before I'm home."

"You're heading home tonight, father?" Sam asked.

"You saw the ice on the road. We still have corn in the fields and there is much to do." Edward joined them at the wagon, pulled his big frame up onto the seat, then looked over his shoulder at Ernst. "Remember you have much to learn. The ship's crew will not know of your lack of success at the university. Don't let yesterday use up too much of tomorrow." He whipped up the team, the strong odor of the hams and souse still in the wagon faded as it rolled away, iron tires clattering over the cobblestones. As an afterthought, Edward called over his shoulder, "Sam, study hard."

Sam waved and the wagon turned a corner out of sight. The boys hurried to the cellar and were well into a jug of West Indies rum when they heard Ernst's father returning home. Tucking the jug behind some old musty trunks, they headed for the stairs.

"Now the trick will be to convince father that I must say goodbye to some friends," Ernst whispered. Then they heard Wilhelm's stern voice.

"There you two are. Have you packed yet, Ernst?" Wilhelm's glance strayed toward the hidden jug, and he smiled, never staying mad at his son for long. Sam wondered if he suspected they'd been celebrating Ernst's farewell.

There is little time left," Wilhelm cautioned. "You say the tide turns at four a.m. Then you must be onboard well before."

"Yes, sir. And thank you for the chest." He'd spent most of the afternoon filling a small leather chest with gear the brig's owners had recommended and his father had provided. He supposed his father had softened at the thought of sending his only son so far away. He'd given Ernst not only the gear and the chest, but enough gold coins to pay his passage home from as far away as California. Uncle Edward had quietly slipped him a twenty-dollar gold piece as well, a month's wages for a young man, and even

Mrs. Foxe had offered him a few pence from her savings, which he magnanimously refused.

"You have your Bible?" his father asked.

"Yes, sir. And a Farmer's Almanac that Uncle Edward brought me."

"Good. Are the rest of your things properly stored? Have you hidden—"

"Yes, father. The little box is magnificent." His father had also given him a black lacquered, mother-of-pearl inlaid Oriental box. Its finest feature was a system of intricate panels which, when moved in the proper sequence, opened a false bottom where he'd stored his gold coins in packed straw so they wouldn't give up a telltale rattle.

"We must leave for the dock by eleven," his father said. "It would not do to be late."

"Father, there is no need for you to be up at that hour. Sam has offered to deliver me to the brig. He would like to see her."

"You know I'm used to being up at all hours."

Turning to Sam, Wilhelm added, "I appreciate that Sam, but I will see my son to the brig. Now let's sup together this last time. We won't be together again for a good long while." He called up the stairs to the housekeeper. "Mrs. Foxe, I hope you've supper enough for some very hungry men."

Mrs. Foxe outdid herself with Ernst's farewell supper, and Ernst outdid himself convincing his father that he should say goodbye to his many friends. Ernst knew the wine and the brandy that followed such a meal would ease his father's restraint—and he was right.

Sam and his cousin waved to Wilhelm, who followed them to the door, and the pair started down the street into the darkness—away from Ingrid's house. They continued around the block, approaching from the other direction. Sneaking down the side yard, Ernst picked up some pebbles and flipped them at an upstairs dormer window. A pale face rimmed with blond hair appeared in the lighted opening and quickly disappeared. In a few seconds the rear door opened and Ernst hurried in. Impatiently, he motioned Sam to follow.

Entering the house they proceeded down a dimly lit hallway then up a narrow-carpeted stairwell, its walls covered with expensive flowered wallpaper. The upstairs door opened onto a well-lit room, and the harsh light revealed two giggling girls, one slightly older than the other.

Both girls had long blond hair and limpid blue eyes. They wore simple woolen dresses, but cut daringly low with a corset that pushed their full breasts together. Sam stared at the cleavage until his concentration was broken by the sound of Ernst's voice.

"Well, Ingrid girl, this must be your little sister. A pretty bit o' fluff—I believe she'll do well enough for my country cousin."

Sam blushed and extended his hand. "I'm Samuel Mueller. Pleased to make your acquaintance."

Ingrid laughed, grabbed her skirt, and curtsied. "Well, if yer not the proper one—for a man who comes a'visitin' in the dark o' night." She giggled impishly. "This is Gretchen."

Gretchen patted the bed next to her. "sit and tell me about your school," she said, pronouncing school in two syllables with the an emphasis on the first. Sam sat down and Gretchen turned to him, putting a knee up on the bed to touch the outside of his thigh. Sam glimpsed a shapely ankle over the top of a dainty lace-up half boot.

He tried to carry on a conversation while glancing from exposed ankle to laughing eyes and back to full pale cleavage. An occasional whiff of her sweet floral perfume made him giddy. Whenever her knee touched his leg, he felt the warmth of her body. Leaning back, she propped herself on an elbow and covered his hand with hers.

"Ingrid, girl," Ernst said, "did you manage to save a bit of the jug I brought the last time I visited?"

Ingrid giggled. "Of course I did."

"Where have you hidden it?"

Pushing aside the patchwork quilt, she reached under

the bed and pulled out a half-gallon jug. She uncorked it, and with one motion, laid it over a freckled elbow. She took as long a draw as Sam had seen any man take, then handed the jug to Ernst, who repeated the process, handing it on to Sam. He imitated them both, coughed and gagged on the high-proof rum, then passed it to Gretchen. Giggling, she drank deeply then passed it back to Ingrid, where the process began again.

As they talked and drank, Sam realized the girls were each older than Ernst. He guessed Gretchen was at least twenty-four. He tried to act mature and was thankful he had just eaten a large meal as the drinking continued. Finally, Ernst struggled to his feet and pulled Ingrid up with him. Sam rose as well.

"Are we leaving?" he asked.

"Hardly, Cousin." Ernst pointed to himself and then to Ingrid, slightly slurring his words. "We are. We're takin' a little walk down the hall. You'll do jus' fine... jus' fine... right where you are." He laughed drunkenly and stumbled out the door with Ingrid close behind.

As Sam sat back down next to Gretchen, she fell back across the bed with her long, slender arms outstretched. "It's sooo comfortable here... don't ya think so, Samuel?"

"Why, yes. Yes, it is," he answered nervously.

She raised up on an elbow, her face close to his. "Don't ya find me the least bit pretty?"

"Why, of course, I do. Yes, I... of course you're pretty." He groped for more words but didn't have a chance to say them as she clasped him behind the neck, pulled him down, and covered his lips with a kiss.

She tasted of rum and sweetness and surprised him by running her tongue into his mouth. It didn't take long before surprise and hesitant curiosity became heated passion and he groped for her, his hand cupping her breast.

Gretchen seemed to know she had a neophyte on her hands and was enjoying it. She toyed with him, pushing his hands away, then pulling them back. Finally, she pushed him off her and rose.

"If yer gonna to do this, Samuel, ye had best be doin' it right."

His eyes widened as she quickly undid the ribbon ties on her woolen bodice and her full breasts sprang from their constraints. The dress and corset fell away, and she stood in her thin pantalets, stockings, and lace-up boots. Bare breasted, her nipples went hard in anticipation.

"Well, ya just gonna lay there looking the oaf? Or are ya gonna shed yer breeches?"

Sam could hardly take his eyes off her breasts as he tugged off his shirt and boots. He rose and shyly turned away, sliding his breeches down his long legs. Gretchen laughed and drew him down on top her in one hasty motion. She had shed the rest of her garments, and he felt the warmth of her rounded curves beneath him.

Cupping his face with her hands, she covered his mouth with kisses, thrust a hand between their bodies, and guided him inside her. "Yust let Gretchen show ya," she whispered against his ear.

As she gripped him with her strong firm thighs and began gyrating her hips, Sam gasped at the surprising heat that enveloped him and at his own instinct which led him on.

Afterward, they lay entwined for a while. When he started to get up, Gretchen pulled him back down and rolled to lay beside him. Patiently, she stroked his chest and thighs, and he felt his interest rise again.

Sounds in the hallway jerked him from her grasp and he scrambled for the door. It was only Ernst, who shoved it open and peeked through a slight crack. He mumbled something, his red hair gleaming in the low light of the whale oil lamp. "How you doin' cousin?"

Gretchen rose and pushed the door shut, banging Ernst's head mercilessly before Sam had a chance to answer. "You will not get off so easy my little rabbit," she said, leading him back to the bed.

This time it was she who shuddered, then moaned a low cry of pleasure and collapsed on top him. When she curled beside him like a contented kitten, he felt like shouting for joy but lay quiet, smiling mischievously instead.

It was another hour, and another more gentle interlude, before Ernst again banged on the door. "Come on, cousin. I got to get to my ship." This time his drunken words rang with a hint of urgency.

Gretchen slid her arms around Sam's neck, pulling him back and kissing him once more. "Goodbye my little rabbit. Ya may be a young one, but it's a handsome buck rabbit ya are." She laughed as he made his way out the door.

"Bye, little Buck," Gretchen whispered throatily as Sam and Ernst left the house.

The two boys made their way down the street laughing and crowing. "I've never met a girl like Gretchen before," Sam said. "She really... really liked me!"

"She really liked the gold piece I gave her, my little country cousin." Ernst slapped him on the back, his freckled face splitting into a grin.

Sam felt his cheeks flush hotly while Ernst continued to beat him on the back.

The entry clock in Dr. Mueller's hall struck eleven when Ernst and Sam stumbled in. It was a good thing it chimed; Sam had trouble focusing on the clock face.

"Father!" Ernst called up the stairs.

Mrs. Foxe peered out of her monk-sized room at the end of the entry hall. "Your father was called out on an emergency. There's a note on the table."

Sam grabbed the note and carefully read it to Ernst.

Dear Ernst:

I may not be able to see you off. Mrs. Ames has started her labor. If the baby comes in time, I will see you at the brig. If not, do proud for yourself.

Good sailing,
Dr. Wilhelm Mueller

Ernst smiled at his father's formality. "Always the doctor," he mumbled. "Well, Sam, it looks as if you win the chore of seeing me off. You'd like to see the brig, wouldn't you? I'll jus' get my things. You get the carriage."

Sam ran to the rear of the house—the carriage was gone. His uncle must have taken it. He thought for a moment, then remembered the little sorrel he'd hired and ran to the stable. The stable boy, asleep in the loft, groggily refused to come down to fetch the mare. Sam left a coin on a work-table covered with leather mending tools and fetched the horse himself.

Ernst stood at the curb when he returned. The boys struggled but were finally mounted, the sack of hams and souse hanging from the saddle, the little trunk balanced on the pommel in front of Sam, Ernst hanging on behind.

"Are you sure you got everysing... everything?" Sam corrected.

"I think so." Ernst pulled a bottle of brandy from his bedroll. "See!" The little horse plodded down the cobblestone streets while Sam and Ernst passed the bottle back and forth.

Half an hour later they reined up at the dock. The brig, Virginia, towered above them, its naked masts cold and ominous, like two giant leafless trees in a winter forest.

Watching from the rail, Henry Tacker, the Virginia first mate, saw the boys arrive. The one in front tried to throw a leg over the horse's neck, but he lost his balance. A trunk he held fell to one side, he to the other. The boy and bedroll on behind, crashed off the back. The two sprawled on the rough board dock, laughing as Tacker turned from the rail and the drunken scene and headed down the aft ladder.

He stopped at the captain's door. "Sir?"

"Yes, Mr. Tacker?"

"If you'll be loaning me a bit of the ship's grog, there'll be

23

no need of a hunting trip. Seems the ginger-hackled boy who signed on," Tacker said, referring to Ernst's red hair, "brought another lad along, and they're drunk as seven lords."

"That'll be fine, Mr. Tacker."

Hard Tack, as he was known to the crew, returned to the deck, where the Mueller boy was authoritatively pointing to the rigging, repeating what he had learned on his first visit to the ship.

"She's a hundred twenty feet from bow to stern, and twenty-two feet in the beam. A full ship carries three masts, but as you can see, cousin," he hiccupped, "a brig has only two."

"God, Ernst," said the dark-haired boy as the first mate approached. "I don' know how you'll ever learn all the ropes, much less all the rest."

"They're not ropes, they're lines," Tacker said with a booming, cheerful voice. "Welcome aboard, Master Mueller. And who's your young friend?"

"Ish' a fine ship you have here, sir," the dark-haired boy put in before Ernst had a chance to reply. "A fine ship indeed."

"Actually, she's a brig, but I'm glad you think so, lad. It's obvious you're a man of the sea, with a fine eye for a sailing vessel." Tacker smiled inwardly at his sarcasm.

"Why, no. No, sir," the second boy said, "To tell the truth, this is my firsh'... my first time inside one... and I've only come to see my cousin off." He finished with a belch. "'Scuse me."

"This is my cousin," Ernst said proudly.

"Pleased to meet you, Mr. Mueller. I'm Henry Tackett, first mate aboard the Virginia."

"Pleased to meet you, Henry," the younger boy said, swaying against the rail. The boys dropped the locker, bedroll, and sack of hams to the deck. One of the hams rolled out onto the holystoned pine.

"Well, what have we here?" Hard Tack picked up the ham

in one hand, admired it, and picked up the sack with the other. "I'll see to these. Now let me show you about."

They descended the aft ladder under the raised aft section of the brig. Hard Tack rapped briskly on the captain's door. "Captain, Mr. Mueller and... and... his cousin... here to pay their respects."

The door opened and the captain focused cold blue eyes on the boys. He extended a long thin hand. "Good to see you men. Come in, come in, I was just about to have my nightly before retiring."

The boys smoothed their coats and stepped through the door. Curled up in a bedroll at the side of the captain's locker was the captain's boy, Ahmed. Asleep, he didn't stir. The room, unlike the musty hallway, smelled of incense and tobacco. A fine Oriental rug covered the floor, and a fur spread draped over a deep goose down mattress. A polished brass oil lamp rested on a rosewood writing desk and another swung from the ceiling.

"Who's this fine-looking young man?" The captain asked, looking the second boy over with a critical eye.

"Another Mr. Mueller... a cousin, it seems," Hard Tack answered.

"Pleased to meet you. You must be a seafaring man, by the look of you." The captain cut his eyes to Hard Tack, trying not to smile.

"No. No, sir. I'm a student. Samuel Mueller."

"We must toast to a fine voyage. It's a custom to bottoms up to a new voyage. Damnable bad luck if you don't." The captain passed a mug of grog to each man. "Gentlemen! To the voyage!" He drained his without a breath.

The two boys looked at each other. "Prost!" said Ernst, and they followed suit.

"Well done, men." Hard Tack smiled. "In fact, so well done, another would suit me. How 'bout it, Captain? It's not every voyage gets started with a fine young man like Mr. Mueller." He took a hefty swig from the mug, then wiped his mouth with the back of a hand. "Do you sing, Master Mueller?"

"I have sung... in church." Ernst smiled foolishly.

"Well, that's a fine thing." The Captain laughed. "On board a brig such as this, not a hand touches a line unless it's done to a seafaring song." He broke into a shanty and Hard Tack joined in. They swung their mugs in time to "Heave To The Girls," and Sam and Ernst clapped to the beat.

Sam eyed the two smiling men and thought what a grand adventure it would be for Ernst.

After three more mugs and another hearty song, the first mate waved them to the door. "Now to see the rest of the brig."

Sam mumbled, "It was good... to make your aquain... to meet you, Captain... er... sir." He made his way the few steps to the ladder, then slipped twice as he ascended. Ernst followed blindly, unable even to voice an objection.

"I'll be showing you to your quarters." Hard Tack led the way almost the length of the ship. He took them down a ladder into the forecastle under the slightly raised fore deck, then shoved them into bunks. "Why don't you boys rest awhile?"

Other men were asleep in the forecastle. Their snoring and coughing disturbed the silence. Hard Tack smiled sardonically, watching to see that the boys made no effort to get up, then listened until their heavy breathing steadied. Laughing and pleased with himself, he headed toward his quarters, whistling a happy sea shanty. It was the easiest Shanghai he'd ever accomplished.

3

SAM AWOKE WITH A START, groggy, but aware that he was not where he should be.

His head throbbed and the bile rose in his throat. He raised a hand to his brow, then dropped it quickly. It reeked of his own vomit.

The bed rolled. Jesus, he was still on board the brig! He rose too quickly and cracked his head with a resounding thump. Dropping back to the bunk, he pulled a splinter from his forehead. Squinting, focusing his eyes on the bottom of the bunk above, only eighteen inches away, he waited for the aching to subside. It didn't. Ignoring the stench, he cradled his head in his hands and tried to gain his composure.

The air was dank and the forecastle dark, but light shafted in through a hatchway. He needed fresh air and a drink of water. Carefully rolling out of the bunk, he staggered for the ladder. The rolling of the ship and his dizziness conspired, and he grabbed the bulkhead.

Finally, he climbed up, momentarily blinded by the sunlight but refreshed by the blast of cool breeze. His eyes adjusted to the brightness, and he stared out over the rail.

"My God!" he gasped. "We're at sea!" Focusing on the brawny first mate standing at the rail amidst coils of hemp line, he remembered some of the night before, and rushed forward. "Henry! Henry, I must have fallen asleep, we must... I must get back to shore!"

The coastline of Massachusetts faded into the mist, aft of the little brig.

The big first mate glanced over his shoulder. His looked turned to one of disgust when he saw who hailed him. He stared back out at the disappearing coastline. "This ship stops for no man, much less a sogger of a boy."

"No! Henry, you must help me. I have to get back home."

The first mate spun, reached out and grabbed Sam's collar with a gnarled, powerful hand. He stared at him with icy eyes. "My name is Mister. Mister Tacker to you. The next time you speak to me, if you have good reason, it's Mister or you'll wish it had been so. Do you understand?"

Sam focused his bleary eyes on the pockmarked, scowling face of the big first mate. He was only four inches taller, but his massive arms and shoulders dwarfed Sam's thinner frame.

"But... but... then I must speak to the captain."

"You'll speak to the captain, or me, only when spoken to. Now get below. You'll serve on the starboard watch and earn your keep while aboard this vessel."

Sam stared at him, unmoving.

Hard Tack spun him toward the forward ladder, shoving him and booting him squarely in one motion. "When I speak you'd best learn to jump!"

Sam stumbled down the ladder to his bunk, rubbing his backside, looking over his shoulder. There had to be some mistake, he thought frantically. He had to be in class. He turned and started climbing back up the ladder.

Hard Tack waited above, the light outlining his massive shoulders and thick bull neck. Sam jerked back, feeling the wind as the first mate's booted foot barely missed his face. He tumbled down the ladder landing flat on his back on the smooth holystoned deck of the forecastle. He stared up at the big, silhouetted figure filling the forecastle hatch.

"Boy!" Tacker yelled into the darkness as Sam retreated to his bunk. "You do just as I say or it'll go hard on you." The husky sailor stalked away.

In the dim light Sam could just make out his cousin Ernst, still asleep or passed out in a nearby bunk.

He's supposed to be here, Sam thought bitterly, I'm supposed to be in school. The family would have no idea where he was. He had to get off the ship.

With a groan, Sam closed his eyes and lay back down on the narrow hard bunk. His stomach churned, and the bile rose up with every roll of the ship. Lying there as long as he could stand it, his stomach threatening to erupt at any moment, he scrambled back up the ladder and crossed the deck to the rail. This time Hard Tack only laughed as Sam lost what little was left in his belly.

Lying in the scuppers, where rough-weather water poured off the deck through the railing, Sam hung his head clear of the deck. Foamy water swept past the hull ten feet below, making him even dizzier, and he had to close his eyes.

He was still there hours later, when the starboard watch was called. As a laughing crewman dragged Sam to his feet, he saw Ernst make his way onto the deck.

"Don't sham Abram with me, you two." The first mate confronted them both.

"I'm not pretending," Sam looked him straight in the eye. "I'm sick as a poisoned rat."

"You're sick all right," Hard Tack said, walking toward them, "brought down by bottle fever. You were both drunk as David's sow when you came aboard last night." He shoved them forward. "It's time to earn your keep, soggers." Hard Tack laughed as they stumbled ahead of him. "Old Dutch there will teach you how to keep your feet under you."

"What are you doing here?" Ernst muttered, his eyes wide and bloodshot. Before Sam could answer, a grubby looking red-faced sailor hurried to their side.

"I'm Swill, the second mate." He hissed foul breath through the opening where his front teeth were missing. Sam was sure the balance of the blackened and yellowed stubs would soon follow. "There's no talking while yer on duty. If you have time to talk I'll be finding a bit more work for you to do." He spun Ernst to face him. "I'm told your name is Ernst, and a hard-headed gentleman you are."

He took Sam's lapel in a rough, callused hand. "And what do you answer to, boy?"

"He's my cousin, Samuel."

"Natty boy. Well, Natty, you and yer cousin follow me."

The last thing Sam wanted was to be known as "Natty boy." Suddenly not wanting to be associated with this vessel in any way, he remembered what Gretchen had called him just a few hours ago. "Buck," he said. "Call me Buck." Ernst looked at him curiously, but held his tongue.

"Ernst," Swill ordered, "you go aft and help with the tarring down. One and Baldy will break you in." He pointed to two sailors filling a bucket from a hogshead full of tar. "Bucko, you follow old Dutch." Swill pointed to a barrel-shaped, red-faced sailor. "He'll learn you how to splice."

"But I'm not supposed to be here."

The man leaned close. "Supposed don't count no more, boy." His rancid breath made Sam's stomach roll anew. Buck, he silently corrected. He was Buck until he got back home. "Follow Dutch, that ol' butter bucket knows the way of the sea," he said, using the sailor's nickname for any Dutchman.

Apprehensively, Buck made his way aft. The hogshead fumes made his eyes water and burned the back of his throat, gagging him. He watched Ernst being hauled aloft, his blue eyes flaring in fear. They'd slung a line under his arms and taken a turn under his buttocks. He rose high in the rigging, a bucket full of tar in one hand, a brush in the other—and a very remorseful, very frightened look on his face.

The men began to sing a sea shanty as they hoisted Ernst

aloft, but the hearty tune only made Buck's head hurt more. I wish I were in school, he thought morosely. The notion was punctuated by a wave of nausea and he ran for the rail again.

"Hang with it, boy," Swill sympathized as he passed. "It won't be long before ye get yer sea legs."

But Buck wondered if he would ever be well again.

BUCK AWOKE the next day without the hangover, but still too queasy from the rolling of the ship to eat. He began to learn a few things from Dutch and to make friends with the rest of the men on the starboard watch.

By evening, he felt like eating. He noticed each man had his own bowl and spoon and took it with him to the chow line.

"Dutch, where do I get a bowl for supper?"

"Boy." Dutch's brows furrowed in his ruddy face. "You had best be worrying about cold weather gear, and what yer bein' paid—and what to do with those boots." A smile crossed his broad face as he studied Buck's work boots, then he turned serious. "The high work will have your soul if you don't have proper foot gear. See Swill and he'll show you to the slop chest. You can get yourself a bowl and spoon, too. Without 'em you'll get only a dog's portion."

"A dog's portion?" Buck asked.

"Aye, a lick and a smell."

Buck laughed for the first time since he'd come aboard, and went to find Swill.

The second mate, complaining as usual, led him to a chest full of old gear where he picked out clothes that came close to fitting, and a battered pewter bowl and wooden spoon. "This'll be comin' from your wages boy, if you prove worthy of any. Now get back to your job."

The brig was being prepared for winter. All permanent lines that stayed the fore and larger aft masts, those that did not run to haul sail or set trim, were covered with tar. Cracks in the deck work were chinsed with sizing pulled from hemp ropes. All lines, blocks, and tackle were mended. Work was a plentiful commodity on the little hundred twenty-foot, square-rigged brig—and Buck was learning. He had no choice.

"Grub!" shouted a grizzled black cook who stuck his head through the narrow hatch of the doghouse at the base of the main mast. Buck ran for his bowl and spoon. A gruel made of cooked raw wheat was ladled into his bowl and topped off with a glob of molasses and piece of salt pork.

Cracker, the cook, a small, wiry, dusky-colored black man with tightly curled steel gray hair and a peach pit complexion, eyed Buck as he filled his bowl and savored the sweet smell.

"Where be your shipmate?" Cracker asked. "You boys need to get that old shore sweet meat out of your gut and get some of this salt pork down, and you be feelin' better. Take your mate this." He handed a large chunk of the stringy but nourishing salt pork to Buck and gave him a wink and toothy grin. Buck immediately liked the man, who reminded him of Tug, the freedman who was his hunting companion. As he walked away, he got a terrible yearning to be home, hunting or fishing with Tug.

Ernst still hadn't made it to the cook house. Buck found him on his bunk in the musty forecastle. "Ernst, get this in your stomach. The sooner you do, the better you'll feel."

"Thanks, Sam. I'll try."

"The name's Buck now," he corrected, crawling into his own bunk. He was asleep almost as soon as his head hit the splintered boards of the narrow slit that served as his bed.

When he awoke, he realized Cracker had been right. After eating and another night's sleep, both he and Ernst were feeling refreshed and thinking they were ready for whatever the little brig had to offer. The weather strengthened and morning found Buck called to the foremast.

"Boy, you just follow One and Baldy, and do what they

say." Buck got a grin from the broad, sun-reddened face of the Dutchman. "Listen to them, and you'll be all right."

Buck climbed up the long, rough rope ladder behind Juan Dominguez and Urbaldo Rodriquez, two thin, aristocratic-looking Spanish sailors who carried the nicknames One and Baldy. They were both tall and lean, and as hard as the cross arms they raced for. Black flashing eyes and long thin noses offset their pure Castilian features. Their coal-black hair was pulled back—Baldy's nickname was not due to lack of hair—and a queue hung to each man's shoulders. They were hard at work, and singing the boisterous sea song, "Cheerily Men," long before Buck had reached what they told him was the fore royal, the topmost sail on the foremast.

"Just keep your mind on your work, Buckito," Juan said, looking through eyes as black as obsidian and down his long aquiline nose.

"Not good to be looking down," Urbaldo advised. "It is just like working on the deck, if you do not look down."

Sail was set, the canvas snapped to work with a resounding crack. The ship heeled with the wind and, failing to heed Juan's advice, Buck's eyes widened as he saw nothing but water and foam below.

"Oh, God," he muttered to himself, his stomach churning like the white water directly beneath him. As he inched his way around in the rigging, the sailors stopped their singing long enough to chide him good-naturedly and holler advice.

Starting back down, once the sail was set, Buck made the mistake of looking for footfalls. The height and the exaggerated motion fifty feet above the deck caused him to cling to the rigging.

"Move it sogger! Move it!" shouted a sailor whose path he blocked.

"Look at me, not your feets!" cautioned Baldy from directly above where he clung.

Buck looked up, feeling his way from line to line as he descended. The next time he dared to look, he was only a few feet from the deck. He jumped, landed with a thud, and fell to the deck. "First time I'm glad to see you," he whispered to the holystoned pine of the brig that held him captive.

Later, after a supper of gruel and molasses, he was able to talk alone with Ernst for the first time. "I know the family will be worried sick. I'm sure no one knows where I am. Do you think we'll be putting into shore soon so I can get a ship back, or at least a letter off?"

"Either that," Ernst replied, "or I understand passing ships trade mail. But don't count on getting off this ship. They tell me there's no quitting once you've signed on."

"But you know I didn't sign on! It was all a mistake."

"Mistake or not, cousin...I think you're along for the trip."

Sounds of the larboard watch singing, "Blow, blow, blow the man down" echoed across the deck as they began one of the many sail changes that kept the brig moving at twelve knots per hour through the choppy seas.

And with each of those passing hours, they drew farther away from Boston and family.

———————

BUCK WORKED the kinks out of his shoulders, back, and legs —sore and aching from his hours in the rigging. But it was his hands which had taken the most punishment. The hemp ropes were merciless. He had to go to Cracker for lard to ease the pain and help heal the thousands of little scrapes and cuts.

As the boys began to show some worth, the second mate, Swill, became more talkative. Seizing the opportunity, Buck began to question him.

"Swill, you seem to know every nook and cranny of this ship. Why is it you're not a captain?"

"I have been, boy... many a time, but I came by this nickname honestly. More than once I've drunk myself out of a cabin aft. My... my teeth hurt a lot and the rum helps." He stared at Buck over a veined and bulbous nose and through watery, bloodshot eyes. "Stay away from the rum, boy. 'Tis truly the demon they say 'tis." His wistful look hardened. "I am good with the stars, so they keep me as an officer... and I earn my keep."

"You're good at just about everything," Buck said.

He nodded. "And the captain caggs me while I'm aboard the ship."

"Caggs you?" Buck asked.

"Aye, I'm not allowed to drink while aboard." Swill explained that the second mate's job was a difficult one. He was an officer, but slept and ate with the crew. His direct command was the starboard watch, consisting of himself and eight sailors; yet he slept and ate with the larboard watch also: nine other sailors under the direct command of the first mate who had a private cabin aft next to the captain's.

Buck continued his questions. He'd seen the captain and the first mate conferring often near the wheel. "Why does the captain never speak with the crew?"

"That's not the way it's done, boy. I'm told our captain was the second son of an English nobleman." Swill lowered his voice. "He decided he was entitled to his father's lands as much as was his older brother. His father banished him when his brother survived an accident and told the tale of how it happened."

"You mean he tried to kill his own brother?"

"I said nothing of the sort, boy." Swill gave him a hard look and glanced quickly over his shoulder to make sure no one heard. "But, I'll tell you true. You'll not have to look far to discover the cloven-hoof aboard this cursed vessel. At any rate, the captain joined the crew of a Brit Man O' War when he had to flee. Ended up being pressed into our Navy, and it 'pears he did well. Got himself a private job... and a soft one, if I do say. But don't get me wrong, he's a hard man. He'll brook no foolishness. He's laid the cat o' nine tails on many a sogger's back." Dropping his voice to a whisper, he added. "And he's been known to be mean as a blood-crazed shark."

He looked around, as if he were telling the darkest secret. "But the worst is, it's said he's a backgammon player."

"A what?" Buck frowned, puzzled.

"A gentleman of the back door." Buck still didn't understand. "You don't think he keeps that young Arab just to empty the piss pot, do ye, boy?"

"I don't see what you mean," Buck said, dumbfounded.

"He's said to be a sodomite, you young fool," Swill whispered. "But if you repeat that, I'll say your dicked in the nob."

"I wouldn't repeat a thing said in trust...what's dicked in the nob?"

"Crazy, lad... crazy as a pet coon."

"What about the other men?" Buck asked.

"Well, God knows there's no cock alley for months at a time." Seeing Buck's blank look, he shook his head in amazement. "Womenfolk, boy. Don't you know nothin'?" Swill smiled, showing the yellow stubs of his teeth. "Some box the Jesuit, but if ye be caught, the captain's liable to make a capon of yer."

Swill shook his head in exasperation at Buck's naiveté. "Tis to play the whore pipe, boy. With yer hand."

Finally understanding, Buck nodded sagely. Later, he watched the captain carefully, looking for some indication of what Swill had accused him of. He didn't see it. The captain was not effeminate, and Buck expected a man of that ilk would be. A tall, blond, aristocratic man, he paced the deck in the pre-dawn hours, never smiling, never saying a word except in low tones to the first mate.

Buck thought the rest of the crew was as interesting as the food was bland. The larboard watch was composed of two Finns, one Irishman, one Bostonian, two Spaniards, two Portuguese, and one Icelander. The starboard watch consisted of Dutch; Juan; Urbaldo; a half-Moroccan, half-

Portuguese called Black Dan; Ernst; two Englishmen who had been pressed into service during the war of Eighteen Twelve and never gone home; Swill; and Buck. Nine men on each watch, including the second mate. Cracker, the cook; Ahmed the cabin boy; Hard Tack, the first mate; and the captain completed the crew.

Buck looked for the chance to make friends with Ahmed, but the strange, diminutive, smooth-skinned boy never strayed far from the captain's side the few times Buck saw him on deck, and he always slept on the deck in the captain's cabin.

The men were not the only occupants of the brig. Foremost on the deck, over the forecastle, was the pigsty. Buck drew the duty of caring for the sow and her six piglets when it was discovered he was a farm boy. He found the pigs to be excellent sailors, much better than the two dozen chickens who occupied cages on each side of the sty. They had stopped laying on the second day out.

Buck lost some of his enthusiasm for their care when Cracker informed him they were kept for the captain's table, and he found out the nickname for the poultry keeper, which he couldn't repeat without blushing.

As the newness wore off and the crew settled down to a regular schedule, Buck could see that Ernst was becoming bored. Unlike Buck, who found more to learn than he thought possible, Ernst looked for mischief or how to get out of work. While Buck delighted in doing a job well, Ernst delighted in being able to avoid work altogether.

Buck began to worry when Hard Tack took notice of his cousin's activities, and overrode Swill's authority with the starboard watch. He sought Ernst to do the tarring, to empty the slop buckets from the mess, and, worst of all to Ernst, gave him Buck's job of swabbing out the pigsty. He had to crawl on his knees through the muck in order to get it clean to Hard Tack's standards, returning time after time to the rail to lower buckets for clean saltwater, then again for buckets to clean himself. Ernst hated the job and began to hate Hard Tack.

The watches were clannish, each trying to better the other when called to all hands. Where the starboard watch would overlook Ernst's irritating traits, the larboard made a point of ridiculing him.

As the brig neared the equator, the breeze began to fail and more and more the little ship was hove to, waiting. On the twenty-fourth day out of Boston, booms and yardarms creaking with the slow roll of the ship as they lay dead in the water. Lifeless lines and dejected sails, now looking brown, spotted, and dirty in their slackness, waited.

Buck was bored and had to look for work for the first time since he'd been aboard. Being becalmed began to try all their nerves. Even the singing was muted and dejected.

Without a breeze, the heat became unbearable. The crew kept busy picking okum and hemp for caulking, mending line, and tarring, but the chief occupation was complaining. The hot sun and humidity also brought another kind of unwelcome life. Flies, roaches, and bedbugs began to proliferate.

And the lack of a breeze brought back the odors of shore. Smells usually carried away on the freshening wind—the hogshead of tar, the little pigsty, and worst of all, each other—now hung over the steamy deck.

The sea did not give a ripple. Indolently, it heaved up and down in great flat sheets of gray. The ship's booms, like batons, led a muted symphony. Only the yardarms creaked, responding with sound.

After days of making only a few miles headway, Dutch, Black Dan, One, and Baldy sat picking okum on the deck. Swill, Ernst, and Horace were aloft replacing a block that was not running properly. Horace was a big Boston boy of Norwegian descent who appeared a bit slow to Buck and a bit of a bully. He continually got more of his share of the gruel and salt pork, and always pushed his way into line.

Buck noticed that even Ernst steered clear of him, excluding him from any of his horseplay.

Buck had talked Cracker into letting him help clean the galley and, since there was little work for the men to do, Swill did not complain about his absence on deck. Cracker teased Buck about his shoes, drawn from the slop chest and already beginning to wear through the sides.

"Boy, those holey shoes is fine for dis weather but dat snow and ice 'round de horn is gonna freeze your toes together like an old duck. If we gotta swim 'round, you gonna be fine."

"With all the hides in California," Buck said, "I'm sure I'll find a pair of boots as good as any made."

"No, dey got de hides, but we got de shoes and boots in de hold, along with all kinds of trade goods. We hauls de hides to Boston, and de shoes back."

The conversation was interrupted by a shout from outside.

Buck stepped out of the cookhouse and looked up at a commotion in the rigging. High above, Horace hung with one arm looped over the yardarm, his flailing feet kicking freely. Swill caught him under his free arm, hauled him up, and helped him regain his footing. He stood on a taut line between Swill and Ernst, then swung a ham-like fist that caught Ernst a glancing blow on the temple and yelled an indistinguishable profanity as the red-headed boy rapidly retreated down the rigging.

Ernst made the deck well ahead of Horace and beat a hasty retreat to the middle of his watch mates. Horace and Swill raced up behind.

"You bloody, buffle-headed bastard," Horace sputtered. "You... you... I almost fell because of this... this sogger sono-fabitch!" Horace directed his tirade to the crew in general.

Ernst carefully maneuvered the whole crew between him and Horace. Hard Tack, who had been near the helm, came to see about the ruckus.

"What's this now? I'll have no fighting onboard this ship!"

"This... he... I almost fell!" Horace shouted. "If it weren't your ship, sir, I'd beat his bloody head in. He kicked me right out of the shrouds!"

"I slipped, sir," Ernst said. "I almost fell myself. It was an accident."

"Well, well now." Hard Tack flashed a tight smile, the closest his pocked face had come to a grin since he'd seen Buck throwing up in the scuppers. "We need a bit of entertainment, and you two have a grudge to settle. Let me have a word with the captain."

When Hard Tack turned and went below, Black Dan pulled Ernst aside. "Boy, you stay away from him. Don't tie up with him no matter what."

"What... what do you mean? What's happening?"

Black Dan looked incredulously at a wide-eyed Ernst. "Why, boy, you've got a fight on your hands."

4

"No GOUGING OR KICKING," the captain commanded, "fight fair as shipmates should." Obviously enjoying himself, he climbed to his familiar place on the quarter deck to watch the entertainment.

Looking like a man sitting down to a feast, Hard Tack pointed to a clear spot next to the galley. The crew clamored to the rail, to the top of the galley deck house, and fanned out across the deck. No one stepped in front of the quarter deck where the captain stood. Hard Tack climbed up to join Taylor-Johnson. Horace stood confidently at the center of the ten-foot horseshoe of men, his shirt removed, tufts of golden chest hair glistening in the sun.

He was only two or three years older than Ernst, but he'd been at sea for over ten years. His shoulders and arms bulged with muscles earned from years in the rigging. Outweighing Ernst by thirty pounds, he stood an inch taller. A crooked smile crossed his lips as the crew shoved Ernst forward.

The larboard watch tried to wager with Ernst's watchmates—there were no takers.

Buck watched quietly. He didn't approve of his cousin's shipboard actions, but, still, Ernst was his friend and cousin. "Be careful," Buck muttered.

A boyish hundred and sixty pounds, Ernst raised his fists in the Queensbury tradition. His only possible advantage was speed. He had been in more than his share of boyhood scraps and managed to maintain an air of confidence.

Horace's smile faded and he lashed out with his fists, missing his target but catching Ernst on the upper right chest with a hollow thump. Ernst instinctively countered with a hard-thrown overhand left that landed on Horace's cheekbone, then quickly followed with a right that caught him squarely on the nose with a smack heard over the excited men. The left hook reddened Horace's cheek, but the right brought a rush of blood and staggered the bigger boy.

Horace's eyes widened, but he was not badly hurt. The blows brought a cheer from the starboard watch. One and Baldy pounded Buck on the back. "He does well, your cousin!" Baldy said.

Buck saw the glimmer of a smile cross Ernst's face as he closed with the larger boy.

"No, no," muttered Black Dan, but it was too late. Horace locked Ernst in a bear hug and squeezed, catching both his arms in Horace's own powerful, knotted ones. Ernst gasped as he ran out of breath and could not catch another. Horace's face contorted and his biceps bulged. Ernst's face reddened, his eyes bugged-out, and he gasped for breath. Horace raised him off his feet and slammed him to the deck as Ernst went slack in his grip.

On his knees, his head hanging forward, Ernst struggled for breath with wheezing gasps. Horace stepped in with a powerful uppercut, catching him squarely on the nose before he could rise. Blood spewed and the blow drove him back to one knee. A solid right smacked to the side of Ernst's head with a sickening crunch, sending him sprawling across the deck. He dizzily struggled to rise, a hand on the deck, blood starting in a thin line below his left ear and gushing from his broken nose.

Horace closed again, bringing his knee up into Ernst's

already mutilated face. The crunch resounded across the now silent deck, and Buck charged forward. But the crew caught him, pinning his arms before he could get to Horace.

Ernst rolled over on his stomach, gasping for breath through a nose and mouth filled with blood. He managed to sit, his legs outstretched on the deck. Horace closed again, kicking him full in the stomach. Ernst slammed back to the deck, unconscious.

Buck struggled against his captors. Black Dan grabbed him, pulling him face to face. "Easy boy... it's over... it's over. No one is much the worse for it. There'll come another day."

Buck set his jaw, blood pulsing with anger, but he stopped struggling. He would even this score, he promised himself as he eyed the laughing crew patting Horace on the back. Maybe not now, he thought, garnering his self-control, but sooner or later.

He relaxed his taut muscles and the crew released him. Stepping forward, he knelt beside his cousin, face down on the deck blowing bubbles in his own blood. Buck grabbed a bucket, went to the scuttlebutt, and began to dip fresh water.

"Don't use the fresh, boy," Dan cautioned.

Again his jaw tightened. He relented and tied a halyard to the bucket, then dropped it over the side, retrieving it hand over hand. He poured the saltwater gently over his cousin. The scuppers ran red as he flooded the deck. Coughing and trying to catch his breath, Ernst slowly regained consciousness.

Buck sighed with relief and glanced up. The captain and Hard Tack stood laughing on the quarter deck. It was the first time Buck had seen the captain smile, much less laugh, since they had left Boston.

Helping Ernst to his feet, Buck guided his stumbling cousin down the ladder to the dank forecastle. As Ernst collapsed into his bunk, Hard Tack's shadow fell across the forecastle floor.

His voice gruff and demanding, he yelled from the top of the ladder, "Back to work you two. You're shift isn't over yet."

Buck ignored him. He tore two small patches from the tail of his shirt, rolled them into balls, and stuffed them into Ernst's nostrils, stemming the flow of blood. Then he turned to climb the ladder. Ernst tried to rise and follow, only to be pushed back into the bunk.

"You stay," Buck commanded.

When he reached the deck, Hard Tack waited, his pocked faced contorted in a sneer. "Where's Ernst? It's back to work for that sogger. He hardly got any exercise."

"He's going to stay in his bunk," Buck said resolutely.

"Why, you little sonofabitch. You'd sham Abram with me!" He lunged for Buck, but Black Dan stepped between them.

"He doesn't understand, Mr. Tacker," Dan said. "We'll fetch the boy to his job. Come on lad." Hard Tack glowered at Black Dan, but made no move toward Buck.

Pushing Buck ahead of him, they descended the ladder into the forecastle. "Boy, don't be forgettin' who's God on this vessel," Dan cautioned. "They can have your hide at any time. Now, get your cousin back on his feet."

For two long days, as Ernst healed and Buck seethed, the little ship bobbed in the doldrums.

Then the breeze began to freshen.

"Sail ahoy!"

The cry rang from a high yardarm. The captain hurried to the deck. He brought out a glass, looked the approaching ship over, then gave Hard Tack the order to come ten points to port. The two ships hove to, not a cable's length apart. The Aries furled smoke-stained sails. The fires under her trypots were quiet. She was one year, one hundred and eighty-five days out of Baltimore and bound for home, lying deep in the water, laden with whale oil.

The mail was gathered from the men of the Virginia and brought to the captain in his cabin. Of the twelve folded and wax sealed letters, six were addressed to Edward Mueller, Kathleen Mueller, or Wilhelm Mueller. The captain eyed them thoughtfully, then dropped them into a spittoon next to his writing desk. He dragged a sulfur head across the pine floor and after it flared, dropped it in on top of them.

Leaving, he turned to Ahmed. "See that they burn to ash."

Hard Tack selected four men to lower the longboat and pull oar. The hair on Buck's neck bristled as he saw a Mueller Manor ham being carried by Taylor-Johnson as a gift for the Aries captain. Buck hadn't seen the hams or souse since the night they had boarded.

Ernst was selected to man the oars, while Buck watched, envious yet pleased—his letters were on their way. For the first time in nearly four weeks he sighed with contentment. He hadn't dwelled on thoughts of home, but now this slight brush with the outside world brought a flood of memories. He wondered who made the souse and scrapple? Who ground and packed the sausage? The thought of the task falling to Edward Jr. brought a smile to his face—there was nothing the young boy hated worse.

As he lay in the equatorial sun, Buck thought of the cool breeze rippling the pond where he and Tug had catfished. He closed his eyes and could almost smell the pork chops and biscuits on his mother's supper table.

"Heave to, boys. Man the yardarms." The order jerked him back to reality.

He raced for the mainmast and led the crew to the foreroyal. Sail snapped to work in the stiffening wind, and they were underway again. The Aries disappeared to the aft, on its way to Baltimore.

After several days, the swelling in Ernst's nose disappeared, and Buck's anger subsided with it. He seethed with quiet resentment, but no real harm had been done, and perhaps Ernst had learned a lesson. Now at least his cousin behaved himself, he grudgingly admitted. No tricks and no dodging work. Still, at every opportunity, Hard Tack hazed him.

Ernst cleaned the pigsty every other day and was given the job of emptying the chamber pots from both the captain's and Hard Tack's quarters, a job formerly assigned to Ahmed. The more withdrawn Ernst became, the more Hard Tack rode him. Swill sent him wherever he hoped Hard Tack wouldn't be, trying to protect him from the first mate's vindictive wrath.

On the twenty-eighth day out of Boston, the Virginia plowed across the equator with a favoring aft wind. Buck and Ernst were the only crew members who had not previously been there. As was the custom, they were initiated into the Honorable Order of Neptune.

The crew stripped them to the waist and ran them several turns around the deck. Blindfolding them, they doused them with buckets of sea water. Laughing, threatening far worse, they tied halyards under their arms and hoisted them up to the first yardarm, then they lowered them with a gut-wrenching rush and spun them until they were so dizzy they could barely stand. Again, they were doused with buckets of saltwater.

Ernst took it resignedly. Buck tolerated it good-naturedly.

Then, as the initiation drew to a close, Horace stepped in close, hitting Ernst full in the face with a load of sea water—and also the heavy wooden bucket. The crew fell silent.

Buck tore the blindfold from his eyes at the sudden quiet. The crew stood watching Ernst and Horace. It was obvious to Buck what had happened. Blood flowed in a small rivulet down Ernst's cheek, dripping onto his chest where it mixed with the sea water, making it look much worse than it really was.

Ernst stood, with an expression of stolid resignation, blindfold still in place.

Buck's heart pounded. He clenched his fists and in two long strides, closed the distance. His blow, backed by shoulders that had now been forty two days in the rigging, caught Horace under his ear at the hinge of his jaw. Horace hit the deck as if he had fallen from the top gallant yardarm. Almost in the same motion, Buck scooped up the bucket on its first bounce, swung it over his head and brought it down flat on Horace's face with a sickening splat as Horace lay on his back, unconscious.

If Ernst's nose had been badly broken, Horace's was horribly smashed. The bucket managed to split one eyebrow and chip his two front teeth. Dead silence reigned on the brig for a moment, then was broken by the sound of Hard Tack running from the quarter deck where he had been watching the initiation.

"Seize that man... seize him!" The crew hesitated a moment, then three men from the larboard watch grabbed Buck. Ernst removed his blindfold and stood wide-eyed, dumfounded by the scene.

"Bare his back and strap him to the mast," ordered Hard Tack, turning and gathering up the tail of a three-quarter inch halyard.

Buck struggled but found himself bound tightly by rough hemp rope. As the line began its first whistle through the air, he realized what was happening. The first blow across his naked back staggered him and he fought to keep from crying out. Before he could catch a breath, the second landed with a resounding crack and he gasped. The third buckled his knees, but he clamped his jaw and made no sound. The fourth blow, falling across his neck, blinded him for a moment but his vision returned. He closed his eyes so he wouldn't see the next blow coming.

He hardly felt the next few. On the tenth blow, he collapsed to the deck. Welts rose in inch-wide, bleeding crosses on his back. His gasping breath, as the crew watched quietly, was the only sound other that the whistling of the halyard through the air.

"That'll teach ye some manners," Hard Tack growled, collecting the halyard into a coil. As he turned away, he overheard one of the crew members mumble, "He's a tough landlubber. Not a whimper."

"I'll show you soggers whimper." The first mate spun back and again the line whistled over his head to come down across Buck's bleeding back. He jerked with a fresh spasm of pain.

"Bastard," Ernst whispered, then, fury sweeping through him he slipped a ten-inch marlin spike out of Dutch's belt. As Hard Tack flung his arm back to deliver the twelfth vicious lash, Ernst closed the half-dozen paces between them. He put the full force of both arms into the blow, driving the iron spike into the man's thick shoulder, sinking it a full two inches into his right joint.

The brawny first mate's eyes went wide. He dropped the hemp line and staggered back, fearing the second blow, then realized the spike was still embedded in his shoulder. Sinking to his knees, his face as white as the sail, he grasped the iron with both hands and tried to pull it free.

Buck missed the pleasure of Hard Tack's moan of pain and the sick look on his face. He had passed out—without uttering a sound.

Dutch stepped forward as Hard Tack lay on his back, still gripping the marlin spike embedded in his shoulder. The big ruddy seaman placed a foot on either side of the spike and jerked hard to remove it. Hard Tack cried out, one arm limp, the other clutching his bleeding wound.

The captain hadn't left the quarter deck. Without raising his voice, he pointed to Ernst. "Bind him to the center of that sheet. I'll scrape the insolence from the bastard. We'll teach this educated sogger some manners."

The men merely stood, staring at Captain Taylor-Johnson.

"I said keel-haul him!" he shouted.

Ernst was pulled to the rail by several of the crew members. One end of a long line was carried forward and passed under the bowsprit and then brought back to the opposite rail, where a pull on that end would drag Ernst under the brig. The hundred twenty-ton ship had a beam of only twenty two feet and a draft of twelve, but she ran under full sail, cruising through the water at ten knots.

White water sang, roiling under her gunnels. Staring at the foaming froth below, memories Ernst had blocked for years flashed through his mind. He could see the little catboat his father had once owned. It lay on its side, knocked down by a gust of wind. His mother was in the water, twenty or thirty feet away from him. He yelled for help as his father swam toward him. His father dragged him, choking and spitting to the boat, hoisted him up on it, then began madly searching for his mother, but it was too late. She had already gone under.

Ernst remembered the taste of sea water, and of fear. He remembered his father crying as they clung to the catboat waiting for help.

Fear lay in his mouth like a copper serpent as he was readied for his ordeal. His shipmates pushed him to the very edge of the deck and hoisted him over the rail. His throat constricted, and his eyes began to water then burn with fear.

"Haul away," the captain shouted.

Ernst's body trembled with fright as he was jerked over the side. He grasped for the rail, fighting to hold onto it, but the power of ten pulling men wrenched him loose and he tumbled into the sea with a scream.

His watchmates had been standing by, observing the proceedings. Now they joined in. The faster they hauled him under the brig, the better chance he had to live.

Ernst's first sensation was one of white, white foam as he passed through the bow wake of the rapidly traveling ship. He cried out, taking in huge gulps of water, its salti-ness gagging him, burning his throat, and finally his windpipe and lungs. The barnacles on the hull tore through his striped shirt and duck pants, ripping and splitting skin and flesh. He rolled and turned as he careened against the hull. Mercifully the rope slackened and he sank away for a moment, only to be slammed back against it. Again and again, he slammed and scraped.

His lungs about to burst, he gasped for air. Receiving only a lung full of burning saltwater and sea trash knocked from the ship's crusty bottom, he blacked out.

The sea spat him up forty feet aft of where he was pulled over as the crew hauled him from rail to rail. They dragged him to the deck unconscious. Draping him over a cask, they began pumping sea water from his lungs. Cracker worked over him until the captain raised his voice again.

"Cook, you tend to Mr. Tacker; his watchmates will see to the sogger."

Each time a man touched Ernst, he came away with bloodied hands. But their efforts were rewarded with a gasp and a choking cough, then several more. Ernst's body had been cut and scraped over almost every inch, his scalp laid open to the bone by sharp barnacles, his pants and shirt torn to shreds.

As William Taylor-Johnson returned to the quarter deck, he spoke casually to Swill. "It seems the hull is in need of a scraping."

"Aye captain, so it would seem."

Ernst had been taken below before Buck came to. Dutch and Urbaldo untied him and laid him face down on the deck, dousing his back with saltwater to cleanse his wounds, but sending fresh pain racking through him.

After tending to Hard Tack and taking him down to his bunk, Cracker returned and gently applied a salve of lard and calomel to the cuts and welts on Buck's back. Cracker had taken great pleasure in Hard Tack's moans of pain as he had packed the first mate's wound, suggesting to the captain that he cauterize it with a red-hot iron.

Unfortunately, the captain had not agreed.

"How's Ernst?" Buck asked as soon as he opened his eyes, then he flinched from Cracker's ministrations and gritted his teeth.

"Don't know, boy; had to go aft first. Let me finish with you, then we go tend him."

"It looked like just a cut."

"No, boy. They done keel-hauled him. I guess you was passed out."

"What do you mean, 'keel-hauled'?" Buck started to get up, but Cracker urged him back down.

"Stay here and let me finish dis, den we go see to dat boy." Cracker finished applying the salve, following Buck as he struggled to his feet and headed for the forecastle.

Swill stood at the helm, Hard Tack and the captain were below, and the starboard watch was on duty. Buck would have been expected back on duty, lashing or no, if it had been his watch. He ran for the ladder, jumping half way down into the forecastle. He stopped and stared, his stomach luffing like the sails on a windless night. He wanted to run from the room at the sight of his torn and bleeding cousin, but instead bent over him.

Ernst lay with one arm hanging to the deck, quietly moaning.

"Jesus, Cracker... Jesus, look at him. What did they...? Those bastards! What did they do to him?"

"I done told you, boy. Dey keel-hauled him. Dey tied a line to him and hauled him under the ship." Cracker stared down at the bunk.

"Ernst... Ernst." Buck softly shook him, awakening him from his stupor.

"Sam... I got him Sam," Ernst mumbled, then faded back into unconsciousness.

"Who's Sam?" Cracker scratched his kinky, steel-gray head. "Dis boy is dreaming of better places."

"What'd he mean, Cracker? Who did Ernst get?"

Cracker's mouth curled into a half grin. "He got Hard Tack, boy. Whacked him good with a marlin spike. Stuck him real deep... in the shoulder. Too damn bad it wasn't a little lower and a little deeper. He done it 'cause it looked like old Hard Tack was just gonna keep on whippin' you." He shook his head. "Dat spike went in real deep. I had to take both hands to pull it out."

Buck knelt beside Ernst's bunk, tears welling in his eyes. He wiped them away with the back of his hand, uncaring if Cracker saw. "What can we do for him, Cracker? He's cut real bad all over."

"We got to clean the trash out, den we gots to wait.... This salve will do a bit of good, but it's not the cuts what gets 'em, it's de coughs, once they gets all dat bad water in the lungs."

They began cleaning out the minute bits of shell and seaweed which permeated the cuts on Ernst's raw, seeping body. As the cuts begun to scab, clear lymph formed little wet spots. Soon Ernst was moaning again, and almost as soon, coughing. He hacked deeply.

"I seen dis too many times," Cracker mumbled, his hands working over Ernst's body. "The lungs keep gettin' full, they coughs and coughs gobs out of em', then de fever comes."

A shadow cast across Ernst's prostrate body. Swill stood in the hatch-way. "Buck.... The captain, he says for you to tend to. You'll have to leave him. I... I'm sorry." His expression and the softness of his voice betrayed the distaste he felt for having to pass the order along.

"Cracker, will you watch out for him?"

The little cook simply nodded. Too affected by Ernst's condition and his own aching and burning back to respond to the anger that now seethed inside him, Buck moved stiffly forward and up onto the deck. His back was on fire, every muscle in his body screaming out against movement. Still, all he could think of was Ernst.

Later, quietly working with Dutch sewing a bolt rope into a main top gallant that had blown out, he spoke his thoughts to his friend. "That son-of-a-bitch shouldn't be captain, Dutch. No man should suffer such brutal treatment."

"Boy, all who own harps are not harpists. He'll meet his comeuppance, but I fear not on this voyage."

"He may," Buck said softly.

"A wise man wouldn't try to swim against the tide, son."

Buck merely eyed him and continued shoving his needle through the line.

5

FOR THE NEXT THREE DAYS, Buck cared for his cousin during every off moment. He couldn't get him to eat, even during his few lucid moments, but did manage to get water down him. Ernst coughed continually, a deep, racking, phlegm-filled cough.

When Buck returned from the morning watch, Ernst lay on his back, one arm hanging to the deck. Spittle and phlegm had run out the side of his mouth and dried. His slack mouth hung open and his sightless eyes stared straight ahead. Buck moved forward slowly, unable to accept what he saw, his heart thudding dully inside his chest.

He stopped at the foot of the bunk, wanting to scream but no sound came. Instead, he crashed a fist into the bulkhead, then slowly sank to his knees.

He sat there for long, pain-filled moments, staring at his cousin and friend, wishing somehow he could have saved him. Finally, he rose and stood next to Ernst. With hands that shook he removed his shirt, dipped it in the bucket of water he kept next to Ernst's bunk, and carefully began to wash his cousin's face. He ran his fingers through Ernst's red hair, smoothing it away from his forehead, remembering times they had spent together through the years.

When he finally glanced up, he saw Swill frozen in the doorway.

"Sweet Jesus, I'll get the captain." He spun and raced for the ladder.

Buck's chest felt full of hot rocks. His stomach churned, feeling oddly hollow. Fresh tears welled but he sobbed only once. His eyes were dry by the time the rest of the starboard watch congregated in the forecastle. They moved aside as Swill returned with Hard Tack.

The first mate watched Buck preparing his dead cousin's body. "Fetch Cracker. Tell him to get a bit of old sailcloth and get this sogger ready to make a hole in the water. You boys divvy up his things. He had nothing the captain or I will be wanting."

"No!" Buck snapped, his grief set aside by a steely resolve. "Any bastard touches my cousin's things will rot in hell before this day is over!"

"'Tis the custom aboard ship," Hard Tack grumbled. "His things will be divided—"

Buck stood not two paces away, Ernst's ten-inch knife suddenly clutched in his hand. Cold, unblinking eyes fixed on the big first mate.

"Well, you are a relative," Hard Tack stammered. "I guess that does make a difference." Turning away, he hurriedly climbed the ladder, one arm hanging limp at his side.

Within the hour the crew gathered at the rail. Wrapped from head to toe in sailcloth, sewed tightly by Dutch's deft stitches, Ernst was offered to the deep. The captain ordered the Dutchman to perform the ceremony. As they all looked on, the shrouded body slid from its bed of tilted boards, hung suspended for a moment as if reluctant to seek the cold depths, then dropped into the foaming sea and disappeared below the wake of the brig.

Buck stood staring at the water, which had accepted his dead cousin body with a nonchalance that equaled its immensity. His chest leaden, his mind reeling with emotion, he returned to his bunk and awaited the next watch. For days he spoke to no one, just did his work, slept, ate, and repeated the cycle.

The breeze remained steady. Each time he returned to his berth, he thought of home—longed for it. Thoughts of the family he'd left behind lingered on his mind now more than any time since he had left Boston.

He reasoned that if a man could die so quickly, without warning, at the hands of other men, maybe he shouldn't plan for tomorrow—but live his life for today. And maybe he shouldn't let others get too close.

He had disliked the captain and first mate prior to Ernst's death, now he distrusted and despised them with a hatred he never before thought possible. At first, he had at least respected them for their competence in handling the ship. Now he doubted even that.

If he was to live, he reasoned, if he was ever going to return to his home, if he was going to survive this voyage, he must learn all he could. Learning must become more than just a way to pass the time, it must become an obsession. Each of the men on board had skills, languages, talents. All had something to offer. He would seek what was valuable in each man, overlook what was not and be cautious of it, and he would be constantly diligent.

He would glean that which he could use.

His mind sorted through the men he knew. Dutch was a good sailor, but more than that, he was well educated. He continually quoted the world's scholars and philosophers, applicable lines for any situation. Buck thought Dutch must have read everything ever written.

Juan and Urbaldo each spoke Spanish as only those raised with a language are able—and this ship was headed for Spanish-speaking California.

Swill was a navigator. He knew the stars, and a man who knew the stars would never be lost—on sea or land. The second mate had intimated to Buck on a late-night watch, that Black Dan had been a pirate and a soldier of fortune.

He wore an earring, whic signified a sinking, or more pointedly, the survival of a sinking.

It was rumored among the men that Dan had sailed under many a privateer's flag and was expert with the cutlass, dagger, and musket. Black Dan had never said a score of words to Buck, but the stout little Portuguese was always willing to work next to him in the rigging. That meant a great deal onboard ship, for a man entrusted his life to his workmate.

Buck was now among the first two or three up the ratlines, working with the best of them. The outside of the yardarm was considered a position of esteem. It was reached by the first man to the top. More and more, Buck was the man on the outside, beating even Dan into the rigging. Black Dan could teach him a great deal, if the rumors about him were indeed true.

Buck resolved that he would winnow the wheat from the chaff.

He began that very afternoon, after the sail was set and the ship was on a comfortable beam run, when the crew had a chance to relax. Most of them congregated on the deck, one with a button accordion, others with cymbals made of pot lids, someone played a mandolin, another a pair of penny whistles. The fufu band, as the sailors called it, played accompaniment to the singing of a full-crewed shanty. Buck joined in for a while, then the men grew tired of playing, and some of them drifted away.

For the first time since Ernst's death, Buck pulled the small leather chest from under his cousin's old bunk. He emptied it carefully, then refolded and repacked the contents. Luckily, he and Ernst were nearly the same size. Even closer now that he had another three months' growth and, more importantly, the development of a neck and shoulders muscled by hours in the shrouds.

Buck laughed softly as he refolded the set of Sunday best Ernst had vainly packed—the first laugh he'd allowed himself since his friend's violent death.

Removing the small piece of line around his waist he'd been using as a belt, he tried on one of fine leather that Ernst had packed away. As he bound it around his trousers, he noticed the weight of the center portion and studied it. The light leather backing folded up, revealing another leather flap which pulled away from the heavier main belt.

Tucked into a small crease were ten lovely little gold coins, each a shiny five-dollar gold piece. Ernst had never mentioned them. Quickly, Buck concealed them again since another crew member sat in the forecastle mending clothes.

The Virginia plowed on.

Buck fell to his work with a fervor. Once again, he had something for which to strive. He questioned Black Dan at every opportunity. Soon he had the ex-pirate telling his many experiences, though never in anyone else's presence, and not before swearing Buck to a blood oath of secrecy.

Dan taught him the subtleties of the use of the dagger and cutlass. They drilled for hours in the cramped forecastle while the rest of the watch was on deck or lolling in their bunks. Dan was a short man, but what he lacked in height he more than made up for in brute strength. Black curly locks, usually bound in a bandanna, and flashing black eyes accentuated the tight curly hair that covered his muscular body and masked most of a swarthy complexion.

At first, Dan laughed at Buck's amateurish attempts to emulate his cutlass moves, using lengths of cargo ricking they had taken from the hold. But soon his laughter became well-spaced with intervals of hard breathing interrupted by grunts, as Buck began to land blow for blow. Within days, both men were marked with bruises where the blunt blows landed.

After weeks of practice, Buck let the older man have some peace, but not until he knew he could best him. Even then, he continued to pump the swarthy man for fighting stories and strategies.

Dutch, the most skilled hand on board, taught Buck the basic skills of the sailor and a good deal of basic engineering. Everywhere onboard ship, blocks and tackles and levers eased the sailor's burden.

The windlass raised a hundred fathoms of wet triple-braided line, ten fathoms of iron chain, and four hundred pounds of iron anchor, using only the broad backs of four sailors.

Dutch carefully explained the use of the block and tackle, where each pull of the line was reduced to one fourth its original length but increased to four times its power by the blocks. During his instruction, Buck lost a wager to Dutch—his molasses ration for the next three days —when he bet that Dutch couldn't break a half inch braided line with his bare hands.

The man deftly secured one end of the line to the rail, looped the end around the foremast, put a harness hitch in the line near the rail and another near the mast, creating a block and tackle without the mechanical blocks. The line parted on his first heave. Dutch grinned and winked and clapped Buck on the back.

The gruel just wasn't the same without the molasses.

Buck questioned the Dutchman every time he came up with one of his profound sayings. The ruddy-complected man quoted the ancient Greeks, the Romans, the Bible, Bacon, Payne, Shakespeare, and dozens of others. Not only could he quote them, but he could usually name the book from which it had originated.

Before they were fifteen days past the equator, Dutch had taught Buck one of the most valuable lessons he would learn aboard the brig. They were sitting on the bow away from the other men reading the Farmer's Almanac, the Virginia on a comfortable run, her spankers and jibs wing and wing with the wind dead aft.

"Buck, would you do me a favor?" Dutch asked.

He looked up curiously; Dutch usually called him boy or son. "Sure. What's that?"

"I... I've got some letters.... I've been carrying them all the way from Boston." He looked around warily, making sure no one stood close by. "Could you read them to me?"

Buck laughed. "What's the matter, old man? Your eyes beginning to fail you?"

"No, Buck, that's not it. I... I can't read," he whispered.

"You can't read! What do you mean you can't—"

"Sssh—I don't want the others to know."

Buck digested that a moment. "How the devil do you know half the world's writings if you can't read?"

Dutch smiled. "Why... I listen, boy." He explained that on many ships, the captain, officers, or one of the educated crew would read aloud to any who cared to listen. Dutch had spent countless hours on endless voyages over the world's oceans, listening.

"I not only hear, boy... I listen. You'll come to learn that the two are not the same. Then I mull it over in my mind. You learn to listen, then you'll come to understand."

Buck read Dutch's letters with a strange new respect for the man and sat pondering long after his friend had left.

He resolved right then that he would teach Dutch to read.

WILHELM MUELLER SAT at his kitchen table fingering the folded parchment that had arrived only moments before, afraid to open it. Equally afraid not to. He would have done it at once had it been from Ernst, but from the captain? That was a far different story.

Finally, he slipped a table knife under the wax seal and unfolded the ivory paper.

Dear Dr. Mueller:

It has come to my attention that a Buck Mueller has accompanied your son onboard the Virginia. He has been considered a stowaway. However, I have consented to pay him a sailor's wage if

he will tend to. He claims to be a cousin of Ernst's, so if his family
is unaware of his whereabouts, please inform them.
  Your obedient servant,
  Capt. William Taylor-Johnson

Wilhelm sat quietly for a few moments then called for his housekeeper. "Mrs. Foxe, please run to the livery and have them harness my carriage. I must journey to Mueller Manor." He walked quickly to the stairway. "I won't be returning until morning."

———————————

"LAND HO!"

The cry echoed from the main topgallant cross-tree, where a sailor sat bending a line and looking for a break on the horizon. The first sight of land in sixty-three days brought a cheer from the crew. The captain ascended to the quarter deck, laid his glass to starboard, and gave the order to come about. The brig had been trying to beat into a fifteen-knot head wind across her port bow since dawn.

"Mr. Tacker," the captain said, "we'll ride this wind to the harbor of Pernambuco. Perhaps we'll get a fairer wind on the turn of the tide."

Nearing the harbor, the order rang across the decks to break out the empty water casks. They dropped anchor in ten fathoms of green water, not a cable's length from shore. They backed the sails smartly and hove to with the anchor line being hauled aft and made fast. They dropped a second anchor forward and the men turned to on the windlass with the aft line until the forward line took hold and they were solid.

Buck scanned the shore, inhaling the musty aromas that came from the land. A few red tile roofs stood out among the many thatched ones. A Catholic church raised its proud bell tower in the center of the little Brazilian town. The lush jungle grew right to the town's edge on two sides; the sea and a river bordered the other two.

Another hundred yards into the harbor a full rigged three-masted whaler, the Noble out of Baltimore, sat swaying on the incoming tide.

Swill called for oarsmen and every man stepped forward. Buck was not selected. The long boat, loaded to the gunnels with empty water casks, made several trips to and from a little wharf at the end of the town's main street. The wind had freshened but not varied a degree in direction. It came from under a gray mottled sky.

The weather was changing. The brig could not leave the harbor against a head wind. If worst came to worst and breeze turned to storm, the brig would seek the protection of the mouth of the river.

Finally, the captain called all hands. "All right men, there will be shore leave for you, but any manjack who doesn't meet his boat will wish he had."

Buck wondered if he would be included. The starboard watch was given first leave, four hours ashore. Buck climbed aboard the longboat with the first load. He was surprised when he was not called back. When his feet touched solid ground, he stood for a moment, gaining his land legs.

Dutch, Black Dan, One, Baldy, and Buck made their way up one side of the main street. Blacks and browns in colorful costumes and wide-brimmed hats went about the business of the city. The crew sauntered the length of the street to a square in front of the church, then around the square and down the other side of the dirt street, enjoying the feel of solid ground.

Pigs and chickens and children gave way as they swaggered forth on their sea legs. Buck, eager to try his Spanish on the Natives, insisted on bargaining for a stalk of bananas. He succeeded in paying twice what they were worth, but at least made the vendor understand.

"I thought I was doing better with my Spanish," he complained to no one in particular.

"You're doin' fine with your Spanish, and so's the banana man—for a Portuguese." Dan laughed heartily. "You're in Brazil, boy. They speak my language here... but a little of it is the same."

Returning to the waterfront, they ducked into the first cantina they came to, a low building with a thatched roof. Openings front and back were left uncovered, inhibiting neither man nor flies from entering, but its hard-packed dirt floor was spotlessly swept, and the rough smell of hard working, hard drinking men only slightly overcame the odor of the strong soap used to scrub and polish the place.

Swill sat at a corner table alone—already well into his cups, his eyes even more bloodshot and watery than usual.

"I'm glad to see you soggers. These Noble boys are looking for their comeuppins'." He motioned to the bar where a dozen rough-looking men stood laughing and tipping their mugs. A huge, red-bearded man towered over the others. He was dressed in a pair of oilskin overalls, the uniform of the whaler.

Baldy called to a black-haired, crimson-lipped girl for a round of ale. She managed five mugs in each hand, barely spilling a drop as the whalers poked and prodded her, taking advantage of her full hands. As the Virginia crew quieted, upending their mugs and ordering more, a gruff voice rang across the room.

"Well, you see now, mates, it's like this." The red-bearded man spoke loudly enough to be sure the Virginia men heard him. "Them Boston boys is not weaned 'til they be at least two score, tis the reason they don't come to sea with the men. They can't bring no tit." This brought a great guffaw from his comrades, drowned out by his own loud guffaw.

Buck and his watchmates sat quietly talking, sipping their grog and eyeing the three barmaids who worked the room. The Virginia men purposefully ignored the Noble crew, while a swarthy man with a full black mustache, about all that showed beneath his broad-brimmed hat, worked the bar; dipping grog from a hogshead barrel and eyeing the sailors apprehensively.

Buck and his friends were well into their second round when the red-bearded man and two of his mates lumbered over to their table. Black Dan sat with his back to the bar and the Noble men. He hadn't said a word since he and his friends had entered. Redbeard, with a Noble man on either side, stopped directly behind Dan, his three hundred and fifty pounds dwarfing them all.

"Now don't you boys be takin' offense," the big man said. "A wee bit of fun don't hurt, do it? Bartender!" he bellowed. "Fetch these boys a drink." Then he turned back to the Virginia crew and smiled devilishly. "Sorry, boys, there's not a wet tit in the place." His shipmates roared, while he laughed and slapped his huge, tree-trunk thick, oil-skinned thighs.

"I might just buy St. Anthony's pig here as much as he can drink." Redbeard motioned to Dan, referring to him as a runt. "He couldn't drink much. Now, his friend there"—he pointed to Swill, who was well into his cups—"is as corned as a brisket already."

Buck saw Dan stiffen but was surprised to see him lower his head. He was even more surprised when Dan's chair moved, almost imperceptibly. Remembering his hours of instruction and Dan's repeated advice, "If there's going to be a fight, take it to them, don't wait," Buck watched him carefully.

Dan's elbow seemed to come up from the floor. Redbeard had his head thrown back. His guffaw changed to a grunt as Dan drove his elbow deep into the big man's crotch, bolting upright in the same quick motion. The full force of his thick-muscled shoulders and compact legs drove the elbow home, lifting Redbeard six inches into the air as Dan's powerful legs lifted him clear off the ground. Redbeard landed flat on his back on the dirt floor of the bar.

The other two men jumped out of harm's way.

Redbeard tried to sit up, retched a quart of foamy ale over his chest, and fell back, grasping his privates with both hands.

A deadly quiet reigned over the cantina as the crews sized each other up. Suddenly, three bar maids bolted for the front and back doors. Every man in the place rose to his feet.

Dan looked the opposition over, his hands resting cockily on his hips. "You boys are out for a bit of blubber. There's enough right here to top off yer casks." He spat on the prostrate Redbeard, who moaned and retched again.

The only answer came from the shuffling feet of the Noble's whaling crew as they began to space themselves in a semi-circle around the men of the Virginia.

Buck stood with his back to the wall, watching silently but tensely. As the bunch advanced, he was surprised to see Urbaldo, not Dan, make the next move. While the whaling crew had their eyes fixed on Black Dan, Baldy, demonstrating incredible agility, kicked a short, squat Noble crewman squarely in the side of the head. His body hit the floor with a solid thump.

Buck's jaw dropped in amazed admiration, then all hell broke loose in the crowded bar.

Tables and chairs upended. Fists, feet, elbows and knees flew. Blood and ale washed the floor as the crack and crunch of blows echoed through the room. For thirty seconds that seemed thirty minutes, the Virginia crew held its own. Keeping their backs to the wall so the Noble crew were unable to take advantage of superior numbers. Two more of the whalers went down to Dan's solid blows and Juan and Urbaldo's talented feet.

Then a well-placed stool drove Dan to his knees and three sailors kicked him into complete submission. Dutch and Buck, side by side, traded blow for blow with four stout whalers. A mug closed Dutch's eye and he was jerked from the wall into a rain of knees and feet.

Buck struggled—arms pinned by two Noble crewmen,

Dan out cold on the floor, and the balance of the Virginia crew in various forms of disrepair in the street.

Redbeard regained his feet. He swayed back and forth, spitting with each word. "These Boston sons-o'-bitches!" He kicked an unconscious Dan squarely in the ribs, rolling him onto his back and up against the wall, then he turned his attention to Buck.

"Well, suckling, it seems you're the only man still on his feet. I'll give you a souvenir to remember the Noble men— to remember who rules the sea!" He pulled a short-bladed skinning knife from a deep oilskin pocket. "I'll notch yer ear a bit. The ladies will be thinking' yer a Sydney Duck, and ye'll have a hard time of it."

The penal colonies of Australia notched the ears of inmates. "A bit of ear should remind you who your betters are."

He moved forward, determination etched on his face.

Buck struggled in vain against the hands holding him immobile. With their attention centered on the act, Redbeard reached to grab an ear. His vicious smile turned to grimace as a chair smashed across his head, dropping him to his knees and sending the knife spinning wildly across the floor.

Horace! Buck stared in amazement.

Horace and three Virginia sailors from the larboard watch had wandered into the cantina for a mug of ale. Swill and Urbaldo were also back in the fray. Buck wrenched free, and drove a fist deep in the stomach of one of the whalers, dropping him to the floor. The four Noble men still on their feet were soon dispatched by the fresh Virginia men.

Buck and the crew surveyed the room littered with prostrate men, broken mugs, tables, and chairs. Then, to the shouted curses of the barman, they gathered their battered shipmates, carrying Dan and One, and staggered along the street towards the wharf.

Horace and Buck walked quietly for a while. Finally,

Buck spoke. "I thank you. Had you not come when you did—"

Horace stopped him, laying a work-reddened hand on his shoulder. "You know I didn't mean for any harm to come to your cousin."

"It wasn't your doing and it's done." Buck's words rang with finality and Horace's tense look eased.

It took four trips in the little shore boat to return all the men to the brig. Before the morning tide, the wind shifted, the offshore breeze putting them on a pleasant beam reach. Dan was put to mending line—his collarbone broken, he couldn't lift his arm, much less climb into the rigging. Horace moved to the starboard watch to help make up for the two sailors the watch was now short.

The Virginia made good time on her run to Tierra del Fuego. More and more, clear skies gave way to mottled, and the brilliant blue of the tropics became gray and cold and windblown. The horizon disappeared in the lifeless iron-colored melding of sea and sky, smooth indolent seas turning to rough-tossed, white caps blowing away to add cutting moisture to the already freezing wind. Rain became snow and then the weather warmed again, only to freeze, forming snow and sleet. Decks froze and men were constantly kept busy chipping the ice away, when they weren't slipping and sliding and desperately trying to keep from being swept overboard to a sure death in a frigid sea. Frozen lines had to be worked until supple enough to tie into the many knots that were the sailor's trade.

Tierra del Fuego! Where wind and currents clashed, venting their anger with forty-foot waves that crashed over the bow, washing the decks with tons of freezing brine. The challenge now was not only to work, but to stay alive doing it. The reward for running the roughest water in the world would, God willing, be the warm blue South Pacific, but first the test of storm and forty-foot waves would have to be passed.

Hot food was a memory; dry clothes a dream.

Clothes were slept in so they didn't have to be thawed. Buck huddled in his bunk at night, too cold to really sleep. At times, he almost envied Ernst.

For seven days they ran at the passage, only to be beaten back by head winds and crashing tons of white water.

Finally on the eighth day the weather cleared enough that they beat far to the west, rounding the rocky headlands whose shores were covered with the skeletons of derelict ships who hadn't been so lucky. Almost as soon as they made the turn northwest, the weather cleared to sparkle as only a frigid sky can, and the wind began to favor the sails. Day to day chores seemed a respite after the trial of endurance of Tierra del Fuego.

As conditions continued to ease, Buck spent hours teaching Dutch to read, but finding time alone was difficult. Dutch was a good student, but he didn't want the rest of the crew to know what they were doing. Still, they were making good progress.

Buck and Horace were becoming good friends, and even better competitors. With each watch, they raced for the outside spot on the yardarm—their bond now as close as the splices they bound. Working hundreds of hours shoulder to shoulder in mutual dependence bred mutual respect between them.

The sky shimmered brilliant blue, the horizon a hard line, giving a man a frame of reference. Eventually, the hard line was broken by a gray-green speck in the distance. As they neared the island, fluky gusts of wind from high deep canyons kept the crew in and out of the rigging as they tried for the second landfall in four months.

The island of Juan Fernandez couldn't have looked better to Buck—unless it had been Boston.

As the setting sun cast its first red glow in the west, the brig neared the island's single harbor. All hands were called several times as the brig tacked with the ever-changing wind. Finally, the crew nearly spent, Hard Tack ready to run with the wind away from the island and try again in the fresh light of morning, the stiff breeze shifted, favoring them and rounding a small headland, they kicked the anchor free in forty fathoms of water.

Eager to go ashore, Buck, Horace, and One stood by to make the anchor rode fast when the proper amount of line had been let out, but a twist in the rode caught in the cathead. The anchor jerked up short of its mark. The brig kept charging forward. Hard Tack shouted a profanity as the rode hung up. Buck quickly slipped a three-foot pin under the kink and pried up to free it.

"Help him with that pin, you sonofabitch!" Hard Tack yelled at Horace.

Anger suffused his features. With a resentful look at Hard Tack, Horace stepped around to lend a hand just as One fed two coils of line to Buck, trying to give him the needed slack. As the kink slipped free with a resounding snap, Horace, angry and careless at being maligned, wasn't aware he had stepped into the coils laying loose on the deck. The coil clamped on his ankle, and he flew over the side of the brig, a fate-applied half-hitch on his leg. He plunged below the surface before Buck could make the rail.

Without thinking, Buck dove in, the water rushing over him, black and cold in the darkening sky. Grabbing the anchor rode with both hands as it plunged downward, the line carried him with it. Down, down, down, into the depths of the sea.

Knives of pain stabbed his lungs. His head pounded and his ears felt as if they might explode. Then the line stopped its descent. The pressure of thousands of pounds of water forced Buck to shed the now still rode and fight for the surface.

As his arms and legs shoved him forward, his vision began to blur. Needing air, desperate for it, his instincts clawed at him to breathe. He fought instinct and the pressure of the depths, grabbing the line instead, hauling himself hand over hand to the surface. His lungs burned and he struggled not to gasp for air, knowing a lung full of black murky water would be his end.

A picture of Ernst sown into a shroud of sailcloth flashed through his mind, but he battled it down. The distance covered so quickly with the help of the four-hundred-pound anchor seemed an eternity to retrace. He wasn't sure he could make it. Then knew he wouldn't. Just when he though his lungs would surely explode, his head broke the surface. Gulping in great gasps of air, he succeeded in taking in mouthfuls of stinging salt water.

In an instant, One was in the water beside him, a blurry vision he was more than grateful to see, and his shipmates were hauling him back onto the deck. They laid him flat and Cracker worked over him. The crew grabbed pins and doubled up on the windlass, trying to recover the anchor... and Horace.

"Belay that!" Hard Tack shouted. "That sailor has canceled his debts. It'll do no good to risk ship and crew for a dead man."

The men stopped recovering the rode and stood in silence. The frustration and sense of loss stilled any comment. The silence was broken only by Buck's sporadic coughing.

Death at sea seemed a closer thing than one ashore. Men who had worked, slept, and eaten gruel together for months became one—various appendages of one efficient body. The loss of a man was like the loss of an arm; the feeling was compounded when there was no physical manifestation of his passing.

He was there one moment; then he was gone. His bunk would remain vacant—a silent yawning reminder. As the ship bobbed in the waves, Dutch read from the twenty-third psalm, hesitantly, but accurately and proudly. He knew the words by heart, but this time he could read them as well: "Yea, though I walk through the valley of the shadow of death, I will fear no evil for Thou art with me. Thy rod and Thy staff, they comfort me."

The words, ringing in Dutch's resonant voice, seemed to settle like a stone in the depths of Buck's soul, as the body had settled into the depths of the sea.

The next afternoon, after several trips ashore for fresh water, the crew returned to the ship and their grisly task of turning to on the windlass. With each turn they made, they expected their efforts to be rewarded by the morbid load of Horace's body. Apprehension became unspoken relief when the anchor chain, then the anchor, appeared. Horace had obligingly sought his own less formal internment.

On Christmas Day the brig crossed the equator for the second time. The sow was butchered and a ham and shoulder baked for the men.

They had sighted no land for forty days since the coast of Mexico and California had prevailing northwesterly winds, they were forced to constantly beat into an uphill course. Buck discovered that fighting the head wind was almost as hard on the nerves as the tropical doldrums.

And there were other problems as well.

If Taylor-Johnson and Tacker had been unmerciful on the first leg of the journey, they were even more cruel and pitiless on this last uphill conclusion. More and more Buck longed for the day he would be free of the absolute control of these men. He determined he would find a way to escape the ship and prepare for his return to Boston. Another ship would get him home or, at worst, he could make the overland journey.

He knew it had been done. Other men had crossed the continent. Lewis and Clark had done it. Buck had read reports of their crossing. And he had heard the Hudson Bay Company reported numerous treks across the continent.

Then one morning, after five and a half months at sea, the brig came hard to starboard and ran easterly. Dawn broke with brilliant bronze promise through billowing clouds over a range of rugged mountains.

At last, California.

6

Santa Barbara, Alta California
March 10, 1828

BUCK PULLED the oars carefully through the floating kelp as
the captain smartly directed the longboat across the surf to
the white sand beach of Santa Barbara. As far as he was
concerned, this was the beginning of the trip home.

Buck was Boston bound.

But first he had to learn the lay of the land, all he could
of other ships, or the way East, if the journey was to be
overland. He was curious why they were landing here.
Dutch had told him Monterey, the capital, was the port of
entry for foreign ships trading in Alta California. Ships
were obliged to land there in order to gain passport to other
places.

The captain strode up the beach to talk with two men as
the boat crew tried their land legs for the first time in
months. Buck watched curiously while Taylor-Johnson
shook hands with the men, one astride a tall gray horse, the
other mounted on an equally tall palomino. They were
dressed in flat-crowned hats with wide brims, ruffled white

silk shirts, and embroidered vests. Tight-fitting breeches with silver conchos down the embroidered outside seam covered boots mostly hidden in silver studded tapaderos, which shielded the stirrups of their fancy high-pommelled saddles.

The flashing metal on their person was dimmed only by that on their tack, which was trimmed by more silver than Buck's mother placed on her holiday table.

As the captain quietly carried on his business, Buck studied the landscape. The beach gave way to gently sloping oak-spotted hills, their beauty marred by the scar of a great fire that had destroyed much of the undergrowth and many of the trees. The hills quickly rose to jagged, granite-shouldered mountains that climbed majestically in the background. Shore birds—stilts, oystercatchers, and avocets with upward curving beaks—scampered on long legs along the edge of the surf; and gulls and terns circled overhead, screeching their displeasure at having their quiet usurped.

A Boston-dressed man, with tall beaver hat, gold-tipped cane, and velvet-collared tailcoat, joined the others on the beach, then returned to the longboat with the captain. A sharply snapped order, and the men were pulling the longboat back through the rugged surf to the Virginia.

Buck was surprised once more when the brig set a southerly course, the opposite way from Monterey. As evening approached, two islands appeared through the mist off the starboard bow. Soon the two became one as the ship dropped anchor off a low isthmus connecting them—it was the island of Santa Catalina, Dutch informed him.

The next morning dawn gleamed through a tarnished gray sky. The holds were broken open, and the men began off-loading cargo. The starboard watch went ashore and the larboard set to hauling cargo in the longboat and in the little shore boat. Crates and barrels were carried and dragged up the beach and hidden in the brush. After a full day of hard labor, they returned to the brig and set sail back to the north, leaving a shore party of three men to guard the stash.

They paused again at the port of Santa Barbara, long enough to put the Boston-dressed man ashore and pick up fresh beef, then they began the arduous task of a north westerly sail into the wind toward the capital, or so the crew speculated as they ate their gruel. It tasted worse than usual since they could smell beef being cooked for the captain's and Hard Tack's table.

After five days of beating into the headwinds, the Virginia tacked east with a favoring breeze and ran for Monterey. Buck stood in the bow with the wind at his back and watched the approaching headland. The landscape had changed. The plentiful oaks of Santa Barbara were replaced by low cypress, their boughs pointing away from the sea, flagged by the prevailing winds. Buck imagined they were pointing inland, inviting him to leave the ship and welcoming him to California.

As they dropped anchor, sea otters floated on their backs in the kelp. Buck admired their playful manner, watching the pups riding on their mother's stomachs. Cormorants dived near the ship, surfacing with sardines and smelt dangling from their beaks.

They spent three days in the port of Monterey while the ship was inspected and trade began with the locals. Assigned to assist a portly government agent take an inventory of the cargo, Buck finally realized the reason for the offloading at the island. No tax could be collected on cargo not inventoried. As the revenue man checked the load, the captain entertained the governor of Monterey.

Afterwards, the two equally tall men said their goodbyes at the rail, then Buck and two of the crew manned the oars, returning the stately graying governor and his portly agent to the quay.

Since there was no one along to gainsay him, Buck boldly introduced himself to Governor Echeandia, then barraged the handsome man with questions. If he had been rowed to Boston, the governor suggested, he would not have had time to answer all of Buck's inquiries.

During the visit to Santa Barbara and Monterey, the crew had been given no shore leave. Shore time on the island was spent working under Hard Tack's watchful eye. After days of sailing up and down the California coast, the men began to grumble—their irritation compounded by the fresh meat and vegetables the officers ate each night. Only fresh wheat was added to the men's diet, replacing their weevil-infested supply. Still they were made to eat the last of the wormy salt pork and weevil laced gruel before the new supplies were opened.

Finally, Baldy complained to Hard Tack, which turned out to be an inauspicious move.

"I'll teach you to complain you sogger," the first mate threatened as he chased Urbaldo from the quarter deck, wielding a two-foot belaying pin and screaming profanities. "You'll all dine with Duke Humphrey on the morrow," he threatened, inferring a day of fasting. He stopped and shook the pin at the retreating Spaniard. "There'll be no gruel or meat for any of you sons o' bitches."

That night the men assembled in the forecastle to decide what action should be taken. Busy making his own plans, Buck kept to himself.

Swill was the officer of the deck, so the men had no worry about talking in front of the second mate.

Black Dan, usually quiet, stepped to the forefront. "I will be damned if I'll work for wages and found, and not receive them both."

"Aye, aye," the men echoed.

"It's not only the grub," one of the Englishmen said. "So long as we're laying out grievances, we might as well lay out the lot. I've been cagged for more'n a month, and it's bloody not fair."

Urbaldo joined in. "And when we do get fed, it is nothing but bug-ridden gruel and slimy salt pork, while the cap'n and Hardtack feed off the fat of the lamb."

"Aye!" the men again chimed in.

The meeting concluded with a decision to present grievances to the captain. A list was drawn up and Dutch, who
had not said a word during the meeting, was selected to be
the spokesman—after much convincing by his shipmates
that he was the man most respected by the officers. They
decided to see what would happen on the morrow. If given
fresh meat and gruel, no grievances would be presented.

Morning dawned and the breakfast hour came and went
with no grub coming forthwith. Cracker sat dejectedly on a
scuttlebutt outside his galley, watching the crew at work,
while the captain paced the weather side of the quarterdeck.
With the dawn, the wind had turned and they were running
for San Pedro, instead of Santa Barbara, their original desti-
nation. San Pedro was reportedly richer in hides, and they
would have had to beat into the wind to reach Santa
Barbara.

Grumbling among themselves, three of the larboard
watch came forward to where Dutch worked quietly on a
jib halyard. Soon they were joined by One, Baldy, and Dan.
Buck continued to work while the men pressured Dutch to
get on with his appointed task. It was clear by his expression that he dreaded it.

The captain stood looking out over the rail, not both-
ering to acknowledge the approaching sailor.

"Captain," Dutch said hesitantly, "the men have asked me
to speak for them."

"Mr. Tacker has ordered no salt pork or gruel," the
captain answered without turning. "'Tis his feeling you men
don't appreciate your rations, therefore you do not deserve
them."

"But, Captain—"

"You'll not speak to me of the problem." The captain
turned to face Dutch, his look hard and uncompromising.

The big Dutchman steeled himself, the muscles in his
hands unconsciously tensing. "Captain, we have grievances
to present. 'Tis my intention to do so."

Hard Tack appeared on the ladder, an eighteen-inch belaying pin in his hand. "You dare belabor the captain over the orders I've given? You bastard—I'll have your hide!" Hard Tack spat onto the deck, and his face turned red. He took a menacing step toward Dutch.

The older man, hands outstretched in fear of the pin, backed into the captain, trying to escape the first mate's wrath. Taylor-Johnson shoved him forcefully back toward Hard Tack, who brought the pin upward in a backhanded motion, splitting Dutch's ear. Blood gushed and the big Dutchman grabbed the ear with both hands, cocking his head just as Hard Tack brought the pin down again, the full force of his massive arms and shoulders behind it.

The first blow sounded like a slap, the second resounded with a hollow thud, smashing the protective bone over the eye socket, popping the eye out onto the cheek, and sending a spray of fluid and blood over the men now gathered at the bottom of the ladder to the quarter-deck. Dutch went to his knees and a crunching kick sent him flying off the quarterdeck into the arms of the crew below.

Buck stood frozen with the others, staring in disbelief. On the deck above them, Hard Tack shook the bloodied belaying pin and cursed them as they carried their uncon-scious comrade in to Cracker. Buck joined them, a feeling of helpless rage pulsing through him. Seeing the empty eye socket and Dutch's dangling eye, his stomach rolled, and the bile rose in his throat.

Backing out of Cracker's deckhouse hatch, Buck stum-bled to the rail, trying to contain both his anger and the contents of his stomach. Hard Tack stood calmly at the head of the ladder, feet apart, belaying pin stuffed through his belt, its coating of blood dripping down the leg of his trousers.

Buck's gaze rose to the pock-marked face of the brawny first mate. "You know, Dutch came on behalf of the whole crew," he said with deadly calm. "At the request of the whole crew." Tacker did not reply but just stood defending his position at the top of the ladder.

His hands clenching into fists, Buck turned and headed back to the galley. "Exodus 21:24," he muttered, just loud enough to be heard.

When he walked into the room, he saw Cracker heating a knife in the glowing coals of the old iron range. The sailors holding Dutch to the floor averted their gaze while the small black cook knelt beside him and carefully severed the eye from its remaining cords. When he had finished, he used the glowing blade of the knife to cauterize the open wound. Buck gagged at the stench of burning flesh that filled the galley as Cracker finished his gruesome task.

Later that night, the brig on a quiet run, Hard Tack sent Ahmed to fetch Cracker's Bible. Lying in his bunk, he found Exodus 21:24. "Eye for eye, tooth for tooth, hand for hand, foot for foot, burning for burning, wound for wound, stripe for stripe." He remembered the stripes he had laid on Buck's bare back, and his jaw tensed.

The threat, he thought, would not go well for the sogger. Setting the book aside, he blew out the whale oil lamp, his sleep fitful when it at last came.

Time and time again, he awakened, startled, at every creak of the rigging.

MORNING DAWNED with copper brilliance over a choppy blue sea. To the west, a line of coastal fog separated sky from ocean and blended in with the blue-green mountains in the distance. Gulls and terns circled the ship, scolding porpoises that joyously jumped the bow wave.

Buck ignored the serenity of the scene and fell to his work. He passed Hard Tack on the quarter deck, wanting to drive his thumbs into the back of the first mate's eye sockets. The urge passed, and he went quickly to the forecastle to see how his good friend fared.

Earlier Dutch had been fitfully sleeping, moaning with his tortured dreams as Buck had been called to his watch.

Now he lay quietly, his left eye open, his right eye covered with a patch.

"How you doin', mate?" Buck knelt on the rough board deck next to Dutch's bunk trying to sound cheerful.

"Buck?" The man swiveled his head back and forth, trying to locate his friend. "Why is it so bloody dark? Has the weather turned?" Dutch tried to sit up but Buck restrained him with a gentle hand. He didn't answer for a moment, trying to understand. It was dim in the forecastle, but a long way from dark.

"It's...it's full light outside Dutch. That sonofabitch hit you awful hard. Maybe it'll take a while for your good eye to focus like it should."

At that, Dutch touched his eyes, probing and feeling the sockets, moving his hands in front of them, trying to see. "That son of a she dog." It was the closest Buck had ever heard his friend come to cursing. "He knocked my bloody eye right out of my bloody head!"

The big, ruddy man turned his head back and forth again, his hands outstretched as if he were walking through a dark room. "Buck, I can't see a blasted thing. You say it's full light?"

"Why don't you get some rest, Dutch? I'll be back as soon as the watch is over." Refusing to confirm his friend's blindness, he gave Dutch's shoulder a squeeze then climbed the ladder to the deck.

The rage in Buck's gut began to boil again. He took several deep breaths and forced himself to calm. In the background, he could hear the racking sobs of his friend and mentor as he lay upon the bunk. He wished he knew how to comfort him but he didn't. What he did know, was that another he cared about had been destroyed by Henry Tacker.

Somehow he had to even the score.

For the tenth time since they had left Boston, he reckoned that he would get even.

Later that day, Buck stood in the bow watching an approaching headland, a well-protected anchorage with high cliffs that fell away to a creek bottom. Far up a gentle canyon that cradled a quiet stream, he could see the bell towers of a large Spanish mission.

Swill walked up to join him. "We'll be making anchor in a minute or two, boy. You mind the rode."

"Is this San Pedro?" Buck asked.

"No, we're a bit south of there. This be San Juan Capistrano. The wind turned in the night. This be one of the richest ports in hides, I'm told."

They hove to in ten fathoms in the lee of high cliffs. The captain gave the order to lower the longboat while Swill went forward to fetch a very unsteady Dutch.

"The captain says you're to go ashore for awhile." Swill gathered Dutch's meager belongings from the forecastle. "'Til the eye gets better."

If he could no longer see, Dutch was useless to Bryant and Sturgis. They lowered the ruddy-faced, grim-featured man into the longboat with a line slung under his buttocks like a cask and pulled for the rocky beach.

An early spring graced the land. A warm sun gently coaxed green shoots from the clay soil and yellow-green willows lining the creek had a fresh coat of new leaves. The hills were shedding their brown winter coats for spring green, like a young deer shed its antlers for a stouter, bigger pair. Gulls, terns, and pelicans wheeled overhead, crying indignant insults at the approaching boat.

Buck would have enjoyed the beautiful day had his task been more pleasant.

The men made a hard climb up to the top of the cliffs. Hard Tack summoned two Indians, naked except for woven grass loin cloths, who were working in the mission fields. He sent them running toward the mission with news of their arrival.

Buck studied the group of Indians who gathered to watch the proceedings. They wore woven shirts and loin cloths, some of rabbit skin and some of reeds or grass, all dyed red. Long coal-black hair was tied back and adorned with shells. Some wore basket hats. The men carried flint knives with hide-bound wooden shafts. Some had small knives tucked into their straight dark hair.

Most of them had fiber carrying nets draped over their upper torsos, with a variety of implements suspended or tied into them. Two of the men carried three-foot bows and small quivers on their backs made from dried rabbit skins. They were filled with straight wooden arrows. On a high rise in the distance, Buck could make out a cluster of woven reed huts partially covered with mud.

Three *carretas* packed with dried hides clattered over a rocky trail on poorly made wooden wheels cut from log rounds. Stiff cowhides were stuffed along the sideboards of the carts, making the sides higher so the load could be increased. The stacked hides rose as high as they were long. Mexican drivers hauled the first few carts to the edge of the cliff and demonstrated the art of sailing the hides the hundred feet to the beach below where a number of the Virginia crew worked stacking them. The men below had to watch carefully since one hide was heavy enough to kill a man if he were solidly hit.

But it didn't take long to learn the trick and soon Buck and the others took turns sailing the hides, laughing and joking as one or the other landed his closest to the growing pile on the beach.

When the first cart was empty, Hard Tack and one of the Mexican drivers helped Dutch climb in.

"Take care, my friend!" Buck called out as the heavy cart clattered away. Dutch merely waved over his shoulder. He would read no more, but being the man he was, Buck believed he would learn to master other skills.

As the cart crested the rise and dropped out of sight, Buck wondered if he would ever again see the friend who had taught him so much. He turned back to sailing the hides, hoping his watch-mates wouldn't notice the mist in his eyes.

As the day wore on, the working sailors and watching Indians were joined by a third group of men. Wearing their hair shorter than the Indian's, their stature larger and stronger than either the Indians or the sailors, this group also pitched in to help.

They laughed often as they worked and spoke in an alien tongue. When a particularly large man sailed a hide almost exactly onto the growing stack below, Buck complimented him in Spanish, "Well done, amigo."

"No talk like Californios, sailor boy," he replied in broken but passable English. "I Sandwich man."

"I'm Buck Mueller, a Boston man." Buck extended a hand, and the huge dark-skinned man took it, engulfing it in a ham-sized callused one. He flashed a huge, white-toothed grin.

"I Tui. Tui mean king in Sandwich Islands, but I not king, just king of the hide boys. King of kanakas." He laughed as he made another almost perfect toss. "What means Buck?"

Buck reddened, remembering Gretchen's christening. "It's just a name." He changed the subject. "How do you like it here in California?"

"Is good here, sailor boy. But for my shipmate, is not so good. Him very sick. He got bad fever. Burn up. He my mama's boy."

"You mean your brother?"

"No, my mama's boy. His daddy a sailor man. My daddy a Sandwich man. I no like him die here. His bones should dry in Sandwich sun." The huge man glanced away, his face no longer smiling.

"Do you have medicines?"

"No, no medicine. We talk to many gods, but he still hot."

"Tomorrow, if we come back ashore, I'll bring medicine

from the ship. You talk to your gods, but perhaps my medicine will help."

By the time the third cart was emptied, Hard Tack had returned from taking Dutch to the mission. They shoved the boats through the surf and pulled hard back to the brig. Buck was glad the Virginia didn't set sail that night. It meant he would have a chance to help his new friend. He set to the task of talking Cracker into slipping him some calomel from the ship's chest.

That night, lying awake in his bunk, Buck thought of home. How had the harvest been? Were the fields still deep in snow? Had his mother received any of his letters? He mentally calculated how many hides they had taken aboard and how large the hold was. The brig would hold thirty-five or forty thousand hides. They could be in California for as long as two or three years.

Buck's jaw tensed. The fact and thoughts of Ernst, Horace, and Dutch, strengthened his resolve. It was time to take his leave.

7

WILHELM MUELLER SAT QUIETLY near his carved smoking table, his pipe long burned to ash. The letter he received had been brought to him via the Noble, again from William Taylor-Johnson. He read it again for the fourth time.

> Dear Dr. Mueller:
>
> I am sorry to inform you that due to avoidable acts on the part of Buck Mueller, your son Ernst has died at sea. If it be any consolation, he received a Christian burial. His body was consigned to the deep. Buck Mueller was appropriately punished for his acts in accordance with the law.
>
> Regretfully,
> Your obedient servant,
> Captain William Taylor-Johnson

Wilhelm refilled and smoked his pipe, his hand shaking, his heart feeling empty and cold and filled with self-loathing. Why had he been so rash in sending the boy off? Why should Ernst have been forced into the same line of work as his father?

Why had he died and what did the captain mean, "avoidable acts?" Was the letter purposefully vague to protect Bryant and Sturgis? Or was it to protect the captain? He had heard much more about captain Taylor-Johnson since he had impetuously sent Ernst off under the captain's care. Or was the letter vague simply to spare a family unnecessary grief?

The following morning, with a heavy heart and eyes swollen from a night of weeping, Wilhelm's carriage plodded toward Mueller Manor, his thoughts still in turmoil. Kathleen was setting the table as the backdoor banged. The counterweight his brother Edward had rigged always took Wilhelm by surprise. Kathleen almost dropped the plates she was carrying.

"Will! For heaven's sake, you scared the wits out of me. What pleasures us with this visit?"

"I've come with bad news, I'm afraid. Where is Edward?"

Her brows drew together, but she didn't press the matter. "He's out at the smokehouse. Do me the favor of calling him to the table. I'll be settin' you a place."

Wilhelm turned and headed out across the yard, finding his brother at work in the sausage shed.

"It never seems to end, does it, Edward?" Wilhelm asked. His brother turned, equally as surprised to see him as Kathleen had been.

"Since Sam left," Edward complained, "I can't seem to get the other boys interested in the souse and scrapple. No one can get it to set quite as well as he did. Edward Jr. has tried, but I might as well get him his appointment to West Point for all the good he has been."

"I didn't mean the work, Brother, I meant... here, read this. Perhaps afterward, you can tell me what you make of it."

Edward read quietly. His features sagged. Finally he looked up. "I'm so sorry Wilhelm. Does Kathleen know? Let's go up to the house."

"Wait.... Wait a moment, Edward. What could they mean... this business of Buck Mueller's involvement? Why is Samuel calling himself 'Buck'?"

"I don't... I don't know," Edward stammered. "Sam

85

wouldn't do anything to hurt Ernst... not purposely. Why would they punish him?"

"The sea can change a man." Wilhelm stared hard at his brother and knew each was afraid of his own thoughts.

Finally, Edward broke the silence. "I must show this to Kathleen." He hurried for the house, Wilhelm slowly trailing behind.

Kathleen was setting bowls of steaming cabbage, potatoes, corned beef, and sausage on the table in front of the boys. "Did you wash up?" she inquired of her husband and his brother without looking up.

"Wilhelm has received some very bad news." Edward handed her the folded piece of parchment. Wiping her hands on her apron, she walked to the wooden sink near the window where the light was better and began to read the note.

Her cheerful expression faded, her lips trembled, then she looked up. "Oh, poor Ernst... what could have happened?" She glanced again at the note. "What does he mean, 'Buck Mueller was punished?' Is that Sam? He must mean Sam. My God, Edward, what could have happened to Sam?"

Wilhelm's shout startled her. "Sam! You mean what did he do? It does not say he was consigned to the deep!"

Kathleen whipped her gaze toward him. "Sam would not.... He loved his cousin.... We don't know anything by this." She flung the letter to the floor.

Edward Jr. got up from the table, walked over and picked it up. "What did he do now?" he mumbled.

Sobbing against her hand, Kathleen ran for the stairs and up to the sanctity of her room.

After the meal was finished, Edward and Wilhelm sat on the porch, talking and smoking until late into the evening. The next morning, Wilhelm harnessed his wagon and left before Kathleen made an appearance.

Three weeks later Edward grabbed his chest and fell among the tall stalks of corn he was checking. He pulled himself halfway back to the farmhouse with one arm, where Tug later found him.

Kathleen and Wilhelm didn't speak at Edward's funeral.

———

AT DAWN, Buck and the men pulled for the rocky beach, the wind wet with moisture and a dark gray sky threatening rain. The larboard watch climbed the cliffs to meet the hide carts, slipping and sliding in the wet clay and grass.

When the sun topped the mountains, the crew topped the ridge. The carts were waiting. Hard Tack set the men to dumping hides to empty a cart then plodded away in it, catching a ride to the mission. As soon as Hard Tack was out of sight, Buck entreated Swill to let him deliver the calomel to the big Sandwich Islander he'd met the day before.

"You make more work for us all," the second mate grumbled. "Go on," he snorted through his bulbous veined nose, "but I'll make no excuses for ye if Mr. Tacker returns before ye get back!"

Buck knew the Mission San Juan was at least two miles away. Hard Tack couldn't get there and back in the slow-moving cart before Buck could make the simple trip to the huts.

As he approached the group of mud and bent willow hovels, he noticed a group of Indian women cooking. They lowered hot stones in tightly woven cooking baskets with the help of bent willow implements until the liquid boiled.

A single hut stood off from the others. Tui stepped from its opening into the now drizzling day.

Buck waved and shouted. "I have some medicine. Where's your friend?"

The huge nut-brown man filled the doorway as he followed Buck into the thatched-roof shelter. Constructed of small willow branches woven around a frame of larger willows, mud and grass had been packed into the larger cracks in a feeble attempt to keep it warm—but still it chilled to the bone. The breeze freshened and whistled through the porous shack. A tiny fire smoldered in the center of the hut. Smoke wove its way through the roof and the hut reeked of sweat and illness. The sick man rested against a porous wall, a wracking cough gripping him. Sweat glistened on his forehead.

"Get some more wood for this fire," Buck commanded.

Tui hesitated. "He plenty hot now!"

"If you want your brother to live—"

"He my mama's son."

"Well, if you want your friend's bones to bleach here, don't listen!"

The huge man responded slowly, skeptically, calling to three others lounging near the hut.

They all started to leave for the task, but Buck stopped them. "Two of you fellows get some mud and start patching these cracks." He knelt at the sick man's side, and his sunken eyes fluttered in acknowledgment then closed again. "What are you feeding him?"

"He no eat," said one of the men who stuck his head in the doorway. He shrugged his powerful shoulders.

Rumaging through the hut, Buck found a handful of dried meat and some dried fruit resembling prunes. Walking outside and back to the other huts where he had noticed the Indian women cooking, he snatched up a deep cooking basket and one of the willow implements. "I'll return this," he promised. He could see they didn't understand him, but only watched until satisfied he wasn't going far.

"Fetch me some water," he called to the working men, who produced a gourd full, and he half-filled the basket. He selected the hottest stone among those surrounding the small fire, fished it out with the willow ring and dropped it into the cooking basket and water. He repeated the process time and again, removing the stones with the hooped willow branch made for that purpose, until the water bubbled and began to soften the meat and fruit. Soon he had a broth. It wasn't his mother's cooking, but it would do.

By the time Tui returned, Buck was propping the man up, trying to get him to drink from a gourd filled with broth. A huge hand grabbed Buck's wrist. "He no want hot drink.... He hot enough!"

Buck had added the medicine to the broth. The calomel was a cathartic. A man who hadn't eaten in days would need a stimulant to get his body functioning. The pallor of death hung on his lean, emaciated frame. He had to have liquid.

"He no want drink," the big man repeated as the sick man coughed and sputtered with the first liquid Buck poured into his mouth. Tui tightened his grip, a rock-crushing one.

Buck looked the huge man in the eye then slowly climbed to his feet. He walked over to the pile of firewood, selected a small dry branch, and offered it to Tui.

"This stick is dead. No drink. Dry. Dead!" He walked to the door of the hut and plucked a weed growing nearby. Returning, he broke the weed in half and squeezed out some liquid. "This is alive. Your friend's bones will be as dry and dead as that stick if he doesn't drink."

Tui hesitated only a moment, then knelt down next to his friend. "I hold."

Soon the man was drinking and mouthing small bits of meat and fruit. It was a slow process but he got it all down. As Tui laid his friend back down on the mat, Buck relaxed for the first time since his arrival.

He had rested only a moment when he sat up with a start, realizing his time was short. "You keep him drinking and keep this fire going strong so it stays comfortably warm in here. He should not be chilled. I'll come back and check on him when I can." Hurrying from the hut, he ran back toward the carts.

When Buck approached his working shipmates, he was pleased to count only two carts at the cliff's edge. He didn't notice the saddle horse tied off to the side in a clump of brush.

Hard Tack was sitting on the grass leaning on a cart wheel. He looked up as Buck grabbed a hide and set to work.

"Did you enjoy the Indian woman, sogger?" The brawny hard-eyed first mate stood and swaggered over to face Buck, coming eye to eye with him.

Buck well-remembered that look.

Hard Tack kept his hands folded behind him, his muscles tense, his shoulders knotted in anticipation. "You bloody sogger, it's time you learned another lesson!"

Buck's eyes narrowed, and he stepped away as Hard Tack uncoiled a leather whip from behind his back and shook it out. It looked deadly as a serpent about to strike.

Hard Tack smiled sardonically. He had traded the Mexican cart driver for the woven leather whip. Now it would come in handy. He flicked it out with an easy motion, then raised his arm high and cracked it.

The resounding snap, like a gunshot, sent chills down Buck's spine and flooded him with memories of the time before. He stepped backwards, but his jaw tightened.

"Seize the bastard and bind him to the cart," Hard Tack ordered.

Not a man moved.

Buck eyed each man in turn.

They were ashore. The authority of the first mate was not as final here as it would have been onboard the little brig. These were the men of the larboard watch, who were commanded by Swill. Men who had worked and risked their lives side by side with Buck for months—and eaten wormy gruel while Hard Tack had partaken of fresh beef and chicken and hams at the captain's table.

"Do as I say!" Hard Tack shouted, raising the whip arm above his head. This time Buck was the target.

But Hard Tack was too close and Buck too quick. He ducked inside and struck the man a glancing blow to the chin while the whip whistled harmlessly over his head. Then, with a resounding thump, he drove another fist hard to the bigger man's solar plexus, doubling him over. For an instant, Hard Tack's mouth dropped open. Then he closed to tie up the smaller man. Fighting in close, Hard Tack's arm extended over Buck's shoulder, the whip still dangling from his hand, the first mate snarled and grabbed the whip with his free hand, trying to encircle Buck's throat to strangle him.

Buck lunged forward and Hard Tack leaned into him, still trying to gain a choke hold with the whip. Buck shifted his weight, grabbed Hard Tack by the lapels, and sat back, instinctively executing a move Black Dan had taught him. He jammed both feet in Hard Tack's belly, flipping the larger man over his head as he dropped to the ground.

Hard Tack sailed above him, eyes wide with fear, out into the void. The whip burned Buck's neck as the leather rubbed away his skin, almost dragging him along with the screaming man. Hard Tack clung to the whip's thin thread of hope as he disappeared from sight.

Buck scrambled to the rocky edge and the rest of the larboard watch clambered up beside him, staring after the careening body. Hard Tack's echoing scream raked a chill down Buck's back.

"My God," Buck muttered, his shoulders knotted, and his arms tensed uselessly. Frustration filled him with dread.

The first mate bounced once, then lay broken and unmoving on the rocky beach a hundred feet below.

Still staring, Buck muttered, "I didn't... I never meant to kill him."

Black Dan clamped a hand on his shoulder. "We know that, boy. It was an accident... but Taylor-Johnson will never condone it as such."

The crewmen on the beach below stood transfixed for a moment. They gazed at the broken body, then up at the cliff, and bolted for the shore boat. Launching it quickly through the surf, they pulled for the brig. Buck stared down at the crushed, twisted form that had once been the first mate.

"I think it would be wise if you weren't here when the captain comes askin'," Dan said.

For a moment Buck didn't move, just stared vacantly into Dan's dark eyes, then he nodded. Without a look back he walked to the saddle horse Hard Tack had hidden behind the shrub and mounted.

"Good luck, Buck!" some of the men called out.

"Good sailing, son!"

"Via con Dios!"

With trepidation, he waved to his friends, spun the little mount, and started off away from the sea.

His decision had been made for him. Like it or not, prepared or not, he as on his way home.

8

BUCK SPURRED the little buckskin mare up away from the cliff, the memory of Hard Tack bouncing on the rocky beach clouding his thoughts.

Knowing the captain would have to get more horses before any real pursuit could be launched, he kept up a steady pace, grateful for the time to think and plan.

He had taken a man's life. He hadn't set out to, but what choice had he had? He was not going to stand and be whipped again. He certainly wasn't going to wait to be hung. He thought of Ernst's useless death. Hard Tack's death was an accident. He hadn't planned it. There was no premeditation—or was there?

Had the hate that began months ago finally manifested itself? Had he killed the man as quickly and mercilessly as possible? He had never underestimated Henry Tacker. Hard Tack had been a dangerous, ruthless, pitiless man. Still, he knew he should be feeling some remorse for his actions. He had taken a human life.

He wondered if Tacker had felt any remorse over Ernst's death, or for Dutch's battered face and lost eyesight. He doubted it. Buck couldn't imagine Hard Tack feeling remorse for anyone or anything.

The little buckskin pranced and worried the bit. She was

heading in the direction of her home. Buck had to use a heavy rein to get her around to the north side of the mission. He didn't have to hurry, just set a pace fast enough to stay ahead of his pursuers. Boston was a long ride. Buck wasn't even certain it was possible.

No man he knew of had yet crossed the continent via the southern half of Spanish New Mexico. There were no maps— like some of Swill's sea charts, the area between California and Santa Fe would only be marked, "Here There Be Dragons."

He didn't know if he could do what he set out to do, but most anything was better than dying at the hands of a man like Hard Tack.

Riding on, he crossed a small creek lined with sycamores and oaks. He stepped off as the little horse passed a pile of rocks dabbed with orange, red, and brown lichen. The buckskin took a few steps, then stopped and looked curiously back over her shoulder at her dismounted rider. Picking up a pebble, Buck threw it, hitting her on the flank. She trotted off in the direction of the mission, kicking up her heels without another glance.

He might be a killer, he thought, but he wasn't a horse thief. Besides, anyone with eyes could track the little horse in this wet weather. It was just damp enough to leave clear tracks with no rain to wash them away.

Picking his way from rock to rock upstream, away from the mission, he began a wide back-track, headed for the huts he had been to earlier in the day. Tui, the big kanaka, was the only land acquaintance Buck had and the only person with reason to help him.

Soon he would leave the stream and strike off across the wet ground, back toward the kanaka's hut. He was sure the captain would track the horse back to the mission. Buck was north of the village and Tui's hut, and he could return far away from the cliff to mission trail. The captain would take the south cut to the mission, and Buck didn't want to chance an accidental meeting.

Farther north he saw another willow-lined stream that cut a ravine to the sea. He made a mental note of it.

After a mile of backtracking, the huts appeared on the horizon, smoke curling up from the one apart from the others. He stayed low in a gully, then crept quickly to the rear of the hut. Conversation in the strange Sandwich Island tongue drifted from within.

Buck waited a few moments until he was sure they had no visitors, then he went in.

The big kanaka looked up from where he sat next to the fire. "Sailor boy, other sailor boys look for you—the tall man... no hair here... like Tui." He pointed to his hairless chest. "With the yellow hair on head." Tui laughed at his own joke. "You valuable man, Buck, worth fifty reals—five hides."

Damn, he hadn't expected them to start looking there, or to arrive there on foot. "You mustn't tell them I've been here, Tui."

"Tui no tell." The big man looked hurt. "Kelolo, better!" He pulled Buck to the woven mat where the sick man lay, his eyes still deep set, but now a little more alert than they had been before. His handshake was still weak.

"Kelolo thanks you, Mr. Buck," the man managed before dropping his head back to the mat.

Buck thought maybe a life returned would help make up for one taken.

"I need a boat, Tui. Soon, before the captain returns. There are things on the ship I must have."

HAVING SENT AHEAD to borrow horses from the mission, Captain William Taylor-Johnson lead a group of ten mounted men to the rear of the adobe complex. Others he had sent to hunt on foot. After tracking the mare from the cliff side, he was astounded at Buck's boldness, or stupidity.

"Why, the bastard has come straight to the mission!" He

followed the buckskin's tracks around the side to an adobe corral. An old vaquero sat on the wall, working a rawhide reata, weaving its frayed ends and watching them approach. He smiled inwardly as the marineros rode clumsily toward the corral. Unfamiliar with horses, they made a comical sight, but seemed in deadly earnest.

The captain dismounted and instructed One to fetch the padre. Then he told two other sailors to ride to the front of the mission and sound out if Buck tried to flee that way. The crew reluctantly helped with the search.

The captain strode into the mission garden, several sailors following behind him. He met One and the padre at the entrance to an inner courtyard. Taylor-Johnson ignored the padre's extended hand, staring hard at the tall, frock-covered man.

The captain stood with his hands on his hips, his long legs spread, Hard Tack's whip coiled in his long thin fingers.

"Padre, a sailor from my ship is in hiding here. I want him."

Father Zalvidea glanced at the Spanish sailor who had come for him and listened as he repeated the captain's order in Spanish. The padre knew French, English, Latin and Spanish, but he wanted a little time to consider the effrontery of the American.

He answered in precise English. "We have had no strangers here since your Señor Tacker arrived this morning, except for the men who borrowed the horses you ride. Your sailor, Dutch, is resting in my personal quarters."

"Not him, a younger man. He's here, all right. We followed his horse to your corral. I demand we be allowed to search for him. He's an American citizen and subject to the laws of the sea."

The priest's black eyes did not waver. "This is a house of God. His laws transcend those of man. Your sailor is not here. If you care to search the grounds, by all means do so. But take two men, no more. I'll not have our gardens tromped flat."

With that he turned on his heel and walked to where three Indians bent over the flower beds. Commenting on their work, he moved from man to man, his graciousness returning as if the captain had never been there.

Taylor-Johnson watched him and felt as if he had been slapped. He had forgotten he was aboard another man's ship. He ordered all but two of the larboard watch back to the horses, then they began a careful search of the well-cared-for grounds.

———

BUCK AND TUI pushed the tiny balsa reed boat into the foaming surf. As they climbed aboard, Buck was surprised how the buoyant reeds supported their combined weight so readily.

Once they left the surf, they skimmed along with coordinated paddling. The sun, halfway consumed by the sea, outlined Tui's big shiny-wet body in brilliant red and orange as he skillfully guided the tiny vessel.

"To the windward side, Tui," Buck said. "I'll have to climb the anchor rode. You stay with the boat. If trouble starts, you row like hell for the shore."

Tui started to complain, but Buck shushed him with a finger to his lips. The sun slowly lowered, orange and yellow giving way to crimson, then purple. It would be dead black soon, with no moon and a high overcast shielding even the starlight.

Buck took a deep breath and hand-over-handed up the forward anchor rode. He paused atop the taffrail. The anchor lantern glimmered on the quarter deck, but the deck watch was nowhere to be seen. He knew at least one man would have been left aboard. As Buck stood quietly watching the reed boat touched the hull, scraping an announcement of his presence.

But no one came running.

The flickering lantern played shadow tricks on the deck,

but still no one came. Buck stealthily slipped into the fore-castle. No one there. The captain must have wanted him badly to have taken the whole damned crew, leaving only an anchor watch. Buck grabbed his bedroll and Ernst's leather trunk and made his way back to the rail.

"Catch these," he whispered loudly to Tui, dropping the items overboard. Tui's huge hands easily caught the load, and Buck made his way aft. Now he could distinguish the outline of a man pacing back and forth behind the helm beyond the lantern, but couldn't make out who it was.

Slipping around the galley, he crept down the captain's companionway, directly below the man on deck watch. He'd been in the captain's cabin only one time, when he had helped to repair the rudder control. He'd made mental note of the muskets, cutlasses, and pistols that were stored in the closet the rudder cables passed through.

He entered the cabin and froze—the squeaking door had disturbed someone. Buck could hear breathing and rustling as Ahmed turned over on his mat at the foot of the bed. Buck waited until the boy quieted once more, then felt along the wall until he reached the door to the storage area.

Quickly he located two big bore Aston .50 caliber pistols and shoved them into his belt, then he grabbed a musket and cutlass and their accouterments. With cutlass in one hand, musket and brass powder horn in the other, brass power horn and ball bag hanging over his shoulder, and a box of caps in his pocket, he made his way back to the deck. Near the end of the galley, he turned to search for the deck watch, expecting a shout at any moment. Turning back, he came face to face with the man. The musket clattered to the deck as Buck struck out with the handle of the cutlass. With a hollow thud, the hand guard caught the man over the eye and he went down.

It was Black Dan, Buck suddenly realized. He sprawled on the deck in the flickering light of the anchor watch, then started to regain his feet.

"Don't get up Dan, please," Buck pleaded. "It's me,

Buck.... The knot on your head is your excuse. Tell them it was the Indians, or something... whatever." Turning away, Buck made his way to the rail.

Sitting with legs spread, Dan looked up and shook his head in resignation. He could barely make out the broad shoulders and lean waist of his friend in the dim lamp light. No trace of the slender boy who began the journey remained.

Black Dan, the privateer, climbed to his feet and walked to the rail, calling out quietly to the disappearing boat, "Good luck, Buck!"

Buck smiled, but kept on rowing.

The boat made no noise as its reed bottom landed on surf-wet weed-covered rocks. "Tui, thank the Indians for the boat," he said. "Take care of Kelolo."

"Where you go, Buck? You welcome stay with us."

"The captain will be looking for me, Tui. I've got to go into the hills, at least until the Virginia sets sail."

"You welcome stay. You welcome come back." The big man helped Buck arrange the load on his back.

"Thank you, Tui, but the captain will come. You've been a good friend, and I'll not forget." He waved at the big kanaka as he made his way along the beach to the cut he'd noticed earlier in the day, then he began the hard climb into the mountains in the black night.

Afraid he was leaving a clear track, he wanted to put a lot of distance between himself and the Virginia before daylight.

The cover grew thicker and the hills steeper as he pushed on, hour after hour. Soon the moon peeked through the clouds and he was able to avoid the vegetation that pulled at his clothes and scratched his face and arms.

When the traversing moon said he'd been traveling for at least six hours, he stopped, taking time only to drop his pack and pull off his boots before he lay down. He was asleep almost as soon as his head hit the grass.

It was the warmth of the morning sun that told him he

had slept too long. Then the events of the day before flashed through his mind and he quickly sat up. Shading his eyes in the bright sunlight, he realized someone was standing nearby watching.

He relaxed as his eyes grew accustomed to the light and he focused on a young Indian boy, clad only in a rabbit skin loin cloth. Coal black hair reached almost to his waist. The boy backed up a few steps while Buck climbed to his feet, working the kinks from his back.

"Buenos dias," Buck offered, glad One and Baldy had taught him the language.

"Buenos dias, señor," the boy replied. "Are you sent to us from Chinigchinich?"

"I beg your pardon?" He stretched and shook down his pant legs, which had crawled up, crowding his crotch as he slept. He turned and grabbed his bedroll, remembering his time was not his own.

He reached for the leather chest and stopped. "Jesus!" he yelled, stumbling backward. He tripped over the chest and sprawled on his back. Quickly, he rolled over and regained his feet.

Directly above him a coyote skin mounted on a stick, its head and paws intact, loomed menacingly. The flanks had been sewn together. Various feathers, arrows, and bird talons protruded from the seams and throat. Over the shoulders, much as a man would carry them, hung a bow and quiver of arrows.

"Jesus, that bloody thing...." Buck grimaced. "Damn near made me yell." He turned and relieved himself in the brush.

"Chinigchinich," the boy repeated, pointing to the skin. "You wait." He ran off into the bushes.

Buck gathered his things, then went to investigate the skin. A rattling of the undergrowth startled him, and he turned to face several Indian men dressed in loin cloths. They carried stone axes and bows, their arrows notched and ready. Buck's cutlass and musket lay rolled in his bedroll out of reach. The pistols rested nearby, but he had failed to load and charge them.

Ernst's ten-inch knife, tucked securely into his belt, offered little comfort.

The boy stepped forward from the group. "My father," he said in Spanish, pointing to the tallest of the men, who was dressed differently from the rest. His hair was plaited and coiled on the top of his head, and a twelve-inch fire-hardened wooden blade was tucked into the braids. He wore a long robe covered with feathers.

Standing to his right was a shorter Indian whose hair hung straight down his back. A feathered head dress stuck straight up, much like a crown. The feathers shown black, but no darker than his skin, which had been rubbed and darkened with charcoal. White stripes on his face and chest contrasted with the black, and a small pouch hung from a thong under his left arm.

The father and the shorter man began arguing in guttural tones, ignoring Buck.

"They argue over you," the boy said quietly.

"Why?"

"My father says you may be the son of Chinigchinich. Is this true?"

"What does the other man say?"

"He says you are just a man, here to steal our women."

Buck eyed the two Indian men. "What do they have in mind?"

The boy shrugged his narrow shoulders. Then he grinned. "Can you run like the coyote?"

"Fast enough."

"Follow me." The boy bolted.

Buck hesitated, not wanting to leave his belongings, but his instincts said follow, so he did. Brush tore at his face and arms; he could hear the Indians behind him screaming, taking up the chase.

Scrambling up a steep trail through tall manzanita, they finally broke into a clearing and he found himself surrounded by huts. His first reaction was that the boy had tricked him. He had run like hell—straight into the enemy camp.

He turned back.

The boy yelling for him to come ahead, and the screaming Indians running up the trail behind, made him retrace his steps. The boy stood at the entrance to the largest hut in the village motioning him in. At the entrance stood a second idol, much like the one he had slept under last night.

"You will be safe here—the vanquech." The boy pointed at the idol.

His options gone, Buck ran into the vanquech, following the boy. He made the entrance just ahead of the pursuing mob of Indians. The narrow entrance of the big hut would be as good a place as any to make a stand. He turned quickly, drawing the knife from its scabbard in his belt. Tense and ready, he waited, but the screaming throng didn't charge into the hut.

"You are safe now," the boy said smiling.

Buck looked at him uncertainly, glancing back to the entrance, but the men were walking away. They seemed disappointed that he had made the "vanquech."

"You are safe now," the boy repeated.

Buck walked to the center post of the hut and leaned against it, still not sheathing his knife. "What is this... this vanquech?" he asked, keeping an eye on the door.

"It is the house of Chinigchinich. He would be very angry if you were harmed.... He will also be angry if you do not put your knife away."

Buck looked at the door again, thought of how many there were outside, walked to where the boy sat, and finally sheathed the knife.

"You are not the son of Chinigchinich... or you would know." The boy looked suspiciously up at him.

"I did not know my father... maybe it was Chi... him."

Just then the boy's father stepped into the vanquech, his tall silhouette backlighted in the opening.

Buck faced him, his hand on the hilt of his knife. Carrying an armful of wood, the man moved forward to a blackened pit near the center pole. As he knelt to build a fire, he spoke to the boy in a guttural Indian language, and the boy translated it into Spanish for Buck.

"As you have sought sanctuary in the house of Chinig-chinich, you will never come to harm at the hand of the Trabuco Juaneros... as long as you obey our laws."

The boy smiled as if to say I told you so, then continued with the translation. "My father would like you to smoke with him. Then he will call the puplem, the elders of the village, and we will cleanse ourselves before we feast to celebrate your arrival."

Buck shook his head in disbelief. Only moments before he had been the fox with the hounds at his heels, now he was invited to share their bones with them.

"Thank you," he said quietly. "I could use a bath and a meal." He was safer here than anyplace he could think of. He needed somewhere to hide for a while. This close to the mission, it was the last thing Taylor-Johnson would expect.

"We cleanse ourselves here," the boy went on as his father stoked the fire. "We cleanse with heat, not like you Spanish."

"I am not Spanish."

"You are not?" the boy asked, looking curiously at Buck.

"No. Where did you learn the language, boy?" No one else in the village seemed to speak anything other than their Native Indian tongue.

"I lived with my mother at the mission... until she died, then I came back here to be with my people."

The sweat and heat of the room continued to build, sapping Buck's strength. As the minutes slid past and his fear receded, his eyes began to drift closed and his head drooped a time or two. Then the chief passed him a small clay pipe. One pull on the pungent tobacco and immediately, he came fully alert. It was different, he realized, from anything he had ever smoked before.

They smoked for a while, neither speaking. Afterward he went out in the cool fresh air and felt great. He guessed sweating was as good a way as any to cleanse. It cleaned from the inside out.

Hidden away in the mountains, he spent almost two weeks with the Indians. He used his musket to hunt game that had been scarce to bow and arrow. In appreciation, they taught him which plants and insects were edible, and which were medicinal. He learned how to tan hides, using an animal's brains and fire ash, and how to snare small game.

Knowing the Virginia would have to move on, he began to feel it was safe to return to the mission. With the boy acting as interpreter, he went to see the child's father.

"Do you have enough game for awhile? I must return to the mission. I need horses before I can continue my journey home."

"My father says you are free to go or welcome to stay, but before you go, he wishes you to join him and the puplem one last time."

Later that afternoon, the boy came to get him, and he once more entered the vanquech. The men were already gathered in a large circle, smoking and sweating. The boy sat behind him, interpreting.

"In honor of your coming," the chief said, "Nocujen, our shaman, will tell the story of the coming of Chinigchinich."

The blackened Indian rose and began to move in a slow methodical dance around the room, speaking as he swayed to the beat of a drum.

"In the beginning, Nocuma held the world in his hands. The world was round, but unbalanced. He gave the world balance by placing a tusuat at its center."

The boy whispered to him, "The tusuat is a black rock from the beach. We collect the rocks to smooth the mud on the walls of our huts, to help with the balance of our lives."

"Nocuma created Ejoni," the shaman continued, "and since he had no woman to bear his children, he created Ae. Soon, sirorut and Ycauit gave birth to Ouiot, whose name means to take root."

The boy was having trouble with the translation and Buck had to listen closely. Every once in a while, the shaman paused to make sure the boy was keeping up.

"They dwelled in Pubuna, a day's walk, there." He pointed to the west. "As a boy, Ouiot was quiet and well mannered. But as he grew and gained strength, he became violent, as many men do."

Nocujen, the shaman, paused, studying Buck closely.

"He was hated by all who lived near him, but still Ouiot was made chief. The people suffered under his leadership. They struggled." Nocujen acted out a great fight, rolling on the dirt floor and struggling with himself.

"And they gained the black rock, tusuat, from the center of the earth. The man Cucumel, saw the people using the tusuat to prepare a poison to rid themselves of Ouiot. Cucumel warned him, but while he slept, a man sneaked into his hut." Nocujen crept from one side of the hut to the other. "And placed the poison on his chest. At last the evil Ouiot was gone and would remain in a state of anxiety and displeasure for the rest of time.

"Attajen then came forth. He was a rational being. He explained to the people that he was the only one who could save them from eventual destruction. He gave some men the power to bring rain, some to grow grain, some to grow crops, some to be great hunters, and others the essentials for living. Attajen made sure the world was right for the creation of a great population.

"It came to pass that this was not to be Attajen's destiny, for Ouimot appeared one day and was turned into Chinig-chinich."

"I thought Ouimot was the bad guy?" Buck whispered to the boy.

"That was Ouiot, this is Ouimot."

"Chinigchinich," Nocujen continued, "was given gifts. He would teach the people of Pubuna the laws of life, and how to get along and live a good life.

"When Chinigchinich died, he was not burned as is the custom of our people. He rose above the stars. He told the people, after dying, that all who obeyed his wishes would have what they wanted. Those who refused him reverence, would remain in a state of anxiety and displeasure for all time, never finding peace within themselves."

Nocujen took his place beside the chief. The chief turned to Buck and again the boy translated. "May your heart become a star of the sky when you go to Tolmac. May you select many wives to serve you." The boy added in a whisper, "Tolmac is in the sky, like heaven."

"Thank you." Buck nodded to each man around the room. They went back to smoking and threw more wood on the fire. Buck turned to the boy. "Did you learn some of this story at the mission?"

"No. The story of Chinigchinich has been with my people as long as there has been a people. Long before the Spanish or the mission. I have often wondered if the padres did not learn some of their stories from us."

Buck couldn't help but compare the legend with Genesis and the story of Christ. It would be something to think on when there was time for such things.

Instead, the next morning just after dawn, he gathered his belongings and prepared to leave. The men of the village clustered around him and Nocujen stepped forward.

The boy interpreted. "At first, I thought you came to steal our women. For that, I feel ashamed. You have brought good fortune." He reached into a leather pouch slung under his arm and pulled out a small, highly polished black rock, almost round and not more than a half inch in diameter.

"As the tusuat balanced the world, may this little tusuat balance your life." He handed Buck the half-inch round highly polished rock, then reached under his left arm and grabbed the leather bag. When he squeezed the bag, all the

Indians stepped backwards, looking as if they wanted to run.

"Thank you, Nocujen." Buck accepted the little rock with some hesitancy. The man turned and walked away, the Indians parting to give him passage.

The boy explained. "The bag is the shaman's aguet. It is powerful medicine. He has placed a spell on you... a good one, I guess—"

"You guess?"

"He put a spell on the tusuat, too. It is very valuable and should bring you good luck wherever you go."

Buck pocketed the little black stone, rolling it around in his palm as he did so. It had been polished to a high sheen and felt good in his hand. His tusuat—maybe it would help. He needed all the help he could get.

As he waved goodbye, the men waved after him, calling, "May your heart be a star in Tolmac." The boy walked with him for a mile or so then turned back with a "Vaya con Dios!"

Buck smiled, as he wondered which God the boy wanted him to "go with."

But he had a good luck piece. Now all he needed was good luck.

9

A LUMBERING wild sow whose broad shoulders tapered to narrow hips, followed by several piglets, broke brush ahead of him. Buck followed behind them, along a narrow winding creek down the mountain. He laughed as he watched her go, thinking she would offer no suet for sausage in her solid two hundred pounds.

Pinon pine, manzanita, and scrub oak gave way to live oak and sycamore as the stream he followed joined with another and another until it ran twenty feet wide in spots, lined with willows. Several times he stopped to watch wild cattle, grazing contentedly with brilliant white cattle egrets sharing their pasture—until he was spotted, and the cattle broke and ran, and the egrets gracefully took flight. Twice wild horses moved out ahead of him.

Finally spotting the towers of the mission in the distance, Buck worked his way up a hillside and into a scrub oak thicket where he could watch the activity below for a while. It wouldn't do to walk in on Captain Taylor-Johnson, though he was sure the Virginia was hunting hides somewhere else by now.

Vaqueros came and went. Indians worked the vineyards and nearby orchards, but there was no sign of marineros anywhere. After more than an hour of watching, and as the sun began to drop behind the hills, Buck covered his trunk, bedroll, musket, cutlass, and bags with brush. Stuffing the pistols under his belt, loaded and primed this time, he untucked his shirt so they would be out of sight, then boldly walked through the mission's main gate.

He passed through a portico next to a wall that embraced four bells in four vaulted openings twenty feet off the ground. The bells diminished in size, the largest weighing at least seven hundred pounds. Behind the wall was a garden where two Indians worked the soil of flower beds. Bougainvillea climbed the nearby walls, breaking their stark white with brilliant purple and green.

One looked up. "Where's the padre?" Buck asked.

"In the sanctuary," one of the Indians answered, both of them stopping their work to stare. He knew they were wondering how he could be there with no ship anchored in the harbor.

Buck entered the chapel through large inlaid doors. Remembering his mother's teachings, he genuflected, though he was never actually baptized Catholic. The pistols pushed into his belly, whispering insistently they were out of place in the quiet dim light of the chapel. He ignored them. He had learned a cheap lesson from the Trabuco Juaneros.

The padre turned from his work at the altar and smiled as Buck crossed himself and rose to his feet. "Hola, mi hijo."

Having heard from the crew that the padre spoke English, he addressed him, "Father, I'm from the brig Virginia. The captain probably told you all about me."

"Do you think the confessional would be a better place for this, my son?"

Buck hesitated. He needed this man's confidence. "As you wish, father."

"No, my son, the question is do you wish it?"

"Yes, sir."

Buck explained what had happened, telling the padre Henry Tacker's death was an accident. Apparently, his word accepted, soon afterward Buck found himself dining with Father Zalvidea and Dutch.

The old sailor's sight had not returned, but already he had discovered a talent he hadn't realized he had. For years, he had been tying knots and braiding line without having to see what he was doing, and the padre had found a job for him in the tannery. The reatas, bosals, reins and romals, cinchas, and whips he made were already being sought after by every vaquero at the mission.

That night, after a well-cooked meal of roasted flank steak, cocida, fresh garden vegetables from the mission, and a generous portion of local rich red wine—vino de pais the padre called it—Buck slept the sleep of the innocent. The soft bed, the thick walls, the sun-blocking shutters, combined with the liquor so generously poured by the padre, conspired to keep him in bed well past dawn.

The echoing thud of axes just outside his door finally brought him to his feet. In the open courtyard outside his room, four Indians took turns chopping at a ten-foot-high, two-foot-thick sycamore stump. The balance of the tree covered half the courtyard, laying askew where it had been felled.

The padre stood near where the Indians worked. He smiled at Buck's approach and motioned to the tree. "I hated to see it go. Its changing fall colors blended so nicely with the oaks."

"You want to leave the stump?" Buck asked.

"No, we'll chop it as low as we can, then we'll just have to wait until it rots."

Buck eyed it carefully before he spoke, "If you'll leave it tall and chop a few of the roots, I'll bet I can pull it over and you won't have the stump in the middle of your garden."

"They are very strong, with a large tap root. We have tried before."

"I can do it, Padre." Buck smiled confidently. Zalvidea looked at him with skepticism, "I would much rather have it gone," he said, but his doubt that it could be done was apparent. Still, soon Buck had the Indians digging rather than chopping.

Grabbing an ax and stripping off his shirt, he began a rhythmic attack at the roots. He was surprised when Zalvidea went to his quarters, changed his robes for breeches and a shirt, and returned to the courtyard. The priest modestly had an Indian remove the women who were working nearby, then took off his own shirt and spelled Buck with the ax.

Zalvidea appeared to be somewhere over fifty, but he gave neither Buck nor the sycamore any quarter. The padre had well defined shoulders and thick back muscles; only a slight paunch testified to recent easy living. It was obvious he hadn't always had someone to do his bidding.

Sweat rolled down their backs and chests as the sun rose higher. Only the ringing of axes and occasional scraping shovels broke the silence. Finally Buck stopped.

"Let's give it a try, Padre."

"We have only begun, my friend. The tap root is very strong."

"I saw some oxen, father. Get me the strongest line you have and two of those oxen, and your stump will soon be firewood."

As Dutch had taught him, Buck rigged a block and tackle from one of the oaks in the courtyard to the top of the broken stump. As soon as the oxen put their backs into it, the sycamore popped, cracked, and tumbled, breaking away a foot below the ground and throwing up a billowing cloud of dust. The feat brought cheers from the Indians in the courtyard—and a large smile from Zalvidea.

The next morning, the padre invited Buck to accompany him on his mission rounds. They stopped at the tannery. Buck was surprised to learn that the cattle were killed, piked from horseback and skinned wherever they were lassoed by the vaqueros. Only the hides, horns, and tallow were taken, the rest of the animal rotted or fed the scavengers. The principal products of the mission were soap, candles, and hides. Tallow was sold in bulk. Whatever wheat, barley, and corn not consumed was occasionally sold.

The rapidly growing hide pile amazed Buck. He had witnessed over a thousand hides taken by the Virginia not two weeks earlier. "How many cattle are on the mission, Padre?"

Zalvidea shrugged his shoulders. "Who knows? Seventy thousand, a hundred thousand? We are over ten leagues on the ocean and a few leagues into the hills." The priest smiled at Buck's amazement, then he shook his head and his expression grew sad. "But when Echeandia has his way, it will all be granted to the Indians. A noble but futile gesture as they are not yet ready. It will not be long before our own people, the Californios, trick the Indians out of it."

"Are you sure this will happen?" Buck asked.

The padre nodded. "One of the results of the revolution was an edict for the secularization of the missions. We must give the land back to the Indians. There have been many changes since the revolution."

"Why would the government do that, padre?" Buck asked.

Zalvidea studied him carefully, as if making a decision about Buck's trustworthiness. "The Mexican government fears the allegiance of the missions, and their priests, to Spain. Their action is, in fact, a way to destroy the power of the church in Alta California and northern Mexico. And it is done under the guise of giving land to the people."

The tall priest opened his arms as he stood among the many Indians at work. "These people have lived in the shadow of the cross for years. They are not ready for so-called 'emancipation.' All we have built... all we have worked for" —he shook his head sadly— "will have been for nothing."

"Is the government right about the church's allegiance to Spain?"

Zalvidea laughed. "You speak with the frankness of youth, *mi hijo.*"

"Is that an answer, Padre?" Buck asked, with only a slight fear of offending this straight-talking man.

"No, Buck. The answer is that the church has only one allegiance, and that is to God."

"As it should be, padre," Buck agreed.

Buck surveyed the hard-working people and thought of all the church had accomplished. The mission was truly a productive place. He wondered how much the Indians had actually changed, living in "the shadow of the cross," as the padre had said.

He smiled to himself as he realized how much he had changed, living in the shadow of the mast.

"Father Barona calls Echeandia an avowed enemy of the religious order," Zalvidea said. "I fear this is an under-statement."

"Who is Father Barona?" Buck asked as they headed back to the kitchen for noon-day meal.

"He is one of the priests who lives here at the mission, only now he is in Monterey getting an edict from the governor. The devil himself directs his Excellency. I am certain this time we will have to divide the mission lands and stock. Each Indian family will have its own small rancho.... On the face of it, you would think it is fair, but I know these people. Most of them will be back in the hills in months, worship-ping coyote skins."

Buck remembered only too well his first sight of just such a skin. He thought of Governor Echeandia and the questions he had asked him that day in the shore boat. He seemed a sensible man, hardly one possessed.

"Even now," the padre continued, "the people leave the mission. They go back to the hills, back to stuffed skins and bird feathers."

"Is that so different from wooden crosses or crucifixes?" Buck challenged impulsively. He could see the priest stiffen at his comparison, but now he was committed.

"During the time I spent with them, I was astounded by the similarity of the story of Chinigchinich to that of the creation as described in Genesis. Maybe the pomp and organization of your... our religion, is no more correct that that of theirs. It's simple and straight forward... so are they."

Zalvidea's jaw tensed. "But they have no reverence for the Son of God, for the holy Mother Mary, or the glory of Immaculate Conception, or—"

Thus began one of many debates that continued over the next several weeks. For each challenge Buck offered, the priest took an implacable stance on behalf of his religion and the mission system in general. He was the quintessence of Catholicism. Buck didn't always agree with him, but his admiration grew. Zalvidea built his arguments on a solid foundation, making each point like interlocking building blocks, until in conclusion, the structure was complete.

On one point Buck was convinced: the mission was at present a benefit to the Indians. Their life in the shadow of the cross was a journey from which there was no return. Whether or not they would have been better off never having had the enlightenment of Christianity was an argument he was not prepared to enter into.

He wondered if his life in the shadow of the mast signified the same irrevocable commitment.

The Indian's tusuat worked well for them. Their life was balanced. They had a profound respect for all things living. If they chose to represent their deity with a stuffed coyote skin, was that so different from crosses and cathedrals, candelabras and holy water?

He wondered if the little lucky piece given him would help balance his life. He was sure it couldn't hurt.

During the next few weeks, Buck started three projects. Hating to see the waste of the steer carcasses, he set up a smokehouse and sausage shack and trained the Indians in its operation. He taught them how to boil the meat and reduce the broth until the bouillon could be dried and stored in crocks for sale to the hide ships. He spent his spare time learning all he could from the vaqueros. Astonished at their skill in horsemanship, he made it a point to listen and learn.

After a day spent teaching the Indians to make sausage casings from the intestines of trapped wild hogs, Buck wandered to the corral and climbed to the top rail to sit among the Californio men.

Sanchez, the head vaquero of the mission, worked a horse on a hand line while the others watched and offered him advice.

Buck had never exchanged more than a greeting with the old man. Stoically quiet, Sanchez went about his tasks with a purity of motion that made every job look simple. He had a face born of years in the sun and wind. His age was indeterminable, his face a peach pit track of crags and canyon-etches. A stoic expression contrasted flashing black eyes that missed nothing and smiled in his face when the horse responded to his urging.

The old vaquero seemed to become as one with the horse when he climbed into the high-cantled saddle. Buck watched Sanchez from atop the corral fence.

"That's a good-looking horse," he said when the Andalusia cantered past.

Sanchez reined up. Leaving the reins draped on the pommel, he dismounted in an easy fluid motion. He swaggered over, climbed up on the adobe fence, and sat next to Buck.

"That 'horse'," he said, pointing indignantly, "Is a sixteen hand pure-bred Andalusia stallion. His ancestors carried Cortez to defeat the Aztecs. They believed Andalusians were gods until they managed to kill two in battle."

Buck eyed the animal. The blue roan seemed to know they were admiring him. He pranced, lifting his knees high and proudly bowing his neck.

"Notice how active his small ears are?" Sanchez said. "The sign of an alert horse.... See how long his neck is... how it blends with his beautiful shoulders.... See how low his tail sets." He dropped from the fence and deftly roped the stallion with his sixty-foot woven reata. He tut-tutted until the horse trotted round in a circle.

"See how he raises his knees? He will train to seven gaits. He will single foot so smoothly you will think you are sitting on this wall. And if you treat him well, and if he comes to love and respect you—with luck, and only if you are deserving—he will charge the gates of hell for you. No other animal, none, will do that. You cannot ride a mule or burro where he does not wish to go. A dog will not do your bidding if it means harm to himself. This horse... this faithful Andalusian, he will do whatever you command. This 'horse'... can turn like a serpent, walk like a cat, and outrun a deer."

Sanchez climbed down from the fence and remounted the Andalusian. With new respect, Buck watched the man work the stallion until the sun went down. The vaquero trained as patiently as the wind and sun that had worked his craggy, ancient face.

Spring gave way to the heat of summer and summer to changing leaves, green to gold. The Virginia called at the point on two occasions, but Zalvidea found it convenient for Buck to be in the back country both times. Zalvidea didn't mention that Taylor-Johnson had offered a reward of one hundred reals for the "killer deserter," and had vowed to pursue the man himself if he learned of his whereabouts.

Instead, Buck rode with the vaqueros at every opportunity. He was becoming skilled with the reata and seldom missed a steer. Tui and a now healthy Kelolo called on the mission several times, laughing and smiling in their infectious manner.

As winter drew near, Buck grew anxious to move on.

Any attempt to cross the great desert in summer was far too dangerous—that much he knew. It was the reason he had remained at the mission this long. Finally, at the end of a long day's work, he approached Zalvidea.

"Padre, I'm afraid the time has come for me to go. I need

to spend some time in Pueblo de Los Angeles and Mission San Gabriel to learn what I can of the desert."

"Again, I must caution you, Buck. We know little of the Paiuches Desert. In the north, the Piute Indians are reputed to be warlike, in the south, along the Rio Colorado, the Navajos are worse. In the far south, the Apaches and Yaquis are feared by all. Beyond San Gabrial, you are in the land of the heathen savage." Zalvidea laid a hand on Buck's shoulder and entreated him not to go. "I wish you would reconsider."

"We have talked this all over before, Padre."

The older man sighed, "You will be missed, Buck. Who will I argue with?"

"I'll miss you, too, Padre. The horses will not be nearly as good company." Buck smiled then turned serious. "Speaking of horses, I'd like to buy one good saddle horse and a couple of pack horses."

"I will ask Sanchez to select them. Can you delay your departure until after Sunday's mass?"

"I fear I may have waited too long now."

"We will bid you farewell in the morning. You will be remembered in our prayers."

MORNING BROKE with a chill in the air. A cold breeze blew up the cut from the Pacific. The wind would be at his back. A good sign, starting a journey with the wind at your back.

Buck's last breakfast with some of the vaqueros consisted of the last of the mission's fresh fruit and a few slices of the sausage the Indians now made with proficiency.

Father Zalvidea laid a hand on Buck's shoulder as he finished his meal. "Are you ready? Pueblo Los Angeles is a long ride and you should get an early start."

"I think you're anxious to be rid of me." He smiled. "I'm

rolled up and ready. I'd like to give Sanchez a shake before I go. Where is he this morning?"

"Gather your things. You may see him as you leave." Feeling a little bit rushed, Buck slung his bedroll and locker to his shoulder. With a priest on each side, he headed for the mission gate.

Outside, the magnificent blue roan pranced near the adobe fence, saddled and waiting. Buck grinned with pleasure at the sight—it was the most magnificent gift he'd ever been offered. Two pack horses, one empty and one loaded with goods, stood nearby. Sanchez was mounted, with a third pack horse trailing.

Father Barona gathered up the roan's reins and led the horse to Buck. "For you, a gift from all of us."

Zalvidea reached behind one of the Indians who had accompanied them to the gate and pulled out a pair of high top riding boots. "These, too. We can't have you crossing the desert looking like a marinero."

Buck pulled his patched and repatched boots off and slipped on the new pair made of finest leather. The Indians packed his personal belongings on the pack horses and he mounted the big blue roan. Feeling the stallion dancing beneath him, he threw his arms back and his chest expanded in pride—the pride of a true vaquero.

"Sanchez will ride with you, until he decides it is time for you to ride alone."

Buck wanted to say thank you, but he was afraid his voice would crack. Grabbing the lead rope of the pack horses, he nodded, spun and spurred the roan.

"Vaya con Dios!" rang out from the padres, Californios, and Indians. "Good sailing!" hailed from Dutch as they all bid their farewells.

Fifty yards from the gate, Buck whirled the roan and shouted, "Thank you!" He hoped Sanchez didn't notice the wetness glistening in his eyes.

Making his way down the trail, he rubbed his hand over his pants pocket, feeling the little round black rock safely in its place. Maybe the tusuat worked, he thought. It seemed lately he'd had more than his share of luck.

As the trail wore on, Buck began to inspect the rig the padres had given him. The saddle was intricately carved in an arch and bell design. The pommel and cantle were inlaid with ivory traded from one of the hide ships. The bridle had large silver conchos on each side at the mouth and ear pieces, Dutch's hand evident in the beautifully braided reins that ended in a finely braided romal that served as quirt. A pair of cantinas, saddlebags, hung over the pommel. The latigo bound a belly cincha woven alternately with red and black hemp. He saw Dutch's hand again in the fine reata, at least sixty feet of intricately woven and tallowed rawhide, bound firmly to a saddle tie.

The pack animals carried sturdy mesquite and leather pack saddles, covered with a mochilla, or Mother Hubbard as it was called in the east—a draped leather that had bags sewn front and back. The rear animal was loaded with supplies, and the front with his personal goods. Two goat-gut water bags hung on each horse. He was well equipped for the long trail ahead.

As they pulled away from San Juan creek, he could see high granite peaks far in the distance and knew Pueblo de Los Angeles rested at their base.

After riding two hours, Sanchez reined up beside him. "Someone comes," he said, motioning to their back trail.

They reined off into the trees.

The rapidly beating hooves of a loping horse broke the quiet. As the rider drew even with them, Buck shouted, "Tui...here!" He rode back onto the trail and up to the panting rider.

"I... I no think I catch you." The huge, brown-skinned man puffed with exertion, his gasps for air exceeded only by those of the little mare he rode. "Tui think maybe you need company. I ride with you awhile. I never go Pueblo de Los Angeles." He flashed his infectious grin.

Buck laughed. "Well, then, let's get on with it."

Dust roiled up as they traveled the dry trail. Soon they were powder covered, and the horses ran with brown foamy rivulets. Not wanting to overwork the animals, Sanchez reined off the trail well before the sun reached the hills to the west.

"It is their first day on the trail," the old vaquero said. "We should make camp early."

The men dropped their packs and Sanchez took the horses to water in the small creek they had been following. The water looked inviting to Buck as well.

"Tui, I'm gonna' scrub off the top layer of this trail dust. Want to come along?"

"No, Tui hungry. I help Sanchez with the camp."

Buck made his way up the creek until he found a thigh-deep pool. He pulled off the striped shirt and duck pants of the marinero, flexed the now corded muscles in his back and shoulders, working out the kinks, threw the clothes over a rock, and slipped into the pool. He hoped the pack lying back at camp contained the rest of the vaquero outfit so he could leave these clothes behind with his memories of the Virginia.

Sinking deeper, he let the cool water flow over him. God, it felt good to wash the grit from his hair and eyes.

"Lose your ship, señor?" The lilting voice startled him and he began to rise, then remembering his nakedness, quickly sank back down. The girl glanced away with embarrassment, her pretty cheeks flushing beneath her high cheek bones.

She had ridden up quietly while he was washing his face. Her horse was lathered—obviously ridden hard. A fine layer of dust covered her clothes as well, but her long black hair shined almost as much as the silver conchos on her saddle. Glossy black tresses fell across a white silk blouse trimmed in Spanish lace. Though the blouse fit loosely, he could easily make out the high full breasts it covered. A red sash circled her tiny waist and cinched tightly over a black leather riding skirt like nothing Buck had ever seen. Split front and back to accommodate the saddle, it covered all but the toes of her fine black leather boots.

He'd never seen a woman ride astride before but decided immediately he liked the idea. He smiled, recovering his composure, but her close regard reminded him of his nakedness beneath the water.

"And you, señorita—do you make it a habit... riding into men's baths?" he asked.

"I see no man, only an arrogant sailor boy." As haughty as she seemed, she couldn't have been more than seventeen.

"Man enough to take you off that horse and scrub away some of the dirt. Maybe I could tell if you're a girl or a boy!" Besides the dust, a smudge on her face slightly marred the fine line of her jaw.

"You are impudent, marinero!" Her chin came up and her dark eyes flashed.

"But I'm clean," Buck taunted. "Maybe you'd like to see." He made a sloshing movement toward her and she backed her horse a little away, but she didn't leave. Buck felt a stirring in his loins he hadn't felt in some time. He sank back down in the water.

"My father has made steers of many who thought themselves bulls for less impudence than yours," she snapped.

Buck laughed but she did not.

"It is the custom in this country to call at the hacienda when you cross another man's land. You would do well to learn manners, marinero. My father's house is a league. There." She pointed upstream then turned away, quirting her horse in the same quick motion. The animal drove its powerful hind legs into the soft mud bank, peppering Buck with mud as she galloped up the slope of the stream.

He watched the spot where she had crested the bank long after her horse's hoof beats were out of earshot. She was strikingly beautiful, her long black hair emphasizing her pale Castilian complexion and crimson lips. For a moment her blush had almost matched their color. Smiling at the memory, Buck climbed out of water, dressed and returned to camp.

Sanchez and Tui had a fire going and side-meat sizzling when he walked in.

"I've been informed by a sassy señorita that we're to call on the hacienda of the rancho we ride across. Do we do that tonight, Sanchez?"

"No, I had planned to stop there in the morning. It will be time enough."

Buck turned in early, tired from their hard day on the road. He fell asleep easily but tossed and turned. His dreams were of flashing dark eyes and raven-black hair.

10

KATHLEEN MCCREED MUELLER sat quietly in her cottage on the outskirts of Boston, rocking and tatting a doily. As on most days since she had left the farm, her thoughts lingered on her son.

If only she knew what had happened.

If only she knew he was safe.

Edward hadn't been gone long. His death had come as a blow which she hadn't expected. She missed him, too, and she was lonely. Soon after the funeral, her stepsons had strongly suggested she would be happier closer to town. Tug and his family moved into the Mueller Manor farmhouse and Kathleen moved into the cottage. Her stepsons hadn't been to see her since the day she had left. Only Ursula, Tuig's wife, stopped by on a rare occasion when she accompanied Tuig to market. Ursula was carrying their second child and Kathleen was happy the girl was living in the big farm house where there was more room for their rapidly growing family.

Kathleen dropped a stitch, which rarely occurred, frowned, and picked it up, her hands resuming the familiar rhythm that always seemed to calm her. With no one to care for at home, she now spent most of her time involved with church and the growing town's activities. She enjoyed renewing old acquaintances from her first marriage. She could make a new life for herself... if only she could stop worrying so much about Sam.

He was still so young and had never been off on his own. Leaving without word was so unlike him. What had possessed him? Over a year had passed without news of him; only the letters from Captain Taylor-Johnson.

She had gone, time and again, to the offices of Bryant and Sturgis, pleading for information, but they always put her off. It was obvious no effort would be made to help her. In the beginning she had cried for hours, worry and fear leaving her barely able to think. The ominous "he has been punished" rolled through her mind a thousand times. If only she knew!

In the end, she had turned stoic. Sam would be all right. He was intelligent, strong, and self-reliant. Sooner or later, he would send word of what had happened. Or he would simply return and explain. She refused to believe he was responsible of any wrong-doing, no matter what Wilhelm said.

Her husband's brother made no effort to mend the breech between them although she saw him almost every Sunday at church. The minister had noticed their relationship, or lack of one. He inquired as to the nature of the rift, but Wilhelm refused to explain. The minister didn't press the issue.

Wilhelm, after all, did tithe well.

MORNING DAWNED CLEAR AND BRISK, and Buck rose before the sun. Going straight to the pack that Zalvidea and Barona had provided him, he investigated its contents. A small hatchet and shovel of precious iron rested across some folded clothes. Buckskin breeches, three folded white shirts, a black leather vest, a wide-brimmed felt hat, and two pairs of moccasins covered other utensils and supplies.

Flour, precious salt, coffee, dried fruit, and several pounds of beef sausage completed the load.

Happily, he pulled on the breeches and shirt. His boots, hat, and new black leather vest finished the outfit. He looked the Californio, the vaquero. He strapped on a pistol and knife, cocked the hat at a jaunty angle, and felt ready to take on a grizzly, or, at least, a sassy señorita.

They broke camp and set out, soon reining up in front of a big corral a few yards away from the back of a large whitewashed, red tile-roofed hacienda. A rawboned vaquero came out to greet them.

"Welcome to Rancho Toro Bravo. Don Pedro has been expecting you." Buck followed the vaquero toward the sprawling adobe. As he neared the rancho, Tui and Sanchez at his side, a portly man in a white silk ruffle-fronted shirt stepped off the veranda.

"Don Pedro Lopez de Seville at your service, señors. Buen provecho." He gave them the most gracious of Californio greetings, 'it is better to be on time than to be invited.' He extended a fat hand to Buck, who accepted the handshake firmly. Then the Don turned to his vaquero, a lanky man with a homely, weathered face. "See that the other two are fed." Buck was surprised to see his friends led away to the rear of the house. "You will join me at my table."

He followed the big man across the veranda into a huge room at least twenty feet wide and forty feet long. A fireplace large enough for a small man to walk into blazed away at one end. Buck trailed Don Pedro on to the dining room, its size dwarfing a long wooden dining table flanked by a dozen tall straight-backed chairs.

Three people sat at the table. Buck's gaze fell first on the señorita he had seen at the stream, this time clean, combed, and even more beautiful. She sat next to an elderly gray-haired, round-figured woman, and across from a tall lean hatchet-faced man with cold black eyes.

"May I present Señora Seville, my wife"—the older woman nodded—"and my daughter, Elena."

Buck nodded and smiled politely, his eyes fixed appraisingly on the daughter. He had to tear his gaze away as the man across from her was introduced. "And her betrothed, Don Eduardo Paulo Juarez."

Buck extended a hand. Damn, damn, damn! The hooked-nosed, hatchet face to marry the beautiful fiery-eyed señorita? The man had a narrow, sallow face that held not the slightest warmth. He looked much older than his 'betrothed.' His handshake felt firm, but cool. His gestures and the look in his distant black eyes reminded Buck of Taylor-Johnson, and he felt immediately repulsed. He forced his attention away and soon became immersed in Don Pedro's questions.

The inquisitive Don quickly learned that Buck had come from Boston and that he was once a farm boy. He was careful not to mention the Virginia or its captain, or that he might be a wanted man. He did however, enjoy speaking once more of home.

The fat don smiled and shoved back his chair. "So your stepfather makes his own brandy.... This is a skill I have long admired. It would be a fine asset to Toro Bravo. Do you also know the secrets of the brandy maker?"

"I often helped my stepfather. I believe I could do it."

"Could you teach it?" Don Pedro inquired. "We have fine vineyards and make reasonable wine... and we have aguardiente, made from cactus, but it is very rough. We have not mastered the brandy."

Buck remembered his surprised at the purchase of casks of brandy by the mission at Monterey, since the mission had its own vineyards, which he could see from the harbor.

"I'm on my way to Pueblo Los Angeles," Buck said. "I need to get into the desert while it is still winter."

"Please consider it, señor." Elena turned toward him, away from her attentive fiancé, acknowledging Buck's presence for the first time since their introduction. "My father would be so pleased. It would be wonderful for him to be able to serve fine Toro Bravo brandy to his guests."

"Elena, if the boy must get on—" Eduardo Juarez interrupted.

The hair on Buck's neck bristled at the reference to him as a boy. He turned to Elena with a slight bow of his head. "I will be happy to help, if the señorita wishes it. It should take less than a week to build a distillery."

Eduardo shot Elena a hard look, which she ignored. She stood and eased back her chair, forcing the men to their feet. "Gracias, señor." She smiled at Buck with warmth. "Now, if you will excuse me, there is a matter I must attend to in the establo."

Her father nodded his permission and she walked out the door toward the stable.

"She has a mare about to foal," the don said. "I know most fathers would not approve of their daughters involving themselves with the livestock, but Elena has always had a mind of her own."

A mind of her own, Eduardo Juarez growled to himself, thinking it an understatement. He glanced at the young marinero who had garnered his fiancée's smiles with such ease. He would have led the hanging party, had this impertinent marinero spoken to a Californio señorita without proper respect and a proper introduction. But his bumptious future father-in-law had brought the man into his home and, worse, introduced him to the ladies of the house. Now he must at least be civil.

"You will have to excuse me, also," Eduardo said. "I must return to a matter of pressing business in Los Angeles." He promptly rose, said his goodbyes to the women, and headed toward the door. Without looking back he added, "Don Pedro, can we finish our business while I pack my things?"

The don shoved back his chair. "Juanita!" he called out, summoning the Indian woman who had been serving them. "Show Señor Mueller to a guest room. He will be with us for the next few days."

Eduardo's jaw tightened—the old fool was going to let the Anglo stay in the hacienda. He gave Don Pedro a disgruntled look but said nothing. He stalked out of the room and the don obligingly followed.

Buck trailed the Indian woman down the hall to small but comfortable quarters. An Indian servant fetched his things and he unpacked them, then went to find Tui and Sanchez to tell them of the short delay. Surprisingly, they were not unhappy about the stay, and immediately began planning a trip into the mountains early the next day with Enrico, the rawboned vaquero who had greeted them when they first arrived. They meant to hunt a grizzly that had been helping himself to Toro Bravo cattle.

Later that afternoon, the don showed Buck the pride of his rancho, his vineyards. They had been planted then left to grow wild—no irrigation or pruning to control growth or production. Buck doubted they would produce more than one ton to the acre and there were no more than twenty acres. He considered several suggestions he might make to the don, but the man was singing the vineyard's praises, so Buck held his tongue.

Instead, they selected a suitable site for the distillery then returned to the house for supper. Elena joined them a little bit later, entering the dining room in a cream-colored off the shoulder gown with a black lace scarf staked in her hair over a high turtle comb. It draped over both her shoulders and tucked into the front of the low-cut dress, partially covering the fullness of her lovely white breasts, which would have been even further exposed without it.

Buck rose while she was seated then sat back down as the don left the room to fetch a bottle of wine. Her mother remained outside in the cocina, kitchen, a smaller building set away from the house in case of fire, directing the final preparations for supper.

"Good evening, señor."

"Good evening, señorita." Buck smiled, his eyes going over her warmly. "Well, there's no question in my mind," he teased, "Now that you've washed the dirt away."

She smiled. "And you now look the vaquero, the caballero. I take it you did not find your ship in the pond?"

The don returned, a carafe of wine in his hand and a very old woman on his arm. Buck rose again.

"This is my mother, Doña Angelina." The don smiled. "Mamacita to us."

Buck nodded at the ancient, wizened woman, whose dark eyes shined, alive and flashing as she looked him straight in the face. She took her seat at the table, slowly but as regally as a queen.

Buck watched her for a moment, waiting for some pearl of wisdom to drop from her aged lips, but she didn't speak. He glanced once more at Elena, but the don began to speak, and soon he was lost once more in her father's endless questions. Buck found himself glad of it. It kept him from staring into Elena's warm brown eyes and at the spot where the scarf was so provocatively tucked between her breasts.

At the first lull in the conversation, he turned in her direction. "Did your mare drop her foal?" Elena's mother, covered her face with her white lace fan, but not enough to disguise her flush of embarrassment nor her subsequent look of disapproval at Buck's highly improper question.

Buck's face grew warm. Too late, he realized he had offended the women, but Elena stepped in to answer.

"Not yet, I am afraid. The mare is young, and I think, still undecided if it is her time."

"Do not be foolish, niña," her father scolded. "Nature tells her when it is time." He turned back to Buck, ending the exchange between them. "Now, Señor Mueller, tell me again why is it you believe the vines should be irrigated?"

Answering the don's continuing questions, Buck wondered at the look of warmth he had seen on Elena's face as she had answered his question. Unhappily, he bid her good night with a small bow, then he and the don went into the main living area, the sala, to test the imported brandy his host kept there.

For the rest of the evening he wondered about her relationship with the hook-nosed man and why she had chosen to marry him.

Dawn brought another day. At first light Don Pedro was waiting with four stout Indians to help Buck build the distillery. They set out on foot but as soon as they got started, a vaquero arrived with the don's big palomino stallion.

For as large a man as he was, Don Pedro swung easily up into the saddle. "I am sorry to leave you, but I must go to Pueblo de Los Angeles to conclude some business. I will return in a few days. Enrico will see that you have what you need." The two men spurred their horses, leaving Buck to his job.

He worked through the day, enjoying the labor that tested his muscles and kept them hard. When he returned to the hacienda for the midday meal, he discovered he had been relegated to eating with the vaqueros in the kitchen. He only saw Elena as she came and went to the establo and as she rode off to exercise her horses. It was all he could do not to saddle the blue roan and ride after her.

As Buck continued his work, Mamacita, as she insisted he call her, came out to watch. She ordered an Indian servant to place a chair beneath a nearby oak tree, then sat contentedly, often making comments and suggestions. Though the work was progressing well, Alta California wasn't Boston and he was often stumped for materials. It was Mamacita who usually solved the problem. The crowning achievement was a large copper kettle she obtained from the kitchen, much to the younger Señora Seville's chagrin, to be used for a boiler.

After three hard days, the job was done and Buck was invited back to the dining room. Don Pedro still had not returned. Elena was not present, and there seemed an uneasiness in the air.

"I'm sorry your daughter could not join us," Buck said to the señora with what he hoped was nonchalance.

"She is not feeling well," Señora Seville said stiffly. "She is...she has been upset lately...." When Buck made no reply but waited for her to continue, she looked embarrassed. "She is very young... you should understand, you are young also."

Buck only nodded, having no idea what she was driving at, knowing only that he wanted to see Elena again. Unfortunately, the next morning she remained reclusive. Buck, unwilling to leave the rancho even though the distillery was finished and already perking, decided to undertake the task of improving the vineyard, even though he had only made suggestions to Don Pedro. He'd received no concurrence from the don, but neither had he received any objections, and he knew it was the right thing to do.

For the next two days, Tui and Sanchez lolled around, grousing that they were ready to leave. Buck ignored them, working with the Indians to bring an irrigation ditch from a little creek that was the main water source for the hacienda to a spot at the upper end of the vineyard. Still the don had not returned, and Buck spotted Elena only once as she rode to a knoll high above them and watched them as they worked. Buck waved, but she only wheeled her horse and rode away.

Once the irrigation ditch was complete, he went to work on the vines. By now they were losing their leaves, and he felt it was time to prune. They had never been trimmed and the growth was wild and uncontrolled. It was difficult to even walk between the overgrown rows.

For the next three days he worked with six Indians pruning the vines, leaving only four major canes on each. From every plant he made a pile of trimmings four feet high. When they had cleared the rows and piled the trash, the vineyard looked like a field of dry limbs stuck in the ground.

Buck smiled at the job they had done, knowing spring would bring new fruit wood and an abundance of grapes, even though the vineyard now looked barren and dead.

As the days continued, Sanchez grew more and more

restless—a caged animal, pacing and speaking to no one. Even Tui grew bored and tired of the waiting. Feeling guilty for keeping them there so long, Buck found them in the late afternoon standing beside the corral.

"You are finished with the vines," Sanchez said crossly. "What will you do now—build the don a new hacienda?"

Buck laughed. "To tell you the truth, I thought it might be time to move on."

A grin lit Tui's wide face. "Time to see what is over next mountain."

He glanced back toward the hacienda, thinking of Elena, and frowned. "Yes, I guess it is." He started back to the house, thinking he wished things could have been different. The sound of pounding hooves stopped him short, and he turned to see horses and a cloud of dust rolling into the yard, and realized Don Pedro had finally returned. His horse at a pounding gallop, the fat man jerked rein and slid to a stop right in front of him, blocking Buck's way inside.

He saw Mamacita totter out of the house and stand nearby. The don dismounted and angrily stomped over to where Buck stood. "You!" he sputtered, his fat jowls shaking. "You have committed an outrage! My beautiful vineyard! It has taken me years!"

"Your vineyard will bear twice the crop next spring."

"You have destroyed it! It cannot possibly recover from this... this rape you have committed!"

Buck started to argue, but in the don's quivering rage it would do no good to try and reason with him. The thought crossed his mind, if he were to rape something of the don's, it certainly wouldn't be his vineyard. He almost smiled, but instead, stepped around him and went to pack his things, leaving the quivering don sputtering behind him, complaining loudly to Mamacita who glared up at him.

Buck hurriedly threw his pack together in the Spartan but comfortable guest room he'd been occupying. As he was finishing, the door creaked open and he turned. Clad in the same outfit she had worn the day he first saw her at the creek, Elena stood in the doorway.

"Mamacita told me. I... I am sorry about my father. He sometimes speaks before he thinks."

"The vineyards will prosper. That I promise."

She nodded, accepting his words for the truth. "He should not be angry. He should offer to pay you for all you have done."

"There is only one payment I want." Buck moved closer, reached over her shoulder, and pushed the heavy plank door closed behind her, pinning her against it in the same smooth motion. Her surprised look softened as he bent his head and kissed her full on the lips. Circling her slim waist with his arm, he pulled her tightly against him, and Elena slid her arms around his neck. She kissed him back, softly at first, then opening her mouth and allowing his tongue inside. She was clinging to him, her nails digging into his shoulders.

Buck groaned. Feeling her tremble, he forced himself away. "That was payment enough for a hundred distilleries, Elena." He picked up his gear and opened the door. Halfway down the hall he turned to look at her. She stood in the doorway, astounded, it seemed, that he had kissed her, even more astounded that she had kissed him back.

Buck shook his head. "You're much too much woman for that soft-handed...." He left the rest unsaid, spun, and set off for the corral. He could still taste her kiss, still smell her perfume.

Damn, he hated to leave.

Elena stared after Buck's tall retreating figure. She watched him stride down the hall, thinking for the first time of the slap she should have given him. How dare he take such liberties! He was impudent and ill-mannered.

And yet she wished he wasn't going away.

Sanchez and Tui had the horses saddled and waiting beside the corral. Buck stowed his gear in his saddlebags, and they all three swung into their saddles. As they rode past the front of the hacienda, Mamacita and Elena stood beside the stout oak front door. Impulsively, Buck galloped over and reined up beside the old woman, the big roan sliding to a stop in a cloud of dust. He was on the ground and, in two strides, scooped her into a big bear hug, as he would have his own mother.

"Don't drink all the brandy, Mamacita," he teased, "leave some to trade, and to wet my throat if I get back this way."

She grunted at the hug and smiled, crinkling the parchment skin on her face. "And you, mi hijo, do not judge all of the Sevilles by one with pig fat filling the space between his ears."

Buck laughed and re-mounted the roan. He allowed himself a last swift glance at Elena, then was saved when his horse spun to join his departing friends.

11

As THEY RODE off toward the hills, Buck couldn't keep his mind off the kiss. If he hadn't been so angry, he would never have been so impulsive. Then he thought of how she had clung to him and kissed him back—as if he were her last chance.

He wanted to turn and ride back to her, take her away from the that bastard Juarez. But where could they go? It was three thousand miles back to Mueller Manor—a farm to share with his four stepbrothers. The thought was foolish. Besides... it was only a kiss.

After hours on the trail trying to ignore his feelings of frustration, they approached the sleepy Pueblo de Los Angeles. Adobes began to pepper fields of crops—beans and squash tangled and dry corn still stood unharvested. Dogs nipped at the horses' heels as they crossed the Rio de Los Angeles, then made their way among tightly clustered adobes to the first cantina. They tied their animals to the rail out in front and loosened the cinches, giving the horses a chance to rest. The long tiring ride had done nothing to ease Buck's black mood.

"If I ever needed a drink, it's now!" He stomped across the board porch to the cantina, his tall leather boots raising dust.

"Tui have dry throat." The big kanaka walked close behind, his heavy weight making the narrow boards creak.

"Tres vinos, por favor," Sanchez called to the bartender, dropping three reals on the bar.

"Unfortunately," Buck said, "it isn't my dry throat or the trail dust that's got me down. It's the thought of that cold-eyed bastard Juarez with Elena."

Sanchez rested a callused palm on his shoulder. "The thing for you to do, my friend, is put a thousand miles of dust and a few señoritas between you and Toro Bravo. The girl and Juarez —that is the way things are done in California, compadre. Her fate was sealed by her father, by agreement with her betrothed. The muchacha has no choice in the matter." Sanchez slid a drink in front of Buck. "You must keep your eyes and thoughts on the trail ahead." He lifted his glass, "Saludos, amigos!" and drained the contents in one long swallow.

Buck took a sip of his drink, feeling the fire burn into his stomach. "You know, this country's not so bad," he said. "The winters are mild. The cattle practically raise themselves. The otter trade continues to grow, and I've heard there are furs for the taking over those mountains to the north."

"No place like Sandwich Islands," Tui said firmly.

"There must be dozens of ways to make a living," Buck continued, ignoring Tui's words. "The hide trade is growing, and the Californios need all kinds of goods." For the first time in a year, his thoughts had turned away from Mueller Manor, from surviving so he could go home.

Pulling one of Ernst's precious coins from his pocket, Buck broke the first of his shiny five-dollar gold pieces, trading them for fifty reals, then blew twenty of those on fiery aguardiente. When the sun lit the west with the soft yellow glow of sunset, they stumbled from the cantina, then made camp in the dark just outside the sleepy little village.

Sleeping hard, he awoke with the dawn, his mouth bone dry and his head throbbing like a hammer against an anvil.

Tui had the fire going, so Buck dug the coffee from his pack and headed toward a trickling stream they had crossed. Finding a place to drink, he noticed another camp through the scrub oak. He walked over and called out in Spanish, "Hola, señors." Two men, dressed in buckskins with fur hats and long Hawkins muzzle-loaders casually resting in their hands, stood to greet him.

"Hello the camp," he repeated in English, realizing they could be Americans. "I got coffee going upstream a'ways. You're welcome to it. Just bring your mugs."

"Obliged," one of them answered, reaching into a small buckskin pack, the only thing besides the weapons they seemed to have.

All three reached the camp at the same time. The two in fringed buckskins hunkered down on their haunches next to the fire.

"That's Tui, I'm Buck, and that's Sanchez." He pointed to each of his friends.

"Tucker Hutchins, and this here's Jed... Jed Taylor. Kinda strange to hear the King's English here 'bouts. You a Boston man?"

Buck didn't know it showed, particularly dressed as he was. He nodded. "And you?" he asked, falling into his Boston, German-tinged brogue.

"Kentucky... and Jed's a Tennessee man. We been takin' furs fer a thousand miles. 'Til the blasted Mojaves decided they needed 'em and our rigs more'n we did. Lucky we kept our hair."

"Mojaves? I take it they're somewhere on the desert east —between here and St. Louis."

"Well, pilgrim, at least betwixt here and Santa Fe," Tucker said. "St. Louie is a fer piece more." He shook his head, moving his long gray hair. "They's the meanest, most conniving bunch of varmints this here ol' boy's ever see'd."

Tucker talked on while Buck fried sausage and pan bread. When it was done, he filled Tui and Sanchez's plates and shared the rest with the two tall, rawboned, obviously hungry men.

"So where do you fellows go from here?" Buck asked, watching them sop up the last of the sausage grease.

"Me, I figure on headin' north, if'n these Mexes don't mind." Tucker looked hard at Sanchez.

"Californios," Sanchez corrected softly.

"I heard they give old Jed Smith a bad time a summer or two ago. I got no hankerin' to end up in a Mexie—" he corrected himself, "Californio hoosegow."

"Jusgado," Sanchez corrected.

"Whatever.... Fact is, we got no hankerin' to tangle with those Mojaves again neither, so I guess it's north for us. I hear the Frenchies been trappin' a big valley up there... called the Tulares or some such. Maybe we can pick up a few furs fer our trouble along the way. How about you fellers?"

"I'm figgering to hang around California for a while," Buck answered, catching Sanchez's look of surprise. "The more I put my head to it, the more a small farm in Massachusetts looks crowded." It was the first time Buck had ever referred to Mueller Manor as small. Everything here was so immense, it changed a man's standards. "I figure a fellow could make his fortune right here if he had a mind to." He grinned. "And a good, strong back."

Hutchins got a faraway look in his eye, "If'n I was a stayin' man, I'd go back to some of that country Jed and I come through, north of San Gabriel. We seen hundreds of head of good horseflesh just for the takin', with no man's mark on 'em. Horses are fetchin' fifty dollars each in Santa Fe, if you can get 'em there."

Buck's head snapped up. "Fifty dollars!" He could buy horses, broke to the rein, for four dollars apiece in California.

"Yes, siree, and they's wild cattle everywhere," Tucker continued. "Might be better than furrin'."

Buck spent the day using his Irish charm and German

practicality to convince the trappers to return to the area they had mentioned north of San Gabriel. Together, the five of them could make their fortunes "wild horsin'". Buck would make himself a stake.

By nightfall, they returned to town and went back to the cantina, where Buck continued working on the trappers. Sanchez, he told them, was California's greatest horse trainer, which was little, if any, exaggeration, and Tui was its strongest man. The latter had to be proven—and was—at least to the satisfaction of the mountain men and chagrin of the locals, by a wrestling match in the middle of the dusty street.

The next morning, with the bargain sealed, Buck spent ten of his forty-five remaining dollars stocking the expedition with flour, salt, coffee, lead, and powder. He spent ten more buying horses for Tucker and Jed. The Mojaves had relieved them of their string.

They all agreed Buck should receive two shares and the first profits to repay his investment, since it was his capital at risk. He'd learned something from watching his stepfather trade in the markets of Boston.

Tucker and Jed carried two flintlocks each and agreed to loan Tui and Sanchez one. The old vaquero refused; his braided leather reata, and his stag-handled knife would do for him. Buck had his own weapons: a fine pair of .50 caliber Aston cap and ball pistols, a fifty-caliber carbine musket, a cutlass he'd taken from the ship, and the two knives he had inherited from Ernst.

The next morning, they rode east, into a bright brisk December day. Buck was convinced he would make himself rich and ride back to Toro Bravo... back to see what his fate might be with Elena, who was obviously unhappy in her situation. He knew she harbored feelings for him. Feelings that had gone unsaid but which were there never the less.

And the fat don would feel far different about him if Buck returned with saddle bags full of gold.

As Buck began riding east, the brig Elk Hound sailed west into Boston harbor. Her captain carried a small packet of mail from ships met at sea and from men in California, where he'd been taking hides for the past two years. Her holds carried tallow, hides, and horns, and the added ballast of California beach rock. The stone was needed to keep Cape Horn's great winds from blowing the ship down with her light cargo.

The smooth beach rocks were destined to become cobblestones in Boston streets, the same ones Kathleen Mueller hurried along to pick up the letter that had come with the ship and was now waiting for her at the office of McCullough Shipping.

She managed to get out the office door and onto the board sidewalk before tearing the wax-sealed, folded parchment open.

"Thank God, he's safe," she whispered aloud, reading in Buck's own hand his troubles, being forced to jump ship, his escape from the captain, then the tranquil life he had led at the mission. He wrote of his friend Zalvidea, with whom he had left the letter, along with instructions for delivery to any Boston bound ship other than the Virginia. He told her of his plan to return overland to Boston.

Kathleen clutched the letter to her breast. Sam could be in Boston by the following summer, if he successfully crossed the Great Basin. Then she thought of the problems he would face, the dreadful blistering deserts and bloody heathen Indians.

Suddenly, summer seemed a very long way away.

Buck rode long and hard that first day, the five men stopping at an occasional trickle to rest and water the horses. The farther east they went, the dryer the country became. Hot desire for the hunt pushed Buck on, and he pushed the stock and men.

They turned north over a pass called Cajon. Late the second day they entered a region of fifteen-foot-tall, gray-green desert trees which pushed spiny branches upward like a man reaching for the sky, entreating his God for relief from the rugged country.

They came upon a trail where a band of horses had passed and turned north to follow the sign along a dry wash. By noon the third day, Tui's mare went tender-footed. They made camp by a salty pond, no more than a rain hole. The water had begun to stagnate, but there was shade from the spiny trees and some grass for the stock. They rested.

The fifth day they entered a flat grassy plain with animal sign everywhere. A large herd of antelope flashed their black tails, showing the men white rumps as they bounded off, stopping curiously to watch before dropping over a ridge and out of sight.

Soon after, they spotted the first band of wild horses. A cold clear spring at the center of a grove of willows had attracted them. Abundant grass waved in the breeze and horse sign covered the ground everywhere. A short reconnaissance produced a wash cut ten feet deep into the plain and varying from twenty to forty feet in width. By blocking it, they constructed a corral between two narrows. The banks of the wash would act as side walls.

The next day they began the hunt. Up before the sun, they breakfasted on hot beans, drop biscuits, and coffee while they devised a plan. They would position Buck and Sanchez along each side of the wash, since they were best with the reata, and Jed, Tuck, and Tui would drive the horses down along the wash so the men could rope them. The plan was sound, yet after the first full day's work, the men had managed to capture only five horses.

It was an exhausted Tui who suggested, "Why do we try to rope them when we can drive them into the trap like Sandwich Island fishes?"

Buck grinned broader than Tui. "Why do we?"

The next day they rebuilt the corral in the wash. They constructed a large wooden gate they could drag closed after the horses had been driven in. By the end of the next three days, they had over forty tough desert horses corralled. Unfortunately, by then even the big blue roan had become footsore, so they decided to rest half a day.

Buck was becoming more and more attached to the horse who never turned away from the wild-eyed animals in the herd, not even the stallions, facing them head to head and turning them even with a rider on his back. He remembered Sanchez's comments the first day Buck had seen the roan. "He will charge the gates of hell for you." Buck named the horse Diablo's Taunt, but called him simply Diablo.

It was February. Buck lost track of the days. He lay awake enjoying the warmth of his bedroll in the cold crispness before dawn, thinking he was satisfied with the week's work. A low rumble far off in the mountains warned of a storm. Intermittent clouds floated overhead, growing thicker in the distance. He could see the stars come and go as they passed. The rain wouldn't bother them here, at least for a while. He dozed.

Something disturbed his heavy sleep, making him toss and turn. Suddenly he bolted upright in his bedroll. He didn't know what it was, but something was desperately wrong. He began to identify a low rumble that vibrated the ground beneath him. Sanchez was sitting up too. Buck shook out his boots and dragged them on.

"What is it, Sanchez?"

The old vaquero listened for a moment, then his face went suddenly tense. "The wash... it rains in the mountains. She floods!"

Buck ran for the wash where the horses had been pinned. The animals milled back and forth the length of the corral, whistling and neighing and pawing at the walls of the cut. They knew the danger far better than the men.

"Dammit!" Buck tore at the gate, which they had placed

on the upstream side. He yelled at Sanchez who hurried close behind. "We've got to tear down the other end. When the water hits, they'll just be swept back into the corral."

They ran to the downstream side and began ripping away at the willows that formed the fence, the horses climbing onto each other trying to scale the walls. Their terrified screams and hoof beats drowned out the sound of the onrushing water.

"Hurry!" Buck shouted.

Just as they opened a five-foot-wide space, the torrent hit. It came in a solid wall, pushing brush and limbs along its crest. Buck boosted Sanchez to the top of the ravine and safety, but his friend reached back for him, a huge branch struck him across the chest, wrenching him from the old vaquero's grip and tumbling him head over heels downstream.

Buck yelled and was gone, the water churning over him, horses everywhere, rolling and plunging in the swirling foam and trash-filled onslaught. Sanchez ran along the bank shouting for his friend, but he was nowhere to be seen in the pre-dawn darkness. He ran until he could barely breathe, till his thin legs were shaking and his sides split with pain. He had covered more than a mile and he still saw no sign of Buck.

Frustrated, Sanchez remained trapped on the far side of the bank away from camp. He couldn't even go for his own horse staked out on the opposite side to continue the search. Finally, he headed back, out of breath, dragging in deep gasps of air. Salted tears found their way down his craggy cheeks as he returned to the corral site, only to have to wait until the torrent receded before he could cross.

12

To Don Eduardo Juarez, Elena Seville meant two things: an attractive wife to operate his household and warm his bed, and the eventual acquisition of Toro Bravo—the latter, by far, the more important.

Elena's father, Don Pedro, was only ten years his senior. It could be years before the fat man would die—much too long to wait before Toro Bravo would be his. Still, there were ways.... Don Pedro was heavily indebted to the Juarez's. He might be convinced to give up control of the ranch if it remained in the family. If he were unwilling to do that, an accident would not be out of the question.

With the revolutionaries in control in Mexico City, Don Pedro had few influential friends left in the Mexican government. He was no longer of use to Don Eduardo—no longer of any political value. Still, the fat man had a shrewd side. Even obese and bumptious, Seville was still a man to be reckoned with, and Don Eduardo knew he must be careful.

Don Pedro had built a beautiful rancho, one to be coveted. It was not as lovely as Rancho Riena de California, the Juarez grant, but it was handsome and productive... and it bordered the Juarez hacienda. He wanted Toro Bravo and marriage to Elena was the easiest way to get it. The least dangerous. And if an accident happened....

Don Eduardo had no qualms about marriage. A woman was something to use, an ornament, if a useful one. Much as the Indians were a necessity for manual labor, a woman was a necessary and expected part of life at the rancho. She was expected to grace the table and the household and see that things functioned as they should in such a grand hacienda as Rancho Reina.

Still he had misgivings about the Seville girl. Elena was headstrong. She had a disgruntling way of speaking when she should be silent, offering her opinion when only men's opinions should be heard. She rode unescorted into the hills; spent time with her horses and the vaqueros out in the stable. But these were problems he could solve. He knew she could easily be brought in hand. Like a good headstrong horse, she would be broken.

Her willful behavior would cease once she entered his household. She would take her place at Rancho Riena de California, overseeing the Indian women and bearing strong Juarez heirs. Castillian heirs. Sons of refinement and breeding who would build the Juarez land grant and holdings, and add even more to that which Eduardo and his father before him had already accomplished.

Eduardo felt destined to build a dynasty.

A Juarez dynasty.

The girl was only the beginning.

A HEAVY BRANCH knocked the wind from Buck's lungs and dragged him deep into the roiling water. He fought for breath, taking in mouthfuls of mud. Coughing and spitting, he scrambled for the surface, only to be tumbled over and over in a roiling maze of brambles and branches.

His strength was almost spent when his hand grasped something solid, something that had direction, drive, was not controlled by the plunging turbulence, not relenting to its tumble and roll. He grasped the mane of a strong, desert-wise mare.

Kicking and plunging, the animal swam and fought to stay on the surface—too busy staying alive to try to rid herself of her new burden. Buck had no idea how many miles they were swept down the ravine, but suddenly it widened and his feet occasionally touched bottom. The mare, Buck still clinging to her mane, found a high spot, and clambered out of the water. They both fell to the ground exhausted, the mare uncaring that the man, her enemy, slept at her side.

They were alive and, for the moment, that transcended hate and fear.

Buck awoke first. He had that and another advantage over the little mare. Though stronger, faster, and eminently more qualified to find her way in the desert—the mare could not reason as he could. And now he reasoned he would need this little horse if he was ever to get back to camp. A camp he wished he'd never chosen.

More than a month's work swept away in a few moments. God, what a waste. And yet he was still alive. Maybe the lesson was cheap.

Pulling off his belt, he fastened it around the mare's strong neck. He wasn't sure he could hold onto her or ride her until she gave in, but he had to try. Odds were, she would throw him and disappear into the desert, leaving him without her needed strong legs, and without the belt to boot.

He found a tough piece of willow and took a turn in the belt. He might be able to choke her down, if he had to. Buck lay beside her for an hour. She coughed and hacked but didn't awake. Stroking her neck and talking to her softly, he implored her to trust him, to surrender herself to him. Just as he began to worry that she might not wake up, might not survive at all, she raised her head.

Grabbing an ear, taking a turn in the belt and choking

her, Buck held her down. If she couldn't lift her head, she couldn't get to her feet. She kicked furiously and struggled to sink her teeth into him, but he was relentless. Pinning her head to the ground, turning the belt until her tongue extended, he held her. Finally, she calmed, resigned that she could not get up. Buck eased the belt, stroked and talked to her, whispering in her ear like a lover until she relaxed and calmed.

Standing quickly, he jerked up on the belt and threw a leg over her back as she sprang to her feet. Immediately she was a child of the desert again, twisting, turning, trying to throw him off. Buck rode as he had never ridden before, digging his fingers into her mane, gripping her hard with his thighs. A labor of necessity—of life itself.

The mare bolted, kicked, spun, tried to turn her head and bite him, but he hung on as relentlessly as a cougar. When she tried to turn and sink her teeth in his thigh, he struck her nose with his fist. When she ducked her head, he dug his heels into her flanks, driving her forward. When she flung her head backward, he grabbed an ear and twisted.

The mare plunged, he clung; she spun, he countered. Finally, she lowered her head and ran flat out, wind sweeping her mane, Buck leaning low, marveling at her speed. God, she was quick! Diablo was strong, steady, fearless. The mare was quick, wary, guileful. Finally, reluctantly, he twisted the willow, and choked her down until she stopped and dropped her head, her tongue lolling down. Out of breath. Out of will.

A bittersweet victory for Buck.

If she hadn't been weakened from her exhausting ride down the ravine, her lungs fret with water, he knew she would have won.

He dug his heels into her side and turned her upstream, pushing her, not letting her recover, knowing she could still win if he let her strengthen. He kept her at the edge of total exhaustion, yet was careful not to hurt her. He wanted this mare to live, to bear Diablo's colts. Colts that would have

Andalusian strength and courage, desert wile and quickness.

He didn't know how long they trudged; he was almost done in himself. He shivered in his still-sodden clothes, even though the sun was up. Knowing he had to keep pushing, to keep her moving, praying exhaustion wouldn't overwhelm him, praying he wouldn't fall asleep and slide off her back.

They passed dozens of drowned horses, feet and legs in grotesque positions, mouths open, tongues distended, pride gone. Had he not been so exhausted, survival so preeminent, he would have sickened and retched at the sight.

They continued upward, finding a place where the water only trickled, and finally crossed the ravine. Tui, Sanchez and the mountain men rushed to the bank as horse and rider splashed through the little stream, now indolent, apathetic in its disregard for life.

Buck tried to dismount but his legs were shaking so hard he collapsed off the horse. Tui picked him up and carried him like a child to his bedroll. The game little mare collapsed and lay on her side, uncaring that she was in the camp of the enemy.

"Sanchez look for you," Tui said quietly. "All look, but no find."

Buck just smiled. He ached from head to foot and his eyes would not stay open. But at last he was safe. He was asleep almost as soon as his battered body touched his bedroll.

Sanchez led the tired little mare to a corral he and the others had constructed to confine the few horses they had saved. He coddled the mare with grass he cut by hand, scolding the other horses and allowing her to eat in peace. Sanchez smiled. She had saved his friend. He felt as if he owed her a debt, and he meant to see it repaid.

ELENA STARED through the shutters of her room. Eduardo was on his way to Toro Bravo to call on her. She was trying to decide what to wear, not that she really cared.

A knock at her door echoed through her room. Mamacita stuck her head in and smiled, seeing Elena standing in only her petticoats next to the carved four-poster bed.

"You must get dressed, child. Don Eduardo will be here soon."

"I do not wish to see him, Grandmother. He is old and ugly, and he treats me like a horse, not a person."

The old woman walked to Elena's bed and sat down. She patted a spot beside her, beckoning Elena to join her. Elena sank down on the colorful quilt, resting her head on Mamacita's shoulder.

"Do you remember your grandfather, child?"

She nodded. "Of course, I do. He always had time for me. He used to let me sit on his lap, and he played games with Luis and me." Luis was her brother. He had been killed when they had escaped the revolution and first come to California.

"Well, I did not know your grandfather until our marriage was arranged. He was not the best-looking man my father could have chosen, but he was reasonably handsome... and, you know, it is our way." She smiled, crinkling the lines in her face. "The first time he called on me I was very shy. He thought I did not like him, and he became angry with me. I did not want to marry him, and I knew he felt the same."

Elena rose and walked to the window. "But, still, we were forced to wed, and over the years, I grew to love him very much. He was a good man, even though he had trouble showing it. And he loved me... or came to love me. By the time I lost him that day on the road, I thought he was the most handsome man in the world." The same day Elena's brother died, her grandfather had also been killed. Though she was little more than a child, Elena had seen her grandmother's pain that day. She would never have suspected there was a time when her grandmother had not loved her husband.

"It is our way, child," the old woman repeated. "Eduardo will change. He is like a small boy, showing off his manliness. He will come to love you, and you will come to love him."

"Eduardo will love me—as he loves his horses." Elena rose and straightened her shoulders defiantly. "I want to be loved as a woman."

Mamacita avoided her gaze. "Get dressed, child." Though she tried to give her granddaughter courage, she, too, did not like this man her thick-headed son had chosen. Her granddaughter was very precious to her. She deserved better. But she knew Pedro had done what he thought was right. And it was right—for the Sevilles and Juarezes.

As she watched her proud Elena, head held high, chin jutting forward with determination, she wondered at the outcome. Finally, Elena moved away.

"All right, Mamacita, for you I will get dressed."

The old woman nodded. "Wear the yellow, child. It makes you look happy, and you will be so." She kissed her granddaughter's cheek and walked out of the room, closing the heavy door behind her.

Elena stared after her, feeling a little guilty, but the lie she had told was only a small one. Grabbing her riding clothes, she dressed quickly, checked to see that no one was around, and ran from the house. At her direction, one of the vaqueros saddled her mare and Elena swung up on its back, riding astride as she usually did, though her parents heartily disapproved.

"Tell my father I have gone for a ride," she told the tall vaquero who had helped her. "I will be gone all day. Tell him I hope he enjoys Don Eduardo's company." The man eyed her with a hint of understanding, nodded and waved as she galloped away from the barn.

BUCK and the men rested only a day.

Muscles and bones still battered and sore, he rode at the rear of the cavalcade, content to let Sanchez worry about their next encampment.

Low hills, backdropped by formidable mountains, blocked the path to the west. To the north, the desert gave way to a grass-covered plain. Though scarce, its water holes were well marked with game trails. Antelope, deer, bear, and elk sign were everywhere... and much more horse sign than marked the country they had left behind.

Sanchez finally reined up in a grove of scrub oak near a marshy lake fed by a clear cold spring. While he and Tucker put together a makeshift corral using the copse of scrub oak as posts, Buck rode out to survey the country beyond the camp. As he crested a dusty rise, Diablo snorted a challenge which was answered by a splendid red stallion, who busily herded his brood of forty mares off toward the next low hill. Surveying the landscape, Buck rested a leg over the saddle horn to relax and watch their departure, and was almost unseated when Diablo jumped forward, anxious to challenge the red.

"Whoa, boy." Buck patted the roan sleek neck. "You want your chance at the ladies? Tomorrow will have to be soon enough." The big horse settled down. Resting quietly once more, they watched the band disappear, and Buck's thoughts drifted to Elena.

After the flood, he had almost resigned himself to giving up this quest for horses, for money. That was what it really was. He wanted to meet her on her own terms, meet her as an equal. But he feared it a fruitless effort. She was a betrothed woman, a woman of property, of one of the most influential families in Alta California. He was dreaming. But then he had been taught to follow his dreams. To meet all challenges.

He would do what he set out to do.

The success or failure of this odyssey meant very little to the rest of the men. To Tui it was just someplace to be and good fellows to be with. Tuck and Jed would spend their money, if they were lucky enough to be successful, in the first civilization they happened upon.

To Sanchez it was the horses, always the horses. He would be happy anywhere there was good horseflesh, and happiest when there was the promise of new and even better stock to train.

The next morning they followed the red stallion west, over a low range of nearby hills, across another valley with a huge humpbacked mountain to the north, and finally topped a ridge. They drew up their mounts and sat in awed silence, surveying a vast valley dropping two thousand feet below, almost as far as they could see to the west and south, and out of sight to the north.

Zalvidea had told Buck of a great central California valley stretching hundreds of miles to the north, beyond where Monterey lay and even beyond Yerba Buena. A land full of grizzly, elk, and Indians. A valley called Tulares, for the reeds that lined the banks of the lakes and marshes in the bottom.

They watched the stallion pick his way down a rocky canyon in front of them, pushing his band and snorting into the air. Finally, as the band dropped from sight, Buck and the men turned away, making their way back along the base of the big humped-back mountain that reigned over all.

Buck pulled Diablo up next to Tui, between two huge live oaks on a rocky point overlooking the secluded valley they had ridden through. A fine little stream made its way around the base of a hill until it was lost in the reeds of a lake at the bottom of the valley. The lake in turn fed a stream that plunged into a rocky gorge. The place was low enough that it wouldn't often be touched by snow yet high enough to enjoy the cover of oaks and an occasional pine.

From where he sat, Buck could see several deer grazing in the distance. Two elk broke from a thick grove of willows bordering the east end of the lake and trotted over a rise, laying their long heavy racks along their spines and trumpeting their displeasure at having their graze disturbed.

At the far side of the valley, over a mile away, two black bears flung dust and pieces of rotten log in the air as they dug for grubs. Suddenly they bolted. The roar of a grizzly carried to where Buck and Tui now watched, alerting the two smaller bears to a charge. They scrambled for cover as a huge grizzly took up their former position.

"Bear Valley," Buck said, the words rolling easily off his tongue. "That's good a name as any." Tui looked at him curiously when he dismounted. "This'll do... this will do just fine."

It was a beautiful spot. A place to build... a place to share.

13

THEY BUILT a strong corral in the bottom of the rocky canyon at the edge of the Tulares. Two steep sandstone walls formed the sides. Now they could begin the hard work of rounding up a share of the hundreds of horses living on the floor of the valley.

Indian track and sign were almost as prevalent as horse sign and they were cautious as they worked. Zalvidea had spoken highly of the central valley Indians who called themselves Yokuts, but he knew little of the mountain tribes. The number of white men who had crossed the big Tulares Valley could be counted on a man's fingers and toes, and even fewer had crossed the mountains. Buck liked the idea that he was one of few men to see such a place, and began to think of it as the land he would call home.

But first they must gather horses.

During the first two days they regained all the stock the flood had taken. The next day they moved their campsite to the hill overlooking the lake at the edge of Bear Valley. When they passed a spot where a travois had been dragged by a band of Indians, Buck made up his mind to seek them out. He wanted to come to terms with the Indians before one of the men blindly stumbled upon their camp while chasing a band of horses.

It would be better if the meeting were planned, better if he had Tuck and Jeds' muskets, and Sanchez's reata to back him up.

As soon as they finished their breakfast of beans and biscuits, Buck suggested the rest of the men stay in camp to begin a permanent shelter while he scouted the Indian camp. He was sure the travois track would lead him straight there. He wouldn't approach if he found them, but return for help after he'd had a look-see. Then they could go in force.

Tracking the drag trail left by the travois poles, he spotted a wisp of smoke in the distance, almost in the center of a larger valley south of his newly named Bear Valley. For over an hour, he crouched in a thicket overlooking the village and watched. This camp was different from the Juanero's. Horses stood staked in a line near huts made of tall saplings covered with hides. Buck surveyed as much of the area as he could, and then returned to Bear Valley.

A little before ten o'clock the next morning, he picked his way across a meadow and up a shallow creek, back to the Indian camp. Two Indians paced him from several hundred feet away as he approached. He carried his .50 caliber musket casually across his saddle, and his cutlass strapped behind. He led a skittish pack horse with the hindquarters of a doe and a small buck strapped in plain sight past the mesquite drying rack and continued in closer to camp.

The children and squaws disappeared into lodges long before he came within musket range. The place seemed strangely silent; even the forest creatures stilled in anticipation.

Buck jumped—startled by an Indian speaking just behind him to his left. He spun his horse and fought the instinct to raise his gun. The Indian held a bow with an arrow notched, but not aimed nor drawn. He was dressed in buckskin leggings, and wore a headband of golden eagle feathers hanging down the back of his neck along a braid of twisted black hair. Behind him, a few feet away, stood several more Indian men.

Buck placed his right fist across his heart, as the men had done in the puplem of the Juanero village. The feathered Indian approached to within ten feet, the thudding of his moccasins on the hard-packed earth the only sound. The Indian studied Buck and the load of fresh game for a few unnerving seconds, then brought his own fist to his chest.

"I have brought meat," Buck offered in Spanish.

The man muttered something in a guttural language in return.

Dismounting, Buck glanced at the ravine where he knew his friends watched, then rested his musket in the grass, careful to keep it within easy reach. Pulling one of the hindquarters from the pack saddle, he offered it to the tall Indian, who turned and motioned for the others to come and take it away. Buck watched apprehensively as they walked forward, but they kept their weapons lowered. Purposely turning his back, he removed the rest of the meat and handed it over, then followed the men back to the village.

Women and children poured from the hide-covered huts as the group entered, swarming around him, curiously touching his clothes and jabbering to each other in their strange tongue.

He glanced around, still uneasy, but comforted a little by the knowledge that Tuck and Tui watched with primed muskets from a ravine less than a hundred yards to the west, while Jed and Sanchez were shielded by a grove of scrub oak on the east.

The tall Indian gestured for him to come forward. Along with several others, they sat down on a thick robe of red fox fur beside a communal cooking fire amid baskets and grinding stones. Waving and speaking to one of the younger Indians, the first man filled a pipe from a small woven basket with designs on the rim, took a twig from the fire, and lit up. As they passed the pipe back and forth, Buck suddenly realized that all the men in the village were either very young or very old. His muscles went tense, but he forced himself to remain calm.

The first Indian patted his chest and said "Cuatcho." Then he pointed to Buck.

"Buck," he said, touching his own chest. The Indian held up two fingers and pointed in the direction of the ravine where Tuck and Tui watched. Next he pointed to two places by the fire. Then he pointed to the scrub oak and to two more places near the fire.

Buck forced a smile. They knew the men were out there. There was nothing he could do but comply and bring them in. Standing, he walked to the edge of the village and waved for Tuck and Tui to join them. As they walked forward, Indians appeared from positions several yards behind and to the sides, and followed them into the camp. Buck went to the other side, repeated the process, and found Jed and Sanchez to be likewise surrounded.

Several more Indians led their horses from where they were hidden, tying them alongside their own in the picket line. Proficient with the sign language of the plains Indians, Tucker found it worked as well with these. They were Paiutes, he discovered, Utes-who-live-by-water, from the high mountains to the north. They wintered here in the mild climate of the lower valleys and would soon return to the high country.

They would feast tonight on the meat he had brought, yet Buck was still uneasy. As the Indian women began to prepare the meat, he pulled Tucker aside. "What do you think of these Paiutes? Are they trouble like the Mojaves?"

"You never know, boy, but we wouldn't be sittin' and palaverin' with the Mojaves. They'd already be drying our scalps, not cookin' fer us."

"Do you think they might help us? These men are obviously horsemen, and they must know the country. Our job would go one helluva lot faster, if they would."

"We'd have to trade with 'em. Indians ain't much fer

workin' fer whites. For that matter they ain't much fer workin' a'tall, and your gold'll mean nothing to 'em."

Buck hadn't thought about trading when he'd provisioned up. It was a mistake he wouldn't make again. He didn't have much to spare. "How about horses, would they work for a share?"

"Maybe that and somethin' to boot. They fancy bright and shiny things, and cloth... but mostly bright falderal and such."

Buck dug into his pocket for the folding knife that belonged to Ernst. He hadn't used it much. He didn't want to part with the ten-inch knife, and the thought of trading either of Ernst's knives saddened him. He had visions of leaving one of them between Taylor-Johnson's ribs.

The smaller knife would have to go, but he needed something else. Buck was sure the Indians would value the iron utensils back at camp. They could spare a pot.

"The horses first, Tuck, then this if you have to." He handed Tuck the folding knife. "And a pot."

Tucker hunkered down and began bartering with Cuatcho. He unfolded the knife and laid it between them. Cuatcho picked it up and looked at it with disdain. He stood and walked over to Buck's gear. Buck was reminded of his stepfather as he'd bartered in the markets of Boston. All people were much the same.

Cuatcho stalked about, surveying what the white men had in sight. Then he returned and sat again. He made a great gesture of pushing the knife back, leaving it lying on the ground. Making a sign to Tuck, he looked away as if disinterested and conversed with a nearby Indian.

Tucker walked over to where Buck sat talking to Tui. "He wants the blue roan."

Buck's jaw went tight. He leapt to his feet. "He doesn't have that many braves!" He stalked away to where the roan was tied, and Tucker walked up beside him.

"Don't get riled, boy. It's all just part of the game." Tucker chuckled and shook his head then returned to the fire.

Buck finally calmed down and went back to his place on the fur rug. He chuckled to himself as he watched the two grown men grunting—with pleasure when they offered, with indignation as they were refused.

Tuck turned to him. "For the cutlass and one out of every five horses, we get six braves all the way to Santa Fe.... And we'll be needin' 'em with the Mojaves and all."

"And a woman to help keep the camp while we're out working," Buck countered.

Tuck returned to the fire, grunted and gestured. After more signing he approached Buck. "Throw in the folding knife, and we get the squaw and seven braves, one to take her to 'em in the high country when we leave for Santa Fe."

"Done!" Buck said with a satisfied smile. And it was.

They rode out of the Indian camp, seven men and an old fat squaw stronger than when they had entered, and less Ernst's folding knife, his cutlass, and a pot. If the braves were worth their salt, they could more than double their catch, at little cost to them.

By the end of the second week, they had garnered over a hundred horses. Sanchez stayed in camp with one of the Indians, breaking as many of the animals as he could to the halter. During the next weeks, the horse hunting slowed. They had to range farther and farther into the valley to find them, then drive them farther, with greater opportunity for escape, to reach the corral. While they hunted the valley floor, Buck saw other unmounted Indians who hid in the brush and watched. They were ignored with disdain by the Paiutes, but not by Buck, who stayed wary.

One afternoon, in pursuit of a small herd, they crested a rise and spotted a village of over a hundred huts built of willows and mud, much like the Juaneros. The crude huts were scattered along a creek at a branch of a river Buck hadn't seen before. Zalvidea had mentioned a stream he had named La Porciuncula, the Jubilee. This river boiled and frothed in gay-but-deadly abandon, crashing rapidly from the high mountains to the east. It must be the Jubilee.

With time growing short, and no need for more Indian help, Buck and the men ignored the village and continued to round up wild horses. By the end of the first month they had two hundred and twenty. The next month added only one hundred—logistics becoming a major problem. Just feeding, watering, and building fences for that much stock became an endeavor. And they couldn't afford to let the animals weaken. Crossing the desert would take all the stamina both men and animals could muster.

Finally at the end of a long, back-breaking day, with few horses taken for the effort, Buck called the men together.

"I've had enough. Tuck, if you think we can make the desert this near to summer, I'm game to give it a try. If these horses will bring fifty a head" —he scratched some figures into the dirt with the sharp end of a stick— "even after we split with the Paiutes... Jesus, that's over ten thousand dollars!"

"The Great Basin's tough enough in the winter," Tucker mused. "I reckon' it's pure hell—and that's the right word— in the summer. But I've been hankerin' to move on fer a spell. Let's get ourselves across before the real heat sets in and what water holes there might be dry up."

Buck looked from man to man. "Jed?" he asked the usually silent mountain man.

"Whatever Tuck says."

The big kanaka smiled. "Tui used to hot. Sandwich Islands get plenty hot."

Even stoic Sanchez agreed. "It is time. Zalvidea will be wondering about me. And the horses need more graze than we can provide here. They will be better off on the trail."

It was settled. They would set out as soon as they were prepared.

14

BY TEN THE next morning they were packed. They waved goodbye to three of the Paiute braves who rode out to the north. The Indians who left drove over forty head of horses in front of them. The squaw walked behind.

Their first disagreement with the Paiutes had occurred the night before when the Indians realized they were entitled to sixty horses but couldn't drive them across the Mojave to Santa Fe and back again, as they had first agreed. Finally Tucker conceded two additional braves to the one who would ride with the squaw, but that the Indians would take one in six horses, rather than one in five. They would leave now, rather than after the trip to Santa Fe.

Buck gazed back as he topped the ridge east of Bear Valley. In many ways, he hated to leave. Late spring sparkled on the land; the valley was blanketed with orange poppies and blue lupine, and the new green growth of the buckeye and scrub oak glittered with morning dew.

They had built a respectable cabin. Straight lodgepole pines found along the creek grew close by, and it was an easy downhill drag to get them to the cabin site. In the evenings, Buck had occupied his time building a stone fireplace into one wall. Its stack already rose well above the thick sod roof.

It was a place he hoped to return to.

As they made their way east, the country rapidly changed, going from grassland and scrub oak to sage and then greasewood desert. Tall cactus, rocks, and rough ravines made his memories of the lush green valley even sweeter. On the third day they made a dry camp.

"From now on," Tucker counseled, "if the moon's willin', we ride by night. We scout ahead and find the next water hole. We don't move 'til we know the next water." Jed tugged on his thick gray beard and put in his usual two cents' worth. He nodded.

The heat was hardest on the horses. They hung their heads, lolled their tongues, and suffered. No shade, save the occasional bank of a ravine offered relief from the burning sun. Each night they hobbled the stallions away from each other to keep them from fighting, or from leading the band back to the grass and water of the green mountains which now shone hazy purple in the distance.

Early that evening as the sun touched the horizon at their backs, painting it gold, Buck and Tui took the first turn at scouting ahead for the elusive water. Following Tucker's advice, they tracked tiny desert bees and wasps who made hundreds of trips each day to whatever water they could find. The men also watched for mourning doves who watered dawn and dusk. With the help of a game trail, they finally found a brackish hole, then returned to camp. Distant coyotes serenaded them to sleep.

The sun rose lemon yellow, climbed to white hot, and hung, torturing man and animal. Driving the horses became second nature as one day wore into the next. At dusk, the blistering sun dropped, flaming orange, behind far away jagged purple mountains.

Buck made friends with a Paiute brave named Toka, who proved to be an excellent horseman. Taller and leaner than his fellow warriors, he had straight, sharp features, high cheekbones, and keen black eyes. The Indian's brown-and-white paint mare almost matched the big blue roan in quickness and daring as he helped herd the wild horses across the burning sands. And the brave had other skills as well: Toka found water twice when Tucker was all but stumped.

They fought the dust and heat for nearly two weeks. The horses' ribs were beginning to show. Grass was scarce and what there was held little nourishment—tall clumps of arrowweed and an occasional wispy smoke tree offered only the barest sustenance. Dust devils danced macabre pirouettes around them, crowning the insult with blasts of hot, sand-laden wind, then left, swivel-hipped, to find others to antagonize—the odds of which were slim.

Still, they rode on.

The morning of the fifteenth day, Diablo tossed his head and pulled at the rein. Tired and irritable, Buck drew him up short.

"Let him have his head, boy," Tucker said. "'Bout the only thing that would get him excited is smellin' water. It's too damn hot to think of them pretty little mares." He grinned. "He ain't no different from us—he's been spittin' dust for days."

Buck eased off on the reins, and the blue roan plunged forward, not running, but keeping up a strong, distance-eating gait. They rode on for more than a mile then climbed to the top of a low sloping rise. Buck reined up, unable to believe his eyes. A small willow-rimmed lake surrounded by sweet green grass lay before them. The horses had smelled it, too. They perked up their ears and picked up their pace, then thundered down to the bank. The thirsty animals sank their muzzles into the warm but refreshing wetness, and the men dropped down beside them, not minding the company, grateful for the thirst-quenching drink.

Tucker sat up and backhanded the water from his long straggly beard. "Don't drink too much, boy. Give your ol' belly time to work loose from your backbone. I reckon mine's dried on tight."

They drank their fill then went to set up camp, riding

into a copper-colored setting sun not nearly so ominous as when water was nowhere to be found. They spent three days at the willow-lined lake, resting until the grass was almost gone, letting the animals regain their strength. On the morning of the third day, a band of Indians approached. They stayed on the other side of the lake, away from the men and the large band of horses. Warily, they watered their animals.

Buck studied them from the distance. They had thick bodies, short broad noses, and straight coal black hair that hung down to the middle of their backs. They moved with efficiency. A dark stain in a geometric pattern was painted on their faces, chests, and backs. Almost as black as Cracker, the Virginia Negro cook, they wore only loincloths, leggings, and moccasins in the blistering sun. They watched the party for a few moments with cautious disdain, then rode back over the rise and melted into the desert.

"Won't be long now." Tucker spat a gob of thick brown tobacco. "They'll be wantin' our horses."

Buck surveyed their disappearing cloud of dust. Damn. They had come so far. They didn't need Indian trouble. "Why don't we offer them a few? Maybe we can buy our way through without a problem. Better to barter a couple than risk them all."

"You don't know 'em like I do, boy. Them's Mojaves. They'll take the ones you offer, then lay in wait fer ye. They's as mean as a rattler an twice as tough. They can live longer without water than any goat or lizard out here. They'll sit quiet for hours, covered with brush, let you come right up on 'em, then come at ye like hell was on their tail. There's no bargainin' with 'em... besides, I owe 'em."

The Mojaves didn't return and that night the men rode on. The country became more difficult. Where before it had undulated with a few rocky mountains, easily skirted, now it was scarred with steep ravines. Soon they would be forced to travel only in the heat of day. The trails were just too rough.

Just before dawn, they pulled up at a muddy seep where a ravine ended in a barren sand wash. The brackish water pooled for only a short stretch then disappeared in the sandy wash bottom. The horses drank quickly, almost draining the seep, then went to graze on what little grass and few edible plants they could find. They strayed farther than usual. The graze was sparse.

Buck knelt beside the campfire, uneasy. The Mojaves hadn't come, yet he knew they were out there. Knew they were watched by dark patient eyes.

———

THE BRIG VIRGINIA backed her sails in the harbor, returning to the Mission San Juan for the third time since the brig had reached California. She sat a little deeper in the water, her hold over a third full of hides and tallow. As the crew lowered the shore boats, William Taylor-Johnson strode the quarter deck.

"Mr. Piedmont," the captain said, showing Swill a new respect since Hard Tack's demise and his promotion to first mate. "This time maybe we'll get lucky. Our deserter friend, Mr. Mueller, must still be somewhere in the area. I've talked with most of the hide ship captains. They've not seen him, and if they do they'll not take him aboard."

"He could have tried it overland, sir. If that's the case, the savages, or the desert, will already have his blackguard hide."

"I think not. The man's no fool. Nor is this papist, Zalvidea, who runs the mission, beyond hiding him. If we didn't have to trade with the pious bastard, I'd bring his mission down around his ears."

"Yes, sir," Swill said, "I'm sure you would."

"I suppose it doesn't matter. With or without the priest's help, we'll find our Mr. Mueller and make an example of him." He fixed a hard gaze on Swill. "I want you to go to the mission. Take a cask of grog and loosen the tongue of your old shipmate, Dutch—and mind you don't get drunk yourself. In the meantime, I shall visit the inland rancheros. Mr. Mueller has enjoyed his freedom far too long. It's time his bloody carcass scraped our hulls, and he joins his sogger cousin." A corner of his mouth twisted up. "'Tis bad for the crew to think of a killer-deserter enjoying the Indian women."

Several nights later, dressed in his finest navy-blue uniform, the captain raised his glass in a toast to his host, Don Pedro Seville. His smile was wide to Seville and his family, and it was sincere, at least as far as his attention to the beautiful young Señorita Elena. He glanced across a branch of candles flickering on the low carved wooden table in the sala, and saw her talking with her mother and grandmother. He wondered if he would ever have a chance to get her alone.

His slick smile faltered at the thought. These Californios watched their women with the same fervor a Bostonian guarded his finest silver. Ah, but in this case he understood the don's concern. The girl was a beauty, and he was as good a judge of women as he was of fine ships. He licked his lips as she bent to retrieve a fallen hanky, exposing the deep cleft between her pale breasts. He had caught her glance several times while he'd been chatting with her father. Perhaps she was as enamored with him as he was with her.

He smiled again, hoping it was the truth.

"Where did you say you were bound, capitan?" Don Pedro took a sip of his brandy, a ruby ring on his thick-fingered hand glinting in the candlelight.

William dragged his gaze from the don's luscious daughter. "I'm sorry, Don Pedro. My mind seems to have drifted. I was thinking of... home. Your gracious hospitality has made me homesick." Or, at the very least, had made him think of the buxom black-haired tavern wench he'd bedded just before he left.

"Sí, I am glad you are enjoying yourself. I asked where

you are bound. I thought perhaps you would be headed for the Sandwich Islands."

"No, sir. There's plenty of trade goods to be had right here on your coast. And now that you've begun making such fine brandy" —the captain raised his snifter and studied the amber liquid— "I'll have some goods to trade in the South American ports as well on our voyage home."

William watched Elena tuck the hanky into the top of her dress. She crossed the room to where he spoke with her father.

"Sí, the brandy is very good," the don agreed. "And the young man you mentioned earlier had much to do with it."

"Everything, I would say," Elena added, smiling as she stepped up and rested her hand on her father's arm.

Taylor-Johnson forced himself to smile. So far he had said little about Buck Mueller, careful to bide his time. But he had discovered the man had indeed spent time at Toro Bravo. Just thinking of it made his stomach muscles clench.

"Mueller helped with the brandy?" he asked. "How so?" He forced the scowl from his face.

"Señor Mueller built the still," Elena said. "And left detailed instructions of how we should use it."

"He also destroyed my vineyard," her father grumbled.

Elena frowned. A spot of color infused her cheeks. "I beg your pardon, papa, but I do not see how that can be. I have never seen such growth as there is on the vines this year."

"Growth is not a crop, niña."

William took another sip of brandy, eyeing the glass appreciatively. "It would seem he served you better than he served the Virginia."

"Señor Mueller was a poor sailor?" Elena asked.

"The man was a sogger and a troublemaker, a deserter, and finally a cold-blooded killer. He murdered my first mate, Henry Tacker, and a fine man he was."

Elena's black lace fan came up to her face. "He... murdered someone?" She stared at him in disbelief. "Surely you are mistaken, capitan."

Elena continued to stare in his direction, her eyes locked with his. She's interested in me, he thought. If only I can navigate this dark-eyed Californio somewhere alone, there'll be a blue-eyed Californio left when I sail.

"Unfortunately, I am not mistaken, Señorita Seville. Mueller shoved the poor helpless man off a San Juan Capistrano cliff. We buried his broken and battered body in a quiet place overlooking the sea... God rest his soul." William sighed deeply. "And God help me to find the man who bloodied his hands with the death of my fine shipmate."

"I can hardly believe it," the don said, shaking his head and making his thick jowls quiver. "He seemed a good young man. Rash, perhaps, but a fine head on his shoulders."

Elena's face looked a little bit pale. "The man you describe... that does not sound like the same Buck Mueller who visited with us here at Toro Bravo."

Taylor-Johnson smiled. "Oh, to be young and gullible again."

She started to say something else, but a slight Indian serving woman spoke from the doorway. "Lo siento mucho, I am sorry to disturb you, but la comida is served in the dining room."

The captain offered Elena his arm. "Enough of this unpleasant topic for the time being."

"Sí, that is true," the don said. "Now if you will excuse me, I will see that things are in order." He left them in the sala.

"I should like to hear more of this, capitan," Elena said as they started forward. "I hope you will tell me the rest of the story."

"Certainly, señorita." He smiled. "After supper, if you wish. In the garden, perhaps?"

"That would be lovely." Then she added, "My mother always enjoys taking coffee in the garden after supper."

The muscles in his jaw went tight, but the smile remained on his face.

Elena urged him forward. "Shall we retire to the dining room, capitan?"

Even with the mild rebuff, he refused to give up hope. All the way to the table, his eyes remained fixed on the cleft between her breasts.

SINCE SIGHTING THE MOJAVES, they had begun to post two guards rather than one. The early morning sun formed a platinum line along the horizon when the first small band attacked. From far across the herd, Tui spotted four of them as they swept down, encircled a small band of twelve grazing horses, and pushed them up a ravine. He fired his flintlock after them, more to alert his friends than in the hope of doing any harm. The small band of raiders was already several hundred yards away.

Buck called the men together over a hurried breakfast of cold beans and biscuits. "I had hopes they'd let us pass, but it seems they just waited until we got to this rugged ravine country. Any suggestions?"

Tucker spoke up immediately, "As I done said, we take it to 'em. If'n we wait they'll just keep a'comin' at us until they got all the horses, then they'll come fer our hair."

"Well, the sooner we get at it, the sooner it'll be done," Buck agreed. "Let's leave the Paiutes here. This fight isn't theirs. Sanchez can watch the horses. The rest of us will track them down."

They collected shot and wad and filled their powder horns. Jerky and dried biscuits filled their pockets. Toka insisted on coming along. It seemed he also had a grudge to settle with the Mojaves. The Indian thieves had been armed with lances and bows. If the pursuers could stay out of arrow range, the job wouldn't be too hard, but that could be a difficult task in this rough country.

The trail was a simple one to follow. Four Indians had herded the horses off. Tucker was positive more were hidden to discourage pursuit. The trail circled up and around the encampment, keeping to the southwest. The sun clawed into a pewter sky, its heat merciless. They followed on through mesquite and cactus, then the trail turned due west.

Buck spoke to Tucker, "You think they're headin' back to the lake?"

"Maybe, but more'n likely they'll wait till we're blinded by the late afternoon sun." Tucker rubbed his whiskered chin thoughtfully. "I think we best ride two an' two.... You an' your Indian fall back a mite. It appears to me they play us with ambush."

Jed and Tucker took up the lead. Tui dropped back more than thirty yards, Buck and Toka another forty. Almost as soon as they had done so, Tui yelled, "Behind you!" He spurred his horse toward his friends.

Three Mojaves rose up behind Tucker and Jed and let fly with arrows. Tucker's mount bucked and kicked as a long-feathered shaft drove deeply into its flank. Tui screamed a shrill cry that echoed up the ravine, then spurred his horse, distracting the attackers who turned to face his charge. Tucker got off a quick shot that clapped like thunder. Buck and Toka from their position behind heard the gunfire and spurred their horses forward. Tui fired before he was close enough for a sure shot, but charged on, swinging the musket to bludgeon one of the Indians. Jed, an experienced Indian fighter, held his fire until Tucker could reload. Tui galloped through the Indians, his massive bulk scattering them. More Mojaves appeared on the sides of the deep ravine and let fly with arrows and lances.

As they rounded a bend and came into sight of the battle, Toka handed Buck his reins and motioned for him to take the left side of the ravine. At full gallop, the wiry brave leapt from his horse, rolling and disappearing into the rocks. Buck turned the roan and clattered up the steep side of the ravine to get above the fight, working his way along a sandstone embankment to the crest. Tying the horsehair lead rope of Toka's little paint to his saddle horn, and dropping Diablo's reins, he slipped quietly from the saddle.

Unconsciously, he rubbed the little black tusuat that rested in his pocket, and climbed to the edge of the ravine. Two more shots echoed. Tui and Jed reduced the Mojaves by two as they raised up to release another volley of arrows. This time Tucker held his fire.

Buck inched along the edge of a sandstone outcropping. From his position atop the ledge, he saw Toka doing the same across the ravine. The Paiute sprang, knife in hand, onto the backs of two Mojaves, his stone knife finding its mark in the back of one with the force of the fall. Struggling with the other for a desperate moment, he kicked the man over a twenty-foot embankment to the floor of the ravine.

Buck continued inching along. He rounded a large boulder and spotted two Mojaves squatting behind another boulder between him and where Tucker and Jed were reloading. Buck laid the sights of his flintlock carefully to the middle of the nearest Indian's back, but didn't fire. Instead he whistled and the man turned, surprised he had been flanked. Buck's musket roared and belched flame, and the big fifty caliber slug knocked the surprised Mojave off the rock. He tumbled to the bottom of the canyon.

Before Buck could jerk his pistol from its sheath, the other Mojave let fly. The arrow creased his cheek, hotly rebuffing his moment of chivalry. The Indian moved to scramble over the rock as Buck's pistol bucked in his hands. The ball took the tattooed brave between the shoulder blades, and he tumbled forward, joining his partner in the floor of the canyon.

Wiping a generous amount of blood from his burning cheek—another lesson cheaply learned—Buck made his way along the rim of the ravine. The desert air smelled of spent powder. Nothing stirred. He waited a few moments, then, slipping and sliding, scrambled down the sandstone embankment to the bottom. He used his foot to nudge the closest Indian over on his back, and found the big slug had taken the man to wherever the Lord intended. Tucker, Tui, and Jed walked up, their faces dusty and grim. "Well, we got us some Mojave, but no horseflesh," Tucker complained. "I still think we should take it to 'em."

Buck surveyed the carnage. Five Mojaves lay dead. One lay moaning. Toka dropped a knee to the middle of the man's painted back and drove a knife into his neck before Buck had time stop him. "Jesus," he whispered, his mouth going suddenly dry.

Jed sat spread-legged on the ground digging at the growing crimson spot where the broken shaft of an arrow protruded from his thigh.

"Hell with it," Buck said. "While we're after ten horses, they could be back at the herd cutting out another fifty. And that leg of Jed's needs tending."

"Then let's be headin' in," Tucker said, pulling his beaver hat down, "Soon as I do a little chore." He climbed up the side of the sandstone to where the first Indian had fallen. Buck looked away as Tucker cleanly took the man's scalp, adding it to the falderal hanging from his saddle.

"They'll think twice a'fore they come after us, if'n their spirit loses its ticket to heaven." The Indians believed a mutilated brave would be denied access, or at least be ugly in the afterlife.

Passing one of the Indians Buck had shot, Tucker advised, "Take his hair boy, he would'a had your'n."

Over a queasy stomach, and without looking at Tucker or the Indians he'd killed, Buck said, "I have no need of that man's hair. He can go anywhere he wishes, as long as it's not back after our horses."

JED LAY IN A FEVERED COMA, babbling in disconnected ramblings. The wound festered; the bandage reeked of puss, green and seeping. Bright red streaks ran up his thigh into his groin. For the second time since he had taken the arrow,

Tucker heated his knife and the rest of the men held Jed down while the old mountain man opened his friend's wound, then cauterized it. The stench of burning putrid flesh made Buck gag.

They rested for two days on the banks of a muddy river. On the morning of the third, they climbed to a ridge overlooking the canyon and buried Tucker's lifelong friend.

"Weren't the Mojaves what got him," Tucker grumbled, helping the men pile rocks on the grave. "'Twas the fever. Never was an Indian could take ol' Jed."

Buck swallowed against the lump in his throat. He'd never come to know the silent mountain man, not as he'd come to know Tuck. But he liked the man and respected him. And he knew how close the two friends were. It was a tough lesson, how fast a life could go. It was one that had changed him, like the other lessons he had learned.

Needing a moment alone, he walked down to the small trickle of a stream they had used to water the horses, and hunkered down beside it, cupping some in his palms to wash his face and neck. His reflection wavered before him. He looked different now, taller, thicker in the shoulders. Rougher. He was different inside, too.

He was a man now, he realized. The boy in him was left in Boston, the youth in him stayed behind onboard the Virginia. Maybe he'd been a man since the day Ernst was killed.

They mounted and rode on. Climbing upward out of the desert, the country changed to low cedars then to stately ponderosa pine, then to rolling grass land, and finally back to desert. They began a steady climb upward through low cedar again.

Three hard riding, hard driving weeks later, they camped outside Santa Fe.

Instead of the welcome they had expected, the Mexican governor informed Buck the men had no business in his territory without passport and only let them stay when

173

Buck offered twenty-five head of horses as a token of his esteem.

The pueblo was crowded with a mixture of Mexicans, Indians, and cautious mountain men fresh from Missouri, or out of the mountains to the north. Before the first day was done, Buck was haggling with two Missouri men. They had gold, ready cash, and were willing to buy all the horses. For two days they dickered and argued. Finally, Buck admitted the desert had taken its toll. Two hundred and forty-three head brought thirty-five dollars apiece. Buck, Tucker, Tui, and Sanchez split up the gold coins. With Buck's two shares, he had over three thousand dollars—a small fortune. With that amount he could buy a half-interest in a brig like the Virginia, if he had any interest in returning to the sea.

That night, after closing a cantina and partaking of the charms of four fiery-eyed señoritas, the men shared a campfire that seemed extra warm and extra friendly. The next day was spent in the pueblo of Santa Fe getting tack repaired and horses shod, then another night in the cantina, and the next day getting over their hangovers, and, finally, they were ready to start back home.

At dawn they left with a saffron sky at their backs, their bellies full of tortillas and beans, their possible bags full of powder, shot, caps, and wads, and their saddle bags full of gold. Their return would be much faster without the horses to push, feed, and water—if the Mojaves let them be.

Five weeks later they waved goodbye to the Paiutes at San Gorgonio Pass, two days away from Pueblo de Los Angeles.

Buck was truly sorry to see Toka go, but now he was driven by a new goal.

Elena, he had to see Elena.

They made camp near a clear stream with Pueblo Los Angeles visible a mile below. The men collapsed to their bedrolls, completely fatigued, but Buck was too eager, too anxious to sleep. Instead, he meant to head into the village.

"Ain't you a'feared a' that sea captain what's lookin' fer ye?" Tucker asked.

"Hopefully, he's given up by now," Buck said.

"From what little I know of that maldito," Sanchez said, "I do not think the man is the kind to give up too easily."

"Don't worry," Buck said, "I'll be on the lookout for him." He almost wished he would see the no-good bastard. His fingers moved to the handle of the Aston shoved in his belt with the thought of Taylor-Johnson.

"Maybe you should wait until tomorrow," Sanchez said. "Tui and I could go in and take a look around."

"Like I said, I'll be careful." He didn't want to wait. He would have ridden straight to Toro Bravo, but he wanted to purchase gifts for Señora Seville and Mamacita, and especially for Elena.

Now that he was so near, he could hardly wait to see her. But Tucker and Sanchez were right about the captain. He'd keep his guard up until he was sure it was safe.

15

Pueblo de Los Angeles
July 7, 1829

ELENA MARIA SEVILLE stood before the polished metal mirror, staring numbly at her reflection, surveying the results of hours of preparation but not really caring.

The wedding costume was perfect, her mantilla properly staked with a beautiful inlaid tortoise shell comb, her long black hair shining. The pale-yellow gown, painstakingly sewn of finest Chinese silk and Portuguese lace, fit perfectly. Thanks to New England whalers, baleen hoops kept it wide at the hem, tapering up and fitting tightly to her narrow waist.

Everything looked perfect, and yet it did not.

It's my eyes, she thought. They look bleak and sad. Somehow she must force a hint of happiness into them. She would soon be the wife of one of Alta California's most prominent citizens. Other women would be envious that she was marrying Eduardo Juarez.

"You look lovely, niña," Mamacita said as she walked into the room and sat on the edge of Elena's bed. They were staying in their small adobe casa in the pueblo, closer to where the wedding would be held.

Elena turned to her wizened old grandmother and managed a falsely bright smile. "As you do, Mamacita. To me you are as lovely as you must have looked on the day you were married."

"So many years ago, Elena." Her grandmother's black eyes softened. She crossed the room and put her arms around her beautiful granddaughter, hugging her tightly. She whispered with encouragement, "And I came to love my husband very much."

Elena moved away to the mirror so her grandmother wouldn't see the tear that suddenly welled and rolled down her cheek. Her lips trembled as she tucked a last tendril of hair under her white lace mantilla.

"Perhaps it is as papa says," she managed without her voice cracking. "I was destined to reign over California's largest rancho.""Sí. Destined." Mamacita smiled, but her smile too, was forced. "Come now, child. It is time for your wedding."

TRAIL WEARY BUT EAGER, Buck headed into the village, a spotted cur snapping at the big roan's heels as they plodded along the dusty streets. The stallion regally ignored them. With the sun beginning its late afternoon descent, Buck was surprised at the activity in the usually sleepy town. It was far more crowded than when he had last seen it almost a year before.

He reined up before the low, thatched-roof adobe of Ernesto's Cantina, noting its two glassless windows, their wide sills, and the potted plants resting atop them, and listened for sounds from inside. He wasn't sure what steps Taylor-Johnson had taken in pursuit of him. He hadn't been back long enough to discover where he stood. He could only hope the captain of the Virginia had given up finding him, or that Buck looked different enough with his hair so long, the scar of a Mojave arrow creasing his cheek, and wearing buckskin clothes—so unlike the sailor he had been he wouldn't be recognized even if the captain still searched.

He sat for a moment on the big blue roan, his weary eyes scanning the cowhide hanging across the doorway then the dusty road leading into the pueblo. His gaze warily searched up and down the village. Adobe houses and stores faced this way and that without regard to the layout of the road, which wove and turned in a haphazard pattern that matched the position of the buildings, rather than the other way around. Dogs and children played in the powder-fine dust of the streets, and donkeys, pigs, and fowl wandered about without the confinement of fences.

Pueblo de Los Angeles was as different from Boston as Buck was from the boy who had left there.

He hoisted the .50 caliber Aston at his waist an inch, making sure it rode free and easy in its holster, another was tucked away, loaded and ready in his saddlebags. He dismounted, his nerves strung taut. He listened for the sounds of English being spoken in the cantina.

Nothing.

He had a thousand miles of trail dust to wash from his throat, and one drink wouldn't begin to be enough, but it would have to hold him. He had other more important things before he celebrated in earnest. If it hadn't been for Elena, he would have continued east from Santa Fe.

East, all the way to Bostontown.

He checked the load in the cap and ball pistol, then led the roan to a hitching rail where the animal could drink from the moss-covered water trough. Even from inside the adobe he could keep an eye on the horse and his saddle bags —bags lined with his share of gold from a year's hard work.

The big horse shook his withers, flinging lathered sweat, then pushed aside the layer of floating moss and buried his muzzle in the water. The roan flicked his ears at gnats that buzzed about them and drank deeply.

Buck mounted the wooden step and strode across the dusty board porch, big Spanish rowels on his spurs announcing his approach. As he reached the cowhide-covered opening, he realized the bartender was closing the door behind it.

"Hold up there, amigo," Buck said, "pour me a drink before your siesta."

"No siesta today. Today fiesta!" The rotund bartender grinned under a full salt and pepper mustache, displaying a missing front tooth. "But I have time to pour you one drink before I close." He removed his sombrero and returned behind the rough plank bar.

Before he followed, Buck took a moment to slap his broad-brimmed flat-crowned hat across his thighs and the back of his buckskins, sending a cloud of dust across the porch. He ran his tongue over his dry parched lips then turned and spat grit into the road. It had been nine months and two thousand miles of tough, hot, tortuous trail since he'd downed a mug of aguardiente in Ernesto's.

Smoothing his thick brown hair, he readjusted his hat and closed his eyes for a moment, knowing the inside of the cantina would be dark. The few seconds necessary for his eyes to adjust could wind up costing him his life.

Pushing aside the cowhide curtain, folding it back so he could keep an eye on Diablo and his gold, he walked inside the room, which lay empty except for the bartender and a few buzzing flies. Buck felt the tension flow from his arms and shoulders. The cool darkened interior welcomed him after so many months in the burning sun corralling and breaking horses.

He smiled inwardly. He'd made it. After the long hours of drudgery and occasional moments of heart-pumping fear on the drive across the Mojave to Santa Fe and back again, Pueblo de Los Angeles was a welcome respite. And the gold in his saddle bags and his new-found pride and confidence testified it had been worth it.

He had something to offer her now.

Ignoring vacant wooden tables and cowhide chairs, Buck bellied up to the rough plank bar. He was hungry for news and a little conversation. He smiled to think this was the same cantina where he, Tucker, Tui, and Sanchez had made their bargain to go horsin' together.

Buck eyed the mug the rotund man had set before him. He upended it and threw down the aguardiente, the strong cactus liquor favored by the Californios. He fought a cough and conquered it. Expelling a breath, he slammed the mug down on the bar, but not quick enough to smack the fly that had been pestering him.

He ordered another. As the Californio dipped it from a small wooden barrel, Buck stretched, trying to work the kinks out of his stiff muscles. He stifled a yawn and realized just how tired he was. He knew he looked it. He hadn't bathed in days. His buckskin breeches were cut, tattered, and stained, and he had several day's black stubble on his face.

Buck winced at his reflection in a dirty polished metal mirror over the back bar then smiled tightly. His deep-set brown eyes stared back at him over circles almost as dark as his stubble of beard. He wondered if he shouldn't just let the beard grow. Would Elena like a beard? Few Californios had one. The still-reddened scar on his cheek, compliments of a Mojave arrow, had taken his youthful appearance. Only by the grace of God and a quick musket had it missed taking his life.

Buck worked his chest and shoulders, now corded with muscles from his hard work on the hide and tallow ship, then his months on the trail. How different he was from the boy who'd left Boston almost two years ago. He wondered if his family would recognize him when he returned. If he returned.

Now he had other things on his mind—most importantly, beautiful raven-haired Elena. One fleeting kiss had drawn him back through a thousand miles of burning desert, hundreds of hostile Indians, and too many other man-killing obstacles to count. But somehow he felt certain she knew he would come. He would have to buy clothes and clean up before his long-planned meeting with her. He should probably be on his way.

"I must close soon," the bartender timidly prodded. "I do not wish to be late."

"Big doin's today?" Buck asked, smiling. "What's the occasion?"

"Fandango at the Public House. Every musician in the country will be there. Tonight we dance till dawn." He flashed Buck a grin and mimicked the dancing, twirling behind the bar. "Even now there are two whole bullocks turning over the coals."

Buck finished the last of the his drink. "Church holiday?"

"No, no, señor. A wedding. The Juarez family and the Sevilles form a powerful alliance.... And the bride, that Elena. What a beauty."

Buck's head snapped up, the words piercing his chest like a Mojave lance. Catching his breath, he spun away, knocking over his mug, the remaining liquid running off the planks onto the floor. He took two steps toward the doorway, then hesitated, turned, and strode back to the bar. He set the mug upright. "Fill it again."

"But, señor, I will be late."

Buck just glared at him.

"The wedding will be ending even now," the barman pleaded, "and then the festivities begin." Without realizing it, the chubby bartender had answered Buck's unspoken question.

Elena was already married. He was too late. After nearly a year, he had missed by only a moment, but that moment might as well have been an eternity.

Insistently he slapped the bar with the flat of his hand, needing something to drown the serpents writhing in his belly. "Fill it again."

A flash of fear widened the bartender's eyes. He responded quickly, topping off the mug.

"Where's the Public House?" Buck demanded, killing the drink in one gulp.

"It is the biggest building in the pueblo. You cannot miss it."

Buck dropped a coin on the rough wooden bar and left with long spur-clanking strides. As he swept through the cowhide covering, the bartender hurried to slam the plank door closed behind him.

Untying the roan, Buck swung into the saddle without using the stirrup then spurred the horse a little harder than he meant to with the big Spanish rowels. Seldom touched with the iron, Diablo leapt forward, digging his rear hoofs into the dirt, sending chunks of earth flying.

Two hundred paces down the dusty street, Buck reined the horse to a trot, the busy building and a gaggle of California's finest carriages in sight another hundred paces ahead. It wouldn't do to make a spectacle of himself—for her sake it would not do. But still... he had to have at least a last look at her.

He slowed the roan to a prancing walk. The horse side-stepped nervously, still wanting to run, sensing his rider's tension. Buck drew rein in front of the double doors of the thick-walled public building. The stallion reared, thrashing his forefeet in the air.

Buck spun him away from the doors and crossed the road, dismounting between a pair of shiny black carriages. He tied the roan in a deliberate motion and headed for the arched carved doors of the adobe Public House.

A group of finely dressed Californios approaching the entrance stopped and stared reproachfully. Brushing by them, he strode inside the foyer, careful to keep his back to the wall as he surveyed the celebration.

Soothing sounds of guitars and violins wafted into the room from the rear veranda, but they only tightened the knot in his stomach. The large room echoed with chatter, filled with guests as it was: women in the finest silks and laces; men in embroidered breeches and waistcoats, silken shirts and shoes with satin bows. The odor of lilac and rose-scented perfumes hung in the air, competing with the savory smell of meat being roasted behind the massive adobe.

It was an affair of excellence.

Buck recognized the short, rotund prefect—the lieutenant governor of the state. Echeandia, the governor, stood near him. Both wore elaborately embroidered waist-length charro jackets, ruffled silk shirts, and intricately stitched calzonevas—the tight breeches flared at the bottom favored by Californio men. Flat-crowned, wide-brimmed hats hung down their backs from finely woven horse-hair lanyards. They stood with the Majordomo of Pueblo de Los Angeles and other well-dressed men.

The Pueblo's gente de razón. Gentlemen of reason.

Buck felt less than reasonable.

Reasonable would be to ride away and never to look back. Reasonable would be to forget about her, and California.

But reason warred with want—and the need of at least one last look.

Condemning glares followed Buck as he strode across the spacious room to a table laden with steaming platters of cordero cabazo, roasted lamb's heads; migas, sour bread sliced thin and fried in garlic oil, pastel de tomal, pies of onion, garlic, corn, tomatoes, peppers and olives, richly spiced, each with a different meat—beef, chicken, pork; mostaza, wild mustard greens in olive oil and garlic; pie cerdo, pigs feet; and in the center, a deep pitted bulls head, its horns festooned with ribbons, flanked by two perfectly roasted sandhill cranes. And these were the snacks. The real meal of roasted bullocks, whole roasted pig, frijoles, and vegetables of many varieties would follow the dancing. His eyes scanned the room and those still staring looked away at his hard glance.

The bride and groom had not yet arrived. Grabbing a

mug, Buck filled it with brandy, wondering if it came from the still he'd built for Elena's father.

If so, on this occasion, it would indeed be bitter brew.

Leaning casually against the whitewashed wall, he took a deep breath, then a long draw from the mug—ignoring the searing burn of the fiery liquid.

A tall whipcord-lean young Californio left his group of friends and crossed the room. He stopped on the opposite side of the table. "Surely you can see, hombre, that you are not properly attired to attend this function. The vaqueros are out in the back. You should—"

"You, hombre, should mind your own business," Buck snapped. The man started to answer, his face turning red, then he cut his eyes away as a big green horsefly buzzed near his head. The Californio wisely followed the fly back across the room, gliding gracefully in his satin-trimmed shoes.

A polite applause started near the door and soon filled the room.

Don Eduardo Juarez and his bride had finally arrived.

Buck's stomach twisted at the sight of her, at how incredibly beautiful she looked. A polished jewel-encrusted tortoise shell comb staked a white lace mantilla that set off her ivory complexion and flashing black eyes. The mantilla flowed down her back, but not far enough to cover the raven hair falling to her waist. The ruffled hem of the yellow silk and lace gown touched the floor.

Buck's chest tightened. He knew he shouldn't be there. He should be on his way home. Back to Boston. As far as he could get from the men who might still be hunting him. He should leave now, get as far from there as he could. Then his anger flared as the tall gaunt man bent to kiss his beautiful bride.

Elena felt her husband's lips cool on her own and dutifully closed her eyes. She was now a married woman, Señora Elena Maria Seville y Juarez. She smiled at her husband and politely brushed a kiss against his cheek, then she turned to the guests who crowded near her. Inwardly, she sighed in resignation. The fine lines at the corners of her eyes were the only indication of the turmoil she'd been through this last year. For months she had fought against her independent nature, trying to be a dutiful daughter, and had finally come to accept the fate her father thrust upon her.

Beside her, Eduardo, twenty years her senior, took her hand. It was an unusual and attentive gesture. She looked up at him with hope in her eyes, her parents' words ringing in her ears. Marry him for the good of the family, her mother had preached. You will come to love him, her grandmother had joined in. It will forge an alliance between two of Alta California's most powerful families, her father had said.

They must be right, she thought, but the queasiness would not leave her stomach. Surely, it was the proper thing to do. She glanced around the beautifully decorated hall to see California's most prominent citizens were there. Dons and doñas from all over Alta California smiled at her in admiration.

She only wished she felt one tenth as happy as they appeared to be. She continued to scan the crowd then stopped her perusal and sucked in a breath, staring transfixed, her mouth gone suddenly dry and her heart pounding to a growing crescendo.

Buck was bigger, wider in shoulder and taller than she remembered. It was a man, not a boy, who stared back at her. His features softened when he realized he had caught her attention, and she felt the warmth his presence had brought her since the first time she had seen him. Though she tried to control it, a flush stole into her cheeks.

It had been so long, almost a year. She thought he had returned to New England, to his own people. She felt a burning behind her eyes just to look at him. Por Dios, he could still make her stomach flutter and her palms grow damp.

Elena   inwardly   shook   herself.   Stop   this,   she

commanded. You are now a married woman. She should be thinking of her husband, responding to his attentive touch —not to the gaze of an out-of-place rough-looking man she hardly knew. She glanced at Eduardo but he was busy talking to someone else, someone of importance to his ambition. She let her husband's cool hand slip away from hers and turned to look back at Buck, her tentative gaze locking with his bold, forthright one.

Buck allowed himself the luxury of Elena's warm look, unashamedly letting his eyes drift from her toes to her mantilla, along the way admiring her full breasts, narrow corseted waist, and flaring hips, then he forced his gaze away.

Reluctantly, he turned and started to walk away, but was brought up short two steps later. Captain William Taylor-Johnson followed the newlyweds into the room. The tall ramrod straight Englishman stopped short, his eyes, cool and penetrating, widening noticeably as he recognized the man he'd been hunting for almost a year. Buck rested his callused palm on the pistol riding at his waist, his blood going hot at the sight of the blond sea captain uniformed with the pomp and polish of a Spanish Admiral. But instead of a confrontation, the captain spun on his booted heel and left the room.

Eduardo Juarez, Elena's hawk-nosed husband, must have felt the tension building in the room for he turned in Buck's direction and speared him with his black foreboding eyes. His bushy brows furrowed so tightly they almost touched. The hard look changed to one of incredulity when Elena left his side to make her way toward the rough-looking intruder. Eduardo's hand reached out to stop her, but she shrugged his grip away.

Every eye followed her progression as she made her way toward him, stopping across the table from where he stood. Above her white lace fan, her dark eyes wavered—uncertain, questioning, worried. He caught the faint scent of roses and the clean smell of soap. He thought she'd never looked more beautiful.

He wished he could tell her, but his chest constricted at the thought that she belonged to another man, and any tenderness he felt fled with the image of her sallow-faced husband lowering himself over her in their wedding bed that night.

Her worried look changed to something else as she noticed the fresh scar across his cheek. "Your face," she said. "You have been hurt?"

"It's not important." Before he could say anything more, she straightened and her dark eyes steeled.

"There will be great trouble. Please. Do not ruin my day."

"No," he said, his look turning hard. "I wouldn't want to do that."

She stiffened. "The captain... he told me what you did. He has told me a great deal."

"The captain lies," Buck said coldly. There was time for no more. He now could see Taylor-Johnson through the broad arched windows of the Public House. Returning with some of his men, the captain strode confidently, followed by the first mate of the Virginia and three brawny sailors—all armed with cutlass and musket. Buck caught the flash of fear in Elena's eyes as she turned to face the door.

"Hurry, you must go!"

He wondered if her fear was for him, of if it was because he might 'ruin her day'. He turned at the sound of the doors crashing open. Five angry men moved into a room of more than a hundred, eyes searching like raptors, eager to corner their quarry.

Buck bristled, his hand coming to rest on the handle of the Aston. He had felt Taylor-Johnson's lash, now he might feel the garroting choke of the noose.

Or the captain would finally pay.

16

"Mueller!" Taylor-Johnson shouted, and the room fell silent.

Buck stared at the tall blond sea captain. He'd waited nearly two years for this confrontation. Ernst's death would finally be avenged. The scars across his back would be avenged.

But at what cost to Elena?

He saw her, from the corner of his eye; her body gripped with tension. Against his better judgment, he relented, acquiescing to her wishes. As the group of marineros marched into the room and everyone turned toward the door, he dropped behind the table, which was covered with a floor-length cloth of fine Spanish lace over one of muslin, and crawled beneath.

The hair bristled on the back of his neck. He wanted to stand and resolve this, instead he hid. What had Taylor-Johnson told Elena? He could well imagine the lies. Buck knew he owed her nothing. There had been no understanding between them, only that warm connection they'd both felt and that one brief, passionate kiss. He moved to where the table coverings came together; a tiny crack parted and he searched the crowd.

The captain talked with Juarez and it appeared they

argued. The tall blond sea captain pointed toward the tables and instructed his sailors to spread out. As they moved across the room, Buck tensed. Elena's wishes or not, it looked as if it would be a fight.

He fingered the ten-inch knife he always carried and slipped the pistol from its sheath. Elena backed into the table as the sailors approached, her layers of heavy lace petticoats pushing their way into sight under the edge of the cloth.

As the men reached the table, Buck saw a way to honor her wishes and avoid the fight. He lifted the hem of her wedding gown, which protruded under the table, and ducked underneath—a hiding place unlikely to be searched until the marriage was consummated. He heard her gasp when his cheek accidentally nudged her thigh, but she didn't move.

In nervous broken conversation, she explained to the sailors that Buck had bolted for the door at the rear of the building. Beginning to enjoy himself, he expelled a hot breath where her well-rounded rump joined her shapely pantaletted legs, and felt Elena's nervous twitch.

As the sailors hurried off, he gave in to an uncontrollable urge and nipped a firm thigh, heard her quick intake of breath, and slipped back under the table. Unknowingly, the women crowded around her, blocking the view from her husband and the sailors.

Once the men were gone, Buck swept the cloth aside and stepped from under the table. The growing chatter stilled. While the guests stared in surprise, he stalked around the table. Searching the crowd, he made for the front door, his pace hurried but deliberate, knife in one hand, pistol in the other.

The crowd parted. Eduardo Juarez made a threatening step toward him. Buck turned to face the hook-nosed man, sheathing the knife and gun, hoping the man would make a move, ending Elena's marriage before it could begin. To Buck's disappointment, the tall man turned on his heel and headed away from him, walking to where Elena still stood beside the table.

Buck met Elena's gaze one last time, then turned and bolted through the tall carved wooden doors. There were things he had wanted to say to Señorita Seville.

They would go unsaid to Señora Juarez.

Crossing the porch, he came face to face with her father, the señora, and Mamacita.

"Buck!" the don exclaimed with a smile of warmth he hadn't expected. "The vines, they did well... the biggest crop we have ever had."

Buck just nodded. Stepping off the board porch, he ran to his waiting horse and mounted. He paused atop the prancing, sidestepping stallion long enough to tip his hat to Mamacita, and receive a broad but confused smile in return. Then he spurred the roan. As he clamped his thighs against the saddle, he could feel the little tusuat in his pocket. Resisting the urge to dig it out and throw it into the thick dust of the street, he galloped out of town.

Buck galloped the stallion all the way back to camp, where Tucker and Tui bent over a fire. Sliding the roan to a stop, he hit the ground with a purposeful stride. As he began collecting his gear the men gathered around.

"You fixin' on leaving before this coffee's done boiling?" Tucker asked. "We were gonna mess up some of Sanchez's beans then head for the cantina."

"Cantina's closed. Big doings in town. Not for me though. You fellows go on and get the dust out of your throats. At the fandango, the drinks are free."

"What about you?" Sanchez asked.

"I've had enough the place already." He stopped and turned to face his friends. "Taylor-Johnson's in town, and now's not the time to settle my score. I'm headin' back to Bear Valley. Maybe catch a few more horses to deliver on my way east. I'll be there till winter comes. If you fellows get a hankerin', you know where I am." He shook hands all around, grabbed up the lead rope to the two pack animals he planned to take with him, and swung up on Diablo's back.

"Say hello to the padre for me," he said to Sanchez, pulling his hat down low. Spurring Diablo into a fast walk, he called over his shoulder, "I'll look for you fellows when I see you comin'."

Tucker stood with his hands on his wide hips and watched Buck ride out, then shook his head and walked back to the fire. "It ain't the captain that's makin' him leave. That boy's got a burr festerin' under his saddle. It ain't like him to just ride out... tain't like him a'tall."

ANGER SEETHED through Buck as he drove his little string of horses into the Tujungas toward the high granite mountains. Zalvidea had told him of a path into the big central valley that was almost due north of Pueblo Los Angeles. He would find it and get as far away as fast as possible.

Three days later he sat in his saddle in a deep cut among tangled wild grapes, overlooking the big Tulares Valley far below. If he worked his way north, along the east rim, he should come into the country where they'd trapped the horses, and from there find his way up the side of the big humped-backed mountain into Bear Valley. The thought of returning didn't have the appeal it had when he had visions of a rancho, a home. A home for Elena.

He forced it from his mind. He would think of Señora Juarez no more.

Now he regretted not buying supplies. He was out of coffee and beans, and down to a quarter of a sack of flour. But he would make do. After learning from the Juaneros and the Paiutes, he could make do anywhere.

For the first time in weeks, he thought of Mueller Manor. He should return to Boston in the spring—he knew his way across the desert. He could make it alone, he was sure. He knew the sea, the mountains, and the desert. And his saddle bags were full of gold.

Still, he had unfinished business in California. He was torn between leaving for home, or staying to settle his debt —Ernst's debt. If he went to any of the California hide ports, sooner or later Taylor-Johnson would show up, and with any kind of luck, Ernst could finally rest easy. What Buck had done to Hard Tack was only a prelude to what he'd do to Taylor-Johnson. But if he missed the captain, he knew the Virginia would head for Boston as soon as her holds were full of hides, horns, and tallow. If the sea didn't claim the bastard, he would have another chance to settle the score there.

The little tusuat still rode in his pocket. Perhaps luck would find him again. He rubbed it through his breeches. It hadn't done badly by him, all in all. He was a long way from having everything he wanted, but he had a damn sight more than when he'd left Boston.

Ernst had nothing but a cold, watery grave.

BUCK SAT QUIETLY, concealed by a grove of scrub oaks, watching a village of woven bark and willow huts in a flat far below. Again he was without trading goods. Quietly he picked his way back along the path he had come until he found a good camp site near a shallow stream with a big live oak shading a grassy flat spot.

He'd worked his animals hard. Taking out his frustrations, he had traveled mercilessly. He would let them rest and graze the afternoon away while he hunted a deer to offer the Indians. He would need their help if he was going to catch another batch of horses.

With a fat young doe on one of the pack saddles, he boldly rode into the Indian village. There was no sign of life among the bark and willow huts, other than a few smoldering campfires. He dismounted, unpacked the doe, and laid it across a rock, then sat down to wait. Half-finished baskets, grinding stones that had been left full of unground acorns, and ember fires were spotted about the clearing. In the trees nearby, high up in the branches, great woven baskets as tall as a man and far bigger than he could reach around held stores of acorns. It was a well-established camp. Fearing his approach, the Indians had left before his arrival.

Only a few minutes passed before they began to show themselves, tentatively peeking out from the scrub oak nearby. Buck stood and placed a closed fist across his chest as the braves filtered slowly out of the brush surrounding the village. A group of adult males, carrying stone headed clubs, small bows, skin quivers of headless arrows and a smaller quiver at their waist with short shafts of different size heads walked forward and sat by the main fire, motioning him to join them. As soon as he sat down, some of the women came forward and began to stoke two of the cooking fires burning nearby.

The women wore reed skirts and rabbit skin vests, but their breasts were partially exposed underneath. They were round-faced and flat featured. Straight, waistless bodies and ample thighs reflected the easy living in this lush valley.

Glancing around, he saw they had no mounts. This tribe would be little help to him in catching wild horses. They carried bows, but much shorter ones than the Paiutes. Along with stone knives and stone-headed axes, they appeared to be the Indian's only weapons.

Continuing to size him up, the women crowded around with baskets of rosehips, pine nuts, and acorn meal, then began frying a dough made from water and the acorn meal on flat rocks heated by their fires.

Buck noticed one girl in particular. She was taller than the rest, and more slender. Her features were not as broad as the others. Buck wondered if she might be from another tribe. When she offered him a basket filled with pine nuts, she would not meet his gaze, keeping her dark eyes shyly averted. He noticed her breasts were not those of a slender girl. They were large and full and eye-catching as she bent to serve him something to eat.

Her skirt was braided in a finer plait than the rest, and her hair was braided and wound around her head in an intricate, time-consuming style. He wished she would look at him with those warm brown eyes—it might help him forget others.

The Indians completely devoured the doe. Through a mixture of sign language Tucker had taught him and the guttural language of the tribe, he learned the Indians called themselves Yokuts, confirming what Zalvidea had told him of the area, and that they had never seen a white man before. That night the chief insisted Buck take a hut near the center of the village. He would rather have been out in the open, but he conceded, not wanting to offend his host.

He slept well, rested well, comfortable with these gentle people.

He stayed for two days, leaving the village only long enough to bring back game each morning. The old chief noticed Buck watching the doe-eyed girl as she worked around the village. That night, when he returned to his mud hut, she sat outside his door. As usual, she kept her eyes cast downward.

Wondering what the significance of her presence was, he entered with only a perfunctory nod of his head. As it grew darker, he continued glancing her way, but got no response. She still sat outside the door, legs primly together, eyes fixed on the ground in front of her. Finally, he caught her glancing over her shoulder and met her gaze. She turned quickly away. He was damn sure she wasn't a guard; she was there for something.

The red orange shadows of dusk slid away, leaving it fully dark. Buck watched the doorway, wondering what the girl outside would do. He moved to his bedroll, pulled off his boots, and stretched out, shoving his hands behind his head. A few minutes later, he heard a rustling, the girl bent over and crawled into the hut. She lay down beside him, not meeting his eyes, not quite touching him but very close.

He didn't know quite how to approach this problem.

He believed the girl had been told to be there. Somehow it took the challenge from the moment. But he certainly didn't want to offend her tribesmen.

Pondering the problem, trying not to compare the girl to Elena, he finally fell into a fitful sleep.

Awakening, he was surprised to see her up sitting behind a small fire she had built in the center of the hut, she watched him. Two small baskets of nuts and wild rosehips awaited him. Buck smiled. He'd been right all along. It was not at all bad, having a woman around.

The hut was so low he couldn't quite stand. Feeling the need to stretch and relieve himself, he stepped outside, into the full light of day. It was seldom he slept so late, but he felt comfortable here. Extending his arms, he worked the kinks from his shoulders then walked behind the hut and into the brush for his morning relief. Afterward he washed in the stream and returned to the village. He was surprised to see most of the tribe gathered by the communal fire, watching him walk toward the hut.

The girl stepped out beside him. Several of the younger girls ran over, giggled shyly, grabbed her by the hands, and led her away. The older women followed. The men beckoned to him to join them by the fire, then produced the ever-present pipes.

Wondering what all of it meant, his glance kept searching for the girl and before long she returned, being led by a group of the women. Now, she was dressed differently, much more ornamentally. Adorned in a long reed cape covered with bird feathers. The women drew her forward.

The men stood up, and Buck followed their example. The old chief began a chant while the girl stood in front of him, eyes still kept carefully down. Then, to his amazement, the women began disrobing her. First the cape, then the rabbit skin vest, fully exposing her breasts. They stripped off her reed skirt and finally, somewhat anti-climactically, her moccasins. Still not satisfied, they unbraided her hair and let it fall to her waist.

They led her toward him and placed her hand in his. For the first time she raised her eyes to his face and stood unflinching. The chief completed another short chant while she stood there, far more beautiful in her innocent nakedness than in the crude, if highly adorned garments.

Buck had no idea how he was supposed to react, but he had a strong suspicion what was going on. He felt the heat in his face travel to his loins as he overcame his initial embarrassment at seeing her nude. She was remarkably beautiful in a primitive, pagan way. The girl quickly recovered her skirt and vest, then came to stand close beside him. Jesus! He guessed he had a wife. Not how, nor where, nor whom he'd planned to marry, but a wife nevertheless. It would take a good scrubbing to find out just how beautiful she really was, but that task would be a pleasure.

The women began dragging baskets forward and building cooking fires while the men produced musical instruments, and some formed a small circle and danced to clattering sticks and banging river rocks. Gourds and turtle shells filled with pebbles softened the rhythm, the feasting and celebration wearing on into the day.

Tired of the dancing, Buck took the girl by the hand and slipped off to where Diablo was staked. From his saddlebag he recovered a small hunk of soap he'd made from deer tallow and ash. The pools near his old campsite would do nicely. She stepped back as he bridled the big roan. It was obvious she didn't want to go near the horse, but just as obvious she didn't want him to leave without her.

Swinging into the saddle, he sat looking down at her, silently daring her to come. With a defiant look she walked forward. Reaching down, he gripped her forearm and swung her up behind him. Diablo, well rested and feeling it, pranced and sidestepped, and the girl clung to him, wrapping both arms tightly around his waist, her thighs pressed firmly against the outsides of his legs. He could feel her tremble, her breasts pressed into his back, and desire snaked hotly through him.

He rode toward the pool, determined to consummate her unasked for bath—and his unasked for marriage.

They reined up downstream. Buck dismounted, swinging his leg over Diablo's neck, then lifted the girl to the ground. Looking into her big doe eyes, he stood there for a moment, wondering if he should kiss her. She shyly averted her eyes, the moment passed, and he led the horse to a patch of fresh green grass where it could reach the water.

When he walked back, she was wading in the creek with the innocence of a child. Thinking how tempting she looked, he sat on a rock by the edge of the pool and removed his boots, then stood and slowly unbuttoned his shirt and pulled it off. His breeches fell to the ground and he stepped out of them, his long johns still clinging to him, covering the lust he was beginning to feel. Retaining that last bit of modesty, he stepped into the pool until it was shoulder deep.

Still wading in the stream, the girl watched with interest, then climbed up on the bank and removed her rabbit skin vest and reed skirt. Dressed as God had made her, she stepped into the pool to join him.

When the Indian girl drew closer, he reached out and drew her to him, kissing her tentatively. Wide-eyed with curiosity, she soon got the idea, and returned the kiss. Buck closed his eyes and so did she, and he began to kiss her deeply. He pulled away from her and she smiled, still a little shy.

Turning his back to her, he swam over and picked up the bar of soap from where he'd tossed it near his clothes, returned to her, and began to soap her waist-length, coal black hair. She stared at the lather in amazement, then giggled at the bubbles, ducked her head under the water, and rinsed the soap away. Her hair hung across her shoulders, teasing the rosy peaks that had risen hard as pebbles from the coolness of the water, or from the nearness of the man who had just become her husband.

Buck hoped it was the latter.

Reaching out, he lifted strands of hair away from her heavy breasts, then slowly began to caress them. The smile faded from her face, and her dark eyes seemed to smolder. His blood began to pound when her hands found the waistband of his long johns and she began to strip them away. He kicked them up onto the bank and lifted her into his arms. She buried her face in the hollow of his shoulder as he carried her to the grass-covered slope.

Pressing her down in the ankle-deep grass, he kissed her tenderly, then rolled her beneath him, using his knee to part her legs and settling himself between her thighs. She encircled his waist with her arms and clung to him as he found her warmth and entered her. When she cried out, he hesitated, but her heels dug into him and she pulled him deeper inside. She was primal and instinctive, and she arched and cried out as they rolled in the grass and he reached his release, spilling his seed inside her.

He tried to move away, but she shifted so her breast touched his lips. Pleased, he kissed her there and grew hard again inside her. This time he rolled to his back and pulled her up on top of him. It was she who cried out again and again, until he hissed a low, primal groan of release, and finally relaxed beneath her.

They lay entwined for a while, then she giggled and rolled off him, returning to the water. They swam, and washed with the bar of soap, splashed, and played like a pair of river otters. After one more roll in the soft green grass, this time more gently, they dressed.

Lifting her onto the big blue roan, they picked their way down the stream toward the village. He had been married for over four hours when he finally learned her name. It was Lali.

ELENA SAT down in front of the polished metal dressing mirror and called for her Indian woman to fetch her a cup of chocolate. It was nice having someone to do your every bidding, as she had never really done at home. She wondered why she felt so restless.

Before her wedding, Mamacita had had many long conversations with her, warning her of the ways of men. She told her it would be years, if ever, before she was able to take pleasure from what seemed to pleasure a man so greatly.

Her wifely duties were the worst part of her marriage. Eduardo visited her alcoba, her bedroom, almost every night. He said little to her, just crawled onto her in her bed, shoved himself inside her, and rutted like an animal until he spilled his seed and slumped satiated on top of her. Then without a word, he returned to his own alcoba.

The first night he had hurt her badly, not stopping when she cried out, the pain knifing through her like a blade. As he left, he told her to call her serving woman to tend her.

It was a duty she abhorred, but it was truly grand being the señora of such a magnificent hacienda. They entertained constantly, and the governor was expected soon. They had received numerous gifts from the great families of Alta California, and more arrived weekly from Mexico and even Spain.

She thought of her wedding day. It had almost been ruined. The American captain who purchased hides from Eduardo had told her about Buck Mueller murdering the first mate. In the past she had thought of him as a boy. It was a man she had encountered at the reception. Still young, but now hard and dangerous. There was no doubt in her mind he would have used his pistol and knife if the sailors had found him. He had hidden as soon as the captain returned. Was he a coward, a murderer as the captain claimed?

Or was he respecting her wishes?

Buck had been bold in coming to the reception—not the action of a coward. Even if he did not know the captain would be there, he was brave to face her father. Don Pedro had wanted to have him whipped for what he had done to his vineyard. She smiled as she thought of her father's surprise when the grapes produced the largest crop ever, and the irrigation system kept not only the vineyard watered, but the pasture above the hacienda also green and verdant. A pleasant change from the summer brown hills surrounding the house and grounds.

No, she did not think him a coward. A coward would have run, or would not have shown up at all.

And she would not have let a coward kiss her.

She had been attracted to him from the first. Months after he had ridden the big roan away, she thought of him. She remembered his boldness in kissing her that day in his room. The same bravado he had shown in hiding under her skirts, his hot breath on her thigh—and nipping her before he slid back under the table, making her gasp and blush. Mother Mary and Joseph, he was brazen!

But Mamacita liked him—she who barely tolerated her own son. After he had gone, she had talked about him until Don Pedro reprimanded her. How she had crowed when the vines produced more than twice the crop ever.

Elena could still recall the look Buck had given her as he'd left the fandango after her wedding. It seemed hard, but she felt it meant more. More than goodbye. She would barely admit to herself that she had thought of him on her wedding night, long after Eduardo had hurt her and left for his room.

She wondered what it might have been like if she had married Buck instead of Eduardo.

17

Buck sat on a hill in the shade of a verdant green buckeye overlooking Bear Valley.

Lali was busily cleaning the small cabin he and Sanchez and the others had built when they were here before. There had been no doubt in her mind about accompanying him when he left the village. He did not complain, needing the companionship, needing the distraction. She was tender, basic, and uncomplicated—and beautiful in a wild untamed way.

The summer crept along unnoticed in its perfect weather. He built a monk-sized smokehouse of boulders against a stone face of the hill, two hundred yards away from the cabin so any bears that might be attracted to the succulent odors wouldn't worry Lali. He filled it with smoked and jerked venison, and elk, and sausage made from both. Almost daily, they walked to the spring which was the source of the little creek and worked at building up a dam as they bathed. They took time to make love in the grass, and Buck enjoyed her innocence. Daily he would cut a lodgepole pine from the grove surrounding the spring and drag it back to the cabin where it would become another rafter to use later for expansion.

He couldn't bring himself to hunt for horses. Collecting

as many as he could drive meant it was time to leave for Santa Fe... and Boston.

Instead, he constructed a dam and the beginnings of an irrigation system, a corral, worked in the smokehouse, and continued to enlarge their cabin. Only the last two rafters of a new sod roof had yet to be put in place. There was no need to leave this valley. The winter would be more than comfortable. And Lali was beginning to learn a smattering of Spanish and English, beginning to become an intellectual companion as well as a physical one.

Weeks passed and the weather began to cool. Fall was approaching. Buck decided to finish the sod roof over the addition they had built and was perched at the ridge beam when he saw three riders crest the rise in the west.

He didn't have to see their faces to recognize the men. Tui's big frame swayed from side to side as he rode. Tucker slouched in the saddle, always appearing to be half asleep but actually alert for whatever might come. Sanchez sat straight in the saddle, one hand lightly on the rein, the other resting on his waist, the epitome of the Spanish horseman.

Buck's eyes misted at their approach. He hadn't realized how much he missed these friends. Returning to work, he ignored the distant figures and finished the last of the sodding as they rode toward the beginnings of his rancho.

But he was down and waiting, the fire in the fireplace roaring, and Lali cutting up huge elk steaks by the time the men dismounted. The water boiled, and Buck yelled at them to bring their cups and the coffee he knew they carried.

Tuck walked up to the little cabin, surveying its additions and the smoke house. "Boy, if I knowed we was headin' fer town, I mighta gone the other direction. You been busy!"

Buck chuckled. "Guess I'll always be the Boston man." He turned to Tui and Sanchez. "How are Padre Zalvadia, Dutch, and Kelolo? Kinda thought you might be bringing Kelolo back with you, Tui."

Tui gleamed, happy that Buck remembered his brother. "Kelolo gone home." The big kanaka flashed his infectious grin. "He and other Sandwich boys catch a schooner, so Tui come back to keep you from trouble."

Buck smiled at that.

"Zalvidea is the same," Sanchez offered, sliding gracefully from the saddle. "He will always be the same." Sanchez shook his head. "He tries to keep the mission together but still the people leave. He asked about you. Sent his best regards. Wants you to know that he prays for you. Dutch, the blind man, he sends his regards."

Buck felt a twinge of guilt. He needed to talk to his good friend the padre, to confess that he was not Catholic. It was a guilt that had been gnawing at him like a dog worrying a bone.

Tucker motioned to Lali. "Seems you caught yourself a wild one. Thought you was huntin' horses."

"Been doin' some scouting, and a little peace-makin'." Buck grinned. "But not much horse hunting."

"Where'd you find this little filly? Don't look like no valley Yokuts Indian to me. Don't look like no Paiute neither."

"She's a valley Indian all right. I just scrubbed her down and dressed her in that Boston-made buckskin." He'd spent the better part of two days making her a buckskin dress and a wrap from the cape of a big bull elk.

"You figger on takin' her back...to Bostontown, I mean?" Tucker's bushy brows lowered, and he scratched his beard.

Buck returned his friend's gaze, but ignored the question —as he ignored it when he asked it of himself. He was growing very close to Lali, a closeness that transcended the language gap. And they were even beginning to bridge that. He avoided thinking past his short range goal—a herd of horses and a ride to Santa Fe. He would cross that other unhappy bridge when he came to it.

He was beginning to depend on Lali.

WITH THE HELP of the three men, Buck constructed another small cabin away from his, on the other side of the corral. It was a good thing for a week later the first blush of snow gave the valley a fond caress.

Sanchez spent time training the little desert mare that had saved Buck from the flood. Buck had been using her as a pack animal, but Sanchez wanted Lali to have a good dependable mount. Tucker scouted the hills, noting the horse sign so they would be ready to collect the animals in the spring.

Buck kept building. He constructed furniture. He continued dragging lodgepole pines down and stacking them. A barn was the next project he had in mind. He made a broom for Lali and showed her how to sweep the slate floor that he laid in the little cabin. A slate floor under which he hid his stash of Missouri gold.

His friends told him of their stop at Rancho Toro Bravo on their trip from the mission. The don's wine vats were full, and he would soon be distilling brandy in earnest. Don Pedro asked them to convey his appreciation to Buck for his efforts and to assure him that he had a claim on a portion of the first commercial batch. Mamacita was overseeing the operation. She had sent him a bottle of fine Spanish brandy with a note attached: "I will do better than this, Buckito." He believed she would.

With some remorse, Buck began hunting horses. Toka and his people returned, and Buck again hired his friend and five braves to help. Priding himself on the skill he had learned with the reata, he swelled with pride each time the big blue roan showed his superiority to the rangy wild horses. But as they gathered a larger and larger herd, Buck's nervousness grew. Each animal they captured brought him closer to leaving, closer to his decision regarding Lali.

Closer to riding out of this valley that had become more a part of him than Boston ever was.

He was making his mark on the land. When he left this time, he would be leaving behind ground saturated with the sweat of his efforts. Leaving physical things he could not take along. The cabin, the dam, the corrals, the smokehouse. But even worse, he would be leaving behind what he knew the valley could become.

And Lali. It pained him to think of leaving her, of sending her back to her tribe.

In his mind the land was already planted and irrigated. A mill worked timber from the mountainside and ground wheat grown in the fields.

All he needed was his hands, and a little luck, to make the dream a reality.

His quandary was solved on the first day it was warm enough to take Lali to the dam for a bath. Beneath the bright warm sun, he realized her lithe shape was beginning a subtle change, her supple waist beginning to fill out. Sweet Jesus! He was going to be a father!

Grinning from ear to ear, he returned with her to the cabin. His decision was finally made. He was staying in Bear Valley.

After they had gathered a hundred and sixty head of horses, the nearby land and surrounding hills were becoming overworked. That night, he invited Tucker, Tui, and Sanchez to join him to share some of the bottle of Spanish Brandy. After they had finished half the bottle, he broke the news to them.

"I won't be riding with you fellas this fall to Santa Fe."

Tucker smiled. "Kinda figured you to be the settlin' kind. It's a right thing you're a'doin'."

Both Sanchez and Tui agreed.

That night as he lay beside Lali, listening to her regular breathing, he pondered his decision, a hundred different thoughts crisscrossing his mind.

He must send word to his family. What would his legal rights to the rancho be? California was Mexican territory and he was an American citizen. Zalvidea had told him that only Mexican citizens could own land. Only Catholics could own land. He did not wish to give up his American citizenship.

The padre told him Governor Echeandia insisted mission lands be granted to the Indians. Lali was an Indian. The Californios assumed he was a Catholic...even the padre thought so. Maybe the lie would have to stand. The thought of deceiving his friend galled him, but not so much as the thought of leaving this valley... of losing land he'd come to think of as his. He would ride to see Zalvidea in the spring. The padre would help him.

The Californios were not interested in the interior. Seldom had they been out of sight of the ocean. None of the ranchos were more than fifty miles inland, and Bear Valley must be over a hundred. He doubted if any Mexican had ever laid eyes on the valley.

He felt sure he could conquer his problems. With just a little more luck.

Lali awoke as he fingered the little tusuat he kept in a small basket of personal things near the bed.

"It is good medicine, this tusuat?"

"The Juaneros think so," Buck said quietly, then dropped it back in the basket and turned and pulled her close, wrapping his arms around her and resting his hands gently on her growing belly. "You're my good medicine," he whispered in her ear.

DON EDUARDO PAULO JUAREZ sat staring out the shutters of his study. The view from the hacienda was an impressive one: the Palos Verdes Hills to the south, Malibu to the north, the great marsh below, and the startling Pacific sunset beyond.

Behind and to the south lay most of Rancho Riena de California. A grant which would almost double in size with his acquisition of Rancho Toro Bravo. The governor would grant no more than eight square leagues to any one man, but a man could acquire more. He would have Toro Bravo, one way or another.

Don Pedro's obligations to the Juarez family were coming due the end of this year and, as Eduardo had anticipated, the old don could not satisfy them. Not unless that damned marinero's brandy still was more than merely successful. Unfortunately, it just could be.

Eduardo knew Don Pedro was attempting to purchase the grape crops from some of his neighbors. He'd added more vats to the two the marinero had built, so more wine could be put up and more brandy distilled. The don employed a man who had lost a foot in an accident off one of the hide and horn ships, but claimed to have the skills of a cooper. A stack of barrels grew behind the establo. The old woman directed the whole project. It had been she who had insisted on the additional vats, the barrels, and the buying of the neighbors' grapes.

It was more than just irritating, the way Don Pedro allowed his women to interfere in men's business. Thank God he had broken Elena of sticking her nose where it was not wanted.

He thought of Toro Bravo and ground his teeth. If the notes were met, he would have to handle things another way. He was determined to build an empire. To hand that dynasty over to his sons—and an old man mattered little in his scheme of things.

The thought was disquieting. More than anything, he needed male heirs, needed to be certain the Juarez name was carried on. He was disappointed Elena was not yet with child. He had visited her alcoba almost every night since they were married. Still she had not ceased her monthly flow, wasting the lifeblood which should be building a strong Juarez son. What was the matter with her?

The sun dropped below the horizon, and the shadows outside Eduardo's window disappeared. She would be in her bed. She had missed the evening meal for days. Eduardo presumed it was to avoid him.

He would not be avoided; tonight he would conceive a son.

Rising from his desk, he made his way down the hall to her door and shoved it open. The alcoba lay in darkness. She rested beneath the covers, seemingly asleep. She had pretended to be sleeping many times when he came to her bed. He knew better. More than one time, he had caught her at the game, but it didn't really matter. It was her duty. He would see that it was performed.

Slipping off his clothes, he crawled into bed beside her. "Elena, I am here."

She made no response.

These damned women of breeding, why were they all so cold? Not at all like the Indian women or the women of the Pueblo. He pulled on her shoulder, rolling her onto her back. Elena made a small sound of protest as he parted her legs and shoved his way in, then lay there beneath him stiffly. When he was finished, he moved to the edge of the bed and dressed, then left the room without a word.

Elena listened as his footfalls faded, then she rose and walked to the shutters. She stared out over her veranda to the ocean beyond. It is so beautiful, she thought, with the moon over the water. She loved this hacienda. She was becoming a part of it. Eduardo had allowed her to make many changes in the house. But something always seemed to be missing.

There must be more than this.

She chided herself. She had everything she wanted, didn't she? Well, almost everything.

She wished she could ride her mare into the country. Wished she could ride astride like a caballero, could feel the wind once more in her hair. She missed that. Eduardo insisted she ride sidesaddle, and then only when she was accompanied by one or more of the vaqueros. It bored her.

She loved to ride—to ride until she and her mare were

both covered with perspiration. She knew the mare loved it too. She still walked to the barn and curried and talked to the horse almost every day, a habit Eduardo despised and one which amused the vaqueros. The mare loved her, was gentle with her, maybe understood her better than anyone here at Rancho Riena de California.

Elena sighed. She must not dwell on these things. She must think of tomorrow. The governor would be here again, and the tall blond sea captain. She wondered what they were planning. They had met several times. The governor was coming to San Pedro aboard the Virginia. She wished Eduardo would discuss his business with her. She would not interfere, but she knew she could help him.

She turned away from the window. She must plan for tomorrow. Tomorrow everything must be perfect. Elena wearily walked away.

SANTOS MONTES, Eduardo's head vaquero, waited patiently in Eduardo's study. He had been the top man on the Juarez rancho for the past ten years. It had been his job to do those things necessary for a major land holding to grow and prosper—things that could not be done by the patron.

Before Eduardo took over, he had worked for Don Ernesto, Eduardo's father, and he had respected the don. He was not particularly pleased with his inherited employer. With the father he had always known exactly where he stood. With Eduardo, it was different. Juarez depended upon no man, and a man who could not bring himself to rely on another man, who could not trust another man, could not be relied upon or trusted himself.

Still, as long as he was well paid and not expected to perform the duties of the regular vaqueros, he was willing to work for the man and consider him patron.

Montes paced the floor, a dangerous glint of anticipation in his eye. He had been called upon a dozen times to face other men and he was good at it. No man was faster with a blade—or better at concealing it until it was time to strike. The men he had used it on had seen only its hilt with their fading eyes as it protruded from their chests.

Santos almost smiled. Eduardo's father had recruited him from the mission guard. He would be grateful to the elder Juarez forever for that. He'd joined the cholos, the guard, rather than go to a Mazatlan prison, and he had hated it from the start. The padres watched every move he made, and turned his miserable life even more miserable.

He had killed many times for old Ernesto Juarez, always men who had gotten in the old man's way, always for business. He wondered what it was the new patron wanted of him.

When Eduardo entered his study, he found Montes seated behind his expensive desk, rolling a cigarillo from his private tobacco stock—a gift from Captain Taylor-Johnson. He would have reprimanded any other vaquero, but not this one. Eduardo would have preferred not having him on the rancho at all. He would have had fired him if he had not been so capable at tasks other men would not undertake.

Though he did not fear Montes, he was wary of the man. But in order to continue the growth of Rancho Riena, using the same methods as his father, Montes was a necessary evil.

"Do you enjoy my tobacco, vaquero?" Eduardo asked, only hinting at his displeasure.

Montes struck a sulfurhead on the leather desktop and took a long draw on the cigarillo, exhaling slowly, letting the smoke drift out through his nose.

"The tobacco is fine, jefe, but I am sure that is not why you called for me." At least he referred to him politely as 'boss' even though he helped himself to his tobacco. Only after he had finished speaking did the tall vaquero give up the seat and cross the room.

"No, that is not the reason I have called you here." Eduardo moved forward and took the vacated chair. "I have a task for you, Montes. A simple one that will take but a few days. Don Pedro Seville is acquiring grapes from all the surrounding ranchos for his brandy distillery. I want this stopped. Inform the owners that I feel it is in the Sevilles' best interest... that this venture is bound to fail, and I do not want my foolish father-in-law to waste his money."

He knew that just by sending Montes the rancho owners would understand he was serious about the matter, knew they risked a confrontation if they did not comply. Seville would be able to buy few grapes.

"That is all?" Montes felt disappointed. A task hardly worth his personal attention.

"Do it well, vaquero. It is more important than it appears. Buenos noches." He excused the man. Montes helped himself to the makings of another cigarillo, then left and quietly closed the door.

Sitting in his chair, Eduardo wiped the ashes from his desktop. The mere presence of Santos Montes irritated him. He felt the man was beyond his control, and he did not like that feeling.

Staring pensively out through the shutters, he contemplated the next day's business. Echeandia and Taylor-Johnson would be arriving and they could conclude their bargain. By this time next year the three men would control the profitable hide trade in California. Echeandia was already moving against the missions. Soon mission ownership of the lands and herds would be broken, their vast holdings distributed to the Indians, and easily taken by intelligent men—like himself.

With Taylor-Johnson having the exclusive contract with California, signed by the governor, to ship all California hides to Boston, Eduardo would have no trouble obtaining financing to purchase three or four ships. Enough to convey all the hides he and Echeandia could collect.

The governor would grant the exclusive contract to Rancho Riena to act as export agent for the hide trade, at least in the southern half of Alta California. Eduardo, in turn, would contract with Taylor-Johnson for the exclusive right to transport the hides to Boston. They would set the price. No more bidding by the various captains, no more driving the price up for the benefit of the ranchos and the missions. Without the competition of other captains, there would be little profit—except for the export company he owned.

It was their plan to launch a coastal schooner with a five-pound gun mounted bow and stern, to patrol the coast of California and stop any illegal activity.

And if his governor-partner gave him any trouble, Montes would take care of him. Echeandia had been the first Mexican-born man to be appointed governor of Alta California, the others being old country Spanish, and now there was much pressure on Mexico City to appoint a Californio, a Native, as the head of state. There was a good chance Eduardo could be that next appointee. If not, it could be as long as a year, maybe more, before one was appointed. And in the meantime he would control the hide trade. Even in that short time the profits could be huge.

He would see that the contract allowed for a unilateral rescission. Without Echeandia to stand in his way he would control it all. The captain would have to accept whatever terms he dictated. As the ranchos struggled for survival, he would loan them money, and eventually own them. Another addition to the dynasty he intended to create. The Juarez dynasty.

All of California was not beyond his grasp.

Eduardo smiled into the dim light of the room. Rancho Toro Bravo would be first. It was his by right.

After all, he had married it.

18

UNLIKE LAST YEAR, there was no Indian summer. Fall came hard, fast, and cutting.

Tuck, Tui, and Sanchez rode out with a cold wind at their backs. With the help of five Paiute braves, they drove over a hundred wild horses ahead of them. Buck agreed to take a half share this time, since he was staying to work the rancho and care for his wife and their coming child.

Lali was heavy with child. He was pleased with her new shape. Though she was quite large, it didn't seem to slow her down. She still joined him in any task she was strong enough to do. Her Spanish was improving rapidly and they had learned to communicate well.

He decided to work through the winter, then make a trip to the mission at San Juan Capistrano to see Father Zalvidea, after his friends returned from Santa Fe.

And after the baby came.

He would enlist the padre's help in getting a land grant. Zalvidea believed the problems he faced with William-Taylor Johnson and Bryant and Sturgis would remain between him and the Americans. As long as he stayed in Mexican-controlled Alta California the authorities would not interfere in the matter. He could return to the valley with seed and an iron plow, plant his crops, then go on to Monterey and appeal to the governor.

Buck spent the fall planning his irrigation system and building furniture, including a tiny willow cradle.

And a baby boy they named Tucker was born on a November afternoon.

A brutal fall foretold and even harsher winter, then it gave way to early spring, the first wild flowers, the greening of the buckeye.

BUCK IMPATIENTLY AWAITED the return of his friends. He was eager for them to see his son and he had missed the male companionship.

He'd hired men from Lali's village to help him with the irrigation system and was almost finished when he saw two riders approaching from across the valley. Soon Tui's distinctive sway and Sanchez's rigid posture were apparent. Tucker wasn't with them. The leathery old mountain man had mentioned the possibility of working his way north into the Rockies from Santa Fe and tying up with some trappers—Buck was sorry he wouldn't see his namesake, for he knew the old trapper would be proud of little Tucker's name.

Old Tucker had already been in one place longer than he had ever been since his childhood. Buck was not surprised that he had gone, but he would miss him.

It had taken a little longer to make the trip from Bear Valley across the desert, since Sanchez had decided to graze the horses for a while outside of Santa Fe. While the animals rested and recovered from their arduous journey, he and Tui broke a number of them to the halter. This time, they got sixty dollars a head from the traders who came from the East.

That night the friends killed the last half of the bottle of brandy Mamacita had sent Buck and celebrated their safe return. The next day Buck pulled up a stone from the slate floor and added another twelve hundred dollars in gold to his stash.

It was time to make his request of Zalvidea. He worried only slightly about leaving Lali and little Tucker at Bear Valley. The Yokuts, Lali's people, were still there and would watch after them, and help with whatever she needed. She had attained a status in the tribe far above most women, since Buck kept the tribe supplied with meat and had taught them to catch and train horses.

Their only real enemy in the valley was the grizzly, but the giant bears seemed content to feed on plentiful berries, small game, and an occasional fawn or elk calf, and seldom came near the cabins. As far as the Yokuts were concerned, the great bears were indestructible—their feeble arrows did them almost no damage. The grizzlies were worshipped by the Indians, the Yokuts knew them as mohoo, a god to them. And they were highly respected, and a little feared, by Buck.

"What do you think, Sanchez?" Buck asked of his friend the third day after the vaquero's return. "You and Tui rested up enough to head back for the mission?"

"I am more than ready," Sanchez said.

"Tui ready to see Indian friends." There was a woman he visited among the Juaneros. Buck imagined he was eager to see her again.

He turned to Lali. "I won't be gone long. Soon as I talk to the padre and buy the goods we need, I'll be back."

She nodded in that sweet accepting way of hers. "I will be waiting," she said simply.

At dawn the next morning, Buck hugged her goodbye, then held for a moment the small wriggling bundle that was his new son. He was still awed by the tiny miniature of himself, and handled the child with much more care than necessary—as if he were fashioned of delicate crystal rather than flesh and blood.

Riding out with only one pack horse between them, the

men made Pueblo de Los Angeles in two and a half days. The sleepy little village hadn't changed, though it was much less busy than when Buck had last seen it almost a year ago. They spent only an hour at the cantina, then, over his friends' complaints, Buck pushed them to go on to the Mission San Juan Capistrano. Even Rancho Toro Bravo, with the hope of seeing the don and Mamacita and collecting the brandy Don Pedro had promised, could not sidetrack him.

The fiery-eyed señorita who had been its occupant was now the mistress of another great California rancho. She was gone from his life for good. Still, far more than he should, he thought about her.

They pushed hard toward Capistrano. Zalvidea was at work in the mission garden, the sun just casting its last furtive rays, when the men rode up, their horses lathered and dusty. The padre greeted Buck with an uncharacteristic bear hug and led them to the mission kitchen for a warmed-up supper of pozole laced with chunks of pork.

While the men ate, Zalvidea updated them on the status of the mission. "It has been a difficult time this past year," he said. "We are constantly pressed by the governor to institute a plan to distribute the land and stock to the Indians. I am sure that it is just a matter of time before a mandate is issued and the governor develops his own plan and enforces it."

"What about the mission guard?" Buck asked, shoveling in a spoonful of the cooked corn meal. "Can't you stop them with the guard?"

"We are not inclined to force and even if we were, the mission guard is, and always has been, under the governor's control." The priest lowered his voice and sat forward on the rough wooden bench. "It is a long-time mistake of the church to have the guard paid by the governor. Even if the cholo's sympathies were with us, their purse strings are tied to the state."

"I see your point," Buck said.

The padre sighed. "I fear we are destined to participate in the destruction of what has taken years of effort to build. Not at all what I had envisioned myself doing—undoing God's work."

"I'm sorry, Father."

He shook his graying head. "Ah, but enough of our troubles. Tell me about you, my son. It has been some time since we have talked."

Buck related the events of the past two years, mentioning the horses they had captured and the place he had discovered in the hills, leading up to the reason for his visit. "So, as you can see by my enthusiasm, I'm extremely taken with my valley in the mountains. I call it Bear Valley, and I'm hoping you can help me make my dream of a mountain rancho come true. I'm going to seek a land grant from Echeandia."

Buck waited quietly for a response from the priest, his palms a little damp with nervous expectation. Finally, brushing the dust from his robes, the padre spoke carefully.

"You are aware of the problems. This Indian girl, Lali... I am sure she has not received Christ. You are not a Mexican citizen, which you must be in order to receive a land grant. Even to even live in Alta California."

"I know that, Padre, but—"

"Many of these things are easily resolved," Zalvidea continued. "Are you willing to become a citizen of Alta California?"

"I would prefer not to give up my American citizenship, but Lali is a citizen. Won't that do? I'll bring her here for instruction so she can become a Catholic. You said yourself, the governor is pressing for the Indians to have land, for whatever motives he might have."

"His motive is the destruction of the missions." Zalvidea said emphatically.

"Even if that is the case, and if you'll forgive me, don't you think I might use that to my advantage? This could be an opportunity for him to prove that is really what he wants. This valley of mine is land no Californios would want. In fact I'm sure no Californios have ever seen it. It's way inland, far beyond any harbors, on the very edge of the great desert."

Zalvidea rested his hand on Buck's shoulder. "It would be good for you to bring your wife here; at least we can baptize her and the baby. Little Tucker, is it?"

"Yes."

"Then we can begin Lali's religious instruction." He rubbed his chin with his hand. "Yes, it is a good thing. I will think on the proper method of approaching Echeandia. As you marineros would say, perhaps we can hoist him on his own halyard."

Buck smiled and relaxed a little on the rough wooden bench.

He spent the next two days at the mission. Sanchez visited with the vaqueros, retelling tales of the wilderness and the great desert. Tui discovered a group of Sandwich Islanders camped on the point where the hides were sailed down onto the beach and rode out to greet them.

Buck spent hours talking with Dutch. Though happy to see him, Dutch warned him emphatically of Taylor-Johnson.

"He calls you the killer deserter," the old sailor said. "Your name was the first word to roll off the bastard's tongue each time he came to the mission."

"Zalvidea says the Mexicans aren't after me. Only Taylor-Johnson."

"Don't underestimate him, boy," Dutch said. "He sent Swill here, with a crock of rum, thinking it would set me to talking... and tellin' what I knew of you. I drank their grog, but I didn't tell 'em nothin'!" Dutch roared and slapped his thighs, then turned serious. "He means to have your hide, son."

"And I mean to have his, Dutch. It's no wet-behind-the-ears boy he'll meet this time. You can tell him I mean to see him dead." Just thinking about it, Buck felt a rush of fury so strong it was several minutes before he could resume his quiet conversation with his old friend.

"Zalvidea says the missions may be destroyed," he finally said, concerned over the future of Dutch's home. "Maybe you should come with me, back to Bear Valley."

Dutch shook his head, his sightless eyes staring vacantly. "This is my home now, son. I know my way around here, even without my eyes, and I'm useful. I like what I've learned to do."

Buck smiled. The beautiful rawhide reatas, whips, and bridles Dutch wove were sought after by every vaquero for miles around. He hoped nothing happened to Dutch's home.

On his third night at the mission, Buck wrote a long letter to his mother while Zalvidea composed a letter of recommendation to the governor. A letter from Buck would accompany it to the capital at Monterey. The padre suggested he request a missive from Don Pedro as well, one that could be sent along with a cask of Toro Bravo brandy.

That was excuse enough for Buck to visit Toro Bravo.

———

Don Eduardo Juarez sat at his desk and tried to focus on the agreement spread before him. The past week had been successful. Taylor-Johnson and Echeandia had left that morning, and Eduardo had been celebrating his success all day. He tipped the bottle of brandy—he was well past the snifter stage—to his lips.

So far things were going smoothly. Montes had returned with assurances that no one would sell more grapes to the Sevilles. The hide agreement had been reduced to writing and signed. In less than a year's time he, the English sea captain, and the governor would control the Alta California hide trade.

The only thing lacking now was a son to carry on the Juarez name, a son to continue the dynasty he was building.

He would have it all soon enough. He was convinced he was more clever than the Englishman, and even more clever than Echeandia, governor or no.

He stumbled down the hallway and paused at the door to Elena's room. He lifted the latch and pushed it open. As usual she appeared to be sleeping. He leaned on the door jamb.

"Do not pretend with me," he said drunkenly. "I am your husband." He stumbled to the bed and reached across it, roughly turning her over. She sat up startled, holding the sheet in front of her. For once, it seemed, she had not been pretending.

"Eduardo, you… you frightened me!"

He stumbled, tried to regain his balance, and fell across the bed, pulling the sheet down to her waist. Her thin white nightgown clung alluringly to her breasts as he made his way clumsily to his feet and stared down at her.

"You are so beautiful… so lovely…" His mood blackened. "It is too bad you are useless, nothing but a decoration. It is time you bore fruit, woman."

She felt the sting of his words. He rarely talked to her in this way. "I am sorry, Eduardo. I am trying to be a good wife, trying to become a mother. Were you not pleased with the household while the governor was here?"

"That could have been done by a camposina, any servant. The test of a woman… a wife, is her sons." He leaned over, grabbed her chin and stared into her eyes. His foul breath repulsed her and she tried to pull away. "I want a son, woman!" he shouted, his spittle spraying her face. He stood, swaying on his feet, and smiled, enjoying her discomfort.

Elena jerked away, rolling from the bed, trying to dodge him and make it to the door. Lunging for her, he caught her by the back of her nightgown then slipped and crashed to the floor, tearing her gown open and pulling her down on the floor.

She screamed and clawed at his face, raking her nails across his cheek. Eduardo jerked back, his hand coming up to the harsh red streaks. Shocked at what she'd done, she pulled herself shakily onto her knees, her face wet with tears.

"You worthless bitch!" he said, standing over her, angered by her weakness and the scratches on his face. He slapped her with a resounding crack, knocking her to the floor.

Elena no longer cried, just lay there, eyes cold and lips drawn tight, watching him as he struggled to undress, barely able to pull his boots from his feet. She knew what was coming and she steeled herself, dreading the intrusion into her body, the humiliation she always felt. Instead, Eduardo fell back across the bed. His eyes slid closed and his arms hung down limply as he passed out.

The taste of blood in her mouth sent a jolt of anger through Elena. And made her determined to get away.

Dressing quickly in her riding clothes, she slipped out of the house and raced to the barn. She grabbed one of the vaquero's saddles, leaving her sidesaddle at rest, quickly saddled her mare, mounted, and rode away.

Home. Home to Toro Bravo. Home to her family.

19

ELENA RODE MOST of the night, too angry to feel the cold. By the time she arrived at Toro Bravo, tired and frightened by the long, dark, lonely trail, her temper had cooled and some of her reason returned.

Perhaps he had reason to be angry. He had drunk too much brandy, and had not been to her bed for some time. Maybe she'd acted impulsively. It was the first time he had ever struck her. And she had scratched him badly.

She was too tired to think about it now. She would sleep on it. Things would be clearer in the morning.

Reining her mare up in front of the barn, she loosened the horsehair cincha and dropped the saddle to the ground. Soon she was in her old bed, beneath the colorful quilt Mamacita had fashioned for her when she was a little girl, fast asleep without disturbing anyone.

She slept till well past noon, then awoke to voices on the patio outside her door.

"I appreciate the offer, Don Pedro, but I must return to my valley. I have much to do."

"I am glad you told me about the first mate... about what really happened."

"I've told you the truth, Don Pedro."

"I believe you, hijo."

"Then if you'd be kind enough to write the letter I've asked for, I'll be on my way. In the meantime I'll be more than happy to explore your problems with the still. They sound like they're easily resolved."

She recognized the voice of course. She had thought about Buck Mueller a great deal. More than was proper, and in a very improper manner. What was he doing back? He knew Captain Taylor-Johnson wanted him returned to the ship. It was not safe for him here. Walking to the window, she peered through the crack between the shutters, searching until she could see him.

He had changed since the last time she had seen him. He was taller and much broader in the shoulders than she remembered. But it was more than that. He moved like an Indian—no, more like a cougar. The scar on his face was no longer purple. It was only a fine white line now and did not distract from his good looks.

Again, she pictured him bathing in the creek. She blushed at the thought, turned from the window, and began to dress. She was disappointed to find him gone from the patio when she came out. She walked to the dining room where her father and mother sat drinking thick black coffee.

"Elena! What are you doing here? Where is Eduardo? Is he also here?" Her father's questions flew at her.

"No, Papa. Eduardo is at home. I rode in last night, alone. We argued. I was very angry... but it is over now, I think. May I take coffee with you?"

"Of course, mi hija, sit. Juanita," he ordered an Indian serving woman, "fetch my daughter some coffee. And bring her something to eat."

"Where is Mamacita?" Elena asked, needing the old woman's counsel.

"She is out at the vats... with Señor Mueller, you remember Señor Mueller. He rode in this morning. He is helping her with some problems with the still."

Mamacita walked about the vats and the still Buck had

built two years back, firing questions at him. He had explained to her and to Don Pedro what had happened aboard the ship and the fight he and Tacker had waged on the cliff. Apparently they believed him and were content to let the matter rest, feeling it was Yanqui business.

Mamacita rapped the barrel with her cane. "Buckito, we cannot get it clear, like the Spanish brandy. I cannot discover what it is we are doing wrong."

"Have you tried to filter it?" he asked. "As you fill the jars, run it through a piece of cloth, or charcoal maybe... or clean sand. Cloth would be the simplest. Get a piece of silk as tightly woven as you can find, and layer it a few times."

"I will do as you say." Nodding her agreement, she turned and made her way back to the house. When she returned, Elena was with her.

Buck took a step backward, his hands dropping to his sides as he stared. His stomach knotted and his hands felt clammy. It was ridiculous for him to react so strongly, but he couldn't seem to stop himself. Perhaps if he'd been prepared... but he had no idea she was at Toro Bravo.

Elena nodded politely. "Señor Mueller, it is nice to see you again."

At least she didn't hate him for his appearance at her wedding. "It's good to see you, too... Señora Juarez." The words nearly stuck in his throat. He managed to nod his head and finally turned back to the still.

He opened the big cask and pretended to investigate the leather coil he'd made, but his mind raced. He wished she didn't affect him so. What a fool he could be! His initial shock and surprise turned to anger. Why should he react this way? He owed her nothing. He could feel the heat on the back of his neck... and in his groin.

Elena and Mamacita strolled about the still as the old woman explained the problem to her raven-haired grand-daughter, and Buck's proposed solution. Occasionally, from beneath her thick black lashes, Elena flashed her eyes at him. He pretended not to notice, to concentrate on the still, but found it impossible. She watched him with a hint of amusement, impishly aware of his discomfort.

Finally, a combination of pride and anger forced him to return her slightly too-bold gaze. He started to inquire about her marriage when Mamacita interrupted.

"I was just telling Elena, Buckito, how you suggested we construct another vat in the ground to hold the finished brandy... so we do not have to watch the jugs continually as they fill. We can distill day and night that way." She smiled, showing her aged yellow teeth. "Our brandy is as good as the Spanish," she told Elena, "just not as clear."

"Better, I think," Buck agreed. "It has an interesting flavor, maybe from the leather coils. I'm sure the Spanish use copper, but your grandmother and I didn't have any so we had to make do."

Elena looked pleased. Buck rightly guessed it was seldom that anyone took an interest in her grandmother, besides herself.

Mamacita looked down at her grandchild. It was obvious that something was troubling her. She could see it in her pretty black eyes. The girl was deeply hurt. Men! God help the poor imbeciles. Elena was so young, not so hard to handle. Why were men so clumsy? She had feared from the beginning it would go badly with Eduardo. He was so much older, and she had always thought him somewhat the serpent. And his mind strayed to many things other than a young and tender wife.

She turned to Buck. "My granddaughter loves to ride and I am too old to accompany her. Perhaps you will grant me a favor and watch over her?"

"I hadn't planned to ride—" Elena started to object, but Buck interrupted.

"I would be more than pleased to escort her, Mamacita. A ride before dinner would be nice." He offered her his arm. Elena hesitated, casting a strange glance at her grandmother, amazed the old woman would allow them to be alone, then she took his arm and together they walked to the barn.

Mamacita watched them go. A ride would do her good. Exposure to a young man—a man closer to her own age— would do her good. It was improper for her to be with a man without her, a proper duena along, but the devil with propriety, if it would do her good. The admiration of a handsome young man does any woman good, even one as old as I, Mamacita thought, then smiled to herself. The don and her mother will not approve, but then maybe they will not find out. She chuckled to herself as she strolled back to the hacienda.

Buck quickly saddled Elena's mare and the big blue roan, afraid that the moment, the opportunity to talk to Elena would be spoiled by some interruption. They rode without speaking through the vineyard and up the hill beyond the creek. After almost half an hour, she finally broke the silence.

"I heard you speaking with my father this morning. You spoke of a valley. I was surprised you were still in Alta California."

Buck smiled. "I've found the most beautiful, most bountiful piece of land anyone has ever seen." His eyes shown warm at the thought of Bear Valley. Then he furrowed his brow. "I wasn't so anxious to leave California as it may have appeared to you... as Captain Taylor-Johnson would have you think."

He clamped his jaw, remembering the hours he'd cursed himself for not settling his grudge with Taylor-Johnson the last time he had seen him. "I didn't run from those men. I obliged your wishes. I'd never run from trouble... not unless I had to." He could feel the heat burning into his neck. "I'm sorry I didn't settle my grudge with the captain right there."

Her eyes turned toward him. "I was about to thank you for your consideration... prematurely, I guess."

Now he felt the fool. Maybe she did realize he wasn't

running. "I didn't mean that... I didn't want to spoil your day... not on purpose, anyway. I should have waited for him, after your... your fiesta." He had trouble with the word wedding.

She smiled. "Good. Then I do thank you. But I still think you are a scoundrel!" She laughed and spun her horse back toward the barn. She quirted the mare as she spoke over her shoulder. "For the place that you hid from the captain—and for the bite!"

They raced to the barn, laughing, and riding hard. Buck was surprised when he was barely able to beat her, having to spur Diablo the last few yards. They jumped down from the horses smiling, and walked side by side into the house.

With the don away for the evening, he ate a lonely supper, relegated again to the cocina out back and the company of the vaqueros.

As dawn broke, he took advantage of the small writing desk in his room, composing a short letter to his mother and a very long and detailed one to Governor Echeandia.

That afternoon, as he directed the Indians in the construction of the collecting vat, he saw Elena make her way to the barn. He quickly instructed the Indians in completing their task, then followed. He reached the barn just as she was riding out.

"Do you return home?" he asked apprehensively.

"No, a short ride... up the creek and over those hills." She pointed. "A ride I used to take often. I circle around and follow a little creek... where I first met an impudent marinero." She smiled and reined the mare away.

He watched her ride out of sight, wondering if her directions had been purposefully detailed so he could find her if he followed. He worked with the Indians for another half hour but could stand it no longer. Grabbing a bottle of Mamacita's brandy, he made for the barn and rode out in the direction from which she said she would return.

In less than an hour's ride, he came upon the pond. Still he had not seen her. He was dirty from his work at the vat.

If she had taken the route she said, it would still be another hour before she came along. He wanted to be clean if he saw her, so he quickly stripped off his buckskins and stepped into the cold spring water.

Above him, Elena sat on the hillside overlooking the pond. She hadn't ridden the way she said, but had come directly to the pond. She sensed he would come here, sooner or later. She'd waited only a short time, picking the first of the spring wild flowers and entwining them in her hair. Finally, from the shade of a grove of buckeye, she watched the blue roan pick his way down to the water.

She didn't know why Buck intrigued her so. It was not proper for her to be here waiting for him, but she had come anyway. She enjoyed talking with him, what little time they found to talk. Maybe that was it, he talked to her, not at her as Eduardo and her father did. And they laughed together. She rarely laughed anymore.

Now as he undressed, she felt a twinge of guilt, realizing just how improper it was. But she did not turn away. He moved like a graceful animal, without wasted motion, his limbs supple and ridged with muscle. It was only moments before he slipped into the pond. Only then did she turn and mount the little mare. She didn't know what she wanted from him, only that she wanted him near.

As she rode up he was vigorously scrubbing the dirt from his hair. "Looking for your boat?" she asked.

She startled him. Buck smiled. It was seldom he could be approached in the woods without his hearing. Not now. He must have been preoccupied.

"You have a talent for catching a man in his bath."

"A marinero should not be difficult to catch. I would think the mountain man, the hombre de la montana, you have become, would be impossible."

A least this time she saw him as a man. "I have a bottle of Mamacita's brandy in that roll behind my saddle. If you'll fetch it, I can climb out of this pond."

He boldly started out, not giving her a chance to answer.

She even more boldly watched until the water reached his waist, then turning quickly, she went to the roan and pulled the bottle from behind his saddle.

"Can I... are you dressed?"

"Enough." He had pulled on his buckskin breeches.

She turned, hesitating at his immodesty, then approached and sat on a rock near the creek, handing him the brandy. He pulled the cork with his teeth and handed it back to her. "I'm sorry there's no glass. I should have thought. Will you be able to...?"

She laughed at his uncertainty. "If you can sit there, bare-chested like an Indian, I can drink from this bottle... but do not tell my papa. He would not approve... of the brandy... or my being here."

She had sipped brandy only once before. Women were allowed wine at supper but brandy was saved for the men. She turned the bottle up, took a drink, then coughed as the hot liquid ran down her throat. She handed it back to him. He grinned then took a long draw on the bottle and set it between them.

She broke the silence. "Tell me more of your valley."

He smiled. "Well, it's not my valley yet, only by right of possession." Once he got started, he continued for thirty minutes, his description almost complete, only Lali and little Tucker were left out.

Finally she said, "I have heard much of your trouble with Captain Taylor-Johnson, much from him, I mean. He says you were responsible for the death of his first mate... that you murdered him."

The heat burned into his face. "Captain Taylor-Johnson and his first mate were responsible for the death of my cousin." He stopped for a moment, clamping down on his temper, working to regain his composure. He wanted this to be right, for her to understand. He carefully explained what it was like on board the Virginia and what they had done to Ernst.

"I was responsible for the first mate's death. He came at

me with a bullwhip. I'd been whipped before." He turned and she winced at the crisscrossed scars on his back, faded now but still visible. "The first time I was tied to the mast. The second time he tried I wasn't. We fought and I won. I didn't mean for him to pay with his life, but he did. And he deserved it."

He waited for a reaction from her, but she had none or kept it hidden, so he continued. "It isn't over between Taylor-Johnson and me. He was the man who ordered the keel-hauling that caused my cousin's death. Someday we'll meet again."

Elena shuddered. "You frighten me when you talk that way. When you laugh you sound light-hearted, but too quickly you become serious. There is hate, the fire of hell, in your eyes when you speak of Taylor-Johnson."

He purposely ignored her comment, knowing it was all too true. He changed the subject. "Have you been north of Pueblo de Los Angeles?"

"No, only the padres and the mission guards have gone there, looking for souls to save or runaway Indians, or for Indians who have come over the mountains to steal our stock."

As they talked, the contents of the bottle disappeared.

When he leaned over to lift it again, they were within inches of touching. Her look softened, and in that moment he knew she was remembering a past kiss, one she should have slapped him for.

Quickly she rose. "It is getting late... I must be going back." More than a little drunk, she missed the saddle horn and stumbled back.

Buck pulled on his knee-high moccasins and stood to help her mount, carefully taking her arm. They both stopped dead still at the contact. Elena turned to face him, leaned forward and wrapped her arms around his neck. He wrapped his around her waist and pulled her against him, his mouth coming down over hers. He kissed her gently.

The kiss was enough, an end in itself, yet almost without

awareness he lifted her into his arms and carried her to the cool spring grass on the bank of the pond. They lay side by side, his kisses tender yet possessive. Tenderness soon turned to need, need to hot desire.

He unbuttoned her blouse and unfastened the tabs that closed up her split leather riding skirt, Elena's fingers digging into his hair. Kissing her all the while, he stripped the skirt away and opened the front of his breeches. Elena gasped one small "no" as he entered her, then was lost to her passion, trapping him with her long, smooth legs and pulling him deeply inside her.

Deeper than he ever would have imagined. She cried out as he moved, a soft animal sound she couldn't contain. Her stomach quivered and heat flooded her loins. A heat so intense that she almost pushed him away, but the thought of the emptiness that would follow made her cling to him instead.

They were alone, the center of the universe. Nothing else mattered. For him, for the first time, emotional fulfillment exceeded physical desire. For her, for the first time, there was physical fulfillment. They lost track of time and place and purpose. All that existed for each was the other. At last they were one.

Elena lay beside him, sated, amazed to be there, but more amazed at what had happened to her. She had no idea she could feel the way she did. It thrilled her and it and terrified her. Finally, reluctantly, she eased herself away from him.

"We must... I must get back," she stammered. Rising slowly, she held her skirt in front of her, embarrassed by her nakedness, waiting for him to turn. He did not. Instead he seemed to devour her with his eyes.

"Elena..." he whispered, but she pressed her fingers against his lips to still his next words. Dressing quickly, she mounted the mare, gave him a last sad glance, and reined away toward the hacienda.

"You belong to me," he called after her. "One day you'll

be mine." She reined the horse to a standstill and looked back at him, longingly, he thought. Then she spurred the horse into a gallop.

Buck watched her ride away. There was so much he wanted to say to her. He knew she was upset, unhappy about what they had done. That was the last thing he had intended. It wasn't right that she had just ridden away. They should have laughed together again.

He sat flipping stones into the little pool, watching the ripples, thinking. Pulling the little black rock from his pocket, he flipped it up and caught it several times, trying to reconstruct the last two hours.

Was it the brandy or the intensity of the moment that blocked his memory?

He yearned for total recall.

And he wished he could forget.

BUCK WALKED the roan all the way back to the hacienda. When he entered the big carved front door, Don Pedro met him. "It is late. You missed your supper, but do not worry. They have something outside in the cocina for you. How was your ride?"

Did he know? Buck thought he was at least suspicious. Surely Elena would not have spoken of their meeting. If she had, and of its consequence, there would have been a vaquero lynching party waiting.

"It was fine, thanks. I rode half way to San Juan before I realized the time. Inspecting your fine cattle. You must tell me how you cull the herds so I can do as well as you have."

"You will be on your way tomorrow?" The don looked embarrassed at the question. "I have finished your letter to the governor. I have some brandy casks for you... if you are planning to leave."

"Yes, early I think."

The don had retired for the evening by the time Buck

returned from the kitchen. He stood for a moment outside his room, looking down the hall at Elena's door. He had to fight to control the urge to fling the door open and take her again right there in her bed. Instead he entered his room and wearily pulled off his clothes. It was a long time before he fell asleep.

She wasn't at the table the next morning.

Buck ate quickly, explaining to Mamacita that he had to return to his valley if he was going to get his wheat in the ground in time to make a crop this year.

Sanchez and Tui sat around an open fire with a group of vaqueros, most of whom Buck had met.

"You fellows ready to ride?" he called out as he walked to the barn. "There are some casks of Mamacita's good brandy to load... then we're off."

Sanchez and Tui jumped to their feet and headed toward the barn. A tall angular-faced vaquero, one Buck didn't know, followed a few steps behind. As they saddled their horses, the man stood watching a few steps away.

Sanchez finally noticed him. "Buck, this is Señor Montes, Santos Montes. He rides for Don Eduardo Juarez."

Buck nodded. When the tall vaquero acknowledged neither the introduction nor the nod, the hair on the back of Buck's neck bristled. Taking a long, hard look at the man, he decided he wasn't one he would turn his back on. He returned his attention to the task of leaving.

The don had eight five-gallon casks of brandy set aside. It would take four pack horses to carry the load. He would trade off six casks in Pueblo Los Angeles and take two home with him. One to enjoy and one to take to Monterey as a gift for the governor.

While he packed, he watched for Elena. He thought he could see her outline behind the shutters of her room, but she never appeared, not even as he rode away. Only Mamacita was there to wave goodbye—except for the tall vaquero, who stood watching silently from the shadows.

20

FIVE DAYS LATER, three exhausted riders leading a string of pack horses and driving twenty head of wild cattle they had collected in the hills north of Pueblo de Los Angeles crested the rise east of the pass Buck had named Sycamore Canyon. The packs were loaded with casks, utensils and supplies, and four fat squirming piglets.

Buck put the roan into a canter the last half mile, leaving the men, pack animals, and squealing piglets behind. Lali ran from the cabin to meet him. He swept her—little Tucker strapped to her chest—up into his arms and swung them around.

That night he had a twinge of guilt as he lay with his wife for the first time in well over a month. It was not so much that he had been with Elena, but that he thought of her at that particular time.

For the next two weeks he worked side by side with the Indians from Lali's village, planting the corn and wheat seed for which he had traded some of his brandy. The corn would benefit from the irrigation system he had built. The wheat should catch the last of the spring rains. A two-foot piece of iron would become a plow, when he had time to build it, and the ground would be properly prepared before the next spring sowing.

The rains came just as he finished seeding. He rubbed the little tusuat in his pocket.

For a week after the rains, he waited for the fields to dry out, eager to use the ditch system he had constructed and bring the water to the fields. It was a little early to irrigate, but he was eager to test the system.

He was engrossed in the job of clearing a ditch when the bear came.

The huge old boar silvertip had dug his den high on the mountain when the first snow came. He'd been fat with grubs and ground squirrels when he entered the little cave. Now his ribs showed.

The first day out he'd managed a few berries and rose hips. One fat field mouse scampered from under a rotted log, and a surprisingly fast paw spatted the little rodent before it made its escape, but the morsel only teased his appetite for meat.

Now he lumbered down the hillside above the cabin and lay beneath a manzanita, listening to the wounded sound of a baby's cry and salivating at the promise of more than a morsel. He snorted and cleared his nose, then carefully tested the scent that wafted to him.

A hundred yards up the hillside from where the keening sound originated, his eleven-hundred-pound bulk was almost indiscernible in the shadowed clump of bushes. Snorting again, he blew the smoke smell from his nostrils. The snort and the flicking of an ear at springtime gnats were the only sounds or movements he allowed himself for the twenty minutes he watched and listened and tested the air. His little pig eyes were of much less value than his nose and ears. The nose told him to leave this place that smelled of fire, but his ears, and the wounded wail, won his resolve.

He rose to all fours and began his descent.

Earlier in the morning, he'd made a quick downhill dash at a deer and found that downhill was not a profitable route of attack. His longer hind legs raised his center of gravity, and his bulk overcame his strength. He had rolled head over heels.

He'd lost the deer, and his dignity. This time he picked his way carefully from manzanita to scrub oak, saliva dripping from his teeth as he anticipated the kill.

A SCREAM from one of the Indian women echoed across the valley, chilling Buck to the core.

"Lali!" he cried. Spinning on his heel, he ran for the cabin.

Cooking berries, the baby in his crib until she finished, Lali heard the scream and hurried to the door of the cabin. She threw it open the same instant as the huge bear reached it, and he plunged in, sending dust, bark, and splinters flying into the room as his massive shoulders wedged in the jamb, his snapping jaws so close she whiffed his hot foul breath and was sprayed with his spittle. His massive, razor-tipped forefeet clawed at her and she screamed.

Reeling backward, trembling with terror, she grabbed the boiling berry pot and flung it into the huge beast's snarling face. The bear backed out the door, bellowing with pain and anger, rising on his hind legs to his full ten-foot height and swiping at the boiling, sticky liquid with his paws.

Lali slammed the door and ran for the baby, crying in his crib. The bear cleared his vision, charged, and splintered the door as if it were paper, again wedging himself in the narrow opening. He backed out, frustrated and growling in pain and rage. Then he readied himself to charge again.

Buck covered the eighty yards to the cabin in a sprint, seeing the bear and praying Lali and the baby had not been hurt. Using the only weapon at hand, he two-handed the shovel high over his head and brought it down hard across the grizzly's massive shoulders.

It did little more than distract him, but that was enough. The bear spun on him, and away from Lali and little Tucker. Buck dashed around the corner of the cabin, the sound of the massive animal snarling at his heels encouraging his flight.

The cabin was partially dug into the mountain. Buck reached its uphill rear side just ahead of the huge grizzly. He leaped onto the sod roof, only three feet above the ground, and raced across it. He feared leading the bear back to Lali and the baby, but his musket was his only chance—and it was inside.

The bear took the three-foot rise in stride and gained a few precious steps. Slapping out with its curved, razor-sharp foreclaws, he buried them deep in Buck's hip. Buck hissed out in pain as the big bear tried to drag him back, but the animal's hind legs crashed through the sod roof between the closely spaced lodgepole pine rafters. The grizzly roared his surprise and fury, and Buck spun away, freeing himself from the animal's claws and throwing himself off the roof to the ground in front of the door.

He landed flat on his back, knocking the air from his lungs, dragged in a couple of breaths, then scrambled to his feet. Gasping, he raced for his musket, but ran smack into Lali, sending her and the baby sprawling into the corner. She was running out of the cabin, sure the bear, whose hind legs clawed the air above her, was tearing his way into her home through the roof.

"Stay inside!" he commanded, grabbing his musket and checking the load. Buck stepped back outside and raised the big bore gun, always primed and loaded, and aimed at the bear just as the furious animal pulled himself free and prepared to leap off the roof. The grizzly towered on his hindquarters on the edge of the cabin roof high over Buck's head, roaring and raising its deadly paws as the musket roared and spit flame.

Buck's single shot took the bear beneath the chin, the big

fifty caliber lead ball exploding on the inside of the grizzly's skull. He staggered back, then forward, flailing his claws, snarling, and slinging blood and spittle, then he tumbled forward.

Buck tried to get out of the way, but his wounded hip gave out beneath him and he fell. The bear crashed to earth, his eleven-hundred-pound weight crushing Buck beneath him. Buck, sure he was going to die, gasped for breath, he struggled for a second or two beneath his suffocating load, then blackness took the pain away.

Lali screamed at the sight of her husband, crushed beneath the weight of the huge grizzly bear. Escaping out the cabin's single window, the baby wrapped in a deerskin, she ran to where some of the Indian women had gathered and handed the baby to one of them. She shouted at the others to get the horses from the corral, then ran to where Buck lay, unmoving, under his crushing burden.

Checking to be sure the bear was dead, she picked up the shovel and smashed it across the animal's shoulders. It didn't flinch. Tying reatas to the bear's heavy legs, the women fought to calm the bolting, rearing horses. Finally, they got a turn of the ropes around the horses' necks. It took little encouragement to get them to pull away from the bear. The giant beast rolled off a deathly-quiet, blood-covered Buck.

With hands that shook, Lali wiped the blood away to discover most of it was the bear's. Buck's eyes fluttered open and she fell across him, hugging him to her.

"Easy... easy," he mumbled, "that last hug popped a few ribs." He looked over at the mound of meat and fur beside him. "You set the men to skinnin' old griz." He coughed and a jolt of pain seared through him. "He'll make a fine rug... for Tucker to play on." He smiled, winced, then passed out again.

ALFONSO VALDES, personal secretary to Governor Echeandia, added a few sticks to the iron stove in the cocina of the governor's casa. He was honored to serve the great man.

As soon as the water boiled, he brewed a pot of tea and strolled in to the study where Echeandia sat, his desk cluttered with a variety of official papers and maps.

Echeandia contemplated the letter in front of him. It was from Father Zalvidea, a man he had met many times. He knew him to be prudent, a man not prone to exaggeration. And even though he knew that as Governor of Alta California he was at the bottom of Zalvidea's list, the priest would not lie. He spoke highly of this young Boston man, Buck Mueller. The same man William Taylor-Johnson, his Anglo business partner, had accused of murder and desertion.

The governor knew if he granted a rancho to this Boston man, an accused murderer, his partner would be very unhappy—angry, in fact.

But it might have a greater advantage. It would establish the fact that he truly did want the Indians to own their own land—since this man's wife was a Yokuts. And the land was far from the sea and would have little value, if any, to Mexican Californios. Besides, he could tell his partner that he did it to keep the Boston man here so he would not be out of his reach, if it became necessary to tell him anything at all.

He did not want any problems with Captain Taylor-Johnson, but the captain had left to carry his cargo to Boston and would not return for the better part of a year. With luck, he would return with three or four brigs on the strength of his exclusive right to trade for California hides.

Echeandia knew he should ask Don Eduardo Juarez his opinion of Mueller, but he had already received a letter from Don Eduardo's father-in-law, Don Pedro Seville. The letter extolled Mueller's virtues, particularly his knowledge of grapes and brandy. Fine brandy-making could be a whole new industry for California, and a new source of taxes for his coffers in Monterey. That alone would be worth the wrath of Taylor-Johnson.

The governor sat back and sipped his tea, satisfied with the way things were going so far. In two years, when the hide profits began to flow in, he would be a very rich man. All his years spent gaining favor in Mexico City would pay off at last.

He decided he would concede Mueller's wish for the worthless grant, but not before he got his pound of flesh and made certain the man knew he was deeply in the governor's debt.

Politics was, after all, politics.

BEING FORCED to stay in bed gave Buck time to think. The incident with the bear made him realize how much he really cared for Lali and little Tucker. Lali left the baby in bed with Buck as she tended her chores, and he played with his son by the hour. The boy slept in the crook of his arm. For the first time, he began to truly realize what it meant to be a father.

He also thought a great deal about his meeting with Elena. It had been an experience so intense it seemed almost unreal. Now, here with his son and his wife, he was able to look at it more objectively. He put his incredibly powerful reaction off to his waiting, his long anticipation, the culmination of the dreams and desires of months spent thinking of her while he was alone on the trail—and to the attraction of her striking beauty. It had all come together in that one act of passion.

She was forbidden fruit.

It couldn't possibly have been as exciting and fulfilling as he remembered it. He would put her out of his mind. She was married and had a life of her own, and so did he.

Maybe he had all he needed to truly balance his life was right here in Bear Valley.

It took two weeks for him to be up and on his feet. The bear had done no lasting damage, but his broken ribs and bruised body took time to recover.

The corn was up, the late spring sun working its wonders. Still, it would be some months before he'd be able to make his trip through the great central valley to Monterey. He was becoming impatient as he watched his crops begin to appear.

He wanted this valley to be his.

KATHLEEN MCCREED MUELLER was turned away at the gangplank of the brig Virginia less than an hour after the ship docked.

She was less than politely informed the captain was too busy to see her and would be too busy for several days. Undaunted, she parked herself in the offices of Bryant and Sturgis, offices she had visited dozens of times over the last three years.

Her vigilance paid off the next day. As she sat quietly tatting, the large oak outer door swung wide and a tall blond man Nattily dressed in a split tail coat, white stock and ruffled shirt approached the clerk at the reception desk.

"Captain Taylor-Johnson—it's good to see you safely returned, sir. I'll let Mr. Sturgis know you're here." The clerk almost ran to an inner office door.

"Captain, may I have a word with you?" Kathleen rose to her feet immediately. "My son sailed with you on your last voyage."

The captain turned to face the handsome woman who spoke to him. She was middle-aged, but very attractive. Silver streaks accented long black hair that curled well below her shoulders. Intelligent gray eyes met his with confidence.

He nodded and smiled a greeting as he approached. "How may I be of service, madam?"

"I'm Kathleen McCreed Mueller. My son Sam sailed with you to California."

The captain's blue eyes hardened, and he stopped short. "If your son is the one who calls himself Buck, then madam, he is a murderer and a deserter. He was responsible for his cousin's death, and the death of my first mate."

"My son wouldn't do—"

"I shall not debate the matter! You were not privileged to be there. A full report on the facts will be filed with the company. They have been carefully recorded here in my log." He patted the leather-covered book he carried. "I suggest you take the matter up with the owners." Spinning away from her, he disappeared through the inner door.

Kathleen waited a moment, reining in her temper. The frustration of years without seeing her son, of not knowing all the facts about what had happened, almost motivated her to follow him and demand an explanation. But she had waited this long; she guessed she could wait another day or so. Turning, she walked through the familiar front door and headed for her cottage—still unsatisfied, frustrated, and unhappy.

WILHELM MUELLER also knew of the brig's return. He had been in constant contact with Bryant & Sturgis and had left a letter in their offices for Captain Taylor-Johnson, requesting the captain call on him as soon as convenient after his arrival.

Wilhelm was more than anxious for a meeting with the captain. He was confident his suspicions regarding Sam's involvement in his son's death would be confirmed. He knew his feelings toward Kathleen and her son would be justified by the captain. The real facts of Ernst's death would finally be known.

On the third day after the brig's arrival, the brass knocker on the doctor's door rapped loudly. Wilhelm answered it himself.

The tall blond man apprehensively extended his hand. "I'm Captain Taylor-Johnson. You requested I call?"

Wilhelm shook his hand. "Come into the kitchen if you don't mind." Wilhelm politely stood aside and let the captain pass. "We can speak more privately there, and have a cup of tea... if you have time, sir."

"Just barely, I'm afraid, Doctor. We're still off-loading the Virginia and my presence there is necessary. I would not be here except that I understand your concern, and feel you deserve a detailed report."

Wilhelm brewed the tea and passed the first few moments inquiring as to the voyage. When the tea was made, he sat down opposite the captain.

"Now, sir, tell me the circumstances of my son's dea... of what happened. Please, leave nothing out."

"Of course. You're aware that I attribute the responsibility to your nephew, Buck... or Sam... which is it?"

"Samuel... my step-nephew."

"Samuel, then. As you may or may not know, he stowed away onboard the Virginia. We didn't discover his presence until we were well underway, or we would, of course, have returned him."

The captain went on to explain that Sam had instigated a fight which resulted in wounding one of the crew members, and that Ernst, in the heat of the battle, had been knocked overboard while trying to help his cousin. His resulting recuperation was complicated by a lung problem. A natural death, but one that would not have come about had Sam not been a continual "trouble maker," a "sogger," the captain said. He fortified the description by relating the murder of his first mate.

"Just as I suspected." Wilhelm shook his head. "Of course you're aware the boy is not a Mueller, not by blood. He's not even a full-blooded German... half Irish on his mother's

243

side, and a papist by inclination. Although his mother forsook that faith... affairs of the flesh were more important to her."

"The Irish have always been the bane of the English," the captain said. "Had I known that, I probably would have put him ashore at the first port." Taylor-Johnson rose and started for the door. "I hope I've been of some help, Doctor."

"Would you say that Ernst did well, while he served? Was he a good seaman?"

"Excellent. One of the best." The captain smiled to himself. There was no use in antagonizing the good doctor. Mueller was a powerful man in Boston. "In fact, I commended your son in my reports to the company." The doctor followed him to the front door. "I'm sorry I haven't more to tell you. Thank you for the tea." The men shook hands.

"And thank you, Captain, so very much.... I can rest easier now. I appreciate all the kindness you showed my son. And I'm terribly sorry... ashamed, that my step-nephew burdened you so. Please accept my apologies. If there is anything I can do...."

"Nothing, sir. Thank you again for the tea." The captain turned and once more started to leave.

"Captain, he did have a Christian burial? I know it was at sea, but you did read over him?"

"There was no priest, no one to say the last rites, but we did our best."

Wilhelm was confused. "No priest? Ernst was not a papist. He was a Lutheran, a good German Lutheran!"

The captain stopped short and turned. "And his cousin, Buck or Samuel... he is a Lutheran also?"

"Of course. As I said, his mother forsook her papist ways. My brother would have raised him no other way. He was baptized in the church just down the street."

"Thank you, Doctor. It has been a pleasure, a real pleasure meeting you." The captain left the stately brownstone, thinking the meeting could have been worse. Much worse. He wondered if the priest, Zalvidea, would continue to hide the deserter, as Taylor-Johnson was sure he had, if he knew he wasn't a papist.

21

BUCK SENSED SANCHEZ'S RESTLESSNESS.

As he had promised, the old vaquero had trained the desert mare to perfection—Lali would have a trustworthy mount. But he longed for the mission and the company of other vaqueros.

The corn was high and drying in the fields, the wheat had made a fine stand and was now only stubble. Buck was glad Sanchez was ready to return to the mission and Pueblo de Los Angeles. There were a number of things he needed, and Sanchez could bring them when he returned.

More content than the vaquero, Tui would remain behind with Lali and Tucker, while Buck set off for Monterey. His friend had settled in with a fine fat Indian girl from Lali's tribe. She was a pleasant happy girl, broad in shoulder and hip, a fitting match for the huge, ever-smiling kanaka.

On the same day Sanchez rode out for the mission, Buck took a little-known route north to the capital at Monterey. He gave Lali a big hug, gave little Tucker a kiss, told Tui to guard them with his life, then accompanied Sanchez as far as the west end of Sycamore Canyon, where they parted.

ELENA SAT in front of the mirror over her dressing table, thinking of the day, months back, she had spent with Buck at Toro Bravo. She had watched him ride away, then spent a confused hour alone in her room, ashamed and embarrassed by what she had done. She had never intended, never even considered that her meeting with Buck would end as it had. Her memories were torn between shame at what she had done, what she had allowed him to do, and her joy at the sensations he had awakened in her body, the feelings he stirred deep inside her.

Then Santo Montes had come for her, telling her he had been sent to escort her home, and she'd decided that what had happened did not matter. Her feelings for Buck did not matter. She was going back where she belonged, to live the life she was meant to live. Her future remained at Rancho Riena de Californio.

Somehow she knew Buck would never speak of what happened between them, would never do anything that would harm her in any way.

Surprisingly, Eduardo did not come to her bed for over two months after her return. He had been insulted and shamed by her actions, by the scratches she had left on his face. He was curt with her—when he spoke to her at all—then Elena discovered she was finally pregnant. When she told him, his attitude immediately changed.

Insisting she let her Indian women do her every bidding, he doted on her—in his own cold, non-affectionate way. And he did not return to her bed. He wanted nothing to risk the loss of the son he was certain she carried.

———

BUCK SAT on a small rise overlooking the most beautiful pueblo in California, Monterey. The red tile roofs of the whitewashed buildings stood out against the shimmering reflection of the sun on the blue Pacific. Cypress he had once admired from the sea reached out to him, flagged by the prevailing off-shore breezes.

The ride had taken eight days of hard traveling through the marshy Tulares Valley. He knew the route from San Pedro to Monterey over the choppy Pacific, but had to guess the distance overland.

It was mid-morning when he reined up in front of the Public House and walked boldly into Monterey's most imposing building, asking to see the governor. Unfortunately, Echeandia was unavailable.

He spent the rest of the morning walking around the little pueblo. Stopping at the wharf he visited with some kanakas who were loading casks of water into a longboat for delivery to a beautiful, low, rakish schooner lying a couple of cable lengths offshore. After Buck helped them load the casks, they invited him to visit the ship.

The topsail schooner, Moonsong, was well worth seeing. She was sixty-five feet in length with a seventeen-foot beam. Her cargo hold was ample and her masts were tall and made of the finest grained sitka spruce. She could carry a lot of sail.

For the first time, Buck realized he missed the sea. If it weren't for his love of the valley, and his wife and child, he felt he could have made a life on the sea. None of the horrible things that happened during the voyage of the Virginia dulled his deep feeling for the ocean. Most of it he could contribute directly to Taylor-Johnson or to Tacker. The rest was fate.

The sea, like the mountains, had a purity that could not be found in the city. A solemnity, and occasionally an intensity, a man either loved and revered, or hated and feared. Or both. He realized how much he missed it.

He helped the kanakas lower the casks into her holds then walked the deck. She was immaculately maintained. He was inspecting the worm gear in a box attached to the helm, when a deep voice startled him.

"Tis attached to a cable that is in turn attached to another wheel which controls the rudder."

Buck turned and extended his hand to the man. "Buck Mueller. Pardon me for taking the liberty of looking... but it's a bit different from the controls on the brig on which I sailed."

"Captain Josh Peckinpaugh." The man was in his fifties. Ashen-gray hair framed unblinking steel-gray eyes. Everything about him spoke of the sea, from his hemp-marked, reddened hands to a deep-creased, salted face. All testified to the work and weather the man had known.

He accepted Buck's callused hand. "And what brig might that be? Ye look Californio by the dress of ye."

Buck hesitated, assessing the weathered sea captain. Relying on instinct, he decided he had nothing to fear from him. "I'm off the Virginia, out of Bostontown."

"Aye, I know of her and the blackguard English bastard who minds her business, if ye don't mind me saying so."

Buck felt the seaman would have spoken his piece whether he minded or not. He smiled. "No, sir, I don't mind your saying so. If you had the better part of a day, I'd be happy to add a bit to your description of" —he grinned—" the bastard... but I would rather speak of your ship... and a beauty she is."

After an hour of walking the deck, Peckinpaugh explaining the subtleties of the schooner's rigging and the many differences between it and a brig, Buck left with an invitation to return that night for supper.

On arriving on shore, he walked boldly back into the governor's office and again was told the governor was too busy to see him. Turning to leave, he paused.

"Would you be so kind as to see the governor gets this?" He handed the slight, nervous man the dog-eared letter that had written be for him months earlier. "It's a letter of introduction from Don Pedro Seville."

The lean man who was the governor's secretary studied

the wax-sealed missive then, in a perfunctory manner, instructed him, "Wait here."

Buck paced the floor nervously. A few moments later the secretary returned. "I have been instructed to set up an appointment for you." He rounded his desk and thumbed through a journal occupying the center of the desk. "Now let me see... here, this should be good... two weeks from today at ten in the morning—"

"Can't you make it sooner?" Buck asked. "I've come a damned long way."

"The governor is a very busy man. If the twentieth is not suitable, I can make it the end of the year. Say late December?"

"No, no... the twentieth at ten in the morning is fine, just fine. Thank you." Wishing he could squash the perfunctory little man, he forced himself to turn away. The man's manner was offensive and he couldn't help but notice the calendar had little on the pages for at least a week prior to the time of his appointment. Still, he nodded, crossed to the door, and discreetly left the office.

Two weeks to kill—not time enough to return to Bear Valley and back. He hoped soon it would officially be the Rancho of the Bears. Until then, he would find some way to pass the time. Tonight would be a start.

As he dined with Captain Peckinpaugh in his cabin aboard the schooner, he vented his frustrations. "I have to handle this thing carefully. There are too many reasons they can find not to grant me the land... so I reckon I wait."

"Why sit here and wait... and worry? We're bound for the Russian fort—Fort Ross. We'll return well before your appointment. I can use the extra hand, and ye'll find it interesting. The Russians have built a beautiful fort, the showplace of California."

"I would enjoy that, but I can't risk missing my appointment."

"We'll be back well before. It's a four-day run up, but only a day and a half back. Add a half day to unload our cargo of grain, and a day to load timber—you'll have days to spare. It'll keep ye out of the cantina, and with the weather turning, I could use the extra help."

Buck grinned, liking the idea.

They sailed on the morning tide—Buck, Captain Peckinpaugh, and three kanaka crewmen. The little hold was filled to the brim with golden wheat from the missions at San Jose and Monterey, and they left with a wind at their backs, always a good omen.

SANCHEZ WAS cold and tired when he reined up in front of Ernesto's cantina in Pueblo de Los Angeles, though his ride over the mountains from the big central valley had been uneventful. He loosened the cinches and headed for a cool mug of aguardiente.

The bartender dipped him a mug of wine from a large cask and passed it to him across the bar. "One real, señor."

A lone vaquero stood at the far end of the bar. He looked up as Sanchez was served.

"Hey, vaquero," Sanchez called out, "did we not meet at the hacienda of Don Pedro Seville?" It was Santos Montes, the Rancho Reina De Californio's head vaquero.

"Sí, amigo," Montes replied, coming over to the bar to join him. They talked and drank for some time. Even though they were men of very different personalities, they had many things in common. Both were fiercely independent men and both had a love of horses, more powerful than any love they might have for another man or even a woman.

The more they drank, the more they talked. They parted late that night and well into their cups. The next day Sanchez wondered what it was they had talked about.

Don Eduardo Juarez listened carefully to the angular-faced vaquero as they took café con leche together the next morning. He was fascinated the ex-marinero had found a valley that suited him. A valley he had begun to improve and plant. A California valley. He hoped the Boston sailor developed it well. It would be one more rancho to add to his list of acquisitions.

The one thing Montes did not tell his patron was the story of the marinero's trip to Santa Fe and the horses he had sold—and about the gold. A great deal of gold that must still be at the rancho the old vaquero had called "Rancho del Oso."

Elena waddled slowly to the barn. She spent a great deal of time these days with her little palomino mare. Eduardo insisted she remain quiet and sedate, allowing her to do nothing but sit and read, or walk about and supervise the Indians, nothing more. He paid less and less attention to her as her waistline grew and grew. He had not visited her alcoba since she first informed him she was with child.

He insisted she refrain from riding. Still she could curry her mare and get a little exercise that way. She bent over to pick up the comb and brush, and felt the wetness gush from between her legs making a small puddle among the straw on the barn floor. She was only a little frightened. Mamacita said her water might break soon. Now she would begin her labor.

Soon she would bring Eduardo the son he insisted she carried.

Before she could waddle back to the hacienda, the first pain hit her. She stood grasping her belly with her hands, waiting for the pain to subside, then she continued on to the house.

Mamacita met her at the door. The old woman had

come to Rancho Reina to be in attendance at the blessed event. Elena was glad she was there.

After twelve hours of hard labor, a baby's cry emerged from her alcoba. One of the Indian women ran from the room to Eduardo's study, pausing even then to knock before she burst in.

"It is a fine healthy girl, señor. A beautiful little girl." She stopped short, shocked at the look on the patron's gaunt face.

"A girl! Mother of Jesus! What good is a girl?" His scowl grew even blacker as he turned to face the window, clenching and unclenching the tightly balled fists at his sides.

22

STIFF BITING winds pulled the schooner Moonsong steadily along the beautiful coast—its pine covered, mist-kissed shores occasionally interrupted by sharp-shouldered granite cliffs that plunged fearlessly into foamy, heaving seas. Pounding waves that relentlessly battered away reached for the pines above.

The shallow-drafted schooner heeled nicely, even with its heavy load of wheat, as they tacked into the harbor well north of Yerba Buena, beneath Fort Ross.

The fort was a study in efficiency. The manner in which the Russians handled their affairs brought Buck an understanding of why Peckinpaugh was so sure he would make it back to Monterey in time for Buck to keep his appointment.

With the help of the brawny Russians, they offloaded the wheat and reloaded with timber in one day, hauled the anchor rode, and were back at sea on the evening tide. All along the way Peckinpaugh tempted Buck with tales of Russian Alaska and the riches that could be made smuggling furs—if they could avoid the Russian gunboats.

The coastal work Peckinpaugh did in Alta California, he informed Buck, was just to earn enough capital to make one good run through the islands off the Alaska coast. The shallow-drafted Moonsong was just the vessel for such an undertaking. The deep-keeled Russian gunboats couldn't follow her over the rocky shoals.

Peckinpaugh offered Buck a piece of the bounty if he would accompany him, but Buck was single-minded. Rancho del Oso was all he could think of.

They were well ahead of schedule and on their way home when Peckinpaugh decided to make a stop at Mission Delores in Yerba Buena. Buck didn't complain. He had heard much of its great harbor and many fine anchorages, and was not disappointed by what he saw there.

The stop was brief. They set sail again and made the wide Monterey bay the day before his scheduled meeting with the governor. Promptly at ten the next morning, the big oak door to the inner office swung open and the governor's secretary, the little man he had spoken to before, ushered him into Echeandia's office.

"You may be seated here." The secretary motioned to a chair across the desk from where the governor sat engrossed in paperwork. Buck sat down in the tufted leather chair and waited quietly while the man finished reading.

Finally, Echeandia, attired in a black broadcloth city coat, regal purple waistcoat, and ruffled shirt, looked up. He pulled small wire-rimmed glasses off his nose. "I have read of you, Señor Mueller. Father Zalvidea and Don Pedro Seville have both sent me letters highly praising your accomplishments."

Buck smiled. "I'm grateful to them, sir, I—"

"But you are in California without passport, illegally, even if you are extremely industrious...."

Buck's hands tightened on the arm of his chair.

"I also have heard a great deal about you from Captain Taylor-Johnson," the governor continued. "Unlike your friends, he does not exactly praise your actions."

"I can explain—"

"I hope that you can. You have a great deal of explaining to do and if you cannot do so to my satisfaction, I am afraid

I must have the guard hold you until Captain Taylor-Johnson or another representative of the Bryant and Sturgis shipping firm can escort you back to Boston for whatever fate the legal system of your country has in mind."

Echeandia's words slammed into Buck's ribs like the kick of a mule. This was not at all what he expected. He had come here to negotiate, to charm and cajole this man into granting him a piece of land. Now he found himself negotiating for his very freedom. His first impulse was to bolt for the double doors leading from the governor's office, but that would lead only to pursuit.

Not to the ownership of Rancho del Oso.

Instead, he sat in silence, calmly collecting himself. The governor waited, tapping a quill pen impatiently on the top of his huge oak desk.

"With your permission, Your Excellency," Buck finally said, "I'd like to tell the whole story. It will take some time, sir."

"I am here for the benefit of the citizens of Alta California, Señor Mueller, and for the administration of justice. You may tell your story."

Buck began with his Shanghaiing that night on the Boston docks, and left out nothing—with the exception of his not being Catholic. That fact would remain his secret. When he finished, the governor sat staring. Only the tapping of the pen interrupted the silence.

Finally he spoke. "I have found all conflicts have two sides, Señor Mueller. You have been highly recommended by one of our most respected priests as well as one of the most respected dons in California." He eased back his chair, got up, and began to pace, his hands clasped tightly behind his back. "It would be improper of me to accept the testimony of the Yankee sea captain, a heathen non-Catholic at that, with greater weight than that of my own constituents." He frowned at Buck. "Even though the captain is here by invitation and with proper passport."

Buck said nothing.

"Frankly it serves my purposes—and those of all Californios—to see our Native inhabitants share in the wealth of this great country. The church has exploited the labors of the Indians far too long."

Buck bit his tongue, stifling the urge to defend Zalvidea and the mission system. Now was certainly not the time to engage in that disagreement with the governor.

"And the grant you seek is in an area that none of my people are familiar with, an area far from any settlements. Please describe, in detail, why you feel it is worthy of development, and what it is that you propose for this... this Valley of the Bears."

Buck talked for the better part of half an hour without interruption from the governor, who read and shuffled papers while Buck extolled the virtues of Rancho del Oso.

Finally, Echeandia held up a hand, palm outward. "Stop! Enough. I am convinced, Señor Mueller."

Buck smiled and sighed in relief.

The governor rose from his desk and leaned forward. "Now, if I concede to this request of yours, there are a few things to which you must concede. First, you will ship all goods produced on this rancho through Monterey. Second, you will pay an export tax equal to twenty percent of all goods sold—"

"Is that normal?" Buck asked.

"Is it normal for a governor to grant land to a citizen of the United States, even if his wife is a citizen of Alta California? Is it normal for a grant to be given to an accused deserter and murderer?"

"I explained all that."

"These are my terms." The governor furrowed brows over deep set dark eyes. "If those terms are not satisfactory...."

"No, sir. I didn't mean to suggest... I was just curious if everyone—"

"You are not everyone, my friend."

"No, sir... of course not. Your terms are acceptable." Buck

was afraid he had almost taken a step backward—a huge step. From the newly appointed owner of a California rancho to a Monterey jail. He said no more.

"You may give your rancho's description to my secretary. He will prepare the grant." For the first time, the governor extended his hand. "I will have another agreement drawn also, an export agreement between you and Rancho del Oso, and the export agent of my choosing." The governor smiled for the first time.

It was obvious the "export agent" would be a company owned, or at least controlled, by the governor himself. But it was of no importance. Buck was going to receive his grant and twenty percent of what he exported would be little enough to pay for his beautiful valley.

That night he celebrated with Captain Peckinpaugh, this time at a cantina, where Buck could be the host. Early the next morning, slightly hung over from the many jugs of wine he had shared with his new friend, he picked up the grant to his rancho.

Seven days of hard, lathered riding and he was once more in sight of the huge hump-backed mountain. The familiar trees and trails of Sycamore Canyon comforted him as he clattered up the rocky trail into the lush little valley. Lali ran excitedly from the cabin to meet him, throwing herself into his arms as soon as he dismounted. He swung her around and happily covered her beaming face with kisses. She looked prettier than he remembered, her long black hair shining in the afternoon sun.

Finally, she broke away. "I think you forget your house and your woman."

"And my son? Did you think I would forget him, too? How is my big boy?" He gave her the ribbons he had bought for her in Monterey, and they went inside the cabin arm in arm. Little Tucker slept in the willow cradle Buck had built for him, his small hands fisted beneath his chin.

"What have you been feeding that boy," he teased, "grizzly sausage?" He chuckled. "His toes are hanging out of the end of the cradle. I guess it's time to build him a real bed."

Buck took Lali's hand, led her to the big bear rug occupying most of one end of the cabin, and pulled her down beside him. "Let's see if we can stir up another occupant for the cradle."

His long, passionate kiss was interrupted by banging on the door. Grumbling something about a man needing his privacy, he stood and opened it. Tui and Sanchez barged in, firing questions faster than he could answer.

"I thought you'd gone to the mission," Buck said to the old vaquero.

"Sí, I did for a while, but soon I missed this place. Besides, I had to bring your supplies."

"It's good to see you. Both of you."

"How did your trip go?" Sanchez asked. "Did you get it done? Are you the don of Rancho del Oso?"

Buck laughed and jostled with them in answer. Finally he went outside to his saddle bags. He stuffed the deed inside his shirt but carried the fine bottle of Spanish brandy he'd guarded all the way from Monterey.

Pouring them all a generous portion, he raised his mug. "To Rancho del Oso. Home of the finest horses, the finest friends, and the meanest damn grizzly bears in all of Alta California!" He downed the brandy and pulled the deed from inside his shirt, rolling it out on the table.

They marveled at its intricate scroll work and the governor's red wax seal, then pumped Buck's hand once more and patted him on the back.

"Don Buck Mueller!" They all laughed heartily. Finally Buck broke the revelry.

"I haven't stopped to light a fire for the last four days. I'm so hungry my stomach's flappin' and chafin' my backbone. Let's eat."

The next day he rode the rancho with Sanchez. Buck asked the old vaquero of his trip to see Zalvidea and the conditions at the mission. Finally, after giving Sanchez every opportunity to speak of her, he had to ask. "Did you stop by Rancho Toro Bravo?"

"Sí, everything goes well. The brandy pours from the still and the vines grow as they never have before."

"And Elena? What did you hear of Elena? Is she all right?"

"More than all right." His usually stoic friend grinned his answer. "She has had a baby... a girl, I think. As beautiful as she is, or so it is said."

Buck felt a pang of frustration, then one of jealousy, and finally warm resignation. He was pleased she was happy. He vowed to himself for the thousandth time he would think of her no more.

EDUARDO JUAREZ SAT STARING out the windows of his study, talking but not looking at Santos Montes, who reclined in a leather chair, smoking one of his expensive cigars.

"Don Pedro is expected here in three days," Eduardo said. "That is when his notes to the Juarez family are due. He has indicated he will satisfy those obligations on time." Eduardo took another long cigar from the wooden box on his desk, bit off the end, and shoved it between his teeth. He flicked a sulfur-head with his thumbnail, held it to the end, and drew deeply.

"Apparently he has done very well with the brandy," he continued. "Or I should say Mamacita has done well. I doubt the fat don could have done it without her—or without the help of that interfering marinero." He stood and faced the gaunt vaquero. "Perhaps Don Pedro will die well."

Montes blew a cigar ring, then he smiled.

"You know the route he will take," Eduardo said. "It would be a pity if thieves on the road killed the good don and took the gold he brings to pay his notes."

"Sí, patron, that would be a terrible thing."

"Do not be seen, vaquero. He will have riders with him.

There is a great deal of gold. Some of it will be yours, if you return successfully."

"Have I ever disappointed you, jefe?" A smug smile curved his thin lips. "The road will hold a surprise for the don. That I can promise you."

———————

Two weeks later Elena and Eduardo sat at the big dining table of Toro Bravo, beside her mother and Mamacita. The meal of cocida, beef brisket, had been sumptuous, but Elena could hardly eat. Now they sat sipping Toro Bravo brandy, a habit Elena had acquired much to Eduardo's displeasure, discussing the matters left unresolved by the death of her father, pressing matters that her husband had come to resolve.

Eduardo spoke to her mother in a quiet compassionate tone. "You know your loss is my loss, Señora. Elena's papa was like a father to me. As to the notes due my family... to Rancho Riena that are now past due... might I suggest I tear them up? They are only a formality. Now that Don Pedro is gone, there is no need for them."

Tears welled in the señora's eyes at the heartfelt kindness of her son-in-law. He had been so considerate, so caring during these last trying days. Even now his segundo, Señor Montes and several of the Rancho Riena vaqueros were on the trail of the thieves. Don Pedro and three of Toro Bravo's finest men had been slain, ambushed as they rode to Rancho Riena.

"Might I suggest," Eduardo said, "since the rancho will one day be Elena's and little Maria's, and will one day go to our sons, and since it will be my responsibility to care for it —one I am happy to take on—that you go ahead and deed the rancho to me. It will simplify the management of things... make things easier on all of us." He gently squeezed the señora's shoulder in a gesture of consolation.

But the look on Mamacita's face grew hard and she rose to her feet.

"Of course, mi hijo," the señora agreed. "Whatever you think is best." Her mother knew so little of these matters, Elena thought. It was obvious Mamacita did not agree, but what Eduardo had said was the truth. Elena studied her husband from beneath her long lashes, a tiny voice alerting her, but she said nothing.

Mamacita turned and walked to her room, her manner speaking the words she refused to utter.

"I will have the deed prepared," Eduardo said. "Do not worry about a thing." He smiled, and Elena felt a trickle of unease slide down her back. She couldn't help but wondered why that smile of Eduardo's had looked so smug.

23

Buck sat on the deck of the five-room hacienda he had built into the hill on top of the old dugout cabin. The original building now served as the fruit cellar and storage. His cache of gold had grown along with the house and was still hidden below the old slate floor.

Tucker, now three years old, sat on his knee firing questions as Buck rocked the boy and surveyed the rancho he and his friends had built. The last two years had been busy ones. He hadn't left the rancho since his trip to see Echeandia. Even when Sanchez took Lali off to San Juan to be instructed and baptized in the Catholic Church, he stayed and worked.

Wild cattle, most of which were collected each time they made a trip to Pueblo de Los Angeles, now grazed the several thousand acres of Rancho del Oso, and the swine herd had grown to over two hundred.

A large barn and a second big corral sat below the house, and a partially constructed mill spanned the little creek just below the dam. The lake had grown to a hundred feet in length and held an acre of water several feet deep at the penstock.

Cuatcho, the old Paiute chief, came each year with his braves, bringing furs to trade and Buck added them to the hides, horns, tallow, and sausage the men hauled in pack trains north to Monterey.

Buck thought of his good friend Tucker Hutchins often. He wished the mountain man were here to see what he had done with the place and to spin tales to his namesake. Buck missed Tucker's yarning, and knew that if his friend returned, he would have hours of new stories to tell.

Buck wrote and received three letters from his mother. He was saddened by his stepfather's death and angry and frustrated at his stepbrothers' actions in sending his mother to live in town.

He was surprised to read that a Boston warrant had been issued for his arrest for the murder of Hard Tack. He had thought that problem would crop up only when Taylor-Johnson was here in Alta California. He felt the document would have little effect unless he returned home but he couldn't be certain.

He spent a great deal of time writing "to whom it may concern" letters, trying to clear his name, and asked his mother to deliver them to the proper authorities in Boston.

He still had Ernst's leather chest. Almost all its contents had been traded or worn out, other than the black lacquer box. It adorned the mantel over the fireplace and still held some of its original cache of coins.

Worry plagued him as to whether the authorities would contact Echeandia regarding the warrant, and if so, how the governor would react. The two years since he'd contracted with the export agent, Mercado de Pacifica, as the governor instructed, had been profitable ones for both of them. That would certainly influence the governor's thinking. Still, Buck worried.

Since hard work was the best cure for worry, he rode to the mill site and began lining the raceway below the penstock with stones, a protection against the water washing it out. After two hours of backbreaking labor, Lali rode up.

"Do you think the timber king could take a break?" she teased. "We have company!"

"Company?" He smiled. "Cuatcho and Toka come to see what they can trade me out of this time?"

"No. Vaqueros. Sanchez knows one of them. They say they are just passing through, God knows to where." She crossed herself, looking upward, silently asking forgiveness for her profanity. She had learned a lot in her short time at the mission.

Buck wiped the sweat from his brow and reached for his shirt. "No time for a little swim, eh?" He winked at her, pleased and proud that her English and Spanish were getting almost as good as his own.

"You faker, you only ask when you know that I can not. How is Tucker ever going to have a little sister if you do not slow down?"

"Let's get to our company, woman… this is an event. Our first Californios. Let's show them what Rancho del Oso hospitality is all about!"

He saddled the roan and raced Lali back to the hacienda, barely able to beat the quick little desert mare.

———————

As Buck walked up, Sanchez leaned on the corral rails talking with two vaqueros. Immediately Buck recognized the taller of the two. It was the same man who had made him so uncomfortable at Toro Bravo. He didn't recall the man's name, but he hadn't forgotten his look. It reminded Buck of the time he had crawled up a rock ledge and come face to face with a black-eyed, tongue-flicking rattler.

As he surveyed the lean vaquero, he couldn't help thinking the man might be even more dangerous. This one wouldn't give the courtesy of a rattle before he struck.

"Ah… Buck, you remember Señor Montes?" Sanchez asked. "Santos Montes, and his companion Jesus Gutierrez."

Reluctantly, Buck extended his hand. They both shook

enthusiastically, making him feel a little ashamed of his earlier reaction. He had no real reason to feel as he did, still, he had learned to trust his instincts. They had kept him alive so far.

"What brings you gentlemen to our little valley?"

It was Montes who spoke, smiling a tight-lipped serpent smile, meeting Buck's gaze with unblinking eyes, "we did not know of your rancho. We were riding the hills, looking for stray stock and wild horses."

"Well, I wish there were more of both. We've just about picked the hills clean. And of course, any stock you find here belongs to Rancho del Oso."

"As I said," the tall man cut his eyes away. "We did not know of this rancho."

Sanchez looked at the vaquero a little strangely. He remembered now that he had told the man of Rancho del Oso that afternoon in the cantina. Possibly the tall vaquero had forgotten, just as he had forgotten their conversation for a while.

"Sanchez," Buck suggested, "why don't you show these men around while I see what Lali is stirring up for supper?" He whistled at Tui and started for the house. The big kanaka had taken a liking to the smokehouse and sausage-making, and spent most of his time there.

"Tui, you and Yolo join us at the table tonight. We'll be putting on a spread for our guests."

Tui's Indian wife was swollen with their second child. He walked over to where Buck stood. "I not much like these vaqueros. The tall one is like the shark—quiet, but very fast and very dangerous, I think. I will send Yolo to help Lali with the cooking."

Supper was uneventful. Buck laid out Rancho del Oso's best for their guests. The table was filled with a huge ham, sausages, bread baked from hand-ground wheat, and a variety of garden vegetables. The major treat was the first of the rich red wine, the first vino de pais, from cuttings Sanchez had brought from the mission.

By the end of the evening, Buck faced his doubts about the gaunt vaquero. The man was quiet and sinister looking, but a man could not help his appearance. He seemed amiable enough. The other man, Jesus Gutierrez, was nondescript, hardly even noticed during the meal.

Still... Buck couldn't quite discard his uneasy feeling. All in all, however, he considered his first evening's entertaining at Rancho del Oso a success, despite his strong apprehension.

DON EDUARDO JUAREZ stepped from his cabin onboard the brig Virginia, renamed the California by Captain Taylor-Johnson after its purchase from Bryant and Sturgis. The city of Monterey was in sight off the bow and Eduardo was ready for land. The five-day sail from San Pedro was too much for him. He spent most of the trip in his cabin, green with seasickness. He'd usurped the cabin from the first mate; as an owner of the vessel, he had that right.

Captain Taylor-Johnson walked the deck on the weather-side of the helm, directing the sail adjustment as they prepared a last tack to make anchorage.

Four brigs now plied the waters of the California coast, all belonging to the enterprising partners—Taylor-Johnson, Echeandia, and Juarez. Eduardo smiled and patted the folder he held beneath his arm. He opened it and thumbed through the contents.

A copy of the warrant issued by the Commonwealth of Massachusetts for the arrest of Samuel "Buck" Mueller was the most impressive of the documents, with its fancy scroll work and wax seal; but it was not the one he prized. The small baptismal certificate from the Lutheran Church of the Township of Boston was the most valuable. It almost guaranteed the Juarez acquisition of another Rancho.

Montes had spoken highly of Rancho del Oso. The man's trip, at Eduardo's insistence, had been well worth the time.

This was one Rancho that would fall to him without the slightest effort. He wouldn't have to foreclose... or murder for it. He would simply insist that his partner, the governor, revoke Mueller's grant. The law was clear. A non-Catholic could not own land in California.

And Juarez knew Taylor-Johnson was on his side. The captain had been furious when he'd learned about the land grant. With his help, governor would be easy enough to convince. The hide contract they owned was worth thousands to the three partners. Echeandia could not risk that relationship, even though Eduardo was positive the governor was making something off Mueller's grant. No matter what ties Echeandia had with the American, he couldn't risk alienating his partners in the hide, horn, and tallow trade.

The governor could overlook the warrant, but not the baptism.

Echeandia met his partners at the beach and walked with them to his office. For most of the day the men went over their accounts. Juarez wanted the governor to be well satisfied with their business relationship before he brought up the Mueller grant.

Before they broke for the day, Juarez said, in a quiet voice, "There is a matter of some importance I wish to discuss. I discovered it in the file our good captain brought from back from Boston. It seems your most recent don has misrepresented himself."

The governor's head snapped up.

"I am speaking of the Rancho del Oso grant," Juarez continued. "It appears Señor Mueller is not a Catholic, but a Lutheran." He smiled tightly and unfolded the baptismal out on the desk. "I am afraid, Your Excellency, that you must rescind his grant. I have already taken the liberty of writing to Zalvidea and Barona and informing them of the facts." Barona was the governor's most outspoken critic.

Echeandia sat back in his chair, digesting this new piece of information. He was fond of Mueller. The man had done what he said he would do. He'd been looking forward to a long and profitable relationship. However, Buck Mueller was certainly not as important as his partners, Juarez and Taylor-Johnson, who had just accounted for hundreds of thousands of reals in profits.

He sighed. Juarez had left him no choice. So far he had carefully kept his movements against the church within the law. This grant to a non-Catholic could be used against him in Mexico City if he did not act quickly to rectify his mistake. Barona would attack full force if he did not take action. He would have to enforce the law.

Still, something might be saved.

"Sí," Echeandia agreed, "it is a travesty that cannot be overlooked." He glanced at his sallow-faced partner and asked a question he already knew the answer to. "And what do you suggest we do with his grant, now that it has been improved and appears to be so prosperous? Shall it escheat to the State of Alta California?"

Juarez spoke up quickly. "That would certainly be a waste. It is so far from anything, it would seem to be of little value. Still, I would be willing to take it on. I could put a few families there. That way it could continue to contribute to the wealth of Alta California. It has contributed, hasn't it, my friend?" Juarez smiled knowingly.

Echeandia studied him closely. "And you would continue to ship all its goods via Monterey... via Mercado de Pacifica? I would not like to do anything to hurt my good friends at that company." Echeandia's ownership of more than half of Mercado de Pacifica was not public knowledge, and he was not about to let it be known in this company.

"Of course, Your Excellency." Juarez bowed slightly.

"In that case, I will have my secretary draw the papers tomorrow. The rescission of the grant, the deed to you, and of course, a new contract between Rancho Riena and Mercado de Pacifica."

"Excellent!" Eduardo smiled broadly. "I will be pleased to see that the rescission is handed directly to Señor Mueller."

"If I were not so busy," Taylor-Johnson snarled, "I would like to deliver that document myself. There is still the matter of the warrant."

"That is a matter for you and the Commonwealth of Massachusetts," the governor said with finality.

"But more easily handled if you would revoke his passport and let it be known he was not welcome in California," Taylor-Johnson countered.

"That goes without saying. The grant also served as his right to remain in Alta California. Eduardo, you may inform Señor Mueller that he is expected to be out of this country by the end of the month."

"I will leave that task to my segundo, Santos Montes. He has always been capable in handling such matters."

Echeandia showed them to the door, closed it behind them, then shook his head as he sat back down at his desk. It was not a matter of choice. Still, he regretted it. He shoved the thought away, thinking that fate was a fickle enemy indeed, and turned his attention to other pressing matters of state.

———————

ELENA RODE her little palomino carefully. Maria, her toddling daughter, shared the saddle with her. Eduardo had come to her bed for a few months after she recovered from her daughter's birth, then stopped. She did not become pregnant again and his interest in her waned.

She had always found him repugnant and did a poor job of hiding that fact in bed, or even across the supper table. He had shown no interest in Maria and that offended Elena and made her dislike him even more. There was no happiness between them.

There was nothing at all between them.

Elena found her happiness with her child. She and Maria made their own life together. What Eduardo did or thought was of little concern. She had a beautiful girl who she could dress in the finest gowns and no matter how unbearable her husband attempted to make her life, Maria was hers.

As Elena rode back to the barn, Eduardo emerged through its wide doors. He disapproved of her riding the vaquero saddle instead of her sidesaddle, and she expected him to reprimand her. He merely nodded as he would to an acquaintance and walked on to the hacienda.

As she put away her mare, Jesus Gutierrez stood in the next stall, saddling his blood bay stallion.

"Buenos dias, señora," he called out.

"Buenos dias, Jesus. I see the patron has returned."

"Sí, señora. He sends me to find Montes."

She nodded. "Have a pleasant ride." Turning away, she clasped her daughter's hand and walked back toward the hacienda, the little girl toddling along beside her.

24

THE LAST THING Buck needed to complete the mill was the most important—the mill stone. He let it be known he would give a fine knife to the man who located the proper slab, and had already gone to look at several.

The buckeye were just beginning to bloom, their fragrant white blossoms drawing bees. Buck and Toka worked their way along a hillside covered with the blooming trees, then on north to a granite cliff where Toka had spotted some foot-thick sheets of rock which had sloughed away from the face.

Buck clapped his friend on the back. "These will do fine, Toka. Tomorrow you come to the rancho and I'll have your knife for you. We'll come back with the caretta and some men to help load them."

Toka rode beside him until it was time to rein off toward Bear Valley. Buck waved and shouted a farewell as his friend left to return to the Paiutes' summer camp.

"Be early!" he called out. "It'll take a full day to load the stone and get back to the rancho." It had been a pleasant ride. He enjoyed the tall Indian's company. He was a good companion and a good man to have at your back, as he'd proven more than once on their trip to Santa Fe.

As Buck neared Rancho del Oso, his thoughts were lost

in the construction of the mill and the grinding and shaping of the mill stone.

He jerked rein on the roan when he saw smoke rising over the hill in front of him—from the direction of his hacienda.

Heart thumping hard inside his chest, he spurred the big roan into a run, leaving the pack animal behind. As he crested the hill, his worst fears were confirmed. The barn was ablaze. Galloping in, he passed two of the Yokuts who worked on the ranch madly running in the other direction —away from the flames.

"Damn you!" he yelled after them, leaping from the saddle as the roan slid to a halt in front of the hacienda. He was on the ground and running for the barn when he saw Lali in the doorway of the main house, her eyes flaring with terror. She was jerked back into the room by unseen hands.

Buck slipped his Aston pistol from its holster as he charged forward to meet this new challenge, and saw a painted Indian, knife in one hand tomahawk in the other, filling the doorway. A Mojave? What the hell were Mojaves doing this far west?

Buck's pistol stared its one-eye into the Indian's face before he could raise his tomahawk. The pistol spit and bucked, and half the man's face blew away.

Kicking the body aside, pistol spent, Buck jerked his knife and charged into the room, his forward momentum aided by a Mojave arrow that smashed through his shoulder from behind. He felt a searing jolt of pain, then was surprised to see the bloodied stone head appear through his buckskins. He'd thought his enemy was in front of him.

All his strength, will, and determination drove him on to Lali and little Tucker.

The living room was empty except for a torch thrown into a corner, its flames licking at the wall. He heard screams from the bedroom and plunged in. Three Mojaves had Lali pinned to the bed. He drove the knife he held between the shoulders of the closest Indian. Another let go of Lali's arms and lunged for him.

Dodging the Indian's knife with a fierce effort, he drove both thumbs into the brave's eye sockets popping the balls out onto the man's cheeks. The Indian screamed in pain, whirled and drove his stone knife into Buck's thigh. The third brave scrambled to his weapons hastily abandoned in his hurry to mount Lali.

Now freed, Lali leaped onto his back, scratching and clawing at his face.

Buck jerked the knife from his thigh and stumbled forward, slamming the bloodied long sharpened obsidian blade into the man's lower belly. The man's eyes flared and he sunk to his knees.

"Tucker!" Lali screamed. "They took Tucker!"

Fear flooded Buck with renewed strength. Blood flowing freely from his shoulder and thigh, he charged to the door, Lali close at his heels. They met four more Mojaves in the doorway. A glancing blow from a tomahawk knocked Buck rolling as he bulled out through them, but he quickly came to his feet.

Single mindedly searching for his young son, he spotted Tucker being dragged through the corral. Passing the big blue roan, Buck tore the long musket from its scabbard behind the saddle. The big horse flared his nostrils and turned on the two Mojaves close on Buck's heels; two others remained behind, preoccupied with Lali.

Buck dropped to one knee and sighted quickly. The musket roared and bucked and slammed a big fifty caliber ball between the shoulders of one of the two Mojaves dragging the frightened little boy. Buck rose and ran to finish the other—with his bare hands if he had to.

He reached the middle of the corral before his knees began to buckle. His buckskins streaked crimson, his head swimming from loss of blood and the blow of the tomahawk, he stumbled, his vision spinning. He tried to fight it, tried to keep going, but blackness ate at his will, and he slumped to the ground.

Across the corral, Diablo's hoofs pounded the earth as the big roan fought on, catching up to the Indian dragging Tucker, ripping with his teeth, tearing into flesh and bone.

Buck tried desperately to regain his senses. He tried to crawl, but his legs wouldn't respond to his wishes. He tried to call out, but no sound came. The last thing he remembered, through his blurred and distorted vision, was the big roan rearing and stomping, beating the Indian into the dust of the corral.

The Indians who stayed with Lali beat her unconscious, then pleasured themselves with her prostrate body. The flaming cabin finally drove them out. They left her to be purified by the ravaging flames.

The Mojaves had quietly surrounded the ranch, taking their time, working their way into position. The work of the rancho had been going on as normal. Tui was in the smokehouse, Sanchez in the corral training a colt; Lali and Tucker were in the hacienda.

Three Indians had gone for Sanchez and four after Tui.

Sanchez stood in the open and saw them coming. He made it to his stallion before they reached him. Instead of running, as they assumed an unarmed man would do, he mounted and drove straight into them, his woven leather reata flying.

He scattered the bunch with the game stallion, then dropped a loop over a surprised Indian's neck. A quick turn around the horn and the well-trained horse sat back, jerking the Indian to the ground. He strangled as the old vaquero used the man's limp weight as an anchor. Then he encircled the other two, who ran into each other, trying to escape. The horse's quick turns around the struggling men soon had them well ensnared in the reata, then Sanchez drove the reluctant horse into and over them time and time again.

The old vaquero turned his attention to the smokehouse.

He had seen more Indians running in that direction. Dismounting, he ran to Tui's aid. The big man had one Mojave pinned in a corner, choking him with a huge, ham-like hand; his other massive arm circled the neck of a second.

Two others beat the huge kanaka with their stone axes. Sanchez drove his thin knife between the ribs of one, but the second turned his ax on the tough old vaquero, knocking him to the ground and crushing his skull with a single solid blow.

Tui went down under a hail of blows from the ax and was finally quieted with one of his own sausage knives.

The big blue roan ran from side to side in the corral, pitching his head, neighing a challenge to the deadly group of raiders. Five Mojaves watched but would not enter to face the devil horse. The little boy ran to where his father lay still and huddled beside him.

Finally, the Indians notched their arrows and let fly at the horse. The more arrows he took, the more enraged he became. He charged the fence, snorting and throwing his magnificent head, flinging foamy blood from his nostrils. The Indians retreated even farther. The big roan straddled the man and boy, hanging his proud head but unwilling to concede defeat.

One of the Indians crawled into the corral. With a half dozen arrows protruding from the big horse's sides, the roan charged again, catching the Indian and tearing a bloody patch of flesh from his back as he scrambled under the bottom rail.

The Indians had been told to take the man's scalp, proof of his death. They let fly another half dozen arrows into the big horse. Still, he stood.

A tall, gaunt-faced Mexican rode down off the nearby hill, approaching the remaining Indians. He had no pity for the man, but great pity for the horse.

"Enough! It is enough. You will be paid, as I have said. Fire the rest of the buildings."

One of the Mojaves notched an arrow and returned to the corral. He pulled the bowstring taut and the arrow whistled across the corral and thumped into the child, who whimpered and collapsed across his father.

The remaining Mojaves rode from the rancho. Before they left, they clubbed one of their own who wandered about the yard, his eyeballs popped from their sockets—the Mojave's own brand of desert mercy.

Montes rode back to where Jesus Gutierrez waited on the hill. Before they began the long ride home, they made a careful search of the ruins, looking as carefully as they could, but they were still hot and smoldering.

Santos Montez plucked a small blistered, lacquered box from a bed of hot coals in front of the stone fireplace that now stood alone, surveying the remnants of what had once been it's shelter. He threw it outside onto the dirt. It broke apart revealing a small cache of melted coins. Disgustedly, he flipped them from hand to hand until they cooled.

If the old vaquero thought this was a great cache of gold, Montes thought as he mounted and they began the long ride back to Rancho Riena, he was more of a fool than he looked.

Diablo stayed on his feet for over an hour. Finally, slowly, he dropped to his knees, then rolled to his side driving the arrows even deeper into his chest. His last breath bubbled with bright, proud Andalusian blood.

AT DAWN THE FOLLOWING DAY, just a few minutes after the sun slipped over the horizon, Toka and two Paiute braves rode into the still-smoldering carnage. He dismounted, his face a mask of stone, and walked into the corral. Little Tucker, his life's fluids drained out, lay across his father, whose torn and bloodied body lay sprawled in the dirt.

The Indian's stoic expression did not reveal the ache in

his chest, nor did the ache create the tears it would have in a lesser man.

Quickly he knelt beside his friend, checked to see if he yet lived. There was still a dull pulse. While Toka packed Buck's wounds with dry grass and bound them tightly with hemp, the braves checked for other survivors, found none, then made a travois. As soon as it was ready, he moved his friend into the shade and forced some water down him, then began studying the sign left by the battle.

Twelve unshod horses and two shod ones had ridden in from above the hacienda. Nine had left to the east, four without riders. Two sets of sharp-heeled tracks spoke of boots, and many softly rounded tracks said moccasins.

All the stock at the ranch had been driven out in front of the raiders. The two shod horses had made their way down Sycamore Canyon. He decided to go after the ones who left to the east, the Mojaves, his long-time enemies.

If Buck awoke, he would recover much faster watching Mojave scalps dry in the wind. It looked as though two Mojaves had burned in the hacienda, two lay dead in the corral, and one lay clubbed in the yard—there would be many more if Toka had his way.

It was several days before Buck regained consciousness in a Paiute camp far from Rancho del Oso. His first sound was a keening cry for Tucker and Lali. The Indian woman who was tending him quickly left the lodge in search of Toka.

"Lali?" Buck whispered after her.

Toka entered.

"Lali?" Buck raised his head and looked at his friend. Toka did not answer, just sadly shook his head from side to side.

"Tucker?" the question was choking gasp.

Again Toka shook his head, unable to meet his friend's eyes. Toka turned and walked from the lodge, leaving him to his grief. Mercifully, he drifted back into uncon-sciousness.

Several times over the next two weeks, the tremendous loss of blood and the emotional pounding he had taken almost pushed Buck over the edge. Then the wounds festered with infection. Toka and the tribe's medicine man used their skills to conquer that, and finally his strength began to return.

With it his resolve for revenge grew and strengthened.

He was sitting up for the first time in weeks when Toka walked into the lodge. "I have a gift for you."

"A gift?" Buck studied his good friend's face. "You have done too much already."

"I have been saving this gift for some time. It is one I do not wish to return to summer camp with, so you must take it now."

Toka turned and walked from the lodge. Buck was startled when an emaciated Mojave warrior was flung into the lodge, his hands bound behind him and his legs hobbled with rawhide. He fell forward onto his face, which was bruised and swollen.

Behind him Toka stood with a coupstick in his hand. Along its length hung several Mojave scalps, the flesh well dried, the hair matted and filthy.

"He is the last of his kind." Toka smiled tightly. "The last of the Mojaves who visited Rancho del Oso. If you were stronger you could enjoy him more. But I will do your bidding, or if you wish, we will have the women do so. This dog deserves only women as enemies."

The sight of the painted Indian brought back vivid memories Buck had been trying to shake from his mind. His son being dragged across the corral, his wife being forced to desecrate their bed. His heart wrenched, feeling as battered and bruised as his body.

"Thank you, Toka," he said quietly. "Do with him what you wish.... I have no need of him." He turned his head away.

Toka knelt and rested a hand on Buck's shoulder. "But you may wish to learn more from him, my friend. It seems his visit to your rancho was done at the bidding of another man. He and his friends were paid twenty head of horses and all the stock they could steal, to burn you out of Rancho del Oso and bring your scalp to the tall vaquero."

It took Buck a moment to comprehend what his friend was saying. Someone had hired the Mojaves? Why? He had enemies... Taylor-Johnson. But he wouldn't come this far. Henry Tacker didn't mean that much to him. Why then?

"What man does he speak of?" Buck's eyes, now deep set and sunken, turned hard. "What man would do such a thing?"

"We will see if he wants to tell the women more." Toka dragged the brave from the lodge.

He would talk, Buck was sure, one way or the other. He lay back down on his bed and rolled over onto his side, ignoring the pain that seared through his body, trying in vain to get comfortable. He winced when something prodded the wound in his thigh. Reaching into his pocket, he removed the little black rock he had carried for so long.

If this is luck, he thought, who needs it? He flung the tusuat across the lodge with what little strength he had left.

EDUARDO STOOD TALKING QUIETLY to Elena. In the past few months, she had acquired several Andalusians and stayed busy with their breeding and training. It was seldom Eduardo spoke to her at all, but it was necessary now.

Echeandia and Taylor-Johnson would be coming the following week. It was time to go over the accounts again. Their exclusive right to export hides was turning out to be only as good as the ability to police it. Other ships still plied the coast, smuggling hides and tallow aboard—the goleta, schooner, they had commissioned to patrol the coast did little good. There was just too much coast and all were willing to sell to the highest bidder.

Even the missions still sold to them. The smugglers paid

more for the product, and the missions were no longer sympathetic to the government.

Eduardo stopped speaking as Montes rode up. "Patron, you sent for me?"

"I have a job for you. You must accompany the families I am sending to Rancho del Oso."

"But, jefe," Montes argued, "I have much to do here!" He did not look forward to the ride back to the valley—ten days without women or wine.

"You have been there," Eduardo insisted. "You know the way. You do not have to stay and see them settled. Just get them there."

It was the first Elena had heard of his involvement in Rancho del Oso. "Why do we send families to Rancho del Oso?" she asked. "Are we helping Señor Mueller?"

As always, it irritated him when she interfered in his business. "It is not Señor Mueller we help. We have been granted the Rancho. Señor Mueller and his family were killed... by the Mojaves... or so rumor has it."

Elena stifled a gasp. Buck was dead! He and his family, Eduardo had said. When he turned back to Montes and continued his conversation, she made her way quickly into the shadows of the barn, her eyes burning and her throat constricting with tears.

She had thought of him so many times.

The tears in her eyes began to slip down her cheeks. It was the first time she had wept since her father died.

THE MOJAVE BRAVE traded his limited knowledge for a running start. Even with a several minute lead, he lasted only twenty minutes after he ran from the Paiute camp.

Winter was long off the land, and it was past time for the Paiutes to return to their summer camp on the slopes of the high mountains. As Buck bounced along on the travois on the long trip north, he remembered a line that Dutch quoted on a cold South American night.

"The villainy you teach me I will execute, and it shall go hard, but I will better the instruction." God, how he wished he were going the other way. The tall gaunt Californio the Mojave had described could be only one man.

Santos Montes. A man who had been to Rancho Del Oso before. A man with serpent eyes.

The travois bounced and jarred. His wounds opened and weeped. But moving was a matter of survival to the Indians. His fever rose and he passed in and out of consciousness. He awoke in a permanent village by a large glassy lake. Trout dried on racks near the fire, and huge granite mountains were the backdrop for the camp.

Slowly, day by trying day, Buck's strength returned. He forced himself to eat heartily and soon was on his feet. But it was well into summer before he was horseback again. Even then he continued to walk, and run, up and down the steep mountainsides until he was able to go anywhere—he was driven to regain his strength, driven by the need for revenge. The high mountain air and good food of the summer camp worked their wonders. Still, it was not until the first cold cutting wind of fall that he was ready to ride out.

As the Indians rolled up their summer camp, Toka came to his hut. "I have some things for you. I have been saving them."

"Not another Mojave." Buck smiled at the tall, straight, square-shouldered Indian. "I've had enough of them for a while."

"No, but it is something you may be able to use again."

Toka handed him his old, scarred musket. Toka had retrieved it from the corral, along with a leather bag of balls, powder horn and a few caps.

Buck rubbed the old firearm lovingly. They had been through a lot together. It was old when Buck had taken it from the Virginia. Now it was also well dented and marked.

Still, it would do. It would serve to fire a few last balls—fifty calibers—that carried the initials of at least three men, and maybe four.

"And this." Toka handed Buck the little black rock. "You dropped it on the floor of the lodge when you were sick."

Buck took the tusuat and rolled it around in his palm, as he had a hundred times before. Maybe it was lucky. He was still alive while the rest of them were dead.

And revenge could be his.

It was a long ride south, back to the Paiutes' winter camp. Buck rode with them. As they neared a place more familiar, he turned to his friend. "It's time for me to see what is left of Rancho del Oso."

"I will go with you, my friend."

"No, Toka." Sadness filled his chest. "This is a thing I must do alone."

He turned west on a strong desert horse Toka had given him, headed for a look at his ranch. He didn't know what to expect. He knew none of the Paiutes had been back to take care of the bodies. He was afraid of the grisly scene he might find. He was physically strong, maybe stronger than he had ever been. But was he mentally strong enough to face what he might see?

As he crested the hill above the hacienda, he reined up, amazed to see a hubbub of activity below him. He watched for a while, until an equally surprised vaquero rode out to meet him. Riders did not come to California from the east. Buck was wary, but determined to discover what was going on.

"Buenos dias," he said to the vaquero. "What place is this?"

"It is Rancho del Oso. One of the ranchos of Don Eduardo Juarez. Come and join us... we are about to sit down to the noon day meal."

"Is Don Eduardo here?" Buck asked, hiding the anger that suddenly gripped him.

"No, the don has many ranchos. He has never even been here."

Buck's heart lurched as he followed along behind the rider, his stomach churning as the memories flowed back. They had cleaned up the burned-out barn but had not touched the blackened twisted hacienda yet. The corrals were still in use.

They sat down at a table beneath an oak tree where little Tucker used to play. They served him a plate of beans and squash. Squash of his own planting. He picked at his food and tried not to think of the past, spinning a tale instead of crossing from Santa Fe and the trouble he'd had with the Mojaves. That much at least was true.

"Sí, they are very bad. This is their handiwork." A stout vaquero waved his thick hand at the destruction around them. "They murdered the family that once lived here."

Buck's stomach rolled. "All of them?" he asked, curious whether they knew he still lived.

"Sí, even un poco muchacho. We buried the remains up on the hillside."

After the meal the men returned to work. Buck walked first to a half dozen graves, each marked with only a simple wooden cross. He paused only long enough to kneel a moment in front of the smallest one and swear a quiet oath of vengeance. He back-handed the wetness from his eyes, then he moved to the burned-out hacienda and picked through the ashes. When he was sure no one was looking, he dropped through a hole in the floor into the room below, then pried up the slate floor covering his gold cache. It was still there. Some of the gold pieces had melted together so he cut them apart with his knife.

Unconsciously he rubbed the little tusuat in its familiar place in his pocket. Then he left the house, packed up and rode out at a distance-eating lope.

The good memories were many, but the bad now outweighed the good. He rode hard, not looking back, ignoring the ache in his chest and not stopping until it was too dark to go on.

All the while, his mind muddled through all he had learned.

Montes worked for Juarez. His rancho now belonged to Don Eduardo Juarez. All his hard work. The blood of his friends and his wife and son. He wondered about Echeandia. Was he involved? Maybe twenty percent hadn't been enough.

It was fall, chilly and cold and the land he crossed was tough. He stopped only long enough to dig a root to chew and at a trickle to wet his mouth and the horse's.

Three hard riding days later he sat on a hill overlooking the Pueblo de Los Angeles. He watched for almost an hour, not wanting to be recognized, determined that this meeting would be on his own terms.

He didn't know how far the matter of the warrant had gone. Could Echeandia have been involved in what happened? Buck didn't think so. Could he still be a friend as he had once come to think of him? The notion of a Mexican jusgado did not warm Buck's heart. Jail was a place he knew he could not stand.

As it began to get dark, he rode in and reined up in front of the first cantina he came to. He didn't uncinch the game little horse—he didn't know how fast he would have to leave.

He pushed open the cowhide doors and walked in. A few vaqueros were drinking quietly in the place, but none he recognized. They gave him a long, thorough look in his fringed buckskin breeches and shirt, surveyed the knee-high moccasins he wore then went back to their drinking.

He ordered a mug of aguardiente, and the bartender accepted the chunk of gold with a quick test of his teeth. Satisfied, he brought Buck the mug and a handful of change. Sitting with his back to the wall, he spent over an hour in the place, quietly drinking, watching and listening. Learning little of what was about in the town, he decided to move on to the next cantina.

As he walked out the narrow door he looked back over his shoulder to make sure no one was taking undo notice, and bumped squarely into a man coming in.

"Excuse me," Buck ducked his head trying not to be recognized.

"No problem," the man muttered back in bad Spanish. "Hey!" the man yelled after him. Buck turned, reaching for the knife at his side.

"You landlubber!" The man laughed, reached out and slapped him in the shoulder. It was Josh Peckinpaugh.

Buck dragged him around the side of the building, out of earshot of any of the men.

"It's good to see you, Captain. How have things been?"

"Mostly fair winds, boy. How about you?"

"Not so fair, I'm afraid. And I'm not too anxious for the folks around here to know my name, not quite yet, anyway. I've had a few problems since I last saw you." Buck went on to briefly describe the events since he'd last seen Peckinpaugh, and the captain shook his head sympathetically.

Then Buck changed the subject. "How about you? I thought you were off to Alaska for a load of Russian furs."

Peckinpaugh shook his gray-haired head. "We barely got out with our own skins, much less a load of otter, but that is another long story. It truly saddens me to hear of your troubles. What can I do to help you?"

"Nothing. This is something only I can do." Buck's look turned hard.

"And just what do you plan?"

"I'm going to settle it," Buck said. "Balance the scale."

"Friend, this old sailor has sailed the world over, but it's a New Englander I am, and a New Englander I'll always be.... I'll stand beside ye."

"It's my fight, Captain," Buck stated flatly. "But I appreciate the offer. Now tell me of Alaska... better yet, tell me over a mug. Just keep my name quiet."

They talked for over an hour. Peckinpaugh finally got around to why he was in Pueblo de Los Angeles. "They tried to lock up the hide trade, lad. Your old friend Taylor-Johnson, the governor, and some don, name of Juarez. The rest of us have been forced to smuggle hides illegally."

Buck flinched at the Juarez name but made no comment.

"The last big fandango of the year is takin' place in a couple of days. I come to see who I could meet... who might sell me a few of their hides."

"You say it's a big fiesta?"

"The biggest, lad. Some harvest thing... half the country will be here for it."

Buck pondered that, his mind spinning with ideas. As they left the cantina, Peckinpaugh turned to face him.

"What about after... after ye settle this debt? What will ye do then?"

"Well, one thing's for sure," Buck said. "If I live... if I don't catch a lead ball or swing from an oak limb, I won't be too welcome around here." He was quiet for a moment. "I guess I could go to Boston, try to straighten things out there."

"How long is this Pueblo de Los Angeles business of yours going to take?" Peckinpaugh asked.

Buck looked at his friend, his decision suddenly made. "By the time the fiesta is over, my business will be finished, one way or the other."

"Good. It's been too long since I've seen the shores of New England. The Moonsong will be provisioned and waiting at San Pedro... say for a week. If ye happen along, we'll be needing a good hand." He extended his.

Buck took it, then added as an afterthought. "We may be needing to leave in a bit of a hurry."

"I'll look for you with a taut anchor rode. Stay out of the oak trees, my friend!"

25

THREE DAYS UNTIL THE FIESTA. An event he knew would be attended by Eduardo Juarez.

It was just enough time to rectify another wrong. Buck rode out before dawn for San Juan Capistrano.

It was well after dark when he approached the mission. He quietly turned the little sorrel horse he rode into the mission corral and crawled into the hay for some much-needed rest.

As tired as he was, sleep did not come easy. He was ashamed he had lied to his friend Zalvidea about his background, even if it was only a lie of omission.

Buck opened his eyes, then jumped six inches as a rooster crowed a few feet from his ear. His nerves were on edge, even in this familiar place. Brushing himself off, he made his way to Zalvidea's quarters and rapped soundly on the door.

"Over here," a voice called from across the courtyard.

He should have known the padre would already be up and about, tending the business of the mission. Before he had taken two steps in the priest's direction, the padre recognized him.

"Buck! Buck, it is good to see you." Zalvidea grasped him

by both shoulders. "And Lali and Tucker, are they here with you?"

Buck glanced away, his insides churning at the mention of his family's names. "No, Padre, they... they were both killed... and Tui and Sanchez." He swallowed past the tightness in his throat and Zalvidea crossed himself.

"Was there a priest? Did they receive the last rites?"

"No, Father." He straightened, knowing the time had come to be honest with his friend. "I have something to tell you, Father. Something very hard for me."

"Well, Buck, I would invite you to the confessional, but since you are not Catholic, would it do just as well to sit out here?"

Buck's jaw dropped. "How did you... that's what I wished to tell you. To apologize for deceiving you. How did you know?"

"I received a letter from Eduardo Juarez informing me of the fact. A fact I already suspected, by the way, so it was no surprise to me. He also told me of the warrant that has been issued for you.... Do you know of that?"

"Yes. One of the letters Sanchez brought from my mother informed me."

"It seems the good captain returned from Boston with the warrant and with a copy of a baptismal," Zalvidea continued. "It indicated Samuel Mueller was baptized a Lutheran at the age of six months."

"And you still greeted me as a friend?"

"My son" —the padre lay a hand on Buck's shoulder— "do you think being a Catholic means you cannot have non-Catholic friends? Did you know that the Lutherans believe that—"

"Wait a minute, Padre," Buck teased, relief flooding through him, "no debates until after breakfast!" Both laughing, they walked to the kitchen. As they drank hot coffee and ate warm tortillas filled with chocolate, Buck related the events of the past two years, interrupted only one time by the priest.

"You know Echeandia is no friend of mine, or of the church." Zalvidea's black eyes flashed. "But he had no choice in the matter of rescinding your grant. It is the law."

Buck was relieved to hear it. Perhaps Echeandia wasn't involved in what had happened at Rancho del Oso. He continued his story, but not until he had mentally erased the name Echeandia from his list. Now only three remained—Eduardo Juarez, Montes Santos, and Taylor-Johnson.

After they finished eating, they walked the grounds of the mission. Buck was saddened by the lack of activity. The sausage works and the tannery were shut down. There were not enough hands to work them. The granary stood at a complete standstill. Most of the vaqueros and horses were gone.

When Buck mentioned the deteriorating condition of the mission, the padre only shook his head.

"I fear it's just a matter of time," he said. Then with typical optimism he added, "But we still do fine, we still save souls... speaking of which, when do we talk of this Lutheran matter?"

Buck smiled. "I have some things to do, Padre, in Pueblo de Los Angeles. When I get back this way again, we can have a real visit. Maybe we could limber up the axes. Your table muscle looks as if it could use a stint with the ax!"

"Aieee...I knew it! Now I cannot even threaten you with excommunication!"

Zalvidea walked with him over to the corral, laughing and joking as Buck saddled the sorrel mare. Suddenly his mood turned serious. "Buck, do you remember the many talks we had when you first left the brig... about vindictive-ness and about revenge? It is not a thing that is satisfying... even for a short while. Lali and little Tucker cannot be helped now." He rested a hand on Buck's shoulder. "I will say a thousand Hail Marys for their immortal souls, but remember, they do not cry out from the grave for revenge. It is only you who wants that."

Buck's gaze was far away and as cold as the nights he had spent in a Paiute lodge, waiting for his wounds to heal.

"You're right, Father. They don't cry out from the grave —for months they weren't given the benefit of one." He swung up into the saddle. "Pray for my wife and son. They were Catholics."

"And for you!" Zalvidea shouted after him as he galloped off. "Vaya con Dios, mi hijo."

BUCK'S MIND was a tangle of indecision during the ride back to Pueblo Los Angeles.

Should he stop at Toro Bravo or not? The Rancho held so many memories of the past. Elena, Mamacita, the don... all had been a part of his dreams and ambitions. Now there was only Taylor-Johnson, Montes, and Juarez.

Buck clenched his jaw as he remembered the hook-nosed, sallow-faced man who was Elena's husband. He was Don Pedro's son-in-law, the father of Elena's daughter.

Whatever Buck might have thought of Elena in the past, whatever he had wished for the two of them, was gone. Gone as Lali and Tucker were gone. Still, just as he would never forget them, he would never forget her.

As his mind cleared, he realized he had been reining the mare along familiar surroundings. He approached a narrow rise overlooking the hacienda at Rancho Toro Bravo. He didn't want to expose himself. He would be taking a chance even letting them know he was alive.

He would watch before he approached, he told himself, make sure no one was there who would be a threat to him. Something might be learned. Something that would make his task easier. They would probably be gone anyway. Already left for the village to attend the fiesta. He was sure they wouldn't miss it, just as he would not.

Buck reined up and sat watching for over an hour. The sun was setting in a gray, dappled sky as he approached the main house. If he kept the sun at his back and anyone was there watching his approach, that man would be unable to make him out clearly.

Buck reined the mare up and left her tied to the corral rail. He felt a momentary hint of satisfaction as he passed the still, its fire burning away, smoke roiling up in the crisp fall air.

He walked carefully to the front door of the hacienda, leaving the long gun on his saddle, but checking the pair of Aston pistols and knife to make sure they were in place. Boldly, he banged on the big carved front door.

"Sí, señor?" greeted the Indian woman who answered.

"I'd like to see Don Pedro, por favor."

The woman looked at him strangely. "Don Pedro is no longer with us. He was killed some time ago."

Buck caught his breath. He hadn't heard a word of the old don's death.

"What about Mamacita?"

"She lives at Rancho Riena de Californio with her daughter and granddaughter... and her great-granddaughter." She smiled.

"Who lives here?"

"The jefe of Rancho Toro Bravo." She was beginning to get exasperated. It was obvious the woman was tiring of his questions. "Señor Juarez's segundo. He is the haciendado now."

"And who might that be?" Buck persisted.

"Señor Montes, Señor Santos Montes," she said with finality, as if she had better things to do. Buck took a deep breath, calming himself, allowing the quick surge of anger to settle in his system.

"Is Señor Montes en casa?" Buck had to force the words through his teeth.

"He is out with his vaqueros. Checking the cattle or something. He will return soon." She looked surprised when he brushed past her and walked into the house.

"I am Señor... I am Señor Samuel." It would be best if the man was unaware of who waited.

He knew his way into the sala. He placed himself in a straight-backed chair facing the doorway and waited. The Indian woman walked into the room several times. Finally she asked if he would care for something to drink. Buck declined. For more than an hour he sat, his only movement the clenching and unclenching of his fist as it rested on the arm of his chair.

Santos' man must have ingratiated himself to his patron to live like this, he thought, his temper rising again. A big clock ticked away, but he didn't mind. This waiting was a labor of love—and hate.

A few minutes later, his patience was rewarded by the slamming of the big carved oak door. Montes didn't notice him. The gaunt vaquero walked right by the entrance to the sala, back toward the rear of the house, calling out the Indian woman's name.

Buck heard her telling him he had a guest in the sala. "Señor Samuel is his name," she said.

Buck heard Santos returning, the sound of his tall boots muffled by the fine Chinese carpet over the hard-packed earthen floor.

Buck stood as Santos Montes entered the room. The vaquero's eyes flared for a second, then became hooded, masking his thoughts.

"Señor Mueller, I had heard that you were dead... that you had some problems with the Mojaves." The man actually smiled at him as Buck stood silently watching, hoping the bastard would squirm, wanting him to be afraid. Wanting him to sweat—before he died.

"As you can see, Montes, I am very much alive."

The tall vaquero walked to a cabinet and opened it. Without turning back to Buck he asked, "Would you care for some of Toro Bravo's famous brandy? But then, you have already tried it... have you not?"

He turned to face Buck, a small pistol gripped in his

hand, leveled at Buck's chest. "I presume this is not a social call, Señor Mueller. It is seldom I receive visitors."

Buck felt like a fool. The man's calmness had surprised him, made him doubt. And he was so anxious to make the man sweat he had underestimated him. He was too eager, too preoccupied with making him pay before he died—now, he might not die at all.

Buck smiled tightly. "No, Montes, this is not a social call, and yes, I would like to try some of Toro Bravo's famous brandy." He walked forward.

"Not too close. I will be happy to pour it for you. After all, what kind of host would I be?" Montes poured two pewter goblets half full, flicking his eyes away only momentarily. He extended one goblet to Buck, keeping the pistol leveled at his belly. Buck reached out for the goblet, still two feet away.

Suddenly Buck lashed out, kicking upward. Urbaldo and Juan had taught him the value of limber legs. The kick was aimed at the mug, not the pistol. Montes jerked the wrong hand away. The kick drove the hand and the mug upward, flinging the strong brandy into Montes's eyes. He stumbled back, wiping his face with one hand, aiming the gun with the other.

The pistol bucked and roared just as Buck dove beneath the weapon. Lunging up, he landed a solid blow to the vaquero's chin as he struggled to clear his vision. Montes's head snapped back and he went down.

Buck kicked the spent pistol from his hand. His muscles taut with tension, he waited for Montes to move into a sitting position.

"Don't bother getting up, Montes. We're going to talk a bit." Buck pulled his own pistol from the sheath at his waist, pointing it in the gaunt vaquero's direction. Racing down the hallway, the Indian woman rushed back to see what had happened. She stopped short, staring wide-eyed into the room.

Buck ignored her, taking up a chair he had occupied

before. "I happened by Rancho Del Oso a week or so ago. I was surprised to see that Don Eduardo Juarez, your boss, now owns that fine property. You wouldn't know the circumstances of his acquiring it, would you?" While he talked, Buck settled his own gun in his lap, picked up Montes's pistol and reloaded it.

"I presumed he purchased it... from you. Did you not own it?" Still cool, Montes smiled his serpent, tight-lipped smile.

Buck's fingers tightened on the grip of his gun. Montes's manner was so relaxed, Buck's jaw flexed in anger. He raised Montes's pistol just as the big carved front door burst open, and he swung the weapon in that direction, leveling it at the man in the doorway, a man Buck didn't know and held no grudge against, so long as he didn't interfere.

"This is not your fight, amigo," Buck said. "I suggest you stay out of it. You know this is not a man you wish to die for." He read agreement in the man's dark eyes. He made no further move forward.

"Get him!" Montes shouted at the stout vaquero. "Get the rest of the men together. We...." He paused.

Buck swung the pistol back toward Montes. "You what?"

He calmly aimed and shot Montes in the knee, blood splattering on the whitewashed adobe wall.

The Indian woman screamed and turned away. Her stomach heaved and she retched all over the carpeted floor. Then she ran toward the back of the house. Buck quickly picked up his own musket, while the stout vaquero remained transfixed in the doorway.

Montes held his shattered knee to his mouth, wrapping both arms protectively around it as he sat rocking from side to side, his eyes full of fear. Buck knew his own eyes glittered with hatred and bitterness, but he didn't care. He was beyond the point of caring.

"You what, Señor Montes? You hired the Mojaves... twelve Mojaves to be exact... to burn my hacienda... to rape and murder my wife... to kill my friends." While he spoke,

Buck reloaded the spent piston, keeping the loaded pistol at the ready. The man in the doorway did not move, but his face paled as Buck talked calmly on, as calmly as Montes had spoken when the conversation began.

"Twelve Mojave butchers," he said. "Hired to murder my son... my three-year-old son. Are you a Catholic, Señor Montes?" Buck knew the answer to the question before he asked. All Californios were Catholic.

"Sí," Montes whispered between broken, gasping breaths.

"Is there a priest nearby... or would you like to confess to me... maybe I could grant you absolution." Buck felt cold inside, brutal—the thought of Lali and Tucker driving him on.

"It was not my doing, I swear it. It was Don Eduardo... he paid them... the rancho is his, not mine... it was Juarez!"

Buck was amazed at the weakness of a man who had always appeared so strong, the ease with which he became less than a man. Looks could truly deceive.

Watching him, an alarm went off in Buck's head. "And what of this rancho? Rancho Toro Bravo? How did Don Pedro die?"

"This... this too was the patron's idea. He paid us to kill Don Pedro. Madre de Dios... I beg you, it was him... him! Not me! He is at the fiesta. With Captain Taylor-Johnson. Please, it was him!"

With this admission, the vaquero in the doorway turned away from the scene, and walked away, closing the door behind him.

As Montes talked, and Buck's attention was drawn to the departing vaquero, the tall vaquero slipped a hand inside his boot, seeking the blade that had taken so many men—men who had underestimated him. Jerking it from its hiding place, he lunged for Buck, but his injured knee gave way and he fell on his face at Buck's feet. Broken sobs racked his lean body.

Buck had felt remorse at Hard Tack's death, a tinge at

least, and that had been an accident. But now the sweet taste of revenge was strong in his mouth, and he felt no pity for the sniveling man cowering in front of him. He had the chance now to kill Montes and take his revenge.

Coldly, he lowered the pistol. At the same instant, Montes made another swinging slash with the knife. Buck saw the movement coming, quickly sidestepped the blade and fired the gun, the ball slamming into Santos's chest.

The gaunt vaquero slumped to the floor, twitched once, then lay still.

Buck smiled grimly. And crossed the first name off his list.

THAT NIGHT BUCK made camp on the trail to Pueblo Los Angeles. He slept more soundly than he had since his Rancho had been burned. The voices of Lali and Tucker and Tui and Sanchez did not cry out quite so loudly.

One more day, he thought, then the fiesta.

26

NORMALLY BUCK WOULD HAVE TRAVELED on without stopping to rest. He had a purpose in going, but there was also a purpose in waiting, in camping here beside the trail.

He knew what to listen for, and even though he slept, his subconscious remained alert. He'd been sleeping for over two hours, so the stars told him, when he snapped wide awake. The sound of rapidly beating hooves approached from the direction of Toro Bravo.

Not expecting to find Montes at the Seville rancho, he hadn't anticipated the events that had taken place. He must adapt, flow with the tide if he was going to accomplish his purpose. He knew the odds were badly against him. They had been from the start. Having the others alerted would turn the odds so desperately in their favor his chances for success would approach zero.

He stood on a rock outcropping and waited for the rider's approach, his reata coiled in his hand. He didn't have to wait long.

As the rider drew near, the galloping horse paused to make a three-foot rise in the trail and Buck's loop deftly dropped over the rider's head. He yanked on the braided leather and sat back, wrenching the man from his saddle, stunning him as he landed solidly on his back in the trail.

The stout man struggled to his feet, dazed and stumbling, hardly aware of where he was. Buck kicked him squarely in the knee, making him dance on one leg while he held the other to his chest with both hands. Buck kicked the other leg out from under him, dropping him to the ground again.

Buck stepped forward and bent over him, placing a foot in the man's barrel chest to hold him down. He was right. It was the vaquero who had come to the door as he held Montes at gunpoint. Buck dragged his pistol from its sheath and cracked the man's wrist viciously when he reached for the knife he carried at his waist.

"You've already lived hours on borrowed time," Buck said coldly. "If you wish to continue to stay alive, you'll return to Toro Bravo and busy yourself putting the garbage I left behind in the ground. Do not pass this way for three days... next time, my pistol will speak, not my reata."

Buck lifted his foot from the man's thick chest. The vaquero groaned and staggered to his feet, then limped off toward his horse.

"Not the horse. You can walk back to the rancho. It'll give you time to think on your good fortune."

"Sí, señor," the man said. "Comprendo!" He ran off limping, back the way he had come.

Buck returned to his bedroll, rolled it up and continued on to Pueblo Los Angeles, the vaquero's horse tied behind his little mare.

He arrived on a hill overlooking the town just as the sun cast its first furtive rays over the mountains to the east, under the early morning overcast. He tied the horses well back into a grove of scrub oak, unrolled his bedroll, and fell into a deep sleep.

Content that the fiesta would not be alerted to his arrival, he had one more day to kill. In his hardened state of mind, he laughed to himself at the pun.

He awoke a little before noon. All day he rested and thought about the events of the last few years. He pulled the little tusuat from his pocket, tossed it up and caught it, recalling a memory of the fresh young marinero who had visited the Trabuco Juaneros.

He pulled his buckskin shirt off and lay back in the sun. It was late fall—the overcast had burned off and the California sun warmed his body. He ran his hands over his scars. The front and back of his right shoulder bore the puckered purple mark of a Mojave arrow. Another had creased his cheek, not helping his already dubious appearance. He reached over his shoulder and rubbed his hand across his back. He knew the marks of the whip were still there.

Angry heat rose to the back of his neck as he thought of Ernst. "The villainy you teach me I will execute...." Now, he remembered. Shakespeare, The Merchant of Venice, Dutch had told him. He would have to read that someday—if he lived to read again.

Buck continued to survey his scars, the one on his thigh from a stone blade rose up from his skin, puckered and ugly. He wished he'd had time to castrate the Indian whose knife had violated his leg... or better still the ones who had violated his wife. He ignored a cold shiver as he remembered the four scars across his hip, left from his grizzly encounter. Those four his mother would never see.

If he ever saw her again, he knew she would worry over those she could see.

As the afternoon wore on, it began to cloud up. Soon a clap of thunder rolled across the lomarias, the low hills, that sheltered the pueblo on the northwest. He hoped the rain would not interfere with the fiesta. But the rain did not come. As it began to darken, he led the horses off the hill to water at a creek behind the town. He was tempted to walk into the cantina but thought better of it. He couldn't take the chance of alerting them. He would find them in his own time, on his own terms.

Sleep came fitfully that night. He had gotten too much rest. He was fully awake when the sun over the mountains turned the horizon iron gray. The big golden orb seemed to rise slowly, as if anticipating the day would not be one it wished to witness.

Buck was waiting as the proprietor of the general store approached the front door. By the time the sun was fully up he had purchased a pair of Californio breeches, calvonevas, with silver conches up the pant legs, a white silk shirt with ruffled sleeves and front, a red sash he wound around his waist, and a black flat felt hat with a woven black horsehair lanyard.

He would dress appropriately for this event. It wouldn't do to be as conspicuous as he had been the last time he interrupted a fandango at the Public House. He was sorry he didn't have Ernst's "Sunday clothes." Ernst would have liked that.

Buck returned to the hillside and shaved with the blade of his ten-inch knife. Then he positioned himself beneath an oak tree on the hillside so he could watch the events of the day. Already men were busy out behind the Public House checking the roasting buried bulls' heads, and turning bullocks over hot oak fires they had been tending through the night. His stomach growled as he caught the odor of the roasting meat.

He watched with interest as carriages and riders began to arrive. By midmorning he could hear occasional notes of music as violinists and guitarists passed among the gathering Californios.

Vaqueros and Indians congregated out in the back of the Public House where most of the food was being prepared. Soon the dons and their ladies would arrive. Buck sat up straighter when he thought he saw Juarez, Elena, the Señora, and Mamacita driving up in a four passenger caleche with a folding top, drawn by four beautiful gray Andalusians. But they were a long way off and he couldn't be sure.

He relaxed once more against the base of the oak tree. He would let the fiesta progress, let the wine flow, before he made his move. There was no hurry. The fandango would go on through the day, well into the night, and through most of the following day.

He had waited for months.

Lali, Tucker, Tui and Sanchez could wait a few hours more.

Besides, the cold knot of anticipation in his gut felt strangely right.

IT WAS the midafternoon when he set out. Carefully, almost ceremoniously, he gathered up his things and saddled the horses. He slowly picked his way down the hill to an oak grove out behind the Public House. He tied the vaquero's horse there, a back door in case he needed one.

Returning the way he came, he began his slow, deliberate ride into the small pueblo down the middle of the dusty main street. Among hundreds of others, he was not surprised when he attracted little notice. He tied the horse to the rail out in front and approached the Public House on foot, recalling his last visit. He was a different man then.

He pushed open the heavy front door, every nerve in his body attuned for this moment. As soon as he crossed the threshold, his eyes widened at the unexpected sight of Captain William Taylor-Johnson. Swill stood beside him, talking to four silk-and-lace clad señoritas. Both marineros were dressed to the hilt in full dress uniforms, glittering even more than the ladies. Buck almost laughed aloud.

This was more than he could have hoped for. He knew Eduardo Juarez would not miss this function, but to find Taylor-Johnson here...

He continued to scan the room. As he walked farther into the hall, several people turned and stared, much as they had done when he had walked into Elena's fandango. This time it wasn't because he was inadequately dressed. His clothes were much the same as the other men in the room.

It wasn't because he was so good looking. Any man there would be considered more handsome than he. Still, he could feel the attention, the women first glancing, then turning away, only to glance back again. Was it the way he carried himself? Or was it his manner? Meeting every look a little too boldly, moving without wasted motion, assessing his surroundings with eyes that missed nothing, keeping his back to the wall. Probably it was the hate that seethed inside him. And the purpose that surged through him with every beat of his heart.

Feeling the stares of the men, he turned toward them, meeting their curious glances, issuing a silent challenge—one that instilled a clear warning to keep to their territory and to respect his.

He caught sight of Elena, but even her presence couldn't crack through his icy facade. She stood next to the Señora and Mamacita, chatting with a small group of women. Eduardo Juarez stood across the room, talking with a group of men near a rough plank bar set up for the occasion. Echeandia stood at their center—he had made the trip from Monterey especially for this occasion, as Buck suspected he would.

The only weapons in the room appeared to be the decorative cutlasses Taylor-Johnson and Swill wore at their hips. Buck had left his musket on his saddle, too cumbersome and too obvious to carry into the fiesta. He crossed the room, his eyes shifting from Taylor-Johnson to Juarez and back to the captain. He caught the disapproving glances of a number of guests when he flipped back the red silk sash at his waist, exposing the pistol and knife he carried.

He walked up behind the captain and Swill, his anger flaring at the sound of their laughter as they flirted with the women. He stopped directly behind them.

Casting one more glance at Juarez, he impulsively jerked Swill's cutlass from its scabbard. Somehow the pistol seemed far too impersonal.

Both men spun and stared at the man they barely recognized as their old shipmate. Apparently they too believed his scalp decorated a Mojave lodge.

"Buck!" Swill exclaimed.

"I'd suggest you take your leave, Swill. I've got business with the captain that doesn't include you."

The first mate flushed, embarrassed at the use of his nickname. He used his proper name now, and captained one of Taylor-Johnson's ships. Swill cut his eyes to the pistol at Buck's waist, to his cutlass, gripped in Buck's hand, then to Taylor-Johnson.

The room lay deathly quiet, all eyes turned in the men's direction. Buck quickly scanned the room, looking for signs of interference, his gaze touching briefly on Elena. He was surprised to feel a hint of the old familiar warmth creep back in.

Elena looked stunned. She took two steps toward him, then Eduardo reached out and jerked her back to his side. She pulled away from him, but made no further move. Her eyes never left Buck, and a soft flush colored her cheeks.

Meeting Eduardo's gaze, Buck clenched his jaw and worked a muscle in his cheek. "Leave, Swill... now! Clear the room as you go... except for Taylor-Johnson and Juarez. They stay."

"Do as he says," the captain said. "I can handle this. For both of us, it has been far too long in coming." Stepping back, standing straighter, squaring his shoulders, the captain drew his cutlass and turned to face Buck.

The crowd quickly began to clear, heading out both front and rear doors. Buck's attention remained riveted on Taylor-Johnson who stood waiting, half smiling, cutlass in hand. Stepping well out of the captain's slashing range, he searched the room for Juarez. He was disappointed, but not surprised, to see the man disappearing out the front door, pushing Elena ahead of him.

The villainy you teach me I will execute, flashed through his mind. He would deal with Taylor-Johnson, then go after

Juarez. He turned his attention to the tall, blond, hard-faced sea captain. First things first.

"Do you know the use of that cutlass," Buck taunted, "or do you wear it just to impress the señoritas?"

"I've washed the decks of ships from here to Tripoli with the blood of men who have stepped before my blade. The question is, do you know its use?"

Buck laughed too, but as he did so, he thought of the hours he'd spent drilling with Black Dan. But this was no drill. And he had never picked up a cutlass in anger. Maybe he had been too impulsive, let anger overcome caution. He'd carried a cutlass for a while before he traded it off to Cuatchu, the Paiute chief. Unfortunately, its use had been restricted to chopping brush and killing a rattler or two, and they were not nearly so dangerous as the man who stood before him.

By now the room had cleared. But front and back, eight big shuttered windows were lined with observers, Swill among them.

Taylor-Johnson brought the fight to him. Buck blocked a ringing slash to the left then a slash to the right before he had time to think. Pure reaction set in. The clanging of the tempered iron blades rang across the room, and echoed out into the front and rear verandas.

The captain smiled as he parried. Buck might have learned something from Black Dan, but the art of the cutlass was not a skill easily attained. The captain believed he would end this quickly and get back to his señoritas. He hacked again, left and then right. The force of the blows was enormous. He wondered why the blades didn't shatter on impact. Then the two men tied up. Relying on his greater experience, Taylor-Johnson deftly slid the blade over as he pulled away, leaving an ugly red gash along Buck's neck just above his white collar.

Buck felt the sharp sting, then the trickle of blood down his chest. He had no idea the blade was that close.

The sight of his own blood angered him. With deadly resolve he decided it was the last he would spill.

Clenching his jaw, he attacked, hacking left then right, right again then left, not setting a pattern, giving the more experienced man no quarter. The echoes of the blows resounded through the big open room. Buck drove forward, backing Taylor-Johnson the length of the hall and into a table loaded with steaming platters of food.

He closed with the captain again. This time, Buck had the advantage. Bending the man back over the table, he tried to drive a knee up into the taller man's groin, but the knee didn't score. They broke and he backed away, careful this time that the captain's blade didn't mark him.

Taylor-Johnson stood there panting, not attacking. Buck realized he was resting. It would be a mistake to let him do so. Buck drove forward and the captain skillfully parried, blocking blows to both sides of his blade. Buck backed away again, thinking, planning his next move, then again he drove forward, slashing high for the head this time.

The captain didn't block the blow, but ducked and thrust with his blade, using a rapier move instead of a cutlass move. It took Buck by surprise. He quickly sidestepped to avoid the blade, but it punctured his side just below the rib cage, and a shudder of pain shot through him.

The crowd gasped, the first sound they had made since the fight began. Buck dropped back, cursing himself for his clumsiness. His vision swam for a moment, then cleared.

Taylor-Johnson smiled, a ghoulish self-satisfied smile that made hot anger pump through Buck's veins. The blood flowed freely from under his shirt, staining the outside of his pant leg.

Taylor-Johnson stepped forward with confidence, moving in for the kill. He tried a direct overhead slash, feigned one way and then the other, and ended with a full circular blow directly from overhead—a blow meant to split Buck's skull from pate to chin.

Buck parried, grasping the cutlass with both hands, one

on the hilt, one on the point. The clanging force of the blow drove him to his knees. He recovered quickly, driving Taylor-Johnson back again. This time the captain's parry was not quite quick enough. Buck's overhead slash landed, missing its mark on the top of the captain's blond head, but catching him at the base of the neck. It happened so quickly, Buck didn't realize it was a mortal blow, until Taylor-Johnson's head flopped to his shoulder at an odd angle. He was stone dead when he hit the floor.

Most of the Californios watching through the shutters turned away, their morbid curiosity more than satisfied by the grisly scene.

Buck whispered, "Thank you, Black Dan," but the bile rose as he looked at what was now less than a man. But then maybe Taylor-Johnson always had been. The score for Ernst was settled.

Buck let his blade fall beside the dead captain's. The crowd parted as he moved through the doors. Almost as an afterthought, he reached out and pulled a scarf from a wide-eyed señorita and bound it around his waist under his shirt, stemming the flow of blood.

She smiled weakly when he thanked her. Turning, he strode purposefully across the dirt street to his horse. He mounted and rode out, searching the street for the carriage he thought he had seen arriving with Juarez and Elena. It was gone.

He rode out for Rancho Riena de California.

307

27

EDUARDO CURSED LONG AND FLUENTLY. When he had realized the well-dressed gentleman standing before Taylor-Johnson, cutlass in hand, was the American, Buck Mueller, he'd been stunned. He knew he had to get away, to get help.

He wished Montes were close by. It had been a mistake to reward the man by allowing him to live at Rancho Toro Bravo. He needed Montes desperately. And he needed him now.

He whipped the four grays into a gallop, Elena arguing fiercely for him to go back for her mother and Mamacita. In his haste to leave, he had forgotten them.

"Do you not understand? This man, Mueller—he is insane."

"If that is so, that is even more reason to go back for them."

"He will not harm your mother or grandmother. You know he is fond of them. Did you not see he carried a pistola and I am unarmed?"

"But why would he wish to harm you, Eduardo? Have you done something to him?"

"The man is insane, I tell you. He probably thinks we had something to do with his losing his rancho... since it has now been granted to me. I knew... I thought he was dead."

Elena picked up the correction. "What do you mean, 'you knew he was dead'?"

"You are distracting me, woman. Let me drive!" He cracked the whip over the horses' backs.

It was an hour's ride back to Rancho Riena, a long hour for Eduardo, who kept looking back over his shoulder. But he would be safe there. He had vaqueros there. He wished Montes were there.

Many of his men had been at the fiesta, out in the back. Perhaps he should have stayed there, but at the time all he could think of was escape. Besides, they were unarmed. The men at the rancho would have weapons. He urged the horses faster and rode on.

At last the rancho came in sight. Eduardo reined up in front of the long adobe barn, and an old Indian ran through the wide doors to grab the lead horse's reins.

"Viejo!" Eduardo called down to him. "Get the vaqueros!"

"I am sorry, Patron," the old man answered. "They have gone... to... to round up the cattle."

Eduardo jumped down to the ground, fear snaking through him as he started for the house. He knew the old man was lying. The men he had ordered to remain had gone to the fiesta against his orders. They would pay for that mistake.

He hurried into the house, Elena close at his heels. Little Maria, standing next to the Indian woman who had been left to care for her, ran to her mother and Elena scooped the child into her arms. The two of them hurried upstairs.

Eduardo hurried up the stairs after them. His study, and his gun cabinet, were there. He loaded two muskets and two pistols and laid them across his oak desk. He had a clear field of fire from the hacienda. No one could get close to the house. And he was an excellent shot.

Elena hastened to her bedroom, her alcoba, with Maria. No one had been more surprised at seeing Buck than she. She had finally accepted his death. But she had thought of him often, missing him though their time together had been brief.

He had seen her. Locked eyes with her. Looked deeply into her as he had done each of those times in the past. But this time his look was different. This time she felt he almost didn't see her.

She had always believed there was something violent about him, something deep within him she feared. Even the time at the pond, the last time they were together. As gentle as he had been, she knew there was something dangerous about him.

But why did Eduardo fear him? She had watched her husband as he dragged her from the Public House. She had never seen him so upset. She had never thought him a coward. It did not make sense that he should fear this man over a simple civil matter, a matter of land. That was a thing to be resolved in court, by the alcaldes.

Still, Buck did look crazy. The look in his eyes was dreadful, frightening. The fact he did not acknowledge her presence, did not seem to notice she existed, seemed unlike him, and that scared her, too. If Buck came to the hacienda, if Eduardo was correct in his fear, would he harm her? Would he harm Maria?

She could not imagine Buck doing anything to hurt her or her daughter. She did not believe she could be that wrong about another human being, especially one who meant so much to her. Still, Maria was all she had. She left her daughter just long enough to walk to Eduardo's study.

"Give me a pistola!" she demanded.

Eduardo jumped as if someone had struck him. "Mother of Jesus! Do not slip up on me like that." He had been looking out the window and hadn't heard her approach.

"Eduardo," she repeated. "Give me a pistola!"

He started to deny her, to tell her how useless she would be, then thought better of it. Who knew, she might distract Mueller long enough to be of help, even if she mistakenly shot herself.

BUCK PICKED his way through brush and scrub oak.

The road leading to the main gate, not much more than a wagon track, lay a quarter mile below him. He purposely avoided it. Juarez would be alert and waiting.

It was no longer planning or reason that drove him but pure instinct, something primal, something deep within him. He was having trouble keeping the scarf in position. The wound still bled, soaking into his clothes. Fatigue settled over him like a shroud. He shouldn't be so tired. He'd rested much the night before. He put it off to the fight... and the loss of blood.

Collecting himself he took inventory. He had his long gun and pair of pistols. The ten-inch knife still hung at his waist. Knowing he was short of powder, lead, and caps, he shook his powder horn. It was only a quarter full. Searching the buckskin possibles bag that held his shot, caps, and wadding, he realized he was down to seven balls, including the two loaded in the Astons and the one in his musket.

It would be enough. He would kill this man with his hands, if it came to that.

After an hour of picking his way along, he sighted the rancho. He had never been there before so he carefully reconnoitered. He circled the building complex, staying as far back in the cover as he could.

It was quiet—too quiet.

The only sign of life was a weathered old Indian working around the barn. The shadows lay long in the yard. The sun was only two diameters above the horizon. He would bide his time.

An Indian woman walked from the hacienda to the barn, joined the old man, and they walked to one of the adobe outbuildings on the far side of the corral.

Buck surveyed the rancho, admiring Juarez's taste. The Pacific was only a mile or so away. The slope gently dropped away to the ocean to the west and a creek marsh to the south. A few thick dark green cedars surrounded the building complex. A beautiful place.

A beautiful place to die.

He picketed the mare where she could graze in a patch of new grass, and waited.

EDUARDO SHOUTED for Elena to light the lamps and tapers on the lower floor. He did not want to move from his study and it was beginning to darken outside.

She delivered Maria to his study and walked downstairs to complete the chore, wondering why he'd sent her Indian woman away. She was frightened by her husband's actions. She wished she understood what was going on. Still she carefully went from room to room lighting every candle and whale oil lamp.

She had known Buck hated Taylor-Johnson. But surely Buck would not come here, not to her home. Once before he had complied with her wishes, leaving instead of fighting, on her wedding day. She remembered that day well—and another—and the color came unbidden to her cheeks.

Still, there was little warmth in his eyes when he had looked at her at the fiesta. She wondered what he had been thinking.

BUCK LEFT the mare for a moment, and moved closer to the hacienda. Through the shutters of the open windows, he watched Elena moving from room to room. Having a baby hadn't affected her beautiful body, her fluid movements. As she reached up to light a chandelier, he felt a twinge of remorse. He had inflicted himself upon her life before. This time he would do far worse.

The searing pain in his side jerked him back to his purpose. He watched Elena return upstairs, certain Juarez waited in one of the darkened rooms above. If he did, the darkness would work in the haciendado's favor. He knew his way around the big two-story adobe. Buck did not. He had to discover exactly where the man was.

Limping back to the horse, he pulled his tinder box from the pack rolled behind his saddle. Picking a spot a little over a hundred paces from the hacienda, he knelt in the grass, put steel to flint and got a tiny flame started.

It was difficult for even a marksman to sight a musket in total darkness. And though it might seem that way, he didn't intend to offer Juarez a target. The little fire gave off just enough light to silhouette him as he moved about it.

EDUARDO COULD NOT BELIEVE his eyes. Mueller was not only out there, but he was making camp. He must be as insane as he had seemed at the fiesta.

The loss of his rancho and his family must have driven him mad. Eduardo shuddered. That damn Montes. Montes had assured him Mueller was dead—that he had served the notice of rescission in the manner his patron directed.

It was only later that he learned the fool had also burned the American out. It was a waste of all the work Mueller had done on the rancho. Montes always went a little too far. He would see to his segundo after he disposed of Mueller.

Eduardo laid the musket across the window sill and carefully sighted. He had trouble lining up the bead with the rear sights in the darkness. Mueller continued moving around behind the fire, his shadow playing tricks on the trees. He kept walking back and forth, changing direction and speed, setting no pattern.

If the bastard would stand still a moment, Juarez thought, he could get a fix on him. He carefully squeezed the trigger. The musket spit its two-foot flame and bucked in the darkness.

Buck caught the flash and dove to the side, the whoosh

of the big ball whipping so close to his head he felt the wind slap as it passed. He smiled as he lay quietly in the brush, sure now where Juarez was, then began working his way through the grass to the side, away from the fire he had built. He propped his own musket in the crook of a scrub oak and watched the window where Juarez had fired.

ELENA RETURNED to the study and gathered Maria to her breast, the report of the musket sending new fear careening through her. "What happened, Eduardo, are you all right?"

Eduardo sat at the window sill. Had he hit the bastard? It looked as if he had knocked him to the ground. As he turned to answer Elena's question, the window sill splintered with return fire, throwing chunks of wood over his chest and face. He dropped to the floor, shaking all over.

"He's out there, Elena," he sputtered. "And he's still alive."

BUCK MOVED QUICKLY AWAY from the spot where he had fired. He headed around to the far side of the hacienda and worked his way to the barn. The Indian man and woman were cautiously moving around the corral toward the hacienda.

"Go back to your frijoles, amigo," Buck said quietly from the moon shadow of the barn. "This is not your fight."

The couple stopped in their tracks, not knowing where the voice came from. They turned and scurried back to their little adobe.

Buck walked through the barn, stopping at the entrance. "Juarez!" he shouted across the yard. He waited a moment, called out to him again, then moved to a new position.

"What do you want here, hombre?" Eduardo finally answered. "You have no business here... go away!"

Juarez had gone into another alcoba. Buck caught a flash

of reflection and tracked the sound from a different upstairs window.

Buck yelled again. "Send your wife and daughter away! I'll let the Indian woman come for them. This is between you and me. Let them go back to the fiesta!"

Eduardo turned to Elena, into whose alcoba he had retreated. She crouched beside her bed, shielding her daughter with her body. Eduardo hid behind the jamb near one of the windows.

"He wants you and Maria to leave," Eduardo said. "He wants us separated... it is a trick."

"I should get Maria to safety, Eduardo." Elena's tone hardened. "Here she could be in danger."

"He wants me alone! He's a madman... you cannot go!" Eduardo turned back to the window, leveled the musket at the barn entrance, and snapped off another shot.

Buck responded instinctively, firing in return. He collected himself. He couldn't continue this long-range battle. He didn't have the ammunition and he was continuing to weaken. Time and distance were on Juarez's side. He slipped out the back of the barn and around to where he had built the fire. It had dwindled to coals. He tore at the brush, stacking it on the coal bed until it was piled as high as his waist, then he returned to the barn and waited. The low bed of coals began to do their work and suddenly the brush burst into flame.

Buck circled to the side of the hacienda away from the burning pile of brush. Running to the adobe wall of the hacienda, he flattened himself against it, trying to ignore the pain burning into his side.

As Buck hoped, Eduardo raced back his study, to watch the fire and search for the man who had built it. A large wisteria wound its way up a trellis on the side of the hacienda where Buck stood in the shadows. When he was satisfied that Juarez had enough time to get to the other side of the house, he began pulling himself upward to the second floor. When he got there, he worked at the shutters on a second story window. They resisted, locked tightly.

He swung the butt of the musket, smashing the wooden shutters, and crashed through onto the floor of a darkened room. He was on his feet quickly, checking the musket load.

"Mother of Christ!" Eduardo shouted, realizing the man was no longer out in the shadows, but was now in one of the upstairs rooms. His hands suddenly shaking, he ran to the door of his study at the end of the long upstairs hall. From there, he could see all six doorways leading off the passage.

Elena sank deeper into the corner, protected by the high four-poster bed in her room, Maria whimpering beneath her.

Buck sank to a knee beside the alcoba door and opened it a crack. Still, Eduardo detected the slight motion and fired, hitting the jamb beside Buck's head and splintering it away. Buck fired at the flash of Eduardo's gun, but he had already scrambled back out of sight. Juarez quickly returned to the doorway, brandishing a pistol.

Hunkered down beside the door, Buck pulled his own pistol from his belt then immediately began reloading the long gun. He heard Eduardo burst from his study. They exchanged shots as Eduardo dove into Elena's alcoba.

Buck could hear him shrieking. "We must get out of here —he is crazy! Loco!... Come!" He jerked Elena to her feet and she grabbed Maria as he dragged her to the doorway and shoved her, Maria sobbing in her arms, out into the hallway. Eduardo stepped out behind them, keeping them between Buck and himself.

Buck flung the door open but stepped back into the darkness of the room.

"What are you doing?" Elena shouted.

"Shut up!" Juarez snapped.

He watched them backing toward the stairway. Eduardo turned as soon as they reached the top of the stairs and fled below, leaving Elena to follow behind. Racing to the head of the stairs, Buck fired his long gun over the rail at Juarez, who screamed and dove behind an overstuffed cowhide chair.

Elena stood at the bottom of the stairs, well out of Buck's line of fire, her fear of Buck replaced by amazement at her husband, then by a rush of anger. Eduardo cowered behind a chair while she stood in the open, shielding her daughter behind her.

Buck stepped back, hidden by a wall, and searched his buckskin possibles bag for another ball. He swore softly when he found none. Instinctively searching his pockets, he pulled out the little tusuat. Testing its roundness, he slipped it into the barrel of the musket. It fit almost perfectly. With two strokes of the rod it was seated, wadding firmly holding it in place. He had one good load in an Aston, and a doubtful one in the long gun.

He took a deep breath, trying to overcome his dizziness. Nausea swept over him for a moment. This had to end and end soon or he would fall from weakness. He would take it as it came. At least it would soon be over—one way or another.

He charged down the stairway.

Elena cocked her pistol and raised it, tracking him as he descended the stairs. He ignored her. Eduardo leaned around the edge of the chair and raised his gun, his pupils flaring with fear.

Another wave of nausea swept over Buck and he stumbled. He and Juarez fired their pistols almost simultaneously. Buck rolled the last few stairs to the floor. His ball had buried itself harmlessly in the padding of the big chair. Juarez's ball just missed taking his head off, instead it lodged in the thick adobe wall of the stairwell.

Buck clung to the long gun. He struggled to his feet and leveled the old fifty caliber musket at Eduardo, who cowered on his knees behind the big chair, his pistol now empty.

"No!" Elena screamed. Her voice calmed. "No, Buck."

She held the pistol in both hands, cocked and primed, aimed directly at the side of his head. "I won't let you shoot him."

He shifted his gaze to meet hers. "Elena, this is something I must do. Your husband was responsible for the death of my son... and my wife." Dizziness assailed him and he dropped to one knee, his head spinning and blackness creeping into the edges of his mind. He collected the last of his strength and looked up at her. "And your father, Elena. He ordered Montes to kill him... so he would have Toro Bravo."

Elena's hand shook. She steadied her grip on the pistol with her other hand. She glanced at Eduardo, tears filling her eyes. "That is not true.... It cannot be true. You are lying. He would not—"

"Elena," Buck's eyes remained locked with hers. "Montes told me—just before I killed him."

The pistol wavered. Elena lowered the gun.

Buck rose unsteadily to his feet, using the musket as a crutch. The he raised it again and aimed it toward Eduardo.

"No! You cannot," Eduardo begged. "I had nothing to do with killing your family. I sent Montes to deliver a notice.... That was all."

"And Don Pedro?" Buck asked coldly.

"The old don meant nothing to you." Juarez held a hand out shielding his face, his voice cracking as he stared at the barrel of the musket. "Do not do this. Not in front of my wife... not in front of my daughter."

Elena stared at him. Eduardo had killed her father! The bitter realization of what he had done chilled and her voice came out cold. "She is not your daughter," she said.

"What? Of course she is my—"

"She is his." A graceful hand pointed in Buck's direction.

Buck just stared, unable to believe what he had heard. His gaze swiveled to the child sobbing softly in the corner, clinging to Elena's skirt. A few feet away, Eduardo struggled to his feet, the enormity of his wife's words infusing his pale face with color.

Glancing toward the child then back to Elena, Buck lowered the musket, letting it slip from his grasp and fall to the floor. There had been enough blood. Enough death. And maybe Juarez spoke the truth, maybe he hadn't ordered Montes to bring the Mojaves down on them, hadn't commanded such bloody destruction. Whatever the truth, it was over.

Buck stumbled to the front door and pulled it open.

Behind him Juarez staggered toward Elena. "You bitch!" he cried out, shoving her backward in a single vicious motion and snatching Buck's musket from the floor. Buck spun toward him, just as the old long gun fired from only ten paces away, blowing him back through the doorway, over the porch and into the dirt.

A thousand lights flared in his head. Lali and Tucker, Tui and Sanchez flashed in front of his eyes. He lay motionless in the dust, knowing he must be hurt badly and fighting to regain his strength.

Elena watched in horror. She turned and screamed at Juarez, "Bastardo!" Then she saw the old musket twisted and lying in pieces on the floor, Juarez's body prostrate beside it.

She ran to where her husband lay, his black eyes open, a thin line of blood running from one of them onto the carpeted floor. He was not breathing. The sliver of metal from the exploded breech of the old musket that had found its way to his brain did its work quickly and well.

Steeling herself, Elena hurried out to where Buck lay sprawled in the dirt. A thousand fine grains of tusuat dust were imbedded in his face and chest, and he bled from several places. He wiped his eyes and struggled to sit up.

Buck dragged in a deep breath. His eyes burned terribly, but he could see. He was particularly glad of that. Elena was on her knees above him, crying, holding one of his hands. He wrapped his arms protectively around her and let her sob onto his shoulder. The little girl, his little girl, ran to her mother's side and snuggled into her skirts.

ELENA STOOD in the garden of Rancho Reina and watched the Commandant of the Guard of Pueblo de Los Angeles rattle and clatter away with his accompaniment of men.

She had relayed the whole story to him, with the exception of little Maria's relationship to Buck and the fact that she had delivered the "killer deserter," lying semi-conscious in the back of a Rancho Riena cart, to Padre Zalvidea at Mission San Juan.

She was tired and worried and confused. She should be mourning over her husband, but her feelings alternated between remorse, anger, relief—and almost unbelievably —joy.

The last thing Buck said to her, as Father Zalvidea helped him into the mission and began to tend his wounds, kept running through her mind.

"I'll be back," he'd whispered, "when things are right." He reached out and tenderly touched her cheek. "Don't let Maria think too badly of me."

Elena had caught his rough, callused hand and pressed her lips against the palm. "Vaya con Dios," she said softly, unmindful of the tears that trickled down her cheeks.

She almost wished she could feel bad about him, could hate him as she should, but that was far from how she felt.

She put her fingers to her cheek, remembering the warmth of his touch, and the gentle way he'd smiled, and believed he would return.

FATHER ZALVIDEA TURNED AWAY from the sea to face the double column of soldiers who rode clanking and puffing up behind him. The captain of the guard quickly dismounted and walked toward him.

"We have a warrant here, Padre, for Samuel 'Buck' Mueller. We have been informed he is here, at Mission San Juan."

"I am afraid he is here no longer." The padre turned to stare back out at the ocean. In the distance, heeling deeply, the schooner, Moonsong, her full sails billowing, cut through the foaming white water as her bow plunged into an azure sea. A look of smug satisfaction settled over his strong features.

Buck stood at the rail of the schooner, her sails snapping to work, her stays taut with the freshening breeze. Josh Peckinpaugh walked up beside him.

"Ye don't look much the sailor in those Californio duds ye be wearin'"

"They'll have to do, Captain. I'm afraid it's all I've got." Buck smiled at his friend, his strength returning with the feel of the wind in his face and the feel of the deck beneath him. "I had no time to buy supplies."

The gray-haired man just nodded. "If ye look in my cabin, ye'll find the slop chest. Take whatever it is ye need. I'll be takin' it from ye wages."

A corner of his mouth inched up.

Buck was back at sea.

AUTHOR'S NOTES

Between 1840 and 1890, 400,000 folks crossed the plains on the Oregon-California trails in wagons, afoot, horseback, or pushing hand-carts. Forty thousand of those flocked to the trails during the gold rush year of 1849. After only ten years of travelling the trail, it averaged eleven graves per mile—mostly due to accident and disease, cholera being predominant.

This is a fictional account of one young man and his family, who set out to distance themselves from the conflict in the part of the country that became a Civil War hotbed, and of the trials and tribulations that family faced—typical of those Argonauts who sought only to make their lives better. This story is fiction, but based on dozens of journals, autobiographies, and reports.

This story only touches on a very few of the actual hardships of the trail.

On September 27, 1850, the Donation Land Claim Act of 1850 came into being. The act created a land-grab incentive for settlement of the Oregon Territory by offering 320 acres, at no charge, to qualifying adult U.S. citizens; 640 acres to married couples. Applicants were required to occupy their claims for four consecutive years. Changes in

1853 and 1854 continued the program, but lopped the size of allowable claims by fifty percent.

Only a small number of Americans resided in Oregon country before 1830, and these were mostly fur trappers— and those mostly Canadians—and missionaries who lived alongside the Indian population. But by the 1840s, government support of western expansion encouraged the coming flood of migration into Oregon territory. To encourage settlement, Congress passed the Distribution-Preemption Act of 1841, which recognized squatters' rights and allowed settlers to claim one hundred sixty acres of land. After occupying and improving the property for fourteen months, a claimant could purchase the property at one dollar and twenty-five cents per acre. The United States government hoped to establish a strong claim of settlement in Oregon country, which at that time was held jointly by the United States and Great Britain.

In 1843 white settlers in the Willamette Valley drafted a constitution and, by a vote of fifty-two to fifty, established a provisional government. Settlers could now claim up to 640 acres of land at no charge, although no treaties had been signed with the Indians.

Population growth was steady—not to speak of our defeating Mexico and acquiring many thousand citizens— and helped bring about a boundary treaty between the U.S. and Britain in 1846 that established a borderline at the 49th parallel and gave the United States claim to the territory. The U.S. had been claiming territory to ten degrees above that line, and Canada to ten degrees below, so it was a compromise pleasing both sides. Oregon Territory was officially formed on August 14, 1848, two years after our war with Mexico and our possession of their lands north of the current border. But with the territory being formed, land grants recognized under the provisional government were cancelled, the provisional governing board had been partially composed of British subjects. Settlers needed and demanded title to the parcels of land they had traveled those two-thousand-rough-and-dangerous, five-or-more-months of Oregon Trail miles, to obtain.

Oregon Territory's first Congressional representative, Samuel Royal Thurston (1816-1851), took on the land issue as his first legislative effort, convincing Washington D.C. legislators of the almost unlimited growth potential of the Pacific Northwest and the need to formulate binding property rights in the Territory. Thurston authored the Donation Land Claim Act of 1850. It recognized past claims granted under the provisional government, created the Office of Surveyor-General, and made land grants to new settlers. The Donation Land Claim Act spurred a huge land rush into Oregon Territory by offering qualifying citizens free land. Blacks, until the end of the Civil War, were not considered citizens. For the purpose of population count—thus the number of Congressmen a state could have—a slave was counted as 3/5ths of a person.

The act took effect on September 27, 1850, granting 320 acres of federal land to white male citizens eighteen years of age or older who resided on property on or before December 1, 1850. If married before December 1, 1851, the couple received an additional 320 acres in the wife's name. A large number of marriages took place during this one year to take advantage of that largess. Claimants agreed to live upon and cultivate the claim for four years, which could be counted retroactively. A certificate was issued to the claimant, granting immediate ownership once the land was occupied. Claimants who located on property between December 1, 1850, and December 1, 1853, (later extended to 1855) could obtain 160 acres of land (320 acres to married couples). Under an extension of the act in 1854, land could be purchased for $1.25 an acre. This policy held until Congress authorized the Homestead Act in 1862.

Early pioneers who settled before the act was passed, normally surveyed their own land or hired others poorly trained as surveyors. The difference in determining true- and magnetic-north descriptions was clearly understood by surveyors, but was often misunderstood by the pioneers, and in 1855 the difference between the two exceeded nineteen degrees. Section 3 of the Donation Claim Act set a clear limit of $8 a mile for surveyors' fees, but this often was ignored. Since claims needed to conform to government standards (and only surveyors recognized by the Surveyor-General were those employed by him), claims surveying became something of a racket, and excessive charges were common. Settlers became outraged at this practice, which eventually led to dismissal of the first Surveyor-General.

Most of the claims under the Donation Land Claim Act were located in the Willamette, Umpqua, and Rogue River valleys. By 1856, more than 7,000 settlers had acquired more than 2.5 million acres of property.

My thanks to Wikipedia for much of the historical information above, and to the authors of dozens of biographies, autobiographies and journals for the seeds of this tale. My undying admiration for those tough folks who made this crossing. They were the best of the muscle, brains, hide, hair, and bone of American pioneers.